HALLELUJAH

Myrtle's voice rang through the church. She was almost delirious with the sensuous carnality of clasping Travis and the magnitude of the moment. Involuntarily, her hips ground into Travis' crotch in time with the music, pushing and rotating in slow agonizing motions ... Myrtle caught the magnetic shudder fusing Travis as her twisting hips answered back. Then, with one final thrust, Travis' loins stilled to lodge deep between the limbs of Myrtle. Heat inundated Myrtle like a raging fire, sweeping her in the throes of desire. Mercifully, by the sheer force of willpower, she managed to tear away from all the ecstasy in the world, secreted in the palm of a few moments of bliss.

BOOKS BY ANN ALLEN SHOCKLEY

LOVING HER (Naiad)
SAY JESUS AND COME TO ME (Naiad)
THE BLACK AND WHITE OF IT (Naiad)
LIVING BLACK AMERICAN AUTHORS: A BIOGRAPHICAL
    DIRECTORY (with Sue P. Chandler) (Bowker)
A HANDBOOK OF BLACK LIBRARIANSHIP (with E. J. Josey) (Libraries
    Unlimited)
AFRO-AMERICAN LITERARY FOREMOTHERS: A DOCUMENTATION,
    1746-1933 (G. K. Hall) (forthcoming)

ABOUT
ANN ALLEN SHOCKLEY: AN ANNOTATED PRIMARY AND
    SECONDARY BIBLIOGRAPHY by Rita B. Dandridge. (Greenwood)

ABOUT THE AUTHOR:

Born in Louisville, Kentucky, where an eighth grade English teacher helped
to give birth to my thoughts of becoming a writer. I have been writing
since that time.

I was a newspaper reporter, free-lance writer and substitute teacher before
entering the field of librarianship. Short stories have appeared in *New
Letters, Black World, Essence, Phylon, Freedomways, Liberator, Sinister
Wisdom, Azalea,* etc., as well as anthologies. Non-fiction in magazines and
professional journals.

Working as an academic librarian, I write on weekends, holidays, and
summer months, with my dogs, Tiffany and Bianca, watching the birthing
pains. I wish it could be different.

Ann Allen Shockley

Say Jesus and Come To Me

Ann Allen Shockley

The Naiad Press Inc.
1987

Printed in the United States of America

First Naiad Press Edition May, 1987

Cover design by Women's Graphic Center
Typesetting by Sandi Stancil

ISBN 0-930044-98-3

Chapter 1

MYRTLE sat as majestic as a black queen in the high, straight-backed thronelike chair in the pulpit of the Hillside Union Church. She made an imposing figure in her red robe with the black braid fringing the collar and sleeves like icicles. Her clerical wardrobe contained gowns for each day's service in a revival week. This was an expensive variation, but the way she *looked* was important in getting *herself* across, along with the word of the Lord.

She could detect by the gaping of the country worshipers that she was creating a strong impression on the packed congregation. Her thick black hair was wrapped in mountainous tiered coils above her head, enhancing the beauty of her rich dark complexion and pointed features. A white missionary who had been to Africa told her years ago that she resembled the Hausa women in northern Nigeria. When the white apostle of the religious faith went on to relate the history of the Hausa who developed pre-European cities and governments, the knowledge nourished her budding, young ego. Soon after this revelation, she began to develop the habit of drawing her lean body up straighter to make herself appear as lofty and regal as a mountain. In the confines of her own imagination, she was a proud transplanted African queen reincarnated out of the past, who possessed an inherent bred-in-the-bone gift to be a savioress and high priestess of her people.

Shifting restlessly in her chair while listening impatiently to the droning voice of the host minister, her sharp black eagle

eyes appraised the congregation. She was still packing them
in, even though it was a Thursday night. The Reverend Tinder
Mills's introductory praises of her, delivered in a monotone,
sifted through her ears: "Yes, indeed, we are es-pe-cially happy
to have with us again tonight the renowned Reverend Myrtle
Black, who came all-l the way from South Carolina for this
three-day revival to help spread the word of the Lord and save
those in need."

Watching him closely, Myrtle wondered how the short,
balding minister, dressed in a shiny, frayed black suit, managed
to hold his church together. By the look of things if it wasn't
for the faithfulness of the congregation, there wouldn't even
be any church building. The walls were peeling and the pews
looked like they had been obtained from Goodwill. Myrtle was
critical of all male ministers because they were a threat to her.
But, no matter how dilapidated a church, she still dressed
elegantly in her expensive, fashionable robes. This was done
to outclass the males and provide an ostentatious show to help
her with her own pursuits—if a thing of interest was around.

One of decided interest had been found on the front row
pew the first night. The girl had been there for all the services,
and Myrtle's experienced and appreciative eyes had singled her
out immediately when she came slinking down the aisle exuding
an aura of sex. The object of her attention was a cute girl,
tawny colored with long eyelashes and a rosebud face. It was
her figure that really got next to Myrtle—the ripening curves
ready-made for tactile exploration. This evening they were
bursting out all over in a tight-fitting green dress. She was
hesitant to guess if the lovely's interests were aroused. The
signs indicated that they were. The girl had kept her eyes glued
on Myrtle in rapture, clinging to every sacred word. Myrtle
blessed her with the pseudonym Magdalen and designated her
seating locality to be the crucial amen corner.

"Befo' the Reverend Black brings her stirring message, let's
turn to page eighty in our hymnals and sing 'God's Goin' to
Help Us On,'" the Reverend Mills said.

The barrel-shaped pianist with a lopsided black wig thumped
out a loud chord on the upright piano, signaling the ten-voice
choir to lead the congregation. There was a heavy scraping of
feet as bodies rose sluggishly from the pews to raise their voices
in song:

> God's go-in' to help
> Us on to glo-o-ry.

Myrtle stood up with them, her voice rising loud and clear above the others. Her father had always drilled into her that she had a good-sounding voice for "preaching the gospel and making it hold." In keeping with this, he started her instilling the word of the Lord at the age of twelve. From church to church in cities, hamlets, and towns, she joined her evangelist mother and father as a propagandist for the faith. When her father died of a heart attack in the pulpit, her mother took the circumstances of his death to be a sacred omen of their divine mission to continue the family tradition of spreading the Almighty's wisdom and carrying on the good work. Through the years, Myrtle developed a proficiency in propagating the gospel and psyching the secret minds of those seeking spiritual guidance.

Not only did she perfect her voice, but herself in dispensing God's word. In line with her skill and training in theology, she also became adroit in the ways of the mortals who sought sexual love. The initiation into sex was subtly given by other lady ministers, churchwomen, and gospel singers who loved to hug, pet, kiss, and furtively fondle the "cute little girl preacher."

She remembered the first one who took her all the way down the path of carnal love. The Reverend Lily Smith was a huge, buxom woman five years older than Myrtle's mother. At the age of sixteen while a guest minister at the Reverend Smith's church in Cloverdale, Kentucky, she spent the night in the small cinder block one-bedroom parsonage behind the church. Here she shared the bed with her hostess minister, and that night there was more than the usual kisses and hugs she received from the sisters during her travels. She got very little rest that night, and the good, good feeling introduced to her never left. From then on, she angled for it with an addict's zealousness.

As she became older, the whispers grew about her on the evangelists' circuits. She had more females following her and filling the pews than males. The men who attended her services did so either out of curiosity to hear a female minister acclaimed as one of the best, or to entice her into their beds. When reflecting upon this side of her nature and sex in the church, she often declared to herself: *If people only knew the extent of the gay life in the black church!*

The song ended, and the Reverend Mills offered a brief prayer: "Dear Lord, we are gathered here again to hear Thy word—"

When he finished, the congregation sat down and Myrtle came forth in her long, self-assured strides to take her place behind the lectern. The church was permeated with a hushed, expectant silence, and she took advantage of the captured stillness to stand dramatically before them like an ominous accuser and savioress. Eyebrows pinching together in a heavy frown, her gaze circled the room, penetrating through the worshipers like the power of God. Finally she rested her sight on the girl staring up at her, lips half-parted, face flushed with admiration. Myrtle realized time was running out. She would have to move in from the pulpit, since tonight was her last chance.

Abruptly she opened her mouth wide to let the words scream a shock, breaking the silence: "Give ear, O heavens, and I will speak: And let the earth hear the words of my mouth."

Oh-h-h yes-s-s!

"Luke, fourth chapter, eighteenth verse says: 'The Spirit of the Lord is upon me because he has anointed me to preach good news to the poor. He has sent me to proclaim release to the captives and recovering of sight to the blind, to set at liberty those who are oppressed.'"

Un-hun-n-n.

Like phosphorous lightning, Myrtle moved quickly from behind the rostrum to the side in full view of the congregation. "Yes-s-s, I *know* there are you who are op-*press*-ed by this unjust society, by selfish family members, and by disloyal loved ones." To this, she saw Magdalen nod her head, and thought: *The poor girl's been deceived by a lover.* Myrtle knew that she must utilize this disclosure. "But, *fortunately*, the world is *not* made of all-l-l oppressors. There *are* people who *can* give help, kindness, and *love* to heal the wounds and make you whole and fre-e-e again. The greatest force for freeing the oppressed is the power of love. *Love* for all-l-l. *Love* is the equalizer, for if you are *filled* with love, you won't have the desire to deceive, betray, be the conqueror or enslaver of humankind!"

Preach!

"Ev-errryone needs *love*. 'Man shall not live by bread alone—'"

Ain't it the truth!

"*I* kno-o-w!" Myrtle bellowed to the rafters, lifting her arms high, the balloon sleeves of her robe falling back to expose a diamond watch given to her by a former lover—a retired minister of the Apostolic faith. "I tri-i-ed to live without sharing human love once—" She paused for effect. The personal confession, whether a lie or truth, invariably aroused them.

At this instant, she saw Magdalen's body jerk upright. Her lips were slightly apart as she leaned forward eagerly to hear. Perceiving the intense exhibition of interest by the girl, Myrtle began to hammer home. "I *know* you can't live without love. All people should have someone to love, hold, share sadness and gladness—"

"Yes-s-s, Lord!" The shrill lone sanctioning voice came from Magdalen, who was bent halfway out of her seat, glassy eyes fastened on the Reverend.

Upon seeing the girl's dress slide up farther exposing the soft, firm thighs pressed together, Myrtle wet her lips. It was time to spew forth fire and brimstone, she thought, to heat up the church and Magdalen. "Jesus-s-s believed that *love* is the key to the goo-oo-dness of humankind. Through love, you can accomplish anything and everything. I have love within *me*. *You* have love within you and *you!*"

"I *do!*" the girl exclaimed, waving her arms excitedly.

Myrtle savored the quickening movements of the full breasts jiggling from the action of her arms. *I'll bet you do,* she mused, envisioning the feel of the twin spheres in the palms of her hands.

"You *got* to have love in your mind, soul, and hearts. You got to love Him who giveth love." On this cue, she began to move, strolling up and down in a prance on the pulpit, the folds of her robe swinging in a billowy cloud. Her arms flailed, punctuating the words spewing forth, while her voice intensified, rising and falling like a singer's without music.

"The world has no *room* for oppressors—white, black, man, woman. *Love* is the key, the *redeemer*. I want to hear this wonderful choir sing my mother's favorite hymn—the song she requested on her deathbed that I have sung in remembrance of her wherever I preached—'Love is Life.'"

The pianist crashed down dissonantly on the keys and the choir rose to sing. "Ah-h-h, yes-s-s, sing about the wonders of love!" Myrtle urged, before stepping down from the pulpit to pace rhythmically up and down in front of the church, spreading her arms in an all-embracing gesture. Suddenly she stopped in front of Magdalen, who was staring at her in a hypnotic trance.

Looking down upon her, Myrtle asked low, "Honey, you got love in your heart?"

The girl stared at her, half in awe, half in adoration, and nodded her head in assent. Myrtle's eyes drew flints of light which pinpointed the young body in a sensuous caress.

As though a signal had been given, the girl leaped out of her seat to fling her arms about Myrtle. "Love! I got *love* in my heart!"

"This child's got *love* in her heart!" Myrtle screamed to the rear of the church, squeezing Magdalen in an embrace. The singing stopped and the congregation belched forth assertions of joy for the girl with love in her heart.

Magdalen was crying and trembling, wrapped inside the batlike cape of Myrtle's robe. Myrtle felt the youthful body pressing against her and swallowed hard. Using the fullness of the robe to camouflage her movements, she tightened her arms around the tantalizing form and ground her hips into the girl, rotating them as she pretended to sway with her holy utterances to the worshipers: "Jesus-s-s is love!"

God, the girl sure felt good, good, good fastened to her like that. Was she imagining it, or were Magdalen's hips answering back, gyrating bone against bone, leg to leg, pelvis rubbing pelvis? What a glorious feeling! It was so magnificent that a slight wetness began to ooze down between her legs as the ache there grew sharper. She sucked in her breath with a hiss, reminding herself that she was supposed to be preaching, not dry-fucking.

To mask her sexual excitement, which was causing her to breathe faster, she looked up over the girl's head at the church-goers, although she really did not see them for she was blinded by her overwhelming passion. Maneuvering her voice to rise and gasp out the words in frenetic passion, she shouted, "Jesus loves ev-errybody. All those great and small, rich and poor, ugly and beautiful—" At this point, she expertly pressed her thumb over the angle of Magdalen's jaw and kept it there. The girl fainted in her arms. "See, *God* has *struck* this child with *love!*"

Two stewardesses in white uniforms rushed forward, but

Myrtle waved them away. *"I* can bring this child back to her earthly home. Child, look at me," she ordered, releasing her pressure.

The girl slowly opened her eyes in the arms of Myrtle, who pretended to bend over to see if she had been revived. Then she whispered without moving her lips, "Meet me afterwards?"

The girl mouthed consent.

"Bless you child," Myrtle said aloud. And under her breath: "My black Buick's parked at the back of the church." Solicitously she eased the girl baçk to her seat, slyly brushing her hand across her breasts.

"Let's *all* follow the example of this child and get *filled* with the spirit of love. *I* can help you to see the light; to *know* God's word by joining in spirit with Him!"

Yes-s-s!

The choir began one of its own homespun rolicking renditions, the pianist thumping out a foot-stomping, earsplitting, body-shaking beat. "Praise the Lord!" Myrtle cried, shaking her head and pulling up her robe to perform some intricate footwork that would have made a professional dancer envious. This part of the service always worked them up. She called it the release of tensions to God. As the repenters filed up to her, she stopped to shake their hands, kiss and bless them.

The music became more rocking, louder, and someone produced a tambourine which added to the beat. Myrtle's face was twisted in delirious holy flight as she began once more to wiggle her body and shuffle her feet in time with the music. She imagined herself an ancient Hausa queen performing religious rites around a fire in the African thicket. The movements and mind-image heated her spiritually and sexually, causing her thoughts to focus around the young thing and how it was going to be later. *So-o-o goo-ood!* With this anticipation in mind, her rhythmic twisting movements happily carried her back to the girl whose eyes were riveted on her in fascination.

Smiling, Myrtle half opened her mouth to dart out her tongue in a snakelike path before she said, "Say Jesus and come to me!"

"Hallelujah! *Jesus-s-s!"* the girl yelled back, standing up wavering, face ecstatically convulsed in orgasmic agitation as she swayed toward Myrtle. "I'm *com-m-ing!"*

Chapter 2

MYRTLE'S eyes opened for the second time that morning in the blind-drawn chalky mist of the motel room. The girl, whom she had named Magdalen but had discovered was Leotha, had had to leave early for work in the button factory. Before she departed, their lips had pressed together in deep good-bye kisses with Myrtle fervently promising to write and keep in touch, murmuring her routine words of tearful endearments and commiserations reserved for such partings. As soon as the girl closed the door, Myrtle, exhausted from the sexual demands of the young thing, promptly went back to sleep.

Now fully awake and leisurely resting in bed ruminating over the past evening, she felt pleased with herself, glorying in the long, stimulating night of lovemaking. The girl, obviously not a novice in the art of Sapphic loving, had been very receptive. Smiling to herself, Myrtle stretched out lazily, still smelling the too sweet fragrance of the young thing's cheap perfume. Streaks of powder and lipstick stained the white of the other pillow like a disconnected face.

The bed and room flagrantly testified to loving. In contrast to her usual orderliness, the place was a mess. Her two-hundred-dollar robe had been thrown in careless haste across a chair, and underclothes and shoes made a helter-skelter path to the bed. On the dresser were a seven-dollar tray of assorted soggy hors d'oeuvres, and a champagne bottle floating precariously in a plastic bucket of melted ice. Champagne was bought to impress the cute things. The room was murky with the odors of wine, Leotha's cigarettes, woman-sweat and sex.

9

The caution of time reared its warning into her thoughts. She reached over to look at her watch on the nightstand. It was 10:00 A.M., which meant that the time had arrived to start moving, shower, and get on the road. She was due in Nashville that evening to preach for a week. She liked the big cities best, for there she could get lost and loose. People in large cities were more broad-minded about interpreting the word of the Lord. She did have some reservations about Nashville, a southern city located in the so-called Bible Belt, where there were purported to be a lot of Christians either in fact or fantasy. From other sources, the place seemed to have an overload of the devil's circuits at work, too. But wasn't that why she had been invited there? To preach against the sins of the times and save souls for Jesus?

Flinging the covers back, she got out of bed and opened the drapes. The sun's glare swept away the dimness, letting the morning's light into the room. Situated on the outskirts of town, the motel was separated from a cornfield by the road. She noticed that the parking lot was almost empty. Last night, it had been swollen with cars. Nobody tarried too long in places like this. For her, they were all right for drop-ins and doing your thing, but not to stay.

God knows, she thought on the way to the bathroom, she had had her fill of country towns when younger. Traveling around no-man's-land with her God-proselytizing parents, sleeping in lean-to church parishes on unpaved streets in the colored parts of town. In those places the backyards invariably housed chickens that seemed to take a devilish pleasure in high-fever crowing at the eye-opener of dawn. By eight o'clock in the morning, colored town, except for the elderly, babies, sick, and those on welfare, was deserted. Everybody crossed over the railroad tracks to work in white town during the daytime transmigration of working souls.

Myrtle went over to the washbowl to brush her teeth, one of her favorite morning regimens, delighting in the fact that despite her age, she had all of her own. After rinsing out her mouth, she pulled off her gown and turned on the shower. Before stepping into the tub, she painstakingly tucked her long hair under a shower cap. Her hair and teeth were her personal pride. Sticking out her hand, she cautiously tested the water. Just right.

Showering, she thought about her father, the Reverend

Elijah Black. He, too, had to have everything just right. He was a handsome man, big and black, with chiseled features, the epitome of black and proud before it became a shibboleth. He never went out of the house unless he had on starched and ironed underwear, and was impeccably dressed in a suit, shirt, and tie. The creases of his pants, even though the material might sometimes be shiny, had to be razor sharp. Complementing his neatness in dress was his deep baritone voice, an asset in capping off his appearance and commanding attention. All of this charm was used to save souls and make a living out of the pockets of worshipers.

Myrtle was almost a facsimile of her father, inheriting both his good looks which gave her a unique kind of comeliness, and the resonance of his voice, which, reflected in her, became a rich, clear contralto. She soon discovered that her voice, coupled with her inherent facility for words, could play havoc in the ears and hearts of people. It served her well, too, in bed as an incitement to lovemaking. Also, just as women were attracted to her father, they were to her. But because she was a woman, too, they blinded themselves to the true nature of the magnetism, preferring to place it in the category of the spiritual.

From her mother, the Reverend Gossie Pinkton Black, she acquired her smooth mahogany complexion and soft, wavy black hair, which was passed along from her maternal half-Cherokee grandmother. Gossie had almost died giving birth to her, and because of this, the doctor had removed her uterus. As a result, being the sole child, she was her parents' pride and joy outside of Jesus.

Scrubbing vigorously, she soaped away the perfume and powder odors of the girl's body and the sweat of her own. Slipping into her underwear, she peered toward the closet at the array of clothes she carried with her. Admittedly clothes were a weakness, stemming perhaps from the painful memory of not having had enough of them in her childhood. Those were the days when the collection plates were thin in small towns during the winters, where the work froze with the ground, then thawed in the spring when the earth bore the crops that provided the seasonal livelihood in fields and factories.

During those difficult times, her mother held the family economy together by working for white folks. Gossie was a good cook and wasn't too proud to join the crossovers to perform daywork when her husband would do nothing but stay home, barricading himself into a stormy, mute silence, face hidden between the pages of the Bible.

Gazing at her own neatly hung clothes, she recalled the two times that she had gone with her mother to the other side of the tracks, supposedly to help by dusting and doing light chores. There had been rows of clothes, too, in those closets belonging to the people who had hired Gossie to wash, iron, clean, and cook. She had been awestruck by the deep rugs, shiny furniture, gleaming silver and china. No one ever seemed to be at home in those places, except the wives who kept a watchful eye on the cleaning process.

Quickly, the Reverend Elijah Black put a defiant halt to his daughter's going to the houses with her mother. In his most authoritative way, he bluntly announced in a manner that defied rejoinder: *"My* daughter is *not* going to clean up white folks' dirt. She is going to stay home with me and learn to preach the word of the Lord." Her father fervently believed that a minister's mission in life was to preach, save souls, serve the Lord and nobody else.

Surveying the clothes, Myrtle chose a two-piece pink pantsuit. Bending to step into it, her legs felt a trifle stiff. The physical exertion last night had done that to her. She wasn't as young as she used to be. But for a forty-year-old woman, taking on a young, fiery thing of nineteen, she had held her own and then some more. It had been a glory-hallelujah night all right. The cries and moans of Leotha were yet starbright in her memory. It all was simply a matter of *how* to do what you were doing. Thankfully, the parting with the girl hadn't been too turbulent. Sometimes they could get messy, crying and carrying on, wanting to stay with her.

But, no sir-r-r-ee. None could do *that,* for she was a freewheeling gospel spirit. She couldn't be bored, saddled down with the same person hanging on to her morning, noon, and night. A steady presence frightened off approaches from others. Besides, variety siphoned juice into the bloodstream of life.

Myrtle brushed her hair a hundred strokes, making the tresses glisten. Recently, she had begun to spot a few flecks of gray, but she combed over them so they wouldn't be noticeable. Smoothing the pantsuit, she viewed herself in the full-length mirror on the bathroom door, pleased at what she saw. She was in excellent shape. Her body was firm without the bulging stomach or drooping tits of the middle-aged. She didn't intend to let herself get fat and out of shape. Those preachers' wives could set the tempting chicken and dumplings, home-made pies and cakes on the table all they wanted, but she knew how to resist.

Fastening her watch, she noted the hands pointed to 11:30 A.M. There was enough time before checking out to go down-stairs and have orange juice and coffee. First, she had to pack and get the telltale party effects out of sight.

She began to straighten up the room, emptying the melted bucket of ice in the bathroom and covering the champagne bottle with a napkin. Furtively opening the door, she peered cautiously up and down the hallway to see if anyone was in sight, then swiftly took the tray midway down the corridor where she deposited it in front of another door.

This was her ritual in towns where there was only one motel. One could never take too many precautions. Some of the black maids could have attended her services. When ordering the champagne from room service, she gave her companion cash to pay while she waited in the bathroom. Granted *somebody* was going to know or surmise *something*, but it didn't have to be the *whole* world.

With the can of air freshener she kept on hand, she cleared the room of odors, then checked for any forgotten items. Lastly, she took one final glance in the mirror to see that her natural lipstick was applied straight and that no stray hairs had escaped from the chignon at the center of her head. All was well and she was looking *good*. She went down to breakfast.

Myrtle's Buick Riviera shone like a polished black panther in the sun's brilliance as the motor purred smoothly along I-40 East to Nashville. It was perfect weather for driving. The clouds made white foam islands in the blue ocean of sky. A lovely May day, the kind she liked to be out in to admire God's wondrous nature. The day's beauty seemed like a blessed sign.

She drove with practiced ease and skill, enjoying the high-powered automobile. She had a penchant for luxurious cars. They complemented her concept of herself: supreme in the sight of herself, public, and Lord. Expensive cars denoted power and affluence, transmitting to people that she was in fact a superior woman who called for respect.

Switching on the radio, she located a gospel program. Clara

Ward's group was singing "Jesus Is Kind." Myrtle began humming along with it. Fortunately, the highway wasn't too congested at this time of day. While driving, she began to plan ahead. It was always good to do this, map out strategies and tactics. She liked to be prepared and not get caught unawares, for sometimes God wasn't able to take care of everybody at the same time.

Her hotel reservations in Nashville had been made three weeks ago, after she had found out that the host minister, Reverend Amos Cross, and his wife had six children, aged from six to fourteen. Immediately she wrote to the Reverend Cross saying that perhaps she had better stay in a hotel because she needed the utmost privacy to commune with herself and her Jesus. Staying in a house with all those children would have driven her out of her mind and the Lord's senses.

The truth of the matter was she preferred hotels to houses even if there were no children. In a locked room, what she did was nobody's business but her own. Most times the churches bore the expense of her lodging, but if they couldn't, she managed to get it through extra collections by pleading "One more time around for the Lord!" again *and* again if necessary.

A long fuel truck, with its body shaped like a rocket, roared along beside her, drowning out her thoughts and the radio. The driver deliberately matched his speed with hers, not passing, but honking his horn. Puzzled, she looked over, frowning at the driver, wondering what was wrong. Cap perched low over his eyes, the man grinned out the oil-smeared window at her and flicked out his tongue in a suggestive wiggling movement.

Incensed, she mouthed, "Go on, you white ass hole!" And under her breath: "Forgive me, Jesus."

The man laughed and gunned the truck past her. Anger at him lingered, a smoldering fire. What made men think all women wanted them? Some could be as ugly as sin and older than Methuselah, yet they believed in their appeal merely because they were men. This was another in the long line of reasons why she chose to stay in hotels rather than with the pastors. Most times when the wives were away, the men thought they should try to get her between the sheets. Just because she was a single woman, they were certain what she needed or missed was a man, supposing a woman could not function normally without a penis stuck in her from time to time. However, *she* had news for *them*. If her libido needed assuaging, she knew how to get it done and without a male!

Only when the towns were too small and without motels did she sleep in the church parish houses. When she did, she kept her door locked, a chair propped against it, and one eye opened. Particularly after that incident involving the fat, sloppy preacher in Albany when she was thirteen. The man, old enough to be her grandfather, would have raped her, if Elijah Black hadn't come back sooner than expected. And that old bear of the cloth had a new baby and wife out working to help make ends meet. The old saying was true: a stiff dick has no conscience.

Men sure took pride in that thing between their legs. This appendage—dicks, pricks, Jones, Johnsons, sprouts, trunks— was the mainstay of their egotism.

Myrtle didn't dislike men. They were here on earth to stay and she had to live with them. Weren't they a part of God's universe? She had male friends. Her best one was Jesus. It was merely that men were not essential to her emotional or sexual needs. They were not significant to her. The only male spirit she required was that of God. But who could prove he was entirely male?

The urge to go to the bathroom possessed her. Time to stop and rest anyway. She was making good time. After passing Memphis, it wouldn't be too long. A green sign ahead alerted her to a restaurant and filling station at the next exit. She would get gas and a bite to eat.

Inside the diner she went to the restroom, then sat in one of the booths by the windows. The place was empty except for the middle-aged white waitress sitting behind the counter reading a movie magazine. Upon seeing Myrtle enter, she rose and came over to her.

"Good afternoon, ma'am," she said with a smile as she placed a menu and glass of water on the table.

Myrtle's cultivated minister's smile beamed warmly at her. "I'll just have black coffee and a tuna salad," she said, pushing the menu away. Her regular luncheon fare, one not heavy enough to make her drowsy and nonfattening, too.

Watching the waitress prepare the food, Myrtle thought perhaps she should have sat at the counter so she could strike up a conversation with the woman. When she was a girl, she had liked older women better. Girls her own age were not sophisticated enough. There had been one, however, in her age group, to whom she had gotten closer than usual. Deborah was smart, witty, and had big tits. One evening she had gone over

to spend the night at Deborah's when her own parents were
going away to preach in a rural chitterling switch town where
the minister's home didn't even have an indoor toilet. Having
been there before with them, she hated the place, and had
feigned illness to keep from going with them.

When she and Deborah had gone to bed, it was Myrtle who
had had difficulty falling asleep in the bed they shared. She
had lain stiffly huddled on her side, conscious of the warm,
soft body next to hers. A tremendous surge of desire had shaken
her, stifling, frightening, making her want to reach around and
touch Deborah like the Reverend Lily Smith had touched her
that summer night in Cloverdale. She had closed her eyes
tightly, staying silent, stiff, restraining herself from turning
over to bring Deborah close to her, to kiss her gently awake.
Something stopped her, warning. What would Deborah think?

In the bed lying rigid, she prayed silently, asking God to
help control the desire, to take away the unnatural thoughts
which to her seemed quite natural. What had they been to the
Reverend Lily Smith? When Deborah murmured something in
her sleep and stirred, foot lightly brushing hers, Myrtle had
held her breath, afraid to breathe, think or hope. Were her
thoughts permeating Deborah's? How would the warm, full
breasts feel against hers? She wished Deborah would move
again, give her a signal of mutual accord. But she didn't.

She found herself starting to do what she had been doing
more and more, conjuring up the remembrance of Reverend
Lily Smith in her mind. As she did, her hand moved slowly
down between her legs, drawn to where the throbbing had sent
an ache throughout her body. There the palm of her hand
brushed against the bristly hair bush, index finger extending
like a boring worm to enter the wet opening where it wiggled
and sank into the hot, sticky crevice. Heat stole over her and
burst into flames. She suppressed a cry, as her body was flooded
by pleasurable spasms. Only after this did she fall asleep.

It was after the night at Deborah's that Myrtle was certain
that it was women who moved her. Unnerved by her feelings,
Myrtle avoided girls to whom she was attracted. They made
her jittery, timid, and ashamed. She shied away from them,
for she did not want them to know, nor did she want to risk
being ridiculed for feelings that she knew had a name.

This name she had learned through her peers, although as
a minister, she was left out of the school's furtive girl talk

groups which transmitted sex information. Nevertheless, she had overheard the words "bulldagger" and "funny" whispered about another girl who was tomboyish. She had also heard about the "right" side of sex in the gym showers over the jetting streams of water and smelly, sweaty shoes and socks. She could hear laughter connected with how it felt to French kiss and snickerings of lost cherries. She eavesdropped hungrily, for sex information at home was only given on Sundays through veiled sermons on the Ten Commandments, Adam and Eve, and the forbidden fruit.

The waitress returned with her order. Eating slowly, Myrtle again reverted to the past, which held her thoughts like a tenacious ghost. She had tried to turn her feelings to the heterosexual side of sex to keep from being different. This she had attempted with LeMelle Goshen in her senior class. Looking back, she could see that LeMelle was dim-witted despite the eyeglasses which gave him a false appearance of intelligence. But he was also egotistical enough to be the only male with the self-confidence to approach her. The rest had seemed frightened off by her indifference, piercing stare, arrogance, and barbed tongue which could deliver an insult or quip as fast and stinging as a whip. Most of all, the fact that both her mother and she were ministers had struck not only awe in the would-be youthful suitors, but the fear of God, too!

It was prom night when things came to a head. In line with striving to be like her peers, she had let LeMelle escort her in his father's five-year-old rusty Chevy. Standing aloof in the gaily decorated high school gymnasium, she was bored. With disdain, she watched the dancing and furtive spiking of punch cups with Seagram's Seven Crown. She felt above it all, older and wiser.

As was expected, on the way home, LeMelle parked the Chevy with its rattling motor on a winding country road hidden by trees, and put his arms around her. *Here it comes,* she had thought, taking a deep breath.

Inexpertly, LeMelle kissed her, bumping their noses. His glasses kept getting in the way, and finally, he placed them in the glove compartment. Coldly she had decided to give in to him, believing that it would turn her away from the other desire and make her like the rest. LeMelle's lips opened against hers, his mouth a pit of liquor and chewing gum. Stiffly she sat still, waiting to be struck by the consuming hotness the girls raved about. She felt nothing, but he was breathing rapidly. Because she did not resist, he grew bolder and rammed his hand down into the top of her dress.

His kisses were hot and strange. He had been the only male she had voluntarily kissed, other than her father. The others had been kissed by demand. They were the lecherous preachers who always wanted "some sugar" from the "sweet little girl of Reverend Black." While her father watched grinning with pride, the men would lean over with their foul breaths and yellow eyes for her to peck them on rough, ill-shaven cheeks and tough dry mouths. When her breasts began to develop into round, conical buds, if her father wasn't looking, the men would sneak a pinch on the nipple along with the kiss.

LeMelle's fumbling hands on her breasts that night in the car had left her cold, hurting as the preachers' had done. As if watching from outside of herself, she let him push her down in the seat. She was going to let him do *it* to help rid her of the private demon. Her body was being offered as a sacrificial lamb.

In his frantic excitement, he tore her dress, throwing it above her to push the panties down. He held his thing in his hand, showing in the moonlight like a thin, short sausage growing long and throbbing with its skinned-back inflamed hammerhead. The thing sought to enter her vagina, struggling against the tightness. She closed her eyes and imagined it a sorcerer's wand inside, ridding her of sin, expelling a depravity. She gritted her teeth against the invasion of her body by his, moaning softly from the bruising pain. Aroused and intoxicated, he came quickly. She breathed with relief. Jesus had been merciful.

There was blood and sticky whiteness over her. With chilling adult command, she said sternly: "LeMelle, take me home." The exorcism was finished. She prayed to the Lord.

Soon she found that her sacrifice had been in vain. The preference for her own sex persisted. She hated LeMelle for his failure to exorcise her, and despised herself for letting him enter the citadel of her body.

In the fall, she enrolled in the state college. She lived at home rather than on campus, leaving on weekends to preach wherever invited. Possessed with an inquiring mind, she enjoyed the challenge of her studies, but her social life was an extension of high school. The students looked upon her as being bizarre. She was not invited to their affairs, for weren't ministers supposed to condemn drinking, swearing, card playing, and unlicensed fucking?

Graduating with honors, she went on to the Interdenominational Seminary for a degree. The college and seminary education, combined with her secular knowledge, developed her into a different kind of minister than her salvation-ranting parents. She was more mundane, but shrewd enough to utilize the old-time religion with the intellectual spirituality of the new.

Gossie lived to see her daughter get her education, then lay down and died. Following the burial in the family plot of the Divine Mission Church, Myrtle wrote to the superintendent for a charge. To her dismay, she was assigned as assistant pastor for the First Holy Church in the coal mining town of Molten, Pennsylvania. There the minister, Reverend James Spears, was sixty-four years old, looked fifteen years older, and was sickly.

The Reverend Spears was glad to have relief from leading the religious lives of the black people in the town for over thirty years. He had grown thin and gaunt, his mustard-colored skin made darker by the coal dust. He seemed as spiritless as his parishioners, who tiredly sat on the hard pews on Sundays, victims of habit to the Lord. The church was their salvation from the monotony of mines, debts, racism, and kin.

Myrtle, fired with ambition, took charge, and the Reverend Spears gladly stepped aside. Curious about the woman preacher, the church slowly began to fill up on Sundays. The men and boys came to gawk and speculate about the good-looking preacher, and the women to frown disapprovingly.

Ultimately, Myrtle won the confidence of the women and the respect of the men. Her services, replete with tambourines, rocking music, and shouts to Jesus, brought brightness into the dismal abyss of her parishioners' lives. The drudgery and everyday sameness were forgotten on Sunday, the day they prayed, sang and screamed away their frustrations in the name of the Lord. No club meeting was ever better.

For a period of time, she derived satisfaction from her accomplishment in reviving the living dead in that dreary town. She prayed over the sick, christened the babies born with doomed faces, and prayed their dead ghosts to heaven.

Inevitably she became restless. She missed the stimulation and concealment afforded by urban living. Before the year was out, she asked to be released, saying that she was developing a cough, so the coal dust must be making her ill. She bought a three-year-old Pontiac with the remains of her mother's insurance money and drove away without a goodbye.

"Would you like anything else?" the waitress asked, hovering above her.

Myrtle's thoughts were severed from the past. "No, thank you." She looked up at the waitress and smiled, thinking she might have been interesting to talk with. Opening her purse, she paid the bill.

"Have a göod day!" the waitress said.

She drove to the gas area to fill up before exiting back to the highway. A sign read "Nashville 200 miles." It wouldn't be too long now. A new place and different faces were before her, bringing new challenges which she thrived on. But she had learned that being God's emissary didn't always point to miraculous success. She mouthed a silent prayer.

Then tossing back her head, she laughed to herself. "All right, you Christians and sinners. Here comes the one and only Reverend Myrtle Black! God's gift to the church and womankind!"

Chapter 3

*T*HE sun had not quite disappeared when Myrtle met the Nashville homebound traffic on the James Robertson Parkway as she headed for the Andrew Jackson. She had chosen that hotel because of its proximity to the Reverend Cross's New Hope Unity Church in North Nashville.

The murky warmth, clinging from the day-heat, washed over her like a dragon's breath when she stepped out of the air-conditioned car. On entering the building, she was confronted by a large tapestry of Andrew Jackson riding a horse in the midst of the Battle of New Orleans, which graced the front wall of the lobby. After checking in, she stopped to buy an evening paper, a habit formed over the years. Newspapers were helpful in finding out about a city, its people, problems, politics, happenings, and morals.

After the bellhop left, she looked approvingly around the room with its reproductions of Jacksonian period furniture. The hotel was relatively new and lacked the overstuffed, musty odor of voluminous past patronage. From the picture window, she could see across the parkway to the white dome of the capitol building on the hill. City lights began to make white glares as traffic sounds emitted a strident chorus of movement.

The first thing she had to do was telephone the host pastor. With the number fixed in her mind, she went to the phone and dialed. His voice came over the wires in a slow southern drawl: "Reverend Amos Cross speaking."

"Good evening, Reverend Cross, this is Reverend Myrtle Black. I have just arrived in your city here at the Andrew Jackson."

"Ah-h-h! My wife and I were wondering if you made it all

right." Myrtle didn't find his voice to her liking—too soft and high for a minister, lacking the sonorous quality of her father.

"Yes—without mishap. It was a beautiful day for driving. God's nature was out in all its splendor."

"It certainly was! Won't you join us for dinner? My wife prepared it with *you* in mind."

"I would be delighted to dine with you," she said, eager to meet and know him.

"Fine. I can pick you up in about—"

"*Please,* don't bother," she interrupted hastily. "I have a city map. I want to get used to finding my way around." Most certainly, she did not want him to come here, intruding upon her private domicile. This was now her temporary home. Such a visit could lead to a habit of "just dropping in." Men were noted for that.

"Well, let me check with Mrs. Cross to find out the exact time dinner will be ready."

Mrs. Cross, indeed! she thought. The uppity black imitating whites: "Mr. Blank will have his dinner at eight," or "Mrs. Blank wants the house cleaned." In the background, she could hear the noisy voices of children.

"My wife says dinner is at seven-thirty. Will that rush you too much?"

"No, that is fine."

"We'll be looking forward to meeting you, Reverend Black. We've heard so-o-o many good things about you. I know-ow with *you* here, we'll have an inspiring revival week."

"Thank you for your confidence, Reverend Cross. I will see you shortly."

Resting before going to dinner, Myrtle propped herself up on the pillows in bed and opened the newspaper. At first, the meaning of the headlines did not penetrate, but reading them again made her gasp aloud in disbelief. The *Nashville Evening News* captioned in blue banner headlines:

TWO PROSTITUTES
SHOT ON STREET
IN NORTH NASHVILLE

Two prostitutes were shot last night on the corner of Seventh and Jefferson Street in North Nashville. The

women, Earthly Treasure Williams, 22, and Heavenly
Delight Brown, 19, were taken to Hubbard Hospital
where they are reported to be in fair condition.

The two women, both with prostitution arrest records,
were hit by gunfire from a speeding car around 11 P.M.
as they stood in front of the Slinky Fox Tavern. Police
believe the shooting was precipitated by a war over the
turf between local and out-of-town pimps infiltrating the
city.

Myrtle read on with glee. This Christian city in the Bible
Belt was embroiled in prostitution, sin and vice! It just went
to prove that the devil never rested and was everywhere. Those
poor, poor girls were so young, too! She should have been
here earlier to preach to them to give up their sinful trade. To
come to Christ, to come to *her*. The horror of it all. Wasn't
there anyone around strong enough to lead sinners in the path
of righteousness?

Lead! That was it. The word was a message, striking like
the fist of the Almighty. The city needed a Lord's shepherdess,
since the shepherds weren't doing anything. The inspiration to
become a black leader brought forth a divine revelation in her
mind, smiting her in a fever of beatific stimulation, like Moses
and the burning bush. Never before had she felt so impelled,
impassioned, aroused! The oracle was before her, commanding, giving her mission here. *Thy Will Be Done!*

First, she had to learn more about this city of Babylon.
Enthusiastically, she began to read the rest of the paper for
information that would provide further insight into Nashville's
condition. The mayor was at war with the city council; a local
country music singer had been arrested on cocaine charges;
food prices were skyrocketing; a massage parlor had been
raided; and Travis Lee was to give a concert Sunday night at
the Municipal Auditorium.

Myrtle lingered on the Travis Lee story. Travis Lee was one
of the most popular rhythm and blues singers in the country.
The Sunday night revival service would surely have her for
competition. She studied the picture of Travis smiling out of
the paper. The singer was certainly attractive in an earthy kind
of way. Smoldering and sexy looking with those almond-
shaped eyes and sensuous, full lips that could belt out a song.
Travis's ample curves placed her slightly toward the heavy

side. Her quick, crashing fad diets were no secret, played up
in *Ebony* and *Jet*. Neither was her mercurial temper which
seemed to fluctuate with her diets and lovers. According to the
gossip columnists, she changed men like shoes. Myrtle felt
some kindred spirit with the singer because Travis had begun
singing in a church choir. This meant that she had church *roots*.

Reluctantly, Myrtle pulled her eyes away from the picture
of the almost bare breasts of Travis Lee, half-spilling out of
a low-cut gown. The gal had some good-looking boobs, only
she couldn't lie here all evening admiring tits. She had to get
dressed. One thing Myrtle believed firmly in was being on
time. She would not allow herself to fall into CPT—Colored
People's Time. Furthermore, time was important to her, especially in this city of iniquity.

The home of the Reverend Cross was a rambling, faded
brick and stone two-story building in a deteriorating neighborhood. An iron fence with a gate that hung lopsidedly surrounded the old house. She walked up the steps to the small
concrete porch jutting out like a swollen lip, and pressed the
doorbell, which sounded an ice cream peddler's jingle.

"Good evening, I am Reverend Myrtle Black," she said,
giving a friendly smile to the woman who answered the door.

"Do come in, Reverend Black. I'm Lucy Cross, the Reverend's wife. It's so nice to have you with us. Come this way,
please." Myrtle was ushered into the living room, through a
narrow, dimly lit vestibule with a tree coatrack. "Make yourself
at home."

"Thank you." Myrtle's eyes swept quickly over the short,
dumpy woman with a puffed robin's breast pushing through
a Sear's cotton print dress. Her hair was graying prematurely,
brushed back from a plain, brown matronly face.

A small boy, dressed in shorts and a striped T-shirt, sat
cross-legged on a rope scatter rug before an ancient black and
white television set. "This is our youngest child, Sonnie," Mrs.
Cross said as her face lit up with motherly pride. Tapping the
boy on the shoulder, she ordered, "Sonnie, speak to Reverend
Black."

Sonnie glanced sideways at Myrtle and mumbled something
incoherent before quickly returning his attention to the set.

"My husband will be down in a few minutes. Oh, here he
is now."

Reverend Cross came into the room, hand outstretched,

smiling. "Reverend Black, how do you do? I trust you found
your way without difficulty."

"No trouble at all, Reverend Cross. You see, I am an old
hand at finding my way around." She shook his hand, deliberately gripping it firmly to convey that she could hold her
own. She discovered that she was taller than he. She always
considered this a decided advantage since height commanded
respect. The Reverend was rotund with a moon face slightly
lighter in hue than his wife. Two gold front teeth polished his
smile.

"I'm going to finish dinner." Mrs. Cross excused herself.

"Sit down." Reverend Cross motioned to the sofa with a
green chenille throw cover.

The couch had a broken spring, which hunched her. The
crack in the coffee table's glass was half-hidden by an artificial
bowl of flowers. An upright piano with sheets of religious
music filled a corner near the window holding an air-condi-
tioner, which did not seem to work since it emitted a low hum
but little coolness. The room was clean and austere, showing
the stiffness of "reserved for company." Children's voices
blared from other parts of the house, a cacophony of shouted
words and retorts.

The sounds must have reminded Reverend Cross of the boy
in the room, for he said, "Sonnie, go upstairs and watch TV
until dinner is ready."

"But Daddy," the boy protested, "that one don't work."

Looking embarrassed, his father murmured, "That's right,
I forgot. Well, go on anyway. Reverend Black and I want to
talk."

Pouting, the boy got up and left the room. "Children must
learn to obey," Reverend Cross noted.

"Yes," Myrtle agreed, thankful that children had never been
one of her problems. Motherhood did not appeal to her. All
women weren't cut out to be mothers even if they were women.

The room was warm to her and the clerical collar made a
sweat band around her neck. She wanted to remove the jacket
of her two-piece dress, but propriety prevailed and she endured.
Obviously he was used to the warmth, seemingly unperturbed
in a suit and tie. Southern black ministers were stifled by the
need to maintain an image of formality. Suits worn during the
week were a mark of distinction, especially among small town
ministers. That was the way people distinguished between high
and low.

"We're looking forward to a wonderful week, Reverend
Black. And to get us *all* off to a *big* start, we want you to start
off the Sunday morning service."

"If you like," she said, camouflaging her disgust at the way
his stomach protruded over his belt, black tie resting lengthwise
on the bulge like a fallen twig. His face was bloated, causing
the features to seem flatter than they were. She noticed that he
had the habit of brushing his hand over the sparse knobs of
hair on his head, pausing slightly at the center as if to feel how
much was still left.

As he detailed the activities for the week, her mind sped
ahead of him. She had already decided that this was not going
to be one of those routine fire-and-brimstone evangelistic
weeks. Hadn't she just received a Holy Communication? It was
time for her to *be* and *do* over and *above* the works of the past.
She wasn't getting any younger.

"Have you made the week's program known to the press?"
she asked.

"Definitely! It's going to be in tomorrow's church section."

She frowned. He had made use of only the usual vehicle.
"Do you know any of the press people personally?"

His hand crept across his head again. "Hum-m-m, let's see.
There's George F. D. Clemons, who is church editor for the
Nashville Morning Sun. He's black."

Myrtle's attention was captured immediately. "Oh?" she
said as a plan of action began to take shape in her mind.

"I mailed the press releases and photographs that you sent,
along with some other items to him."

"I would like to meet Mr. Clemons."

"Well . . . I'll try to contact him tomorrow. He's rather hard
to catch up with."

"Can't you call him now?" she persisted. How well she
knew that the best way to get things done was to start at once,
since delays only caused uncertainties and needless confusion.
When she caught his perplexed look, she smiled sweetly. "It
is just that I would like very much to talk with him. To tell
him of *our* work to save souls for Jesus. We don't have too
much time, do we? This *is* Friday."

"You're absolutely right." Although he spoke in agreement,
he acted as if the urgency had not really penetrated. He continued to sit and look down at the floor.

God! She almost lamented aloud. The man was slow-think-
ing and slow-moving. These were traits that she found ex-

tremely irritating. He needed prodding. Women could outthink
a man any day. It was simply a matter of letting *them* think
it was *their* idea.

"I am glad you realize the importance of getting things in
the newspaper, Reverend Cross. Couldn't you try to reach Mr.
Clemons now? If he isn't there, you can leave word for him
to call me at the motel."

"I suppose I could—" He got up hesitantly. "The phone's
in my study."

Myrtle rose also. "I will go with you in case he *is* there,
so I can talk with him."

"Of course—"

His study was a small one-window room with a sequence
of handmade wooden bookshelves lining the walls. He had to
clear the piles of books, papers, and notepads on the desk to
find the phone book. The room was warm, and collected the
odors of the kitchen not too far away.

"Let's see—"

Squinting under the desk lamp, he thumbed through the
phone book.

Waiting, she tried to contain her impatience at his dawdling.
"Here it is." He dialed the number. "This is Reverend Amos
Cross of the New Hope Unity Church. I'd like to speak with
Mr. Clemons, please."

Myrtle strained to hear, pretending that she had moved
closer to get one of the Thurman Funeral Home fans from the
desk. At least in this weather she could be certain it was the
heat of the room and not one of her infrequent hot flashes.

"He isn't in?" she heard him say. Annoyed, she jerked on
his sleeve. "Leave word for him to call me at the motel."
Squeals of children playing in the dusk outside intruded wor-
risomely through the open window. Children seemed to crop
up everywhere, reminders of careless fecundity.

"His wife's going to tell him," Reverend Cross said.

"Dinner's ready!" Mrs. Cross announced in the doorway.

The dining room table was long and wide, causing Myrtle
to suspect that beneath the white linen cloth lurked what was
once a communion table. Odds and ends of chairs encircled
it. Not all of the chandelier lights were turned on or else they
didn't work, creating unappealing shadows. Weighing the
house and its poor state made her wonder whether the church
was in similar shape. If so, she would need to have the baskets
passed more than once to pay the hotel bill. But as the old

saying went: "The Lord takes care of those who take care of themselves."

"This should give us a little breeze while we eat," the Reverend Cross panted, dragging in a floor fan. "A typical Nashville evening," he puffed, setting the fan in front of the room. "These are our children," Mrs. Cross said proudly, then proceeded to introduce each by name.

The oldest one, a girl who looked like her mother in a more attractive way, stared openly at Myrtle, admiration showing for the nylon dress with the multiple pleats.

Myrtle smiled in acknowledgement.

"Now, Reverend Black, you sit right here next to my husband so you two can talk," Mrs. Cross said, pointing to the chair to the left of the head of the table.

When they were all seated, Reverend Cross asked, "Reverend Black, would you please bless our table?"

"It would be an honor. Let's bow our heads—" Myrtle gave one of her short, but elaborate home blessings for the family, house, food, and the Lord.

"Amen," Reverend Cross appended. "Now-w-w, what part of the chicken do *you* like best, Reverend Black?" he questioned, face lighting up as he surveyed the array of food on the table.

"The leg will be fine," Myrtle replied quickly, having learned long ago that if there wasn't a preference, she would automatically be generously served the choice piece of meaty breast.

It took some time to pass the individual plates to be filled with two kinds of chicken—fried and stewed with dumplings—sweet potatoes, macaroni and cheese, turnip greens and ham hocks, beets, cole slaw, and hot-water corn bread. It was a Sunday fare on Friday evening. Myrtle was adept at eating like a sparrow by taking small quantities of almost everything except for the starches which she passed over, yet appearing to have as much as the others. She knew it was an affront to the church sisters if plates weren't filled and emptied with pleasure.

The children bickered among themselves, reaching out greedily for what they wanted, spilling food on the tablecloth in the process. Myrtle excused them, reasoning that it must be hard on Mrs. Cross, if all of them ate at the same time everyday. Now that she had fulfilled the courtesy of sharing a meal with them, she knew this would be the last eaten here.

While eating and half-listening to the uninteresting conver-

sation of Reverend Cross, who obviously never read a newspaper or a book except for the Bible, she focused her thoughts
on George F. D. Clemons who was earmarked to help her set
the first stage in her ordained personal mission.

George F. D. Clemons telephoned her at ten o'clock that
night. In anticipation she had sat up watching TV. "Mr. Clemons, it's so nice of you to call. I'd like *very* much to see you
tonight, if it is at all possible." A pliant note of urgency was
injected into her tone.

"Tonight?" he echoed, unable to control his surprise. "Can't
it wait until tomorrow? I just got in."

"Mr. Clemons, the business of the Lord must be taken care
of when the *need* is there."

She heard him sigh, promising to get there as soon as possible. For this particular pursuit, she reasoned, the best place
to carry on business was here in her own environs without
outside office spectators and eavesdroppers. Pleased with her
success, she got up, smoothing out the folds of her silk lounging
robe and went into the bathroom to refresh herself. She hoped
he wasn't a stubborn male chauvinist.

Within the hour, George F. D. Clemons called her on the
house phone. Opening the door, she put on her most charming-
for-Jesus smile. "I am so pleased that you could come, Mr.
Clemons." She could see that he was impressed by her appearance, which was certainly an asset she intended to use.

"At this time of night after a hard day's work, I would only
do it for a female minister."

"In that case, I am flattered," she said, scanning him in a
furtive way. He had probably been rather handsome in his
prime. At this stage, his wavy hair was salt and pepper, but
still heavy in texture. His light beige face was the shade of his
tired-looking summer suit. A strong smell of tobacco emanated
from him, mingling with a hint of liquor on his breath. He
walked with a slight limp, favoring his right side.

"My, my! First time I've been in this hotel. Real nice. Good
as the Regency," he commented, easing into a chair.

"Would you like a cup of coffee? If it isn't too late, I could
order—"

"No, thanks. I had a cup before I came over."

He reminded her of a henpecked husband with his scuffed
brown shoes. Red socks, incongruous with his yellow tie,
showed straggling down around his spindly ankles. The color

of the socks caused her to speculate.

"Mind if I smoke?" he asked, watching her turn off the television.

"Go right ahead." She allowed this concession, although she disliked smoking.

"You're the second ordained female minister I've met this year. I find it quite refreshing after some of the males I've met," he laughed.

Observing and listening to him, she felt he should not prove difficult. Ministers had to learn to be lay psychologists in order to deal with all kinds of people. Those of the Lord and otherwise. "I am glad that you find us so." She pushed an ashtray over to remind him of the long ashes accumulating on his cigarette.

"What's on your mind, Reverend Black?" Ashes were dutifully flicked into the receptacle.

For effect, she hesitated before replying, shaking her head and making her face pained. Inhaling a deep breath, she began: "Mr. Clemons, I just arrived in your city—"

"Yes," he said softly, his response indicating he was already in sympathy with whatever was distressing her.

"This evening, I read the paper and was appalled by what happened last night. Two *young* girls shot out in the open on the streets. Deplorable! If they hadn't been in the business of selling their bodies, they could have been leading respectable lives."

"It was a terrible thing."

She pressed on: "*Someone* needs to get the people here together. Bring them back to God! *Convert* them from their sinful ways before it is too late and the wrath of God falls upon this city of Babylon." She leaned closer, eyes locking onto his. "Mr. Clemons, in *this* room just a while ago, I received a divine revelation to make the people here *free* of the power of the devil! The Lord has empowered *me* through his Holy Vision to begin one of the *biggest* evangelical crusades ever seen in this city." She paused to observe the effect of the words. His face was inscrutable. Her voice softened. "I can tell you are a Christian servant of the Lord, Mr. Clemons. Do you have a family?"

"A wife and daughter."

"Hum-m, wife and daughter," she repeated gravely. "How old is your daughter?"

"Beth is fifteen."

"Fifteen—" A low expiration. "Almost as old as the girl who was shot on the street. Surely, Mr. Clemons, you don't want to raise a family in a place where the devil is clearly running rampant, do you?" That should put him on the spot, she thought. Males always expected their families to be sacrosanct.

"No, certainly not." He looked away from her to put out the neglected cigarette, a nub between his fingers.

"Good! Because I need *your* help."

"*My* help?"

"Yes! Through *you*, we can open eyes. I want a *big* article in the Sunday paper about my personal divinely inspired crusade to rid this city of sin."

"I—I don't know about Sunday. The church page is already filled."

"The *church* page? Oh, come now, Mr. Clemons. Such news as this Holy Divination should be on the *front* page."

Shielding anger, her eyes narrowed. Here personified was a stupid, prosaic man who didn't know the smell of a good story or even how to create one. With restraint, she said tightly: "If you play it up, Mr. Clemons, I'm *sure* they would put it somewhere other than the church page."

He looked doubtful. "I don't carry that kind of weight. After all, it's a *white* owned and run newspaper. The only way I became church editor was because no one else wanted to be— excuse me—buried there, and as usual, they needed a token nigger."

"*But*, Mr. Clemons, must you *remain* in the background? Isn't the news about those who work for Christ just as important as the rest? Billy Graham isn't dispatched simply to the church pages. The story of *my* Holy War to liberate this city—our black brothers and sisters—from the throes of paganism isn't *news?* Ridiculous!"

His eyes were downcast. "I can write it, but I don't know what they'll do with it."

"They will *run* it, Mr. Clemons," she said confidently. "You know why?"

He uncrossed his legs and shook his head.

"Because first, I am going to *pray*. Secondly, I am going to lay the groundwork tomorrow by going to visit those poor young things lying in the hospital."

"They're under lock and key," he said lamely. "For protection."

"That's where *you* come in. Tell the chief of police, or whomever, that the women have asked to see a female minister. Namely me."

"What?"

"The Lord tells me they are in need of a minister's ear," she added quickly. "And *think*, Mr. Clemons, this would give you the inside track on a human interest story while it is hot. You will have your name someplace other than the church page. By-lined George F. D. Clemons. What does the F. D. stand for?"

"Frederick Douglass."

"Ah-ha! Your mother must have known you would be a great man!"

Silence muted the room as he thoughtfully focused on a spot beyond her. She could tell he was seriously pondering what she had said. She had reached him, unleashing a submerged and thwarted ambition. Her instinct about the red socks had proved correct. He had a touch of boldness.

Finally he said, "I can try." When he got up, his body was a trifle straighter.

"Good, Mr. Clemons. I *know* you will be able to arrange it and any other things that may be of help," she assured him.

Outside in the hall, there were sounds of loud voices and people heading toward the elevator. A dark, stocky man of medium height, dressed in a pinstripe gray suit, white wide-brimmed hat, and pointed gray shoes with stacked heels, led a cordon of bellhops pushing carts of luggage. He carried a small, white poodle in his arms.

"What's going on?" George stopped one of the perspiring black porters.

"Travis Lee and her band are here. We changin' her to a bigger suite on the third floor. She ain't satisfied with the one she's in."

Turning back to Myrtle, George said, "It's Travis Lee's group. You know—the singer."

"Un-hun. Now don't forget in the morning, Mr. Clemons. I must see those girls," she reminded him, wanting to leave her work foremost in his mind.

"I'll do the best I can," he promised, leaving to trail the Travis Lee entourage to the elevator.

"I know you will!" she called out, closing the door. She would go to bed now and let her strategy rest in the hands of the Lord.

Chapter 4

WHILE Myrtle slept, Travis Lee was throwing a private party for her retinue in suite 304-A above her. Travis's own voice blasting from the TEAC-A100 cassette deck that she carried with her on trips provided the entertainment in the background. The living room was distended with people, spirited talk, and gaiety. A table, lavishly spread with food and drinks, was pushed against the wall to make room for dancing. As the evening wore on and the drinks flowed like water, the talk and laughter grew louder. Marijuana smells hazed the air, drifting from corners and the bathroom. A typical Travis Lee party was in progress.

After countless vodka and tonics, Travis began to get a high buzz, which bred touchy thoughts. Usually, drinking with her group was fun, but tonight, probably because of Rudy, one of her ugly moods was creeping up, and the more she drank, the nastier she was getting. Glass in hand and swaying with the pulsating beat of one of her numbers, she tried to contain the bitchy itch by singing along with her taped voice: "Ma-an and wo-man got to lo-o-ve!"

When the tape ended, she went over to change it, calling out above the heads: "Where's Agnes?"

"'Round here someplace," an anonymous male voice answered. "Hey, Agnes. Travis wants you!"

A slim, light-faced Creole-looking woman with short, black hair molding her head like a cap, emerged from another room. She had on a pair of slacks and sheer white blouse that appeared

33

freshly changed into. "Here I am, Travis," she said, zigzagging
her way through the clusters of people draped on sofas and
chairs and the floor.

Frowning, Travis complained peevishly, "Agnes, why's it
taking Rudy so damn long to walk Rhoda? He's been gone
over an hour. I know full well she isn't constipated. He must
be walking her all around Nashville."

"He's probably met up with some friends," Agnes said placatingly, heedful of Travis's impending stormy mood. "You
know how Rudy knows somebody everywhere."

"Yeah, too *many* somebodies sometimes," Travis murmured
under her breath. "Seen Gloria?"

Agnes picked up a black olive with a toothpick and bit into
it. "She's probably in her room resting."

"No, she isn't. I just tried to call her a while ago." Travis
refilled her glass with more of her special Stolichnaya.

Watching her uneasily, Agnes said, "Maybe we ought to
close out the party now so you can get some sleep. You have
a busy day tomorrow with the *Celebrity Special Noon Show*
over WTN, plus the recording session with Willie Frye."

"You my mother or manager?" Travis snapped, bringing
the glass to her lips again. "I haven't had any fun since I had
to go on that grapefruit and cottage cheese diet four weeks ago.
I lost ten pounds, so for God's sake, let me have some fun for
a change."

One of the band members with a Charlie Chan moustache
who was wearing a sleeveless red tank shirt, began to dance
the hustle with a woman in a hip-hugging sunback dress. They
had the floor with a group of onlookers clapping in time with
the music and egging them on: "Git down-n-n with it!" The
couple danced fluidly together in graceful, rhythmic movements with no strain. The woman's body rippled and wiggled
sensuously.

"Louise, you lookin' goo-oo-d!"

"Hustle now!"

Watching the dancers, Travis said, "Agnes, guess what I'd
like?"

"No pot, please."

"Some barbecue ribs!"

"Ribs? With all this food here? You have chicken, turkey,
shrimp—"

"*Ribs*, Agnes."

"For this time of night, it's so heavy." Agnes tried to dissuade her because she knew that if Travis got on that soul food kick again, the diet would go down the drain. She never knew when to stop gorging herself.

Flashing her a warning look, Travis answered levelly, "I am certain there ought to be someplace in this southern city open all night selling barbecue ribs. Even in Detroit where I grew up, they had ribs twenty-four hours on call."

Realizing that Travis was not in the mood to be defied, Agnes relented. "Okay, I'll see what I can do. I'll get Bobby to check with one of the black bellhops."

"Please don't let Bobby get lost with him. Bobby goes ape over uniforms and I need him on the keys tomorrow."

A stocky man with too bright eyes and a Superfly hairdo came up to Travis. "Wanna dance?"

"Sure, Reggie. We going to do the worm. *Yeah!*" Putting her glass down on the table, Travis moved into him, shaking her hips and snapping her fingers. "Can't nobody do it like me-e-e!" She threw back her head and laughed to the ceiling.

At 1:00 A.M., when the party was in full swing, a knock sounded on the door. Agnes, the only one not drinking, pushed through the dancers and stepped over the nodding weed smokers on the floor to answer it. The white hotel manager smiled frostily at her. Remaining outside the room, he politely requested that the party quiet down because people were complaining about the noise.

Agnes apologized, conveying understanding and giving assurance in the refined manner she had cultivated for dealing with similar complaints over the years. In a way, she was glad, for it gave her an excuse to end the carousing.

"Gang—the party's over!" she announced, serving notice by blinking the light switch. "We got things to do *today.*"

"Party pooper," someone sneered good-naturedly.

They began to filter out, taking with them their half-filled glasses, beer bottles, and plates of food, flinging final wisecracks to each other.

"Say, man, you goin' to sleep with that beer bottle tonight?"

"Naw. I'm sleepin' with your old lady. She likes it stuck in her hoochie-coochie. Hah, hah!"

"Louise, baby, how 'bout me comin' up for a nightcap?" The man in the red tank shirt put an arm around the woman with whom he had danced.

"Not tonight, sugar. Tired as I am, ain't nothin' I can do
for you!"

When the last one left, Agnes drew a deep sigh of relief.
The place was a shambles with glasses, spilled food and drinks,
and run-over ashtrays. Too much smoke blended with body
and liquor odors, smogging the room.

Travis was curled up on the couch, half-wasted, nibbling
drunkenly on a plate of barbecue ribs. "Damn good," she commented, washing the food down with a bottle of Millers.
"Where'd the fag find them?"

"Bobby got them at a place called Mary's on Jefferson
Street."

Abruptly, as if the thought had shot up in her mind like a
second bolt of thunder: "Where the hell is Rudy with my dog?"
Some of the rib sauce had stained her white slacks. Noticing
it, she dampened a paper napkin with beer and rubbed. "How
long's he been gone anyway?"

Agnes knew Travis was on the way to being out of it. Fearful
of giving a truthful answer, she said evasively, "He should be
here shortly." With that, she prayed silently for Rudy's quick
return from wherever he was. She didn't want Travis to get
upset *this* morning of all times.

As though magically summoned, a key turned in the lock
and Rudy walked in with Rhoda on a leash, white hat rakishly
pushed back on his head. The gray tie, reflecting the shaded
gradations in his suit, was loose at the neck where the top of
his off-white monogramed silk shirt was unbuttoned. "Party
over so soon?" Lifting his hat, he tossed it on a table by the
door.

Rhoda broke away, leash trailing, to jump happily on the
couch and lick Travis's face. "Hi, babykins," Travis said, kissing the dog back. "You miss Mommie?"

Seeing Travis engrossed with welcoming Rhoda, Agnes
seized the opportunity to sidle closer to Rudy and whisper,
"She needs to go to bed."

"I do too. When we goin'?" he winked slyly.

"Go to hell," she hissed, suppressing the urge to smack his
face, half-hidden behind a forest of moustache and beard. This
facial hair, combined with his fanning Afro, made him resemble
the Hairy Ape to her.

"You don't know what you missin'," he sneered at her
retreating back as she left the room.

"Rudy!" Travis yelled across the room. "Where the hell you been all this time?"

"Rhoda and I been communin' with nature," he replied, going to kiss her on the cheek.

Attempting to focus steadily on him, she asked suspiciously, "You high off something?"

"Just high bein' near you, baby." He pushed her down on the couch and lay half-across her. Rhoda jumped down to the floor.

"You didn't answer my *main* question. Where you been?"

"Aw, I met some old buddies I used to be in the army with from Memphis." His finger began a slow seductive crawl on her arm.

"Just like that!" she smirked. "Seems like everywhere we go, you're always meeting people you used to know someplace."

"Popular nigger, baby."

"Popular my ass! Sometimes I think *too* damn much for *my* taste." Sitting up, she shoved him off. "How is it you and Gloria always seem to disappear at the same time?"

"What you mean?" He leaned back against the sofa.

"*You* know what I mean," she said pointedly, eyes hard.

"Shit! You wanna bitch tonight, I'm goin' to bed. I'm tired." He got up, shedding his tie and coat on the way to the bedroom.

When she rose to pursue him, Travis found herself staggering, something she rarely did no matter how loaded she got. She realized that it was too much too soon coming off that diet. But her speech wasn't slurred as her mind struggled to control her words and delivery.

"Tired from *what?*" she retorted. "You haven't done a damn thing all day but sit your ass on a plane, drink booze, and show off your per-so-na-lity."

"A man gits tired." He sat on the edge of the bed, slipping off his shoes.

"If I hadn't taken you out of that damn bar on Harlem Avenue in Atlantic City when I had, you'd be more tired than you *think* you are now."

Ignoring her, he stepped out of the gray pants down to his purple bikini underwear. Pulling the covers back, he got in bed.

Watching him with venom in her eyes, she went to pick up the phone on the nightstand. After two unsuccessful fumbling

tries, she finally dialed the correct number. "Hello—Gloria?
Just checking," she said into the receiver. Hanging up, she
looked down heatedly at him. "Nigger, get the hell out of my
bed," she commanded icily.
"Come off it, baby. I want to go to sleep."
"I *said*, get out!" When he didn't budge, she reached down
and flung the covers back. *"Out!"*
"Woman, what the fuck's *wrong* with you? You been
drinkin' evil whiskey?" Defiantly he covered himself again.
"The matter with *me* is no nigger man whose clothes, food,
booze, shit, *I* buy and pussy I *give* is going to two-time *me!*"
"Now just a minute, honey," he soothed placatingly, raising
up on one elbow. "How you figure I been two-timing you?
You seen me with anybody? Don't I take care of business really
good in bed whenever you want it? You said yourself ain't
nobody fucked you as good as me. Now come off it."
"I should have left your black ass serving drinks and hustling
whores where I found it," she flung back, swaying drunkenly
above him. Self-pity welled up in her. Here was another male
son of a bitch she had fallen for not worth a piss in hell. "I
know you been screwing Gloria." The last card in her deck
was hurled.
He blinked, dropping his gaze from her eyes to a point
beyond her shoulders. "I ain't been screwin' nobody but you."
"Should of left you where you were," she repeated drunkenly. "Right there in that bar!"
In one swift movement, he threw back the covers and swung
his legs out of the bed. "Now *you* listen here, bitch! I didn't
ask to live with you! You got a Jones on and *begged* me to!"
"Nothing but a two-timing nigger man." Anger and sickness
boiled up in her. A queasy feeling oiled her stomach, but she
went on in spite of it: "Don't you think I don't know about all
those women in Dallas, L.A., New York, San Francisco and
Chicago you been fucking and giving *my* money?" The thought
ran through her head that just because he had one of the biggest
dicks she had ever seen didn't mean he had to stick it in
everybody, did it? "I know all about them. You motherfucker."
"Bitch! Don't you call me no motherfucker—"
"Motherfucker! Motherfucker! *Mo-ther-fuck-er!*" she
screamed.
"Shut up!" His fist shot out, hitting her in the face again
and again.

She hollered out and Rhoda started a series of frantic yelps. "Get out!" she shrieked, tears rolling down her face. Unexpectedly Agnes appeared from an adjoining room, hastily fastening her robe. "Hey—hey, you two! I can hear you all the way in my place. Cool it!" She stepped between them, pushing Rudy off and dragging Travis away. "You better go, Rudy," she ordered, attempting to calm Travis.

Throwing them a savage look, Rudy began pulling on his trousers. "All right, goddammit, I'm goin'. That woman's crazy." He jerked his head toward Travis.

"Get out—*now!*" Travis began again, hounding him to the front room with Rhoda trailing, barking furiously. Stopping, Travis picked up a beer bottle and hurled it at him just as he closed the door. The bottle hit the wall and landed with a thud on the red carpet.

Still crying, she went back to the bedroom, falling across the bed. Agnes shook her head in dismay. She could have murdered Rudy herself for upsetting Travis. When Travis got off balance, she put the entire group in a dither. Rhoda hopped on the bed to snuggle against her mistress. Reaching out to pat her, Travis sobbed, "Rhoda's the only one who truly loves me."

"We all love you, sweetie," Agnes said, wishing she could see Travis's face which was half-hidden behind her hands. She was concerned that Rudy had left bruises. "Look, honey, you got to get some rest." Tactfully she removed Travis's hands from her face. What she saw was awful! The left eye was swelling already and there was a cut over her upper lip. "Let's go to the bathroom and wash your face."

Gently she led the weeping Travis to the bathroom. There she left her momentarily to go to her adjacent room and get an ice bag and first aid kit. She filled the bag with cubes from the party buckets. Returning to Travis, she put iodine and a Band-Aid on the cut. "Here, now put this ice pack over your eye."

"That motherfucker gave me a black eye," Travis cried, docilely permitting Agnes to lead her to bed. With the angry stage of her drunkenness subsiding, Travis had begun to feel nauseated. The convergence of too much liquor, beer, and greasy food churned bile in her stomach. She gagged. "Got to go—" Supported by Agnes, she rushed to the bathroom to vomit convulsively.

"Try to sleep," Agnes advocated, mulling over whether to give her sleeping pills on top of the liquor.

"Imagine! That son of a bitch *hit* me."

Agnes made no comment, believing it best to stay neutral in lover's quarrels. They could kiss and make up tomorrow and there she would be, caught in the middle. "Lie still. Go to sleep." She sat on the bed, keeping the ice pack intact and patting Travis at intervals like she would a baby.

"Men," Travis sniveled, "aren't shit!"

"Some aren't. Now go to sleep."

The liquor taking its final toll, Travis fell off to sleep in a drunken stupor.

Travis slept, but Agnes, beset with worries and anxieties, found sleeping difficult. Lying in bed with the light on, she was dismayed about Travis. Of all the times for her to have a free-for-all battle with that no-account Rudy. This was Travis's first time to perform here, in what Bloomsbury Booking Agency had said was Music City, U.S.A.

For seven years, she had been Travis's business manager, secretary, friend, and confidante, feats all in themselves. She had started out as a secretary and traveling companion, but after seeing the raw deal Travis's business manager and lover, Jules Forbes, was giving her, she convinced Travis that she was getting cheated. Jules was filling his pockets, and that was why she couldn't make ends meet, despite her growing popularity. With diplomacy, she apprised Travis that she had finished business school and was confident that she could do a better and above all, more honest, job than Jules. Firing Jules, Travis gave her the opportunity. She worked hard at it, paying off debts and feathering Travis's nest as well as her own. Taking care of business overruled everything else.

She had learned this from watching her schoolteacher mother and waiter father in New Orleans struggling to live from paycheck to paycheck with nothing saved up. She was determined not to live that way, and more so, to look after the future. She viewed Travis as an investment, which required time and much energy, particularly for cleaning up after nasty scenes like the one she just went through with Rudy.

Rudolph Valentino Jones must have been named by a mother who thought that she had given birth to another of the world's greatest lovers. He probably had a big rocket showing even then in his diapers.

Unluckily, Travis was a magnet that drew the same type of man over and over again—the husky, macho stud with no qualms about living off his woman and slapping her around.

Agnes reached for the pack of thin, brown More cigarettes on the night table. Cigarettes were her solitary indulgence. Sometimes, when inclined, she would take a drink, preferrably scotch. Also, on occasions, she smoked a joint in company with self.

Being constantly surrounded by the band conglomerate of drunks, cocaine sniffers, and needle punchers, all with attitudes, she took the approach that somebody had to keep sane. She also had to keep a level head to ward off the young dudes who made frequent passes at her to get to Travis. Not that she wasn't sufficiently attractive to get male attention by herself, but when young guys began to talk trash to a woman of thirty-six, she felt it was time to pause and assess the situation.

Staving off the young fellows, or anyone else, wasn't too much of a problem for her, she acknowledged, pulling reflectively on the cigarette. Normally, people did not warm up to her, mainly because of her design to keep them at a distance. This was true, too, of the few lovers whom she let get just close enough to share the physical but not the emotional side of her life. The lovers eventually bored her with their beguiling hoax of male and her responding female games that had to be played. Futhermore, the attachments became imprisoning. She found this out in a young marriage, which was dissolved within a year. After a while, she grew to prefer being alone, for self was agreeable with self. In this, had she reached the highest pinnacle of asexuality?

The cigarette tinged her fingers. Meticulously she put it out in the ashtray. As usual, she was careful about everything. Like tomorrow, she had to be protective of Travis's reputation and be sure that dark glasses hid the black eye.

The sluggish light of dawn began to creep through the window. She had better get some sleep before the day bloomed. Reaching to turn off the light, she hoped that Travis wouldn't be too hung over when she woke up.

Chapter 5

*T*RAVIS did wake up with a formidable hangover. As soon as she opened her eyes, she flung back the covers and rushed to the bathroom, gagging. She flushed the toilet, rinsed out her mouth, then groaning with the weight of her fiercely throbbing head, dragged herself back to bed.

At 7:00 A.M., Agnes went in to see about her. The sight of Travis lying sprawled on top of the covers with the stale smell of sickness permeating the room caused Agnes to shake her head in exasperation. What made her more aggravated was the black and blue mark clearly visible under Travis's eye. The ice pack had stopped the swelling only somewhat.

"Oh, Agnes, I feel awful and I must look it, too," Travis moaned. As if in sympathy, Rhoda leaped on the bed to lick her mistress's face. "Rhoda needs to go wee-wee."

"I'll get Bobby to walk her."

"He'd love to do that, so he can look for the nearest gay bar."

Agnes's lips tightened to block a retort. Sometimes she got tired of Travis's signifying about Bobby. He was a nice guy and a hell of a piano player. "Rhoda likes him," she appended defensively.

"My head. Je-e-sus!"

"I'll get some aspirin," Agnes offered, going to the bathroom.

Immediately after swallowing the pills, Travis jumped up again to flee to the bathroom. Talking to Bobby on the telephone, Agnes could hear her heaving sounds.

43

"I can't do anything today, Agnes," Travis murmured weakly, falling back on the bed. "Nothing will stay on my stomach and I feel like holy hell."

For the first time in a long while Agnes felt like strangling Travis, who rolled over, fumbling for the dial of the portable radio. "Music. Maybe if I hear some music, I'll forget the way I feel. It'll get me in the mood."

Not hardly, Agnes thought, but perhaps it would remind her of her responsibilities for the day. The nasal twang of a country music singer came over the air:

> I'm a tra-vel-l-ing man-n
> On the road
> 'Way a-a-w-ay from my
> Po-or, po-oo-r fa-mi-ly

"My God, where's the soul station?" Travis groaned, fiddling with the radio.

"WLOT," Agnes replied at once, having found out for advance publicity releases.

A fast talking news announcer flashed on in a streak of words: "WLO-T new-w-w-s *just* in! The Reverend Myrtle Black has arrived in the city to conduct what *she* says will be one of the *biggest* revival meetings of the times at the New Hope Unity Church. Today, the Reverend Myrtle Black, at the request of Heavenly Delight Brown and Earthly Treasure Williams, two alleged prostitutes shot Thursday night on Jefferson Street, will visit to pray with them at Hubbard Hospital."

"Who shot them?" Travis mumbled dully, head buried in the pillow.

"I don't know."

"Agnes, I don't even feel like talking, let alone singing today."

"Honey, you've got to get yourself together. There's the *Celebrity Special Noon Show,* and later, the session with Willie Frye."

"After last night, I don't want to see *no* nigger man today."

"Willie Frye isn't just *a* nigger man."

"He turn white overnight?"

A knock at the door interrupted them. "That's probably Bobby to get Rhoda."

"All I want to do is sleep."

"Okay, sleep." Whistling to Rhoda, she said, "Com'on, Bobby's here to take you for a walk."

Rhoda barking happily, jumped off the bed to follow Agnes. But it was just the maid with her cart of fresh linens at the door, not Bobby. "Ready to have the rooms cleaned, ma'am?"

"Just the front room right now. Ms. Lee is still resting."

Bobby arrived, styled for walking, slim and neat in his plaid Bermuda shorts and short sleeve red sport shirt. A matching red cap was perched over his sunglasses. He was almost girlish-looking with his soft, smooth baby face. Upon first glance, the combination of fair skin and brown wavy hair made him appear white.

"Here's Rhoda." Agnes attached the leash to the dog's gold collar.

"Travis up?"

Agnes shook her head, wondering if she should confide in him. She liked Bobby better than any other member of the band, mostly because being gay, he wasn't a male threat. Glancing sideways at the maid cleaning up, she motioned him outside in the hallway, closing the door behind them.

"Travis isn't feeling well."

"Hangover?"

"And how!"

Bobby looked concerned. "She's made it before with them."

"Yeah, but this one's real bad." Agnes looked into his eyes, a warm, clear brown with long, curly lashes. To her a waste on a man. "She and Rudy had a fight last night."

"I thought so. He's half-drunk downstairs in the dining room." Rhoda barked restlessly, anxious for her walk. "Okay, in a minute," Bobby said, patting her.

"Rudy's still here? He's got to go. You seen Gloria?"

"She should be in her room."

"Listen, while you're walking Rhoda, try to get the name of a good private doctor from a bellhop. I don't want the hotel's. Then hurry back; I need somebody to keep an eye on Travis."

"Will do. Let's go, Rhoda. This is going to be a short one."

Agnes went back in to watch over Travis.

When Bobby returned, he gave her the name of a doctor in Highview Towers who was reputed to be used by the country music stars. Immediately Agnes telephoned him to come as soon as possible. "He's on the way," she said with relief, hanging up the receiver. "I'm going to talk to Gloria. Don't let anybody in unless it's the doctor."

"All right." Unhooking Rhoda's leash, he went over to sit down on the couch and, unfolding the morning's paper he had picked up, read.

Agnes found Gloria in her room sitting down to a breakfast of poached egg, dry toast, orange juice, and black coffee. Dressed in a multicolored robe, she looked young and fresh, copper skin glowing with makeup. Her tinted auburn hair was in a ponytail, tied back with red ribbon. Gloria was twenty-one years old with a mind twice that age, ambition and shrewdness hidden behind her exterior of innocence.

She had used all she had to advance her singing group, which she had started at the age of seventeen, so that it swiftly passed the competitive female backup groups to top place. Gloria's four Ding-a-Lings had captured the dream of the hundreds of similar young, black ghetto girls who hoped to win fame and fortune the quickest way—through their voices. The beat, rhythm and blues, had been a steady diet in their lives, sounds that drummed incessantly over the air waves, spilling into rooms and streets and minds in the teaming, black stretching blocks of the city. Music expressed and fashioned their hopes and dreams. Gloria and her Ding-a-Lings were a product of this.

Gloria looked at Agnes in surprise. "A visit this early? Sit down. Want some coffee? I ordered a big pot and an extra cup in case somebody dropped by." She smiled, dimples curving angles in her cheeks.

"No, thanks. I'm in a hurry and this is strictly a business call." Agnes's eyes slanted at her, taking in how rested she looked compared to Travis. Anger needled her. "How do you feel?"

"Great. Why?" Gloria bit delicately into a piece of toast.

"Get a good screwing from Rudy last night?"

Gloria continued to nibble calmly on the bread. "Come off it, Agnes." Her tone was conciliatory. "You have a lewd mind."

"Not lewd, dearie—knowledgeable." Agnes leaned back in the chair. "Gloria, Travis *knows* what's been going on between you and Rudy. They had a fight last night and Rudy's ass is out. *Out*, do you understand?" Then coldly: "You're going to be out, too, as soon as we wind up here."

"What do you mean?" Gloria asked testily. "Travis sounds better with my group than any in the past."

"I agree, but don't start thinking you're indispensable. Travis was singing long before she met you." Reaching in her pocket, she took out a More, lighting it with a gold lighter. The cigar appearance of the cigarette gave her a sense of power when talking business. Deliberately blowing smoke out in Gloria's direction, she continued: "Travis is so mad at Rudy now, she hasn't had a chance to get around to you yet. I'm beating her to it. The purpose of this visit is to make a deal with you."

"A deal?"

"Yes. You see, I don't feel up to going downstairs and telling Rudy he's got to get out of here. Pronto. His liquor just might tell him that he's got a right to stay on. I want you to go down there and get rid of him. Take him to the bus station—the fart doesn't need to fly—and buy him a one-way ticket back to Atlantic City where Travis picked him up in the beginning. For all concerned, he needs to be far away from her. Understand?"

Gloria calmly refilled her coffee cup. "Why should I do all of that?"

"Because you have a choice of doing it, or you and your Ding-a-Lings's tails are going to be back on the streets auditioning."

Gloria stirred sugar in her coffee, slowly raised the cup to her lips, and set it back down in a prolonged movement before saying acidly, "We have a contract, sugar, remember?"

"Shit on a contract. I can make it so damn unpleasant for you that you'll wish to hell you never had one."

Gloria remained silent, thoughtfully looking down at her plate. "Rudy can be difficult at times, as you know—"

"That's *your* problem. Just get him out of the way."

"I'll see what I can do," she answered resignedly. A feline smile creased her lips. "I wish that I didn't like men so well. It can make problems."

Casting her a contemptuous look, Agnes extinguished the cigarette. Flinging some bills on the table, she said, "Here's five hundred dollars. Buy his ticket first and give him the rest as he steps on the bus. Better get busy, dearie."

The silver-haired, expensively dressed white doctor came and gave Travis what he facetiously termed his "Celebrity's

Special Drunk Cocktail," an intravenous injection of fifty percent glucose and a prescription for a massive dose of vitamin
B complex and other minerals and vitamins. Amphetamines
were left in reserve. Travis dozed in bed with the radio playing
beside her.

Later when Agnes entered the room to awaken her, she
found her lying on her back staring up at the ceiling. The radio
was blasting with a loud singing group making a righteous
noise in the gospel sound.

"Still feeling bad?" Agnes asked, peering anxiously down
at her. The doctor had guaranteed that the shot would work.

Travis lay there immobile, eyes fastened on the cream-colored ceiling, saying nothing. "Honey, are you all right?" Agnes
questioned fearfully. Travis seemed in a trance, still and silent.
Only the voices of the gospel singers stirred the room:

> Jes-us walks with us
> Talks to us
> He-e-lps us through
> The dar-ark of night

Slowly Travis's lips moved, mouthing the words in tune
with the singers. Her voice harmonized with them in a clear,
controlled soprano. A flower among raw weeds. Breaking off
in the middle of the song, she whispered, "That's right."

Agnes frowned. "What's right?"

"Aren't you *listening?* The music—hear it? Listen!"

Agnes turned her attention to the gospel choir singing in a
thunderous rocking beat:

> Jes-us hel-lps us through pain
> Trou-ble and sor-row
> Heals our minds
> For He walks with us and
> Talks with us

"That's it—Jesus!" Travis shot up in the bed, grasping
Agnes's hand. "Fooling around with all those no-good nigger
men, I've forgotten Jesus—the *man* above!"

"Sure, Travis, but let's talk about that later. We got to get
ready for the *Noon Show.*"

Travis rolled over to turn the volume of the radio higher.

"That's the true black music, Agnes. Gospel! The kind I used to sing as a child years ago in the choir at my momma's church."

"I'm going to get out your clothes and run the bath water," Agnes said, deciding that Travis must be feeling better since she was more alert. She wished the ice pack had helped as much, but Travis would have to wear dark glasses and extra makeup to hide her cut lip. Damn Rudy.

Travis began singing spiritedly along with the radio again. Agnes went into the bathroom to draw the water, sprinkling it with Travis's favorite bath powder. Suddenly behind her, she heard the music close upon her, and turned to see Travis standing nude in the doorway holding the radio.

"Agnes, I need to get cleansed once again to purify myself of past sins," Travis said in a hushed voice, eyes staring at the bath tub. "Take out that smelly heathen stuff. I want *pure* water for my Holy Regeneration."

Agnes gaped at her in bewilderment. What in the hell was the matter with Travis now? Was she having a nervous breakdown? Had the doctor doped her up? Or was she drunk all over again?

"What are you staring at? Let that water out and put in some more. I'm going to get pu-ri-fied in body and spirit. Dipped in the waters all over again—right here. Praise Jesus!"

Since there was no time for delay, Agnes yielded and let out the soapy perfumed water and refilled the tub. Business was business. Whatever was the matter with Travis, she would play along. Anything to get her out of here on time. "Here you are, honey. The river's all nice and clean for you."

"Je-sus is our savior—" Travis sang with the choir. *"More* water, Agnes. Fill it to the *top!"*

When the tub was full, Travis set the radio on the floor and stepped gingerly in. "Now, I want you to say 'I baptize thee in the name of the Father, and of the Son, and of the Holy Spirit.'"

"*What!*" Agnes gasped.

Travis's light amber eyes grew large, swallowing Agnes. "I want to be *purged* of my sins!"

"Your hair. Christ! It'll take too long to dry and set it again."

"*Under*, Agnes," Travis commanded.

She's gone crazy, Agnes thought wildly, *stark nuts!*

"Agnes!"

"Here we go," Agnes replied hurriedly. "In the name of the

Father, and of the Son, and the Holy Spirit." Quickly Agnes
dipped Travis down, under and up.
Dripping wet, Travis spluttered, "Agnes, I've found Jesus
again!"
"Great," Agnes said heavily. "But let's get a move on."
"I'm going on the *Celebrity Special Noon Show* and tell the
world I've been born again! I'm a *new* woman made over in
his image!"
"Un-hun. Here's the washcloth and soap."
"I'm going to forgive *all* my enemies—even Gloria for
making it with my man," Travis said, soaping her body. "But
not that Rudy. My forgiveness doesn't extend that far. Turn
the radio up."
"It's loud enough now for the world to hear," Agnes rep-
rimanded.
"Turn it *up,* I said!"
Agnes twisted the volume higher. The gospel group had
stopped singing and a woman was making church announcements in a southern drawl: "Highlighting our church news for
this morning, the Reverend Myrtle Black, evangelist, will begin
a week of preaching the gospel Sunday at the New Hope Unity
Church, the Reverend Amos Cross, pastor. All persons are
invited to come out and here this wonderful minister of God."
"Isn't that the one who is supposed to see those prostitutes
in the hospital today?" Travis said.
Agnes nodded absently. Sometimes she was amazed at
Travis's memory. Quickly she handed her a towel and started
bringing in her clothes from the bedroom.
"Well," Travis's voice rose to follow her movements, "I'm
going to church in the morning to hear her. And I'm going to
tell her *and* the world that I have found me a *new* man—
Jesus!"

Chapter 6

S ATURDAY at 10:00 A.M., Myrtle entered Hubbard Hospital followed by a bevy of news reporters and TV cameras. Provided with the pass George Clemons had secured for her, she was permitted to see the two women. The sterile hospital room smelled of medicine and disinfectant. Sunlight strained through the double-pane window, bestowing the only cheer in an otherwise bland room.

When the guard opened the door for her, the two women eyed her curiously, staring at the white clerical collar that topped off her lilac pantsuit. "Good morning, sisters. I am the Reverend Myrtle Black who has come to see you and give divine guidance."

"My my. Don't she look pretty," the one closer to the door marveled. "You a woman preacher?"

"Yes, I am. And which patient are you, my dear?"

"I'm Heavenly Delight Brown, ma'am." Heavenly Delight was the younger one. She was apparently faring better than her companion in the opposite bed, who was propped up with her leg in a cast. "That's my friend, Earthly Treasure Williams. She ain't feelin' too good today."

"I hope before I leave, you will both be feeling better in body *and* spirit. I have come to help you, my sisters, who have fallen by the wayside, and to forgive. Didn't our Jesus say: 'He that is without sin among you, let him first cast a stone at her'?"

Earthly Treasure groaned uncomfortably as she tried to turn to get a better view of Myrtle. She looked older than twenty-

two, her dark face tightly lined. The toughness of living
swathed her like a weed grown up in the crevices of asphalt
streets.

"'Scuse me for sayin' this, Rev, but I could sure do with
a cigarette," Earthly Treasure mused wistfully.

"I'll see what I can do," Myrtle said, making a mental note
to send up a pack from the machine downstairs when she left.

"Wish my King would come to see me. He knows I got to
have my smokes layin' in here like this," Earthly Treasure went
on, lamenting in a voice already made husky from too many
smokes in the past.

"*My* Stick, he sent *me* a box of candy," Heavenly Delight
chirped superciliously, pointing to a pound box of drugstore
chocolates on the table. "Stick say: 'Sweets for the sweet'!"
she simpered childishly.

Heavenly Delight seemed to be more concerned with her
appearance. Her blonde colored hair was combed in fresh curls,
contrasting exotically with a pretty olive face. Despite her street
existence, youthfulness still clung to her. "Want some candy,
Reverend?" she offered.

Myrtle looked at her in compassion. "No, thank you, my
dear." She went over and stood between the beds to talk with
them from a more advantageous position. "Sisters, I have come
to pray for you." The words came out, deep and profound, but
smoothed with kindness.

"Oh, Rev, you can sure pray for this leg of mine!" Earthly
Treasure groaned. "I won't ever be able to turn— —work
again if it don't git better."

"I'm going to pray first for you to change your way of
living."

Earthly Treasure's large, bulbous eyes blinked sorrowfully.
"I know it's wrong, Rev, but I don't know nothin' else to do."

"That's right," Heavenly Delight seconded. "But Earthly,
it *do* git kind of rough sometimes in the life. All you got to
contend with, 'sides tryin' to keep Stick happy. Stick got more
women in his stable in town than anybody."

"'*Cept* my King," Earthly Treasure broke in haughtily.

"You certainly are proud of your men, but where are they
now in your time of need?" Myrtle questioned bluntly.

"Somewhere tryin' to git us out of here, I hope!" Earthly
Treasure remarked, raising her bed upward to pour a glass of

water from the pitcher on the table. "Keeps my fever down," she said offhandedly, drinking a glassful.

"They find out who shot us?" Heavenly Delight's voice descended to a whisper. "They don't tell us nothin', except when *they* want to find out somethin'."

Myrtle shook her head. "I haven't heard."

"Don't make good sense, somebody shootin' at us like that. Me and Earthly Treasure was just havin' a friendly spell together 'fore goin' to work. We been knowin' each other since high school days. We'd just had some beers at the Slinky Fox Tavern 'cause we know Dice, the bartender there real good. Just havin' a good time talkin'—. You know, Reverend, how women can talk about things. Afterwards, we went on outside, still talkin' and laughin', standin' there in front of the place when this big, black Cad'lac come zoomin' down the street and somebody started shootin'. Bang, bang, bang! For no reason at all! Ain't that somethin'?" Heavenly Delight wagged her head in disgust.

"Yes, it is," Myrtle agreed. "But you don't have to lead a life of fear. You can still have a future. A good future by putting your faith and trust in the Lord."

"Like King!" Earthly Treasure responded knowledgeably.

"*No,* not like King!" Myrtle's voice rose. "Jesus is kind and merciful."

"King kind—sometimes."

Myrtle's hands sought those of the two women, grasping them tightly in hers. "We women must learn to take care of ourselves, to lead our own lives without becoming a slave to men or anyone else."

Earthly Treasure's rough palm went sweaty and limp. Myrtle suspected holding the hand of a woman in close friendship was new to her, and had caused her embarrassment. She had been led too long by men. The hand of Heavenly Delight was trusting, that of a child's clasped in its mother's. The locking of hands always gave the opportunity for reciprocal closeness, providing through simple touching a kinship of togetherness. Warmth and compassion flowed through Myrtle, inspiring her with the desire to save.

"I am going to pray for your recovery in body and spirit. Let us pray: O Lord, our strength and redeemer, help these two young women with Thy truth and courage to see the light. Help

them, O merciful savior, to come to Thee. *Purge* their sins so
they can begin life *anew*, dedicated to Thee in Thy service.
Wash them free of sin in the goodness of Thy love and wisdom.
Let them remember that God is the rock of our salvation and
our deliverer. Nourish them for a speedy recovery and full
return to good health. Let those cowards who performed this
dastardly deed upon them be brought to justice. We ask this
for these two sisters who need Thy love and grace and forgiveness, in Jesus's name, amen."

"Amen," Heavenly Delight wiped away a tear. "Reverend,
that was sure a pretty prayer. I ain't heard nothin' like that
since I used to go to the Hill Street Baptist Church."

"And you must go to church again, my child."

"Where's your church here, Rev?" Earthly Treasure asked,
withdrawing her hand.

"I'm a visiting evangelist conducting a week's revival for
Reverend Amos Cross's New Hope Unity Church. I *am* my
church, which goes with me everywhere. I intend to keep in
touch with you," she promised them, squeezing Heavenly Delight's hand, nestled birdlike in hers, before releasing it.

"Yeah, Rev, please help to git us out of jail. Those cops
tryin' to say we was standin' there hustlin' and all we was
doin' was havin' a real friendly time. Women can't even stand
on a corner to talk without those bastards—oops! 'scuse me,
Rev—cops sayin' you peddlin' tail," Earthly Treasure be-
moaned, shifting slightly, her face reflecting anger. "Do me
a favor, Rev."

"If I can."

"Tell that King of mine to come see me. Anybody on the
block can tell you how to find him. He's the handsomest, big,
muscles and all. The real Jim Brown type."

"*My* Stick's just as good-lookin'. He's got the prettiest
smile—like Billy Dee Williams," Heavenly Delight rhapso-
dized.

"I will continue to send up prayers for you," Myrtle con-
soled, evading a direct answer to the request. The only way
she would look up that King would be in hell.

"You keep on prayin' for us, Rev," Earthly Treasure said.
"We goin' to need all the prayers we can git to help us out of
this mess. If you come again, bring some cigarettes—Kools."

Outside the reporters excitedly questioned Myrtle about the
visit. Standing ramrod straight before them, she replied in son-

orous tones reminiscent of Elijah Black, "I have tried to make them see the error of their ways. Those women have been led astray by men. I shall preach tomorrow morning about women used by men, and shall say a special prayer for them and *all* women involved in such lives in this carnal city." Then smiling tightly, she shouted: "Praise God! See you in church!"

Then she turned her back and left them staring at her, an image of a female David facing Goliath.

Chapter 7

M INDFUL of her bargain with Agnes, Gloria looked for and found Rudy in the Bottom-of-the-Glass Saloon down the street from the hotel. He was propped over the bar on a stool, smoking and nursing a watery scotch on the rocks. No one else was in the place except the yellow-coated white bartender filling time by polishing glasses for the expected noon crowd.

Gloria paused in the doorway, adjusting her eyes from the hot morning glare of the sun to the dark, cavernous coolness of the room. Drawing a deep breath, she started over to Rudy, realizing that what she had to do called for artful cunning and feminine wiles. She had dressed for the scene in an off-the-shoulder yellow dress, which showed her to best advantage. Knowing she looked good gave her morale a boost.

Feigning surprise, she called out, "Rudy! Am I glad to see you!"

Wavering from the effects of his drinking all night into morning, Rudy turned to look at her, eyes blurred and red-rimmed. Slowly recognizing who she was, he spat out angrily, "Bitch! You the 'cause of it all!"

Gloria managed a pretty smile for him, ignoring the stormy outburst. Since he didn't seem to be as belligerent as the outcry sounded, she slid onto the stool beside him, gluing on her smile.

"What'll it be, ma'am?" the bartender asked, face a cold mask.

"I'll have a screwdriver," she said, not really wanting anything, but thinking that at least the orange juice would supply vitamins.

"Why?" Rudy sneered, putting out his cigarette in a cluttered Bottom-of-the-Glass ashtray. "'Cause it's got screw in it?" A smug grin lighted his face.

"Rudy," Gloria began gently, countering his surliness, "I'm sorry Travis found out about us."

"Hah! Thanks to you, I've been knocked out of the best set-up I ever had."

"I'm sorry, but glad too, Rudy."

"Glad? What the hell you glad about?" The fingers around his glass tightened.

Gloria moved closer so he could breathe in the sweet fragrance of her perfume, and let her hand lightly caress his. "Because now I have you all to myself. It's just *us* now, darling." The cliché came easily: "What we had was *good*, Rudy." Lord, she thought, this sounds like a soap opera.

He stared at her, trying to comprehend what she was saying. Taking the last cigarette out of a crumpled pack, he tossed the empty cellophane on the bar.

"The times we had together, Rudy, making love were wonderful," she whispered, voice husky. Making a man feel he was a great lover always had an effect. "I fell in love with you, darling. My fine, beautiful, strong, black man."

The bartender served her drink and emptied the ashtray. When she opened her purse to pay with a fifty-dollar bill, Rudy's eyes became riveted on the roll of money. "You want another drink, Rudy?"

Shrugging, he pretended indifference.

"Give him another drink," she told the bartender.

Still looking into her purse, he said, "Got any change? I'm out of cigarettes."

"Sure, honey, I'll get some for you." Sliding gracefully off the stool, she gave him a flash of shapely legs. Buying two packs of cigarettes at the machine, she handed them to him. He stuck one in his coat pocket. With undisguised interest, he watched her reach into her purse again to extract another bill from the stack.

Drawing on the cigarette, he said, "She said that she loved me, too, then kicked me out. No woman ever did that to me before. *I* do the kicking. I'm damn glad I went upside her head before I left."

"We never fought, did we, Rudy?" she breathed in his ear.

"It was always sweet and tender moments for us, like it should be with a man and woman." She omitted pointing out that she knew they never fought because they were only together long enough for the brief, furtive, stolen moments. She doubted that she could tolerate any longer ones with him. Rudy was good purely for stud work. It was just the fact that he belonged to Travis that had made her curious.

He sipped the fresh drink, hand tracing a shaky path to his mouth. The diamond ring Travis had given him flashed ominously in the shadows. "She thinks she's better'n me," he continued indignantly, "'cause she's a big star."

"Travis just doesn't understand you, Rudy, like I do. I know you. What you need is me. Together, we can do big things. Let's leave here, Rudy. I have money. I'm well enough known now to make it as a single without the Ding-a-Lings. I found a promotion agent who says he can put me on top. Past her, even!"

He straightened up, tossing down the drink, suddenly appearing sober. "That right?"

She nodded, bringing the glass to her lips, but barely drinking. "With a man like you beside me—good-looking, smart— I can make it."

Rudy crunched down hard on a piece of ice. Two white salesmen wearing seersucker suits and carrying briefcases came in and sat at the opposite end of the bar. The bartender greeted them familiarly, bending over to talk confidentially to them. Gloria was certain that the s.o.b. was relaying her conversation with Rudy to them. She knew she must seem like a nigger bitch pleading with her man.

"Where we goin'?" Rudy asked, sly interest in his eyes.

"Back home to the Big Apple."

"You got money?"

She took the cigarette from him, drew sexily upon it, and handed the wet, red-ringed tip back. "Plenty. And it's all for you, sugar."

"You ain't gittin' no cheap dude, baby. I come high. Expensive!" He sucked hard on the cigarette one more time before deadening the burning end in the tray.

You sure don't look expensive now, she appraised silently, observing the rumpled gray suit and spot-stained silk shirt. "I know you are, Rudy. Don't worry, I'll take care of you. But we have to get away. Today!"

He gazed at her suspiciously. "What for? I'd like to stick

around awhile. I just might be able to get back with *her* again. All she needs to do is miss me a little while."

Grudgingly she had to admire how even from the bottom, his arrogance shone through. But she resented that he was going to be so stubborn. She motioned to the bartender to give him a refill—fire to weaken. "Not from what I heard this morning," she said warningly, half swerving around on the stool to cross her long legs in front of him.

"What'd you hear?" He half closed his eyelids to shutter the questioning alarm in his eyes.

She waited for the drink to be served and the bartender out of earshot before she whispered: "That if you brought your ass back in her door again, she was going to blow your balls off!"

Rudy snorted loudly in disbelief. "She wouldn't hurt *me*. Not there!" He laughed, his mouth a pink, wide gap in the tangle of beard.

"Un-hun. And Agnes is going to get the cops on you for trespassing." Gloria was amazed at the adroitness of her lies. They came smoothly, easily without hesitation or forethought.

"Agnes? That bitch better not mess with me. She's just jealous 'cause she ain't got a fine prick like mine layin' it in her," Rudy bragged.

"We need to go this morning, Rudy. I'm not kidding. For my safety, too! Surely you don't think Travis wants me around anymore after—"

"Maybe you right."

"I know I'm right. Let's get out of here." She took his arm.

"Wait! Lemme finish my drink," he snapped, pushing her hand away. He downed the drink quickly, belching noisily. Reaching for the pack of cigarettes, he almost fell getting off the stool. She put a protective arm about him to improve his equilibrium. The men in the seersucker suits grinned disdainfully as they went out the door. The outside heat quickly sponged away the coolness of the bar.

"I have to get my things from the room," Gloria said, leading him back to the hotel. In the lobby, she caught sight of Bobby talking to a tall, muscularly built white man with coal black hair combed high, and long sideburns. The man had on the country music outfit—Texas-sized hat, black sequined levis and shirt, and short western boots—straight off the rack from the Alamo. Running into Bobby was a godsend to her.

Turning to Rudy, she said, "Now you sit right down here

on the couch by the door until I get my stuff together. I'll be right back." She rushed over to Bobby and pulled him aside.

"I need your help to get Rudy to the bus station. He's drunk as an owl."

"So I see," Bobby said, looking over at Rudy half-slumped on the sofa. "My friend Clyde has a car." He pointed back to the man with whom he had been talking.

"Good." The thought surfaced that Bobby could collect friends faster than anyone she knew. "That's better than getting a cab. Too public. Have your friend drive around to the front in about fifteen minutes. I want Rudy to think I've been packing my bags. I'm going to call the bus station about getting him to Atlantic City. Keep a distant eye on him for me. Sometimes he can hold a lot of liquor, but sober up faster than anybody I know, if he thinks somebody's trying to put something over on him."

Gloria went hurriedly up to her room, grabbed an empty suitcase and cosmetic kit, and went back down to Rudy. She saw Bobby moving discreetly from behind a tall rubber plant near the Andrew Jackson tapestry to ease out a side door. "I'm all set, sugar."

"Okay." Rudy pushed himself up heavily.

Carrying the empty bags, she led him outside. In a few moments, the man in the western hat drove up to the curb in a cream-colored Lincoln Continental. Bobby hopped out quickly. "All set to go?"

Rudy stiffened, glaring in surprise at Bobby. "Where we goin' with that fruit?" He had never liked nor gotten along with Bobby, whom he said should be castrated.

"Bobby's friend is going to give us a lift, sugar." She could see the man at the wheel peering curiously through the tinted windows. Fortunately he could not hear what they were saying. Gloria opened the door and pushed Rudy inside as Bobby loaded her suitcase into the trunk, placing the cosmetic kit in back with her as requested.

"Start it up," Bobby said, getting in the front seat.

Wallowing in the air-conditioned plushness of the car, Rudy seemed to momentarily forget his aversion to Bobby. "Some wheels, hun? Goin' 'way in real style. We got to git us one like this, baby."

"Sure, anything you want." She kissed his cheek.

Clyde put on a tape of country music. "That's my group,

the Country Stompers," he identified proudly. "We're playing at the Grand Ole Opry tonight." Mistaking the silence for admiration, he turned the volume higher. "That's me playing the guitar and singing the lead," he bragged in his deep, southern nasal tone.

"I hate country music," Rudy mouthed drunkenly under his breath.

"Sh-h-h," Gloria hushed him.

"Bobby says you folks are musicians, too."

"That's right," Gloria answered.

"Wish I had a joint," Rudy muttered, leaning his head back and closing his eyes.

Noticing that his fly was open, Gloria tactfully zipped it. In a few minutes, he began to snore softly. The smell of stale liquor mixed with fresh wafted through the car. Since neither she nor Bobby seemed to want to make more than noncommittal replies to Clyde's attempts at conversation, the rest of the ride passed in the plucking of guitars, beating of a drum, and twanging voices.

"Here we are—Greyhound Bus Station." Clyde turned left at the light on Eighth Avenue South into the parking lot.

Rudy woke up instantly when the motor stopped. "Where we at?"

"Bus station," Clyde repeated, looking in the rearview mirror at them.

Blinking, Rudy shot up straight on the seat. "*Bus* station? What the hell we doin' at the bus station?"

"We're going to get a bus out," Gloria said patiently.

"I thought we were goin' to New York," he stabbed accusingly at her.

"We are," she stated.

"Well, Rudolph Valentino Jones don't ride no buses!"

"This is the fastest thing out of the city, Rudy. A plane to New York doesn't leave until later. We'll get off in Knoxville and catch a flight from there."

Rudy frowned. "Why?"

"We have to get away from here in a hurry. Remember?"

His face grew more confused, trying to remember what it was he was supposed to remember.

Cognizant of the urgency of the moment, Bobby jumped out of the car and opened the door to help Gloria get Rudy out. Giving him a hateful look, Rudy yelled, "Take your goddam faggoty hands off me!"

Bobby reddened while Clyde's lips tightened in a face gone dark. "Bobby—" Gloria interceded quickly, casting a remorseful glance at Clyde whom she was certain was as faggoty as Bobby, "get my bag out of the trunk, please. We're going on in to get the tickets."

"This place got a bar?" Rudy sniffed, calming down now that he was away from Bobby.

The station was busy with spring tourists and vacationers. "You rest right here on this bench, Rudy, while I go get the tickets."

Luck was with her, for the ticket line was moving swiftly. The schedule showed that the bus to Knoxville was to leave in ten minutes. Bobby waited at a safe distance with the suitcase, keeping his eyes on Rudy, who had begun a friendly conversation with a young, dark-skinned, hip-heavy teenager in tight, blue denim shorts and halter. A smile slowly covered the girl's face as she listened to him, hand resting protectively on the cardboard red and black checkered suitcase bursting at the seams at her feet. She held a three-year-old boy in her lap.

"It's leaving now, Rudy," Gloria said, approaching him with the tickets. "We can get in line."

Rudy got up more steadily than he had gotten out of the car. Smiling down broadly at the girl he said, "You be sweet now, doll. 'Member what I said about men and women."

The girl giggled, pleased by his male attention. Gloria hurried him along to the gate. "I ain't been on no bus since my grandmomma sent me to live in Atlantic City from Arkansas. She put a sign around my neck sayin' 'Atlantic City' in case I got mixed up. After that, I swore I wasn't goin' to ride on no more poor man's buses."

"Buses have changed since then, Rudy. It won't be a long ride."

"You got all the money we're gonna need? I got to buy some new threads. Everything's left back there in *her* room."

"You'll get all the new things you want." The line pressed forward to board the bus. The girl in the shorts who had been talking to Rudy was behind them with the little boy.

"Oh, Lord!" Gloria slapped her forehead in exasperation. "I forgot! My cosmetic case is in the car! It has the rest of the money in it!" she cried frantically. "I checked my other bag."

"Hun?" The word money caused Rudy to look as distressed as she sounded.

"Here, you take the ticket. I'll have to run back and get it. Save a seat for me, sweetie. I'll be right back."

"Your wife forgit somethin'?" The girl sidled up next to him.

"Ain't my wife."

"May I have your ticket, sir?" the driver said. "We got to get rolling on time."

Together Bobby and Gloria fled through the station and to the car. Throwing her bag on the seat, Bobby slammed the door. "Let's go, Clyde."

Clyde looked back at Gloria questioningly. "Thought you were going, too. He get off okay?"

"There's the bus pulling off now," Bobby interrupted, pointing.

Gloria laughed nervously. There went Rudy with a one-way $79.95 ticket to Atlantic City and without the rest of the five hundred dollars. She patted her purse comfortingly. A little extra cash never hurt any woman.

"We ought to get back in time to catch some of Travis on the *Celebrity Special Noon Show,*" Bobby said, looking at the digital clock in the padded dashboard.

"Sure should," Gloria replied, congratulating herself on an act well performed. Still, she wished that she had defied Agnes and gotten Rudy off on a plane. Rudy in the air would be safer any day.

Chapter 8

*T*RAVIS sat beside Don Owens in the red guest chair on the Saturday *Special Celebrity Noon Show,* looking demure in a plain tailored white dress chosen to emphasize her new image. The expensive Yves Saint Laurent sunglasses that she wore offered a deceptively fashionable accessory to her attire.

For the first seven minutes of her segment, Travis talked enthusiastically about her born-again self. This dismayed host Don Owens, who had assiduously researched and read up on Travis's career and the music of black people. He did not like to appear uninformed or ignorant on his show. Now he found himself totally unprepared and embarrassed. Fidgeting nervously in his seat, he tried to deflect the conversation back to what he had planned to be the main topic.

"Travis, your musical roots have been in the church, haven't they? You first started out singing in the choir."

"Yes, right there in the church as a little girl in Detroit, where I went every Sunday morning."

"Black church music stems from black folk music with its spiritual and gospel songs. Wouldn't you say that gospel music has had a decided impact upon blues and jazz, since many black rhythm and blues, rock and roll, and popular singers began singing in the church? There are those identical rhythmic patterns." Ah-ha! He sat back in his chair, pleased to have gotten this in.

"Definitely. And, too, Don, there is a common thread of emotional experience in gospel music which is carried over

into our secular musical forms. When I sing, I try to impart
my true and undiluted feelings."

"This you most certainly do—in the way you give vent to
a song, unlike many other female vocalists! You are not called
the Pristine Goddess of Song for nothing! However, now that
you have been... uh... born again, do you intend to keep on
with your current style of singing?"

"I suppose so," Travis said slowly, frowning. "I'm going
to keep on singing those songs that *my* people have *always*
sung. Songs that reflect *black* people. Music is also recrea-
tional, entertaining, a release from everyday cares, as well as
a lament about our race's injustices in society. All kinds of
black music mirrors black life, living and soul! It's my private
self, which will be dedicated to the teaching of Jesus." She
smiled sweetly, a little surprised at her articulateness. The Lord
was with her.

Don Owens cleared his throat. "You stated that this revelation occurred early *this* morning."

"Yes."

Don leaned closer. "Can you describe it?"

With eyes half-closed, head thrown back, and face ecstatic,
Travis breathed: "Beautiful! Gripping, intense, yet peaceful,
like being enveloped in a pastoral scene. And, I want to add,
that it came during a time of listening to gospel music!"

Don looked down at the cuffs of his tailor-made trousers
and Florsheim shoes, then up again. "How will this now affect
your visit here? This new insight?"

"I'm going to church in the morning," Travis answered
brightly. "Something I haven't done in a long while. I want
to hear that woman evangelist, Reverend Myrtle Black. You
know, the one who took time to visit those poor women shot
on Jefferson Street in the hospital?"

"Uh, yes," Don said hurriedly. Time was fleeing and he
hadn't talked about the African influence on black music. "Isn't
it true that black music—spirituals in particular—have origins
of African influence? West African in their tonal forms and
rhythmic structures in particular?"

"Decidedly. And I *do* love spirituals."

"But you sing rhythm and blues!"

"I love to sing *all* types of music, Don, anything that people
want to hear. Why, after this show, I'm going over to Country
Music Sounds to cut a record with Willie Frye."

Don gasped, unable to contain his surprise. He was furious that *he* hadn't been informed; he'd been bamboozled again! He pushed his curly dark hair back and swallowed. "Willie Frye is one of our biggest country and western music stars. Will changing your style be difficult?"

"Well, Don, country and western music does have black influences," she added significantly.

"You are indeed a versatile singer," Don said too quickly, veering away from such a controversial topic. Enlarging upon her comment might cause offense to those staunch country and western music devotees who argued that the music was pure, undiluted Caucasian.

"Don, if anybody wants to hear me sing spirituals, they can come to the New Hope Unity Church in the morning. I'm going there because I admire a woman minister who seems to *care* about other women, regardless of their lot in life." Travis tugged demurely at the hem of her dress.

Don looked dumbfounded, at a loss as to how the discussion had strayed again. He usually handled the women easily, through flattery, paternalism, laughs and jokes. This had somehow gotten out of hand. He had to end it quickly, smoothly.

Travis beat him to the draw. "So, any of the brothers and sisters who want to join me in singing the praises of the Lord in the morning can come to the New Hope Unity Church!"

Myrtle sat transfixed before the TV screen in her motel room. She had caught the show by accident, because she'd just happened to turn on the set, hoping to find some news while she ate her jello salad and drank her orange juice. She was flabbergasted. All of this free publicity was a stroke of fate. Travis Lee was giving her promotion beyond her wildest dreams. It went to show that the Lord worked in mysterious ways.

Whoever would have thought that the great Travis Lee would come specifically to hear her preach? That their paths would even cross? Why, she was going to get together the best sermon she had ever preached. She couldn't miss out on this golden opportunity to rise, shine, and give God and herself the glory!

Myrtle was so excited that she stopped eating to listen carefully to Travis. She was storing away all that was said for future use—particularly the woman caring about women part.

To her surprise, she found herself relating to Travis in a personal way, entranced by her sexy, earthy allure on the screen. Although Myrtle was wise enough in the ways of the world to see that Travis's dress had obviously been selected for its demureness, her pendulous breasts were highly visible, rounding out the flimsy material each time she twisted or leaned. Myrtle had no qualms about feasting her eyes on her. The Lord had certainly bestowed those luscious tits to be enjoyed. Myrtle's sharp eyes speculated about the dark glasses and small Band-Aid over the lip, wondering if they were outward indicators of the reason for Travis's instant religious conversion.

As usual, she began planning ahead. She would call George F. D. Clemons to make certain he would represent the press at the morning service. The eyes of Jesus were obviously upon her. In the meantime, she continued to gaze appreciatively at Travis's curves. She found herself thinking that *that* would really be a thing to preach to in the morning. Yes, indeed!

"My, God, Travis has gotten religion!" Gloria exclaimed, half in surprise and half in derision, as she and Clyde watched the program in Bobby's room. "Just goes to show how a bad experience with a man can sure change a woman."

"I knew a country music singer who got born again," Clyde said, sipping from a can of beer. "He quit singing to preach."

Travis's earnestness as she talked about being born again made Gloria flinch.

"Sure nobody wants a beer?" Clyde asked, popping open another can.

"No, thanks. Bad for my girlish figure."

"Bobby?"

"After hearing this, I think I need something stronger."

"I can go to the car. Got some Chivas Regal in it." Clyde picked up the motel's plastic bucket. "I'll bring back some ice."

"I hope she doesn't expect us to get religion with her," Gloria grumbled when Clyde left. "You know how Travis can be when she gets something into her head. She may try to reform us all."

Bobby's eyes were glued to the set, and he looked preoccupied. He was only partially listening to Gloria. "I doubt that," he murmured absently. Turning to Gloria, he said, "What do you think of him?"

"Who?"

"Clyde," he replied impatiently.

"Well-l, from a black woman's perspective looking at a *white* man"—and homo, too, she smirked to herself—"I suppose he's handsome in a rugged sort of way. Looks like he ought to be in a shoot-'em-up playing the tough guy." She neglected to mention that he also gave the impression of being heavily hung. "Where did you meet him?"

"In the motel bar."

"Scotch and soda!" Clyde boomed, opening the door. "Me, I prefer beer." He deposited the bag on the table.

"Damn!" Gloria almost toppled into the TV. "Did you hear that? She's cutting a record this afternoon with Willie Frye!"

"I know," Bobby said, eyes monitoring Clyde's pouring. "Whoa-a-a, Clyde. Not too strong. I got to do a country music set which I know nothing about."

"And with *the* Willie Frye!" Clyde said, impressed. "He's one of the biggest."

"Nobody told *me*," Gloria bristled.

"It's to be just Travis, Willie, the studio backup group, and myself."

"But you just said that you don't know nothing about country music," Gloria steamed.

"Maybe she wants me there for support. After all, she doesn't know anything either," Bobby laughed, shaking the ice in his glass.

Gloria got up to leave when the image on the set changed to a woman in an apron demonstrating how to cook veal cordon bleu. "I'll see you guys later. Got to confer with the Ding-a-Lings. Let me know how the session goes, Bobby."

"Sure will." Bobby raised the glass to his lips, marveling at the thick dark hairs on Clyde's wrists.

When Gloria closed the door, Clyde smiled, resting a hand on Bobby's knee. "Now, let's hear all about *you*."

At this, Bobby laughed coquettishly, warmth seeping through him from Clyde's touch. "There's really not much to tell—" The telling came easily, for he had told the same story following such preliminaries many times before.

Willie Frye, cinnamon-handsome in a white suit and black shirt opened at the collar, greeted Travis warmly in the plush office of Abe Apstein at Country Music Sounds. Face clean-

shaven and hair neatly trimmed, Willie gave off a semblance
of youth belying his forty-five years of age. Possessing a natural, easygoing, down-home personality on and off stage, he
immediately made Travis feel comfortable.

"Here's my favorite rhythm and blues singer," he smiled,
kissing her lightly on the cheek. "With your talent, honey, we
can't miss. We should make a lot of money off this one."

"Nice to finally meet you in person, Willie. I wish that I
could share your confidence. You're taking a big chance with
me. I might ruin your career forever."

"Not a chance, honey. Old Willie's got it all figured out.
Songs picked with you in mind. Arrangements won't pose
problems because we usually play the way we want to anyway.
Sometimes it turns out the writers don't even recognize their
own songs when the sessions are over!" He laughed. "How did
you like the one I sent to you—'Baby's Long Hard Road'?"

"All right, but kind of sad."

"Billy James, one of the best country music composers, did
it just for us."

Abe Apstein, an obese man in shirt sleeves with red, white,
and blue suspenders holding up light blue trousers that spilled
over white buckskin shoes, rose laboriously to shake hands
with Travis. His office walls were plastered with awards, photographs, and publicity items on his record stars. Willie's picture dominated.

"With your combined talents, we automatically got a win-
ner," Abe announced confidently. The smell of stale cigar
smoke and bourbon clung to him. "Glad to have you aboard,
Travis."

"Thank you," she smiled back. "This is Bobby Blane, my
piano player, and Agnes Saunders."

"I've talked with Agnes a number of times over the telephone, trying to set this up," Abe smiled expansively to include
them all. "Sit down, everybody."

"This will be a new experience for me," Travis told him.

"Also for me," Bobby inserted.

"Nothing to it," Willie waved away their fears. "Singing
country music is just like singing the blues or gospel, except
the emphasis is on the lyrics rather than melody."

"Willie's my top star," Abe boasted, lighting the cigar.
"He's come a long way from picking tobacco in Kentucky and
working on the roads. Eh, Willie?" Abe threw an arm affectionately around him.

"Yeah, that's how I got started liking country music. Born into it. Heard it around me all the time. My granddaddy was a white hillbilly. Grew right up in the hills alongside his half of the family. Hah, hah, ain't that a bitch?"

"According to our telephone conversation, Abe," Agnes began, "you mentioned that you were going all out for promotion."

"Right!" Abe confirmed, cigar a stubby, brown tubular roll stuck in the corner of his mouth. "Plenty of publicity. We don't do things halfway here in Nashville. No sir! As one born and raised in this city, I helped make country music a booming business. I *love* it! Why country music's now international." Abe perched on the edge of his desk, bald head glistening like polished silver under the fluorescent lights. "I'm trying to get a Grand Ole Opry stint lined up for you and a few talk shows!"

Agnes extracted a pad from her purse and began making notes. "Fine, Abe, but I hope you can hit the black market. Black people aren't into the country music bit."

"Don't worry. *This* record will have something for everybody!"

"Bobby, looks like we got a lot of work to do today," Travis said. She was beginning to feel peaked, and would have to get some dexamyl from Agnes to keep up the pace.

"Nothing to it," Willie soothed. "Just concentrate on the lyrics."

Abe looked out the window. "We should have a gold record in no time."

"We'll have to pray and trust in the Lord," Travis intoned solemnly.

Everyone was silent until Willie grinned and said, "A-men."

At 11:00 P.M., Travis, exhausted from the lengthy recording session, had Agnes order a light supper from room service. Pensive and quiet, she picked at the turkey salad on her plate. The day had been unusually long for her, and if it hadn't been for the pills, she wouldn't have gotten through.

"Agnes, I'm beat. Willie acted as if we should record all night."

"He wants this first record you two do to come out right, so there'll be others."

"I'm going to take a hot bath and get you to give me one of your back rubs. You haven't done that in a long time."

"A good idea. I want you to get good and rested. Take a Valium and stay in bed all day tomorrow until practice time."

"No, I'm going to church."

Agnès kept her eyes down on her plate. It was time for her to ask: "Travis, are you really serious about this newfound religion?"

Travis stopped eating to stare at Agnes in wide-eyed amazement. "Why, Agnes, surely you didn't think I *wasn't?*"

Agnes fortified herself by pouring some Beaujolais into her glass, saying nothing.

"The world, Agnes," Travis commenced in a didactic tone, "is in a mess. You know why? Because the people in it are a mess. They are not in spiritual accord with the teachings of Christ. People are selfish, thinking only of themselves and how they can *use* each other to benefit themselves." Like Rudy, she added silently. "Do you remember the first thing Willie said to me this afternoon? How much *money* we could make. He was thinking about money, while I was thinking about the quality of my performance. I have fans and I owe them something."

Buttering a roll, Agnes offered no specific comment. "Apparently you have given them something. Didn't you say that the session was terrific?"

"Yes, with the help of Bobby's backing. He can read me like a book. He catches on fast. Bobby's a genius." Travis resumed eating, tasting the shrimp. "Too bad he's a fag. Just think, all those cute looks going to males!"

"Regardless, he's a damn nice guy," Agnes vindicated her faithful friend.

"Maybe I can reform him—through Jesus."

"Anita Bryant, leave him alone. He seems happy the way he is."

"It would be better if he wasn't so obvious at times. Oh well, most people expect male musicians to be queer." Travis sipped her tea. "They say May Brooks is like *that.*"

"She's a good actress," Agnes said tersely.

Travis was quiet for a moment. "I almost got into it once when I was a kid. Experimenting with mama and papa games—playing with each other," she giggled. "But the boys just swept it all away." She made a face. "Dykes turn me off, trying to imitate men when they know they don't have what men have down there. Wonder why some women go that route?"

"Because they *prefer* it, I suppose. You never know which way your heart will go."

"Did you—ever?"

"What?"

"Do *that* with anybody."

"No," Agnes said sharply, and she hadn't. Funny women, as they called them, had never been of concern to her.

"Well, why do you take up for Bobby so much?"

"Because," she said, getting a little tired of the subject, "I believe in letting people's sex lives alone—whatever they might be."

Travis watched her quietly. "Agnes, do you ever get lonely?"

"I don't have time," she said abruptly, finishing the wine and lighting a cigarette.

Travis pushed the ashtray over. "You seem so independent." She could see Agnes withdrawing, and felt hurt, wishing that they could be more intimate as friends. Agnes was everything to her but a lover. It was like being close to a dog that was wagging its tail but growling at the same time.

"Being independent, you don't have to worry with giving-ins or giving-outs." Agnes concentrated on the burning end of her cigarette.

"It's nice, though, to have someone to share things with, turn to, be with."

"It's getting late." Agnes extinguished the half-smoked cigarette.

"Go to church with me tomorrow," Travis invited.

"Sorry, but I have to see that everything's in shape for the concert. I'll get Bobby to go with you."

"Always business first." Words in a cave.

"That's what you pay me for." Agnes's face appeared thin, gaunt in the shadows.

"We're friends, too, aren't we, Agnes? I don't know what I would have done sometimes without you. Like today, getting Rudy out of my hair."

"Fait accompli."

"Are you religious?"

"As a child I was brought up in the church—if that means anything."

"I mean, *believe?*"

"Belief is a state of mind. Come on, now. Better get ready for bed. It's getting late. Still want your back rubbed?"

"No, and I don't want the Valium either. I think I'll relax by reading His word. It's nice that they put Bibles in hotel rooms, isn't it? I hadn't thought about it before."

Agnes got up. "Get your sleep."

"I will, and tomorrow I shall worship in the House of the Lord."

Chapter 9

*T*HAT Sunday morning, the small, brick New Hope Unity Church, situated on a narrow side street contouring remnants of once modest, fine houses, overflowed for the first time in its thirty-five-year history. The hard pews were filled with a congregation consisting of the faithful who habitually attended each Sunday; a multitude who hadn't attended church in a month of Sundays; admirers and curiosity seekers to see and be near Travis Lee; outsiders wanting to hear the Reverend Myrtle Black; and a trickling of those who came to be saved.

For company, as well as protection, Agnes insisted on Bobby's accompanying Travis. He went reluctantly, fretting over the lost time he could have spent in bed with Clyde. In deference to the occasion, he dressed in the most conservative manner he could—in a light plaid suit embellished with a red tie and handkerchief. As soon as he and Travis arrived, they were promptly surrounded by the lay minister, heads of the steward and stewardess boards, and ushers. Flanked by this corp of attendants, they were led down the narrow aisle before rubbernecking heads to take a front row seat beside Lucy Cross.

Watching them, the Reverend Cross sat awkwardly on the pulpit with the choir. He was surprised at the crowded church, a feat he had never been able to accomplish. In nervous stupefaction, he gazed down at the crowd, singling out scattered faces of whites. A few of the young white males had long hair and beards, and the girls next to them had on ankle-length dresses. He placed them as the "Jesus freaks" he had seen and read about, who passed out literature and love on downtown

Church Street and the outlying shopping malls. Other young
people—black and white—looked like students from the city's
cluster of colleges and universities. At the front and sides of
the church were TV cameras and reporters with George
F. D. Clemons among them. One of the white photographers
came up and snapped a picture of Travis.

A transplanted country preacher six years out of Cookes-
ville, Reverend Cross was overwhelmed and awed by it all.
The idea occurred to him that his church had been turned into
a theater. Feeling alone and abandoned before a situation he
could not readily grasp or cope with, he wished Reverend Black
would hurry and come. Women were always late for the most
obscure reasons. He would have to start the service soon, with
or without her.

Sounds of restlessness stirred the air: bodies shifting, mouths
mumbling, and babies crying. The warmth in the church added
to the rustling overtones. Although all the high, narrow, painted
windows were opened wide to a picturesque summer morning,
the scattered floor church fans, going full blast, and hand fans,
donated by the Thurman Funeral Home, offered little relief.
When more of the mortgage was paid off, Reverend Cross had
told the church, an air conditioner would be bought. But collection plates were quite paltry these days.

He could see the waiting had caused worry to line his wife's
face, and her fingers to squeeze the hymnal in her lap. *Don't
blame me, Lucy. It was you who wanted a woman minister for
a change.*

Suddenly there were loud exclamations of "Oh-o-o-" and
Ah-a-a-" hissed throughout the church. Turning, he caught
sight of Reverend Myrtle Black emerging onto the pulpit from
the side entrance. Blinking hard, he stared aghast at the sight
of her in a glittering, silver-sequined robe, her hair looped in
a twisted cone. She entered with the visage of royalty, a queen
about to take her throne. The pulpit was transformed by the
spectacle of her entrance. Reverend Cross was temporarily
immobilized.

Sharing her husband's soporific state, Lucy Cross's mouth
was ajar as she gaped at the woman who completely obfuscated
her husband in his shabby black robe. Travis gasped in admiration while Bobby assessed the robe, which was more expensive than any he had seen worn by the most celebrated of
evangelists.

The organist began a prelude. Recovering his wits, the Reverend Cross breathed in relief. The burden was off him. Standing up stiffly, he positioned himself behind the rostrum. His voice came out a thin reed in the hot stuffiness of strangers.

"Let us all stand, please." Looking down, he began to read: "'The hour cometh, and now is when the true worshipers shall worship in Father, in spirit, and in truth, for the Father seeketh such to worship him.' Let us pray. Our Father..."

Head bowed, repeating the Lord's Prayer, Myrtle covertly eyed Travis. She was more attractive in person than in the pictures. The large hat partially hid her face with head bowed, but did not hide the smoothness of her skin, the tint of an overripe peach. Myrtle instantly recognized the man beside her for what he was. No matter how conventionally gay men tried to dress, they seemed perpetually to wear something that gave them away by color or design.

Myrtle was satisfied that the church was filled to her expectation. This Sunday was going to be an event to remember. If only the place had air conditioning. Even heathens should not have to be cast out in this heat. Already she was beginning to be aware of the ventilation. Natural heat flashes combining with the church's warmth flushed through her. Those antiquated fans merely spread tepid breath. By the time she finished, it was going to be made hotter in mind and spirit.

"'...the power, and the glory, forever, amen.'" Reverend Cross picked up his hymnal. "Please turn to page twenty and sing 'Jesus, Lover of My Soul.'"

The organist struck a dissonant chord and Myrtle diagnosed that the instrument needed tuning. But Travis Lee's voice stood out strong and clear in contrast to the mechanical singing of the remainder of the congregation.

Following the hymn, Reverend Cross began his introduction of Myrtle, stumbling over and mispronouncing words on the paper. Listening to him massacring her distinguished record, Myrtle realized why he was pastor of a two-bit church. He had no flair, or depth. He was dull, insipid, and unexciting. Her renowned credentials sounded flat and uninspiring from his mouth. He was one of those who should have been simply a lay minister.

"I'm pleased to present our guest evangelist for a week of revival, the Reverend Myrtle Black."

With the silver robe a radiant coruscating vestment about

her, Myrtle rose slowly, loftily, erect, impenetrably supreme
above the congregation. An automatic hush stilled the church.
Breathing seemed to cease and babies stopped their crying.
Posing in silent grandeur, an apparition from a holy mist,
Myrtle, intuitive of her mastery for capturing and holding attention, felt her power bridling the congregation. She knew
that she possessed a natural facility for dramatics. A minister
was crippled without it. Pausing for effect, she remained quies-
cent for what was solely a quiver in time, but the vacant instant,
charged with electricity, made it seem an eternity. Her black,
hawk eyes stared straight ahead, seeing all collectively, but
surreptitiously studying Travis at rapt attention. Sucking in her
breath, Myrtle snapped her head to the ceiling and let her
eloquent voice vibrate to the rafters.

"I am reading from Proverbs, chapter fourteen, verse thirty-
four: 'Righteousness exalteth a nation: but sin is a reproach to
any people.' Yes-s-s, my brothers and sisters, sin-n-n is *re-
proach-ful* to all people, and this is what my message to you
this morning is about—*sin!* Here in *our* nation's towns and
cities—*this-s-s* city—sin *abounds!* But few pay heed, for
'Fools make a mock of sin.' And this mockery will be the
downfall of all-l-l. This nation, as Sodom, will fall by God's
wrath because of its wickedness. *No-o-o* city can survive in
sin. *This* city cannot survive in sin—"
    Preach!
Myrtle's heavy eyebrows furrowed together, clouding her
face in a frown as she moved on the side of the rostrum to
tower before the congregation like an oracle of damnation.
"There is the sinfulness of the flesh. The *using* of our sisters'
bodies for the selfishness and greed of others. The *greed* of
men-n-n who take advantage of women in a *sinful* way. Those
poor sisters shot down right out there on the streets—*your*
streets—which would not have occurred if they hadn't been
in the business of selling their bodies to men-n-n for the *lust*
of men-n-n! Men-n-n who put them *out* there to satisfy their
own materialistic needs and for appeasing the animalistic ap-
petities of *men-n-n.* Yes-s-s, I say *ani-ma-listic,* for there is
nothing tender or sweet or beautiful in the sexual act of prostitution. When I visited those two women in the hospital, my
heart became heavy with pain for those poor, poor victims of
a depraved society. Sin is in the streets of Nashville. Sin-n-n

is in the *hearts* of those who sell, buy, and use bodies immorally!"

Ah-h yes-s-s!

Reverend Cross began to squirm uncomfortably in his seat. He could not believe what was being preached in his church by this woman. Why, there wasn't a man in the church, including himself, who hadn't paid for it one time or another. At this rate, he wouldn't have a male in attendance for services the rest of the week. To make him fume more, there was Lucy with a satisfied look on her face—one known to him as her condemning pleasure.

"In black North Nashville, *black* women are afraid to walk the streets night *or* day for fear of being robbed, killed, or raped! More *black* women are raped by white and their *own* men than white women because *black* women are not looked upon in a humane or respectful way, but *selfishly*, since tra-di-tion-al-ly, that has been the plight of *black* women—to be used and abused!"

Ain't it the truth?

Preach on!

"This selfishness must be *stopped,* for selfishness is the prime motivation of sin. It must be stopped by following the teachings of Jesus. Sisters must become sisters, and brothers must become brothers in *spi-rit!* We must learn to love and respect each other *and* ourselves-s-s. Yes-s-s, I say *love* and *respect!*"

Love and respect!

That's right!

The rich, compelling cadence of Myrtle's words spun a web around the congregation. She had them in the palm of her hand. Her words came out in the rhythm of a song, words like notes falling harmoniously in place, captivating, arousing. She was an espouser of truths, provoking, invoking an internal examination of self.

Travis sat spellbound on the edge of the pew, mesmerized by what she was hearing. It was all so true, reaching back to her own basic tenet of people using each other. She had been used and used and used. A burning sensation of remorseful self-pity swept over her. Straightening up, she blazoned out in a gale of passion: *"Preach!"* along with the rest.

Myrtle's eyes whipped down quickly on Travis's enraptured

face and back over the congregation again. Edging closer to
the fringes of the pulpit, she drew herself up to her full height,
letting her voice rise to octave pitch: "All-l-l must *unite* in
Christ to rid themselves and this city of sin-ful-ness. Nashville
ranks as a city having one of the highest statistics of venereal
disease among the youth of this nation. Doesn't this *prove* that
something is *wrong* here in a city *supposedly* in the Bible Belt?
Where indeed are all the so-called Christians? Instead of parading with placards in front of adult bookstores, they should
be holding hands and praying with those who need help and
guidance in the way of the Lord. *I* have never heard of anybody
being raped, robbed, or killed by a book!"

Truth!

A-men!

"I am wondering as I look around me, *where* are all those
holier-than-thou hypo-crites called *Christians* in this city? I will
tell you *where* they are: Standing around with one foot in
heaven and one foot in hell! What they *need* to do is get those
feet to-ge-ther in *one* place—the *Lord's!*"

Rave on to Jesus!

Yes-s in-dee-dy!

Myrtle ceased for a theatrical respite; the church waited in
a deathlike silence. "My brothers and sisters, I am going to
organize a crusade to start cleaning up this city—our black
community—starting with the vicinity of where those poor
women got shot!"

Hallelujah!

At last!

Start, sis-tah!

"I am starting there because it is a ghetto of broken spirits,
homes, families. Some of our most prestigious black institutions line that thoroughfare. Schools that are training our black
leaders of tomorrow—the young and impressionable. Are our
white institutions fringed by physical deterioration?"

No-o-o!

"Brothers and sisters, I tell you without a doubt, the sin in
this city has got to go-o-o! And the only way it *can* go is for
all-l-l of us to go-o-o in the *way* of the Lord!"

A-men!

The only way-y!

"Got to go-o-o!" Myrtle shouted, suddenly sweeping down
off the pulpit to stand before the congregation. In one quick

movement, she spun around and pointed a finger at the organist. Taking the cue, the woman began thumping out a rhythmic beat to which Myrtle started clapping her hands and swaying to the sound of the music. "Got to go-o-o!" she sang out, body twisting and gyrating to the thumping beat.

Got to go-o-o! the congregation responded, caught up in the incantation. Feet stomped, hands clapped, and at the same time, the choir burst forth in a spontaneous musical rock of "Got to go in the way of the Lord."

"Oh-h-h, yes-s-s!" Myrtle screamed, eyes half shuttered, simulating a trance, perspiration moistening her face and dampening her armpits. Initiating a dip and swinging fast turn, she pranced and sashayed in time with the music, bellowing as she did: "We are going to *change* our way of living in our hearts and minds!" Shaking her shoulders and shuffling her feet, she danced before Travis, looking beyond her. The TV cameramen came closer.

Members of the congregation, fired with her spirit, leaped up and began dancing in the aisles along with her. The organist pounded a frenzied beat while hands and feet made accompanying drumbeats.

"Got to go in the way of the Lord!" Myrtle held her arms high, crying above the music: "Those who want to know-w-w your Jesus—'Depart from evil, and do good, so shall you abide forever'—*come,* come and I shall lay His blessings upon you. Say Jesus and come to me!"

"Jes-us!"

To Myrtle's amazement and delight, Travis was the first to come directly to her, crying out. A slight lull hovered over the congregation when they saw who it was going to Myrtle. "My-y-y sister!" Myrtle stretched out her arms and Travis fell right into them like a homing bird flown home to rest. Myrtle smelled the delicate sweetness of her perfume and felt the warmth of her body as their breasts touched in a way only a woman can greet a woman. Myrtle's breath quickened as heat suffused her.

"I was a sinner," Travis cried, tears in her eyes, head buried on Myrtle's breasts. "I've done wrong."

"All that is behind you now, my dear." Myrtle squeezed her, basking in the soft curves melting into her. "You have my spiritual blessing."

"Could I see you after the service?" Travis whispered an entreatment half-smothered in the robe.

"Certainly—the back room." Myrtle gave her another holy squeeze.

Now men and women and children began to come up to be saved, join the church, and get a better look at Travis Lee. "Praise the Lord!" Myrtle shouted, feeling good. "Ev-errybody join hands together. Touch each other. *Touch* each other in hand and spirit. We are all-l-l *one! Love* one another. Touch and let love flow through you. Then say Jesus and come to me!"

When the service was over, Bobby lingered while Travis, slightly shaken from her confession to Jesus, graciously signed autographs, met budding, young aspiring singers, posed for pictures, and talked to the press. Finally tiring of the fanfare, he urged her away to wait for Myrtle.

The church social room where they were escorted was sparsely furnished. Peeling yellow paint on the walls boxed in a floor covered with spotty, cracked linoleum. An ancient sink, two-burner gas stove, and rusting refrigerator made a unit in the corner.

Bobby was pleased to find it was cooler in this room on the tree-shaded side of the church with a breeze coming in from the tall windows. They sat down at a wooden table covered with a plastic cloth and stacked with old Sunday School lessons.

"Whew, it's hot," Bobby said, taking off his coat and wiping his face with his red handkerchief. "I'm ready for another shower."

Travis managed to remain cool-looking despite the heat. "Wasn't she wonderful?"

"A real female black Billy Graham." The red tie was loosened next.

"She's a good-looking woman, too. Dynamic, impressive, powerful!"

Bobby had to admit she was. He wanted to murder the organist, an amateur who had nothing going for her except chords and a beat. She didn't even have sense enough to realize the organ needed tuning.

Myrtle swooped into the room, locking the door behind her. "To keep out your public," she explained, smiling.

"Reverend Black, I enjoyed your sermon so much!" Travis breathed rapturously.

"It was a pleasure having someone like *you* present to hear me."

"Reverend, this is my piano player, Bobby Blane."

"It's good to have you, too, Mr. Blane."

"Thank you, Reverend. It's seldom I get to hear a woman minister." Or any other for that matter. His Sundays were always taken up with other pursuits. Bobby stuck out his hand and felt it pressed hard. His eyes met hers and held. An instinctive recognition stirred him. He withdrew his hand from her hard grip. Forceful women upset him, like overprotective mothers. She reminded him of someone he had met a long time ago in a gay bar.

"Reverend Black, could I have a talk with you later on tonight?" Travis asked, the question conveying urgency.

"Anytime. I am always at the service of those who need me. As a matter of fact, I am staying at the same hotel as you." She was pleased to impart this information for convenience' sake.

Travis hesitated, then said, "Will it be against your beliefs to come to my concert tonight? I would like very much to have you there. This will be my last one—ever—on Sunday. God's day!" The Reverend's presence would give her comfort.

Myrtle thought over the request quickly. It was Reverend Cross's turn to preach this evening. It would not be difficult to get out of being here. She could discern Travis's ambivalence about the concert and her new religious birth. A minister in attendance would give her spiritual support. "I am a flexible woman of God, my dear. If you want me, I will be there."

"Then we can talk afterwards?"

"Certainly."

Bobby occupied himself by gazing out the window. Knocks sounded on the door. "I'll have to open the door now," Myrtle said, looking at Travis as if it were the last thing she wanted to do.

Reverend Cross came in, followed by his wife, George, and a black photographer. George smiled at Myrtle. "Bud wants to get a group picture for *Jet.*"

Bud motioned for Myrtle, Travis, Reverend Cross, and his wife to stand close. "OK—hold it."

Perspiring heavily, Reverend Cross seemed dazed. In contrast, Lucy, bright-eyed and flustered, had a perpetual smile on her face, enjoying the limelight.

"See you in the morning's paper," George waved back at Myrtle.

"You two had better leave by this door," Myrtle said to

Travis and Bobby. "You will get away faster." Locking arms
with both of them, she walked to a door at the rear of the room.

"I'll see you later?" Travis asked anxiously.

"Without a doubt, my dear. I shall be there."

Chapter 10

WITH the reserve ticket Travis left for her at the hotel desk, Myrtle bypassed the long line of ticket buyers at the Municipal Auditorium and walked right in. She was immediately intercepted by Bobby, who was on the lookout for her.

"Reverend Black!" he called, pushing through the crowd. "Travis wants you to come backstage."

"Is anything wrong?"

"No, she just wants to see you." Bobby led her to Travis's dressing room and left them.

Travis was seated at the dresser applying finishing touches to her makeup. Myrtle thought she looked stunning in a skintight, strapless black dress. When Travis turned from the mirror to her, she saw a face powdered and rouged to perfection. Blue eye shadow brought out the long lashes and amber brown of her eyes. A quickening surge of physical attraction assailed her.

"I'm glad you could come, Reverend Black."

"You look very pretty," Myrtle complimented.

"Here's Agnes." Travis's gaze went to the door. "Reverend Black, this is my business manager, Agnes Saunders."

Agnes's eyes measured Myrtle. "How do you do, Reverend."

Myrtle returned the scrutiny in kind while saying, "A pleasure to meet you."

"I wanted Reverend Black to come tonight to give me spiritual support. I don't intend to do any more Sunday concerts after this."

"Sure, baby," Agnes said, thankful that at least she hadn't

reneged on this contractual obligation. There would have been
hell to pay. "Go out there and give them your best, as usual.
You look gorgeous."

"I told her." Myrtle's eyes were drawn again to Travis's
voluptuous curves. A joy to behold.

"Will you pray for me, Reverend, before I go out there? I
need the Lord's blessing."

Agnes turned her back to them, busying herself with
straightening up the cosmetics on the dresser.

"I will." Myrtle kneeled down beside the chair, glad she
had worn the pantsuit, which made kneeling easier.

"Agnes, come and pray with us."

To keep the peace, Agnes went to stand stiffly behind Travis
while Myrtle prayed. "Dear Lord, we ask Thee to bestow Thy
blessings on this talented young singer who has found goodness
in Thee. Help her to go forth tonight and share in all her glory
the gift of song Thou has given her. Let your sound be heard,
for in music, your goodness shines through for making it possible. There is beauty and worthiness in all kinds of music—
every bird has a different song. We ask Thee to give this singer
Thy inspiration and blessing tonight—amen."

"Oh, that was beautiful, Reverend!" Travis stood up. "I feel
so relieved now."

"It's time to go on, Travis." Agnes moved toward the door.

"Reverend Black, would you stay backstage with Agnes?
I need to have you near me."

"If you like."

"Let's go," Agnes urged impatiently. "The contract states
we start promptly at eight."

"Give them your best, my dear," Myrtle whispered to Travis
going out the door.

Watching Travis perform, Myrtle readily perceived why she
was called the Pristine Goddess of Song. She was extraordi-
nary, whether executing a wailing blues, melodic ballad, or
cataclysmic rock and roll number, all flowed from her mouth
as smoothly as breathing. The Ding-a-Lings provided a background of melodious tones, tying in rhythmically with her nuances, shifting moods, and movements.

The auditorium became quiet when Travis, twisting sensuously around the stage, sang throatily of love and loving.
Myrtle was entranced by every bit of her. During a tune of

panting of love and belonging, it seemed that Travis was looking directly at her standing in the wings. Warmth kindled her, a low torch of flame. Feeling an effusion of desire welling up in her, Myrtle eased out farther from behind the curtain toward that which was arousing her, ignoring the sidelong curious glances of Agnes.

At intermission, Agnes tended to Travis's needs while Travis in turn sought bracing from Myrtle. "You are doing beautifully," Myrtle praised, finding the excuse to do what she had been itching to do all evening—touch Travis's warm, smooth, bare shoulders. The contact was like stroking galvanized heat.

"Do that again, Reverend." Travis glowed.

"What?"

"Touch me. It felt so *spiritual!*"

Myrtle held her breath, smothering the exhalations of internal excitement as her fingers repeated their feather-grazing pattern across Travis's skin. Did she feel Travis tremble under the touch, or was it a wish of her imagination?

"Time to go on again," Agnes said brusquely.

"Agnes, this is by far my best concert. See what prayer can do?"

Agnes made no comment.

"Prayer *and* talent, my dear. The latter of which you have an abundance," Myrtle supplied.

For the remainder of the concert, Travis worked the audience into a frenzy. The people whistled, clapped, stood on their seats and called for more. At the end, whooping for an encore, Travis was given a standing ovation.

Blowing kisses of gratitude, Travis acknowledged the Ding-a-Lings, the band, and gave special recognition to Bobby. Then gripping the microphone, she raised her voice over the clamor to say: "I want you all to know this is my last Sunday concert. While here in Music City, I found love. Love in my Jesus and His word."

Myrtle heard Agnes emit a loud gasp. "Damn, what's she doing?"

"I want *you* in the audience listening to me tonight to find Jesus like I did. Now, please join me in singing a hymn—'The Old Rugged Cross.'"

"The band's probably never heard of it!" Agnes shook her

head in disbelief. "She's ruining it. They could have gone to church for that."

The audience was temporarily stunned as a shocked silence prevailed. Mistaking the silence for reverence, Travis began to sing. She sang alone, the hymn coming out hollow, deserted, a travesty over the microphone. The band was paralyzed, not knowing the music, not knowing what to do. In desperation, Bobby searchingly fingered desultory chords on the piano, trying to aid, wanting to cry, curse, and scream at the same time. People began to leave amidst a diffusion of talk and laughter. One or two remote voices drunkenly off-key, attempted to join her. Travis continued to sing until the ending. By that time, the auditorium had emptied.

Back in her dressing room, tears of helplessness and anger filled her eyes. "Did you see what they did, Reverend Black? They walked out! Right in the middle of a hymn!"

"Travis, they didn't pay to hear hymms," Agnes said, unable to conceal the disgust in her voice.

"There are those who do not keep the face of the Lord before them," Myrtle sermonized, "and for them, we ask forgiveness."

A knock sounded on the door and Agnes faced a florist's delivery boy. "Flowers for Travis Lee, ma'am." Agnes took the bouquet of roses.

"Who're they from?" Travis asked, wiping tears from her eyes.

"Willie Frye." Agnes read the note: "Sorry I couldn't be there, but had an engagement in L.A. Knock them dead."

"You take them for the church, Reverend," Travis said.

Another knock and Bobby rushed in, quickly closing the door behind him. "Agnes, there're reporters galore out there waiting to pounce."

"No interviews for her now."

"I'll keep them occupied while you two slip her out," Myrtle volunteered.

"And how do you intend to do that?" Agnes half scoffed.

"By telling them about Jesus," Myrtle quipped triumphantly.

After bidding Agnes good-night, Travis went down to Myrtle's room. There she sat in the lamp's dimness with the sweet scent of Willie Frye's roses permeating the air. Quietly, effortlessly, she talked to Myrtle.

"Shall I put on more light?" Myrtle asked.

"No, I like it this way. The shadows make it soothing."

"Would you care for a glass of wine?" The bottle was waiting, iced in a bucket on the table with two glasses. "Wine to me occasionally is relaxing. Jesus served it to his disciples."

"If you think it's all right."

Myrtle expertly uncorked the bottle she had purchased the day before and filled their glasses. "To our meeting," she toasted.

A smile curled around Travis's lips and stayed. "Yes, at the right time."

Myrtle settled down in a chair, quietly watching Travis.

"You know, Reverend, I was a hell raiser," Travis admitted. "Getting high on booze and pills—props, I suppose, of the grind of show business." Travis's forefinger made imaginary circles around the rim of the glass. "And men! I always had to have one around. I felt that I needed them. Now, I wonder why. Just for sex, I guess, for that was all they were good for."

Slowly Travis sipped the wine. "Even my daddy wasn't any good to have around. He worked on the railroad and was gone most of the time. My little brother and I used to hate to see him come home from his runs, for all he did was fuss at Mama. Later on, I figured that was an out to get into the streets."

Myrtle did not interrupt, letting Travis talk.

"When he was away Mama didn't have any men coming in and out of the house. She was a wonderful Christian woman. She worked as a practical nurse at the city hospital, took care of us, and went to prayer meetings on Wednesday nights and church every Sunday."

"Where is your brother?" This was new to Myrtle.

Travis gazed beyond Myrtle into the dimness of the room. "Sam was killed in Vietnam. He joined the army to get away from home."

"I am sorry."

Travis held out her glass to be refilled. "Going back to men, this is the first time I haven't had one hanging around. I put Rudy out the other night." Her face tightened. "Men can be such bastards." She shot an apologetic look at Myrtle. "Excuse me, Reverend."

"That's all right. Express yourself, my dear."

"You know, I really admire Agnes. She's so self-sufficient—a loner, needing nobody."

"No one is really a loner. Independent, yes."

"Are you married, Reverend?" She tried to picture a husband.

"No. A husband would require too much of my time from the Lord." The stock answer came glibly to a question frequently posed to her.

"I almost got married once, at the age of seventeen while in high school to a boy I thought I was in love with. It was puppy love—or a matter of being in love with love. Thank God my mother put her foot down. I went on to college for a year. Then when my mama died, I gave it up for a full-time singing career. No more stints here and there. I'm glad that I did. But sometimes it's made me feel so jaded at twenty-eight."

The wine spread a heady warmth through Travis, making her want to confide in the woman who was listening sympathetically, compassion heavy on her face. "Have you ever been in love, Reverend?" Quickly she chastised herself. What an intimate question to ask a minister! But under these circumstances, she seemed more a friend.

Love? Myrtle digested the question. She preached about love all the time, but the mortal kind of love Travis was speaking of was a different kind. She had never really been in love with anyone like that. Love was a strong emotional and physical attraction for another. The succession of women in her life had been fleeting and feelings toward them had not given rise to love. Love has to be stabilized by proximity. Mobility from place to place doesn't sustain it. The business of her life called for movement. For this reason, she settled for the brief physical encounters. Love, too, required thinking more of another person than of yourself.

She sidestepped the remark: "I suppose all of us go through some kind of love stage for somebody at one time or another in life."

Travis leaned her head back, half closing her eyes. "I feel utterly drained."

"Why don't you lie down?" Myrtle got up to turn the covers back on the bed. "Rest a while from it all."

"You're a very peaceful person to be with." Travis kicked off her shoes and stretched out on the bed.

Myrtle gently covered her. "Close your eyes. Don't think of anything. Just sleep."

The remainder of the night, Myrtle sat up in the chair, keeping vigil over Travis while finishing the wine.

Chapter 11

MYRTLE watched over Travis until early in the morning when Travis awoke to return to her room and prepare for the flight back to New York. Bleary-eyed and tired from her lack of sleep, Myrtle showered and called room service for breakfast and the paper.

Over coffee, toast, and juice, she read about her beginning crusade to clear the city of its criminal elements. A picture of her in church with her arms outstretched to heaven accompanied the article. Elated over the publicity, Myrtle read quickly, soaking up the words and congratulating George for getting it in.

The phone rang and she picked up the receiver to hear the voice of Felicia Howard, who wanted to tape her later in the week for her TV *Sunday Ebony Roundup*. As soon as she hung up, the Women's Aid In Crisis called to invite her to offer prayer and guidance to the women and girls at the center. A succession of additional calls from admirers and supporters— as well as cranks mouthing threats—further interrupted her breakfast.

Stimulated by it all, but overtired, Myrtle decided to take a nap, and then make a second trip to the hospital to see the girls before the evening's service. She asked the desk clerk to hold her calls.

At the hospital, Heavenly Delight and Earthly Treasure were in low spirits, but looked and felt better physically. Earthly Treasure was sitting on the side of the bed with her hair combed. A half-empty pack of Kools was on the table.

"Why, hello there, Reverend Black," Heavenly Delight smiled, glad to see her. "It's sure nice of you to come again."

"Hello, my sisters. How are you?"

"Fine, 'cept now we worried 'bout goin' to jail," Heavenly Delight grunted.

"The lawyer my King got," Earthly Treasure said, a gleam of pride lighting her face, letting Myrtle know she had communicated with her man, "tolt me they might try to git us on the prostitution thing, but we cert'nly didn't shoot ourselves!"

"I brought some things for you. Candy for Heavenly Delight—"

"Oh, thank you, Reverend!" Heavenly Delight eagerly took the box of Nashville Candyland chocolates.

"And cigarettes for you." Myrtle handed Earthly Treasure a carton of Kools.

"I *do* 'preciate this, Rev," Earthly Treasure beamed. "The Lord must've seen me 'bout to run out!"

"You come to pray for us again?" Heavenly Delight asked, prying open the candy like a child at Christmas.

"Yes, and to talk," Myrtle said, pulling up a chair at the foot of their beds. "I think we all can be a big help to each other."

Driving back from the hospital, Myrtle was appalled at what she had heard from the women. Stories about police graft, payoffs in money and sex. The clientele of the prostitutes distressed her—pillars of the professional and religious communities. She would preach another fire-and-brimstone sermon this evening to whip them awake to the evils in the city.

Before dressing for service, she read about Travis in the *Nashville Evening News*. The article lauded the concert, but hinted of its ending in a travesty with born-again Travis Lee's surprising sermonizing and hymn.

Reading it made Myrtle feel more depressed, for it brought back how Travis had been affected by it all. She wished that Travis could have remained longer, so she could be with her in this crucial time of need. A selfish reason, too, loomed in her thoughts, for she was attracted to the singer. It had been all she could do last night to keep from getting into bed with her and holding her close in her arms. She had acted with God-given restraint, for if she hadn't, the gesture could have destroyed the growing friendship.

Travis might have been shocked or disgusted by the advance. How to know; how not to know? An invisible albatross around the lesbian's neck. Life could sometimes be unfair. Putting down the paper, she got up to go to church.

The service was filled again with worshipers anxious to see and hear her. The word had been spread in beauty parlors, barbershops, pool halls, greasy spoons, beer joints, and corner grocery stores that the Reverend Myrtle Black could really "git down."

She did "git down" by preaching out the Police Department, City Hall, pimps, dope pushers, and middle-class hypocrites. She gospeled them to repent in the arms of Jesus, and those who would not she exhorted straight to hell.

Physically drained and damp with perspiration from the hot church and her hell-fire sermon, she took the stack of messages from the smiling female hotel clerk who artfully apprised her of their secretarial service for guests.

Upstairs, she threw off her sweaty clothes and showered for a second time. Pouring a glass of Bristol Cream, she noted that she was sipping quite a bit of late, justifying it by being more worn-out than usual.

Just as she settled in bed to read the messages, the phone summoned her attention. The Reverend Cross urgently wanted to see her first thing in the morning at the church. She set the appointment for 8:00 A.M., immediately dismissing him from her thoughts. All she wanted now was sleep.

In the humid confines of the back meeting room of the church, Reverend Cross pulled out a chair for Myrtle at the table where on Sunday Travis had waited for her. The Sunday school lesson books had been removed to a corner on the floor, and a new white plastic cloth replaced the old one.

Reverend Cross seemed out of character dressed in a pair of khaki pants and short-sleeved print cotton shirt. The room was stuffy with the everlasting stale aromas of past bodies and church suppers. No air stirred from the outside where the temperature was hot and the day muggy. The sky was gray and bloated with rain clouds.

Reverend Cross sat down and crossed his legs. Taking out a handkerchief, he wiped his damp forehead. "Going to buy an air conditioner one of these days."

You will have to bring in better collection plates than you have been, Myrtle thought scornfully. "Yes, an air conditioner would make it nicer," she said, moving her chair closer to the window.

"The way you have been getting money for us, Reverend Black, it won't be too long," he smiled fleetingly at her. "We are grateful. Yes, indeed!"

"Thank you, Reverend Cross." Myrtle managed to squeeze a smile back. At least he was astute enough to realize the difference.

Uncrossing his leg, Reverend Cross cleared his throat of an imaginary irritant. "Reverend Black," he began slowly, frowning down at the floor, "I asked you here to talk about something very important." He paused, face grave. "It concerns the direction of your sermons."

"What about my sermons?" Myrtle asked testily.

"Well...you see...we have a kind of simple church here—homespun—where people come to hear the word of God as it is written in the Bible." His eyes lifted to settle on the tiny gold cross around her neck. "I'm afraid that those things you are preaching about—selling women's bodies and such—must stop. We stress in our revivals the saving of souls!"

Myrtle straightened up in her chair. "In order to save souls, Reverend Cross, you have to get sinners to repent," she reasoned pointedly.

"True," Reverend Cross agreed, nodding his head in assent, "but what I'm trying to say, Reverend Black, is the *kinds* of people who you are saving through your sermons are not exactly the ones we want in our church pews. They are, shall I say, not the *ordinary* sinners." There! It had been said. He did not want the dregs of society in his church. Only the regular parishioners whose past, and even present, sins were those run-of-the-mill transgressions of adultery, fornication, drinking, and gambling.

Myrtle looked at him in confusion. "I don't quite understand what you mean, Reverend Cross, by selecting the types of people you want to be brought into the church. I thought all-l-l sinners must be saved—regardless!"

Reverend Cross's square, overweight hips fidgeted in the rickety chair. "Ah-h-h, yes-s-s! All sinners are to be saved. But we don't need certain sorts of saved sinners in *this* church." He clasped his hands together in a prayer lock on the table, then unfastened them again to spread his fingers forbiddingly.

"Reverend Black, I cannot have reformed prostitutes"—his eyes shifted beyond her—"or perverts"—for there were *those* now swishing up and down his aisles—"sitting next to children and the good old sisters and brothers who have for years been the foundation of my church. It isn't right!"

Right? The word exploded in her ears. What was wrong with this man? Setting himself up to be a judge as to which sheaves were to be brought into the fold? All repenters were children of God and had a rightful place in the church of their deliverance.

Her silence at his chastisement gave him back a sense of authority, which he felt had been lost since her arrival. Empowered by this, his voice raised to a half-Sunday sermon octave: "Also, Reverend Black, the preaching against our fine police department and city officials must cease. I cannot allow it!"

The silence that he had mistaken for subduedness was a cauldron of anger boiling within Myrtle. The nerve of *him,* she seethed, telling *me* what to preach about. Who did this pitiful imitation of God's servant think he was, talking to her like that? The raging storm claiming her lashed her face, threatening like the sky outside simmering with God's brewing storm. Nobody dictated what she should preach about except the Lord.

Seeing the wrath exposed on her face, Reverend Cross attempted to ward it off. "Reverend Black, please look at it from *my* point of view," he said placatingly. "I have to *live* here. You preach and leave."

Drawing herself up like a ruffled lioness, Myrtle spat out, "In all of my years of serving the Lord, I have never encountered the likes of this. You have the audacity to order me to help you promote bigotry within your church. Then next you tell me what I should and should not preach about." Her eyes bore through him. "Reverend Cross, as long as I am able to open this mouth of mine, I shall preach, shout and scream what *I* want to. Either I do this, or I shall *not* preach for you at all!"

Reverend Cross was so taken aback by her ultimatum, that his nostrils flared over his half-opened mouth where the edges of his two front gold teeth emerged rabbitlike beneath a trembling upper lip. The woman incensed him with her arrogance. If she hadn't been a minister of God, he would have sworn she was a witch in disguise.

She had made a fool of him in the two days she had preached.

Wearing those outlandishly unholy looking robes, getting in
the newspapers and on TV—things he had never been able to
do, which had seeded jealousy in his heart. Even if she had
drawn people to crowd the church and fill the collection plates,
it was still *his* church and *he* was the one to determine what
was to be said and done in it. He shouldn't have listened to
his wife's idea of inviting her here in the first place.

His eyes narrowed speculatively at her. There had been
hushed rumors, which too had made him hesitant about having
her to preach. He couldn't see any outward signs that might
confirm the rumors he had heard of her. But those kind of
women were masculine-looking, weren't they?

Finding his voice, he said hoarsely, "I'm sorry you feel like
that, Reverend Black." Actually he was relieved. His church
need no longer bear the burden of excitement, notoriety. He
could finish the revival in an uneventful, peaceful way of saving
souls in the good old usual way.

"I, too, regret it had to end in this manner," Myrtle said
stiffly, standing up. "Good-bye, Reverend Cross. I shall pray
for you and your church."

When she stalked out the door, a clap of thunder drummed
in the pasty sky, as though heralding the departure of a female
warrior.

Seated pensively at the cluttered table in her room, Myrtle
tried to organize her thoughts. She definitely did not want to
leave Nashville. Not now, anyway, when she had it by the tail.
There was no stopping at this point. Adding to the somberness
of her brown study, the rain was coming down hard against
the windowpane.

Maybe a sip of wine would lift her spirits. True, it was
early, but just one. She got the bottle hidden behind the clothes
in the closet and filled a hotel glass. It would be nice now to
have a woman to talk to about problems, and some loving
which did a lot to banish depression. Drinking slowly, the
liquid began to relax her, causing some of the tension to vanish.
She listened to the tears of the rain. She liked to make love
with the rain beating against the window, cuddled in bed with
the warmth of wine stimulating her passion. To have someone
now to stroke, kiss and be near. What was wrong? She rarely
was lonely. There had never been any need to be lonely when
a sweet young thing was always available someplace.

But here, there hadn't been time to look out among the congregation and pluck one from the pews. She had been too busy, too cautious. She couldn't ruin it, because for the first time she had the attention of the news media, more than a church page announcement or ordinary article. This was the chance to make it big, and she couldn't blow it over a pair of drawers.

She kicked off her shoes and lay down on the bed. A one-nighter would surely help to ease the craving. She chastised herself. She had to stop thinking about sex and get to the business at hand. Certainly the press should know of her being silenced. What she needed was a good follow-up, an attention getter to keep her alive in the news.

She had to think. The rain pushed harder against the window, throbbing like her thoughts. A loud thunderclap rumbled the sky, attended by a bolt of sharp crackling lightning that forked uncomfortably close to the room. At that instant the idea was formulated.

Stupendous! Straight from the heavens and her own acute mind. A March! She sat up excitedly. This was the answer, the gimmick needed. She would organize a Women's March on City Hall to protest vice, crime, and corruption in the city. A March of women of all colors, who would join hands to demonstrate against a male establishment of crooked and selfish lawmakers and lawbreakers. Fantastic!

She would require help, for this demanded organization and support, the aid of local women's groups to rally around a March cry to "Get the Bad Notes Out of Music City!" A shibboleth born. Praise the Lord!

First she had to get a secretary to assist with establishing a base office. She had some reserve funds that could be used. Then she needed to call George F. D. Clemons right away, to let her followers know that the truth cannot be stifled. She was still in command. The trumpet had to be sounded to marshal the forces of women in this city who believed as she. Her work was cut out for her. Now to begin.

By 11:30 A.M., the hotel had sent up a secretary, who to Myrtle's dismay was white. She would rather have had a black one, but that would be reverse discrimination. It was only that she didn't like to let white folks in on too much of her business. The secretary's name was Barbara Katz. In her

early twenties, she had a dingy white complexion and was
plain-looking with stringy brown hair parted in the center,
falling in pleats halfway curtaining both sides of her long face.
She had a coated regional accent. Her efficiency was promptly
demonstrated.

An IBM typewriter, which Barbara claimed made letters
look more professional, was rented, and typing paper, pencils,
pads, envelopes, addressing labels, file folders, paper clips,
and a stapler were purchased. Within hours, the hotel room
had become an office.

With the girl occupied, Myrtle went downstairs to meet
George in the coffee shop. She spotted him swiftly in the
crowded room by the rumpled beige suit he favored. His eyes
had heavy pouches beneath them and the hand holding a burning
cigarette trembled slightly. The waitress came and they ordered
coffee.

"My wife is in love with me again. You've gotten me someplace other than the religion section," he grinned.

"I may soon get you on the front page," she bantered back,
carefully measuring a packet of artificial sweetener into her
cup. Stirring the coffee, she proceeded to tell him about Reverend Cross. "Mr. Clemons—"

"George."

"George, I will *not* be silenced!"

"I've heard that you stepped on some toes. The chief of
police is miffed at you for taking his boys to task. He thinks
that they can do no wrong."

"No wrong? All you have to do is read the newspapers.
Somebody's always yelling about police brutality. It never pen-
etrates until a white person's head gets bashed in."

Glancing furtively around, George extracted a half-pint flask
from his coat pocket and poured bourbon in his coffee. "If I
may, Reverend. I use it for medicinal purposes," he said sheep-
ishly.

A lush, she observed, storing away the information for future reference. "George, I am an open-minded minister." She
put him at ease. "As for Reverend Cross or anybody else, I
intend to keep on saying what I have to say and what should
be said. I thank you for all you have done so far."

"Think nothing of it. I'm getting famous." He swallowed
the coffee laced with Jack Daniels. Alcohol fumes floated over
the table like ether.

"Here are some points I want brought out in your story."
She handed him a sheaf of handwritten notes. "I am going to
instigate one of the biggest women's protest marches in this
city."

"Say, this is great news!" George scanned the notes.

"I need backing, George. Who are some of the key women
in this city? Women with the know-how and know-who? I want
women who are willing to stick out their necks. Can you provide me with any contacts?"

"Don't worry. When all this hits the media, they'll be coming to you. For starters, I'll see if I can get you an interview
on the evening news." He raised his cup in salute. "Reverend,
you're a remarkable woman!"

Myrtle found that Barbara was not only a competent secretary, but neat. Before leaving at five-thirty, she covered the
typewriter, had Myrtle read and sign letters for her to mail on
the way home, and stacked pencils and papers in a tidy pile
on the table.

Alone, Myrtle waited impatiently for the ten o'clock news
to see the interview she had done with the black newswoman,
Cherry Roberts. It came at the end, briefly covering the dis-
continuance of her preaching at the New Hope Unity Church
because of "pressure to silence her."

The following day, the morning paper carried the story of
the March on page five:

CENSORED EVANGELIST BLACK
PLANS WOMEN'S MARCH
ON THE CITY
By George F. D. Clemons

The Reverend Myrtle Black is no longer conducting
revival services at the New Hope Unity Church because
of what she contends was pressure brought to silence her
fiery crusading evangelistic attacks on crime and vice in
the city.

Not to be stopped, the Reverend Black is planning
an all-out local Women's Protest March...

* * *

Reading the paper over Myrtle's shoulder, Barbara gasped, "Reverend Black, I think it's terrible what they did to you."

"I have the good Lord on my side, dear," Myrtle reminded her. The girl was close and the female vapors of warmth and perfume made a heady, inviting fragrance around her. Barbara had her hair in a bun today, and eyeing her, Myrtle could see the outline of her small pink mouth and short chin. A sting of desire burned her by the nearness. All work and no play was not a good prescription for anybody. The pain in her groin was piercing, and she pressed her legs tightly together to ease it. Thankfully the phone rang and Barbara moved to answer it, dispersing the web of female excitement.

Turning to Myrtle with her hand covering the receiver, she said, "It's Wilma Freelander, president of Women United for Action."

"I'll take it," Myrtle said. Wilma Freelander had just read the article in the paper and wanted to know if she could come over for a little chat about four o'clock. Myrtle would be delighted. "Well, that's one contact," she said, hanging up the phone.

"Reverend Black, that is *the* contact. Wilma Freelander is one of the most influential and powerful women in the city!" Barbara exclaimed, spontaneously hugging Myrtle in her happiness. "Oh, I think this is so-o-o *exciting!*"

Enjoying the hug, Myrtle still wished the girl had stayed her distance, hoping the quickening of her breath, brought on by the young body pressing hers, wasn't apparent. Reluctantly she pushed breasts, stomach, and hips away in a pretense of busying herself. "We have work to do. I want you to get a list of women's organizations in the city—civic, social, and religious—to contact."

"All right."

"Black and white."

"This is really going to be something. I'm so glad to be a part of it, Reverend Black. To have the opportunity to work with *you!* I think it's time women should band together."

"Yes. Now let us get busy. We have a lot to do."

Wanting to know something about Wilma Freelander before meeting her, Myrtle called George, who provided a brief account. Wilma was a well-to-do divorcee whose money had come from her family's Walking Horse Farm in Bedford

County, and her own real estate investments gleaned from her former banker spouse.

A unique white southern woman, she had an inherent rebelliousness against the conservatism of the South. When the Civil Rights Movement swept the region, she became filled with remorse for the wrongs perpetrated by her own color, and volunteered to work with the black student demonstrators at Fisk, Meharry, and Tennessee State. As the Jim Crow barriers crumbled, so did her marriage to a dyed-in-the-wool southerner who blamed the breakup on his wife's "love for the niggers."

With the coming of the second movement wave for women's rights, she took the helm as one of the South's pioneer leaders, founding the local chapter of the national organization Women United for Action.

The information George had communicated to her flowed through Myrtle's mind as she walked into Wilma Freelander's spacious office downtown in the Sudekum Building. In the flesh, Wilma was a large-boned athletic type woman with short, straight fading brown hair brushed carelessly back from a round, youngish cherub face with gray eyes and a ribbon mouth. She was adept at putting visitors at ease with a friendly smile and down-to-earth heartiness.

"Glad you could come, Reverend Black," she welcomed Myrtle cordially in a voice bordering on hoarseness. "I've been reading and hearing about you." She got up from behind the desk to shake hands. "Sit down and make yourself comfortable. There's no protocol in my office."

"Thank you for asking me to come," Myrtle said, settling in a chair opposite the desk.

"As soon as I read in the morning's paper about your March, I said to myself: 'Freelander, this is *exactly* what needs to be done.' Reverend Black, you are a woman with insight and imagination. Just what we need in this city, and that's why I called you. To see how we can work together to get your March on the road!" Wilma stopped to reach for a cigarette from an opened pack on her desk. "Mind if I smoke, Reverend? Some folks these days don't like it. Smoke bothers them."

"No, go right ahead."

Wilma lit the cigarette and blew out a heavy cordon of smoke. "I can just visualize an army of women marching in unity on the male patriarchs of this city."

"I can, too, but as you know, I am new here and not familiar

with the various women's groups. I will need all the support
I can get."

"Mine is the largest feminist group in the city, and will be
one hundred percent behind you!"

"In that case, would you serve as cochairperson for the
March?"

"Reverend, I would be honored!" Wilma flicked ashes and
swung her swivel chair to gaze thoughtfully out the window.
"It's going to take a lot of work—planning, meetings, at least
two to three months."

Myrtle sucked in her breath. "Do you really think that long?"

"A lot of work will be involved."

Myrtle frowned, thinking about the time frame. She had to
have money to remain in the city to meet daily expenses. "Mrs.
Freelander—"

"We're going to be partners—please call me Wilma."

"Wilma, I came here as a visiting minister. I do not have
a charge. I make my living by preaching in different churches
in various places."

By this time, Wilma Freelander had balanced the cigarette
on top of an ashtray, tossed her glasses down on the desk, and
had begun writing furiously on a long legal pad. "Hum-m-m,
in other words, you need a livelihood to keep you here," she
murmured understandingly. "Mundane things." Looking up,
she said, "I have a vacant church building—modest. The congregation moved to new and larger quarters recently. It's yours
to rent, if you want it. All you have to do is find some parishioners and you can start your own church!" she laughed a
gravel thunder boom.

Myrtle stared in disbelief. Just like that! All these years and
finally her own church, something she had never really thought
about, for it seemed so far out of reach. Then, too, she had
liked being itinerant. But she wasn't getting any younger, and
with her own church, she would have security, the opportunity
to preach what she pleased, and moreover, do likewise. As-
sembling a congregation should pose no problem. She would
begin by raiding the church of Reverend Amos Cross.

"I would like that," she said, her assiduous mind already
working out details.

"Good! Now let's see, you're staying at the Andrew Jackson—"

"Yes."

"I can locate you an apartment in the Southern Terrace Arms on West End. I own it. I'll make the rent nominal. We girls have to look out for each other, don't we?" she winked conspiratorially. The cigarette was brought to her lips for one last puff and crushed.

"Wilma, I am deeply grateful." The Lord was with her today, sending a white savioress. It paid to know white people of means, for they were a part of the inner circle of haves and how-to-gets.

"Nothing to it, Reverend. I haven't been this excited about anything since I ran for the legislature two years ago. Lost by a narrow margin. Couldn't get the women behind me. They were too occupied with voting for their friends' husbands," she snorted. "That's why we have all those—pardon the expression—mostly shitty male legislators gumming up things. Call me in the morning. The apartment should be ready by then. Meanwhile, you might want to go and see the church. I would go with you, but I have another appointment. Here're the keys and address." She tore the paper she had been writing on from the pad. "From my directions there, you shouldn't have any trouble finding it."

"Thank you again, and God bless you."

"Nothing to it. We got to get you settled so we can move on to the task before us!"

Chapter 12

"*T*HANKS for coming over this afternoon, Bobby," Agnes said, setting out liquor and glasses on the marble-topped coffee table in her living room. "I had to talk to somebody I can trust."

"What's she doing?" Bobby asked, sitting down on the sofa.

"That's it—days and weeks of nothing." Agnes mixed a drink and handed it to him. "She reads the Bible, takes Rhoda for a walk and comes back. *The Tonight Show* wants her and Willie Frye to appear together, but she acts as if she's in another world."

Bobby tasted the drink. "I thought she was really going off that night in Nashville at the concert."

"I can deal with earthly men, but when it comes to the divine—" Agnes strengthened her drink with more scotch and lit still another cigarette. "Yesterday, I tried to get her to sign a contract for a Labor Day weekend engagement in Las Vegas. We all could use the money."

"Why wouldn't she sign?"

"She wants to *think* about it."

"I'd like to get things rolling again," Bobby said. "Anyway, it's good you live here with her. You can keep an eye out."

"That was the idea when I suggested that we invest in an apartment building. Of course, she has her own place upstate to get away from it all."

"She needs to fall in love again."

"Love!" Agnes scoffed, watching him pinching the already sharp creases in his pink and white checked slacks before crossing his legs. "What's love got to do with it?"

"Don't knock it, Agnes. The feeling has helped a lot of people. Especially me!"

"What she needs to do is get back in the swing of things. Work!"

"Or a fun trip to Bermuda, honey. Vacations help too, don't they?" He gave a high-sounding laugh, fanning his hand in the air.

"I suggested a trip and it was vetoed."

"You're just going to have to try harder to get her back to work. The gang's getting restless. Music keeps us going."

"I'll do the best I can," Agnes said despondently. "That's all I can do."

Upstairs in the third floor apartment Travis sat in the summer evening light of the room with Rhoda asleep at her feet and the Bible open on her lap. She had turned on the six o'clock news and to her astonishment, the Reverend Myrtle Black appeared before her on the screen in her clerical collar standing beside a white woman. The Reverend was talking impressively about organizing a Women's March to "get the bad notes out of Music City."

Taken aback at seeing Myrtle on a national news hookup, Travis listened, spellbound, to her expounding on Nashville's sin, vice, and corruption. A spring of excitement swelled up in her. How thrilling! A women's March to be led by a black female minister, one she knew and respected. Leaning closer to the set, she strained to hear every word. The other woman was as absorbed as Travis in what Myrtle was saying. Myrtle's words and posture classed her as a leader who could instill faith in others to follow her and Jesus. Listening eagerly, she wished that she were back in Nashville, standing, too, at the side of the Reverend Black.

The white woman, whose name was Wilma Freelander, spoke briefly, pleading for funds, volunteers, and marchers. The word "volunteer" triggered a response in Travis. That was what she would do: telephone Reverend Black tonight to offer her services.

A laundry detergent commercial foamed on when Agnes rang the doorbell. Rhoda awakened and let out a profusion of loud barks. Vexed by the interruption, Travis placed the Bible carefully on the table and got up to let Agnes in. The smell of fresh scotch accompanied her entrance into the room. Travis wrinkled up her nose in distaste.

"Reverend Black was just on the news," she said, returning to her seat to hear the news commentator rattling on about spiraling prices and the cost of living.

"Oh? For what reason?"

"She's organizing a Women's March on Nashville. Isn't that something?"

Agnes looked at her sharply. For the first time in a long while, Travis was exhibiting some interest in what was going on in the world. "Yes, more power to her. I came up to see if you wanted to go out to dinner. Are you hungry?"

"No—only for the word of the Lord."

Agnes thought that Travis must certainly be out of it when she set aside food. At least being born again was holding down her weight. Rhoda licked Agnes's hand when she sat down. "Everybody's anxious to start working again. The Labor Day Vegas deal sounds good." Travis did not respond, showing no interest in anything except the TV. Agnes conceived it was like talking to air. Rhoda even gave better responses. She disliked seeing Travis this listless. She would have rather had her half-high and raising hell like of old.

"Agnes, do you have to drink?"

Now a moralist! "I just had a couple with Bobby, who stopped by." She had to acknowledge that drinking was becoming more of a habit lately, which did not conform with her usually self-contained behavior. She was losing control of herself and Travis.

Propping her feet on the hassock in front of her, Travis's face closed forebodingly upon Agnes. "I've been doing a lot of thinking lately, Agnes, and I've decided to sing nothing but religious music."

"What? But, baby, you were made on rhythm and blues! On the Don Owens show, you said that you were going to keep on singing what you had been singing."

"I know, but I've changed my mind. From now on, I'm singing just for the Lord."

"Look, Travis—" Agnes tried to restrain herself, be careful, use tact and subtlety so as not to offend or appear too affected. "You can still have your religion and sing rhythm and blues, too. Didn't that—that Reverend Black say something about all music coming from Jesus?"

"I want to sing His music only," Travis confirmed adamantly, lips crystalized in a hard firm line.

Agnes groped for a reply. This was a crucial moment. Travis

couldn't toss her career away on a whim. That was certainly
what it was—a vagary in mind. "Well, mix it up. Make a
gospel record, but keep on singing the other, too." She congratulated herself. Travis could cut a gospel record and show
her versatility. It would be another score for her career. She
pushed on: "You have fans—people out there who adore you,
love you for the way you sing, which makes them happy. You
owe it to them, baby."

This must have penetrated, for Travis looked pensive as her
face changed into a contemplative frown. "I wonder what the
Reverend Black would say."

"She'd agree," Agnes answered quickly.

Travis was silent. "I need spiritual advice. I'm going to call
Reverend Black."

"If you must," Agnes sighed, wishing she wouldn't. Who
knows what that preacher would say.

"I'll do it later," Travis added, glancing sideways at Agnes.
She wanted to do it when no one else was around.

"You're sure you don't want to go out to dinner?" Agnes
asked again, attempting to hide her distaste for the old jeans
and faded shirt Travis had worn for the past three days. Dressing
up and going out might give her a lift.

"I'm sure," Travis said coldly.

"Whatever you say." Agnes gave Rhoda a pat. "I'll check
on you before going to bed."

Travis was glad when Agnes had gone. Sometimes she could
be a nuisance worrying about her and giving advice. All she
wanted was to be left alone to meditate on her religious
thoughts, and not be bothered by her entourage of hangers-on.
Most had begun to drift away anyhow, now that she talked to
them about Jesus. It didn't matter. She felt better being isolated
and apart from those who did not think or feel or believe as
she.

The late evening was closing in on the room with its gradations of darkness. She would feed Rhoda, make a cup of tea,
and call Reverend Black. Getting up, she turned on the lights
of the fashionable apartment where everything had been custom
made. Now the sinking of her feet into the thick, off-white
carpets no longer gave her the satisfied esteem of luxury. She
had a new spiritual realm for self-glorification. The material
artificialities of life no longer mattered.

After feeding Rhoda, she sipped the tea, thinking this was a good time to call Reverend Black. To her dismay, when she contacted the Andrew Jackson, the operator informed her that the Reverend Black was no longer a guest. Upset, she quickly dialed information, knowing the Reverend had to be there someplace in the city. Hadn't she seen her on TV? She felt relief when the operator supplied her with a number. The transient bewilderment of not knowing where the Reverend was or how to reach her had almost caused her to panic.

Upon hearing a young, female voice answer the phone, a trace of something akin to annoyance nudged her. "I'd like to speak to Reverend Black."

"Who's calling, please?"

"Travis Lee," she replied impatiently.

In a few seconds, the Reverend Black's familiar rich tones greeted Travis warmly over the wires. "Travis Lee—a pleasant surprise! Oddly enough, I had been thinking about you. Is everything all right?"

Did something have to be wrong to call a minister? "Everything's fine," she laughed shakily, wondering why she felt girlishly excited and nervous. With a jumble of words, she told Myrtle about seeing her on television and wanting to help.

"Merely to have your name connected with us is a tremendous boost," Myrtle declared.

Travis hesitated before going on to her next reason for calling. "Reverend Black, there's also something I'd like to talk to you about. If it's convenient, I'd like to fly down to see you this weekend."

Myrtle's voice softened, reaching out to Travis like a crutch. "Certainly, my dear. Come and stay with me."

"Thank you, I'd like that very much," Travis said, taking down the address. "I'll be there Friday." When she hung up, a smile broke across her face, brightening it like the sun. She wanted to shout and kick up her heels. It must be the spirit reaching out to her. The thought of seeing the Reverend again brought a song to her lips—a spiritual filled with gladness.

While eating breakfast with Agnes in a kitchen bright with sunlight, Travis asked her to make a reservation for a flight to Nashville on Friday.

Frowning, Agnes quietly filled their cups with the hot, strong coffee she had freshly made. The request caused some

consternation within her. It would make for more chaos to have
Travis go back to Nashville and get tighter on the glory train,
particularly when there was business to attend to.

"I want to confer with Reverend Black," Travis resumed,
filling in the silence.

"What about?" Disturbed, Agnes forgot that the coffee was
steaming hot and the liquid scorched her tongue.

"Agnes, I don't have to tell you everything," Travis shot
back, slamming the pewter mug down hard on the table. The
sound spilled anger between them.

Grasping at calmness, Agnes stuck two pieces of bread in
the toaster. "What time do you want us to leave?"

"I'm going alone."

Mindful this time, Agnes blew on the cup before raising it
to her lips. She invariably traveled with Travis, even when the
no-good bloodsucking dudes were aboard. Travis was so vulnerable—a sitting duck for a likely shooter. "With the way
you've been feeling lately, maybe I ought to go with you."

"What do you mean, the way I've been feeling? There's
nothing wrong with me. I'm fine."

For a nerve prop, Agnes lit one of her brown cigarettes.
"Look, baby, you're a star. Stars don't travel around alone.
Not these days. Anything can happen. Why, last week, a coun-
try music singer was snatched right off the streets there. If not
me, what about Bobby going with you?" she proposed, handing
Travis a slice of unbuttered toast.

"Bobby?"

"He would be around if you needed anything—like walking
Rhoda." At the sound of her name, Rhoda got up from beneath
the table to stare expectantly up for a handout. "Just toast this
morning, Rhoda," Agnes said.

Travis's eyes stayed on the burning cigarette. "You're smoking too much."

How on earth did you ever notice? Agnes wanted to say.
Challenging times and bent nerves called for some kind of
sustenance.

"Rhoda's not going this time either." Travis dropped her
gaze. "I'll be all right. I'm staying with the Reverend. I'll be
as safe as in church."

"Nowadays, even church isn't safe anymore," Agnes
warned sarcastically.

Looking across at Travis, Agnes felt a warm gush of affection rise. Naturally she was going to worry about her. All the years they had traveled together, being close, closer than some husbands and wives. It was strange how she was feeling about her—too anxious, overly protective, too caring in a way. She tried to analyze it, equating the feeling of mother and daughter, but she wasn't old enough to be Travis's mother. It had to be the strong bonds of woman friendship. Too, she rationalized objectively, Travis was an investment. She was supposed to care. "Call Willie Frye while you're there."

"Call Willie?"

"To remind him to have them push the record more. It isn't doing as well as we had hoped." She knew it would if Travis would get off her butt and plug it. The reviews had been satisfactory, if not overwhelming in praise.

"I could have told them. Black people don't go for country music—with or without black people singing it."

"Give it time. It'll be a crossover. Wait and see."

"No more country music for me. I don't even like it."

Agnes stubbed out the cigarette, grinding it meticulously to a crushed tobacco pulp. "Let Bobby go with you. He could stay in a hotel." After all, what did they know about that woman, even though she was a preacher?

"Oh, Agnes, if it'll ease your mind," Travis gave in.

"Good!" Agnes looked happy.

"I'll be perfectly safe with Bobby. Like being with a woman, if she isn't queer," she grinned, dipping into the butter. "Make my reservations for an early flight, and wire the Reverend Black about my arrival. I'm going to start getting my things together."

Chapter 13

*I*N the distance, Myrtle saw the silver streak of the plane approaching to land. Quickly she started toward the gate. Travis, dressed in a white pantsuit and snappy hat, was one of the first to appear, walking in her rhythmic sexy way as if to music. Behind her, Myrtle saw Bobby, handsome in dark glasses with an ascot around his neck. Disappointment stung her. She was not going to have Travis alone to herself after all.

Travis spotted her immediately. "Reverend Black, it's good to see you again!"

"Hello, Ms. Lee," Myrtle smiled, repressing the urge to hug her.

"Please—Travis. You remember my piano player, Bobby Blane?"

"Of course, how are you, Mr. Blane?"

"Just Bobby here, too, Reverend Black. I'm fine."

"We'll get the bags and off we go."

"If you don't mind, Reverend, would you take me to the Andrew Jackson?" Bobby asked. "I came along as a sort of traveling companion. Agnes doesn't like Travis to go around by herself."

"No problem," Myrtle said, made happy by the news. "Would you like to join us for dinner?"

"Thanks, but I'll let you know later. I have to call a friend."

"Bobby has friends everywhere," Travis laughed.

Myrtle hurried them to the baggage area. "Here we are. Pick out yours and we'll be on our way."

* * *

"Are you tired?" Myrtle asked, taking Travis's bag to the guest room.

"Not a bit," Travis said, settling on the couch and looking around. The room was tastefully furnished and spacious.

"How's your new church coming along? I heard about it on TV."

"Fine," Myrtle replied, coming into the living room to sit down beside her. Proudly, she proceeded to tell Travis about her Universal Church for All People. In it, she had the discontented members of the Reverend Amos Cross, along with those who had come to hear her and decided to remain. She did not relate about the conspicuous gays among the congregation who attended because she did not make them feel uncomfortable.

"I want to go Sunday and sing in the choir, if I may."

"No, a solo!" Myrtle laughed, making a mental note to call George. Such news should get to the media. It would entice visitors who might be potential members.

Travis grew pensive, a frown darkening her face, debating whether to bring the subject up now or wait until later. Best to get it over with, she reasoned, and empty her mind of its burden. "Reverend Black—" she began hesitantly.

"It's my turn to ask you to call me Myrtle."

Travis smiled slightly. "I've never called a minister by a first name before."

"Think of me as a friend, too, please," Myrtle said kindly.

"Before anything else, I must tell you why I came."

"Go right ahead, my dear."

"I'm so *confused!*" Travis burst out in anguish, face strained. "I'm thinking of quiting the rhythm and blues field. Only sing spirituals and gospel music from now on."

"I see," Myrtle said softly.

"Agnes doesn't want me to. But I feel with my new conversion, I should just sing for the Lord. I owe it to Him, don't you think?"

Myrtle slowly turned over the question in her mind, probing for a plausible answer. One that would combine the pragmatic with the divine. She had to be careful, for her reply would surely have ramifications.

"At this point," Myrtle said cautiously, "I believe you should allow yourself more time to think it over. Singing secular music doesn't make you a non-Christian, if that is the problem. It is how you live and treat your fellow human beings and yourself, which is what is meant by carrying out God's word. But, on the other hand, you should sing what makes you feel good inwardly."

"I'm so mixed up!" Tears clouded Travis's eyes.

"Please—don't get upset," Myrtle soothed, venturing to take Travis's hand and hold it like a child's. "Your confusion is stemming from an ambivalence about your new life. This frequently happens to the self-converted. It may be that deep down inside, you are not ready to accept it. Or again, you might think you should be acting in a more restrictive religious way." She squeezed Travis's hand reassuringly, liking the soft warmth of it in hers. "My dear, people can be Christians without being fanatics about it. Born-again people seem to think they are cloaked with some special kind of mysticism or mission."

When Myrtle released her hand, Travis wished that she had held it longer. The contact had imparted a closeness of strength to her. Travis gazed wonderingly at Myrtle. "Have you always been religious?"

Myrtle resisted the urge to touch her again. She swallowed hard before answering. "Both my parents were ministers. I was born unto Jesus. Preaching the gospel has been my life. It is just that I am a different kind of minister from my parents. More broad-minded, so to speak. Not a strict interpreter of the Bible, which a female minister cannot afford to be. It would be disastrous, if she were, for sexism abounds!"

"I'd like to see your church—now, if I could." Travis was eager to see what this fantastic woman had fashioned as her own.

"By all means," Myrtle smiled. "We will go to *my* house of the Lord."

"For the first time, I have my own church," Myrtle said, showing Travis around. "It isn't as large as I would like, but the pews are filled each Sunday." Her dark eyes seemed to catch fire. "Soon, I am going to be out of here into something bigger and better!" She had to, for mediocrity never satisfied her.

Slowly they toured the building. "We repainted and I had
another red carpet put on the pulpit," Myrtle said. "Heavenly
Delight made the curtains for my study."

"That name rings a bell."

"She was one of the women shot on Jefferson Street," Myrtle
refreshed Travis's memory. Heavenly Delight was a source of
pleasure to her, having repented and renounced her old life.
Regrettably, Earthly Treasure returned to her King. "I have
given Heavenly Delight the job of keeping the church clean
and in order."

"How nice of you!" Travis's eyes widened with admiration.
Myrtle was indeed a woman of God's substance.

"Over there," Myrtle continued to point out, "is a brand
new piano. My parishioners like good soul-stirring music with
their preaching. Those who don't can go to the Episcopal or
Unitarian Churches," she winked. "One of these days, we'll
work up to an organ."

Travis sat down at the piano to strike exploratory chords on
the stiff keys. "Good tone. How's the choir?"

"Not bad. Twenty-five voices, thus far. A little raw yet, but
they have that good old rocking beat. Ta-ta-tata-ta . . ." Myrtle
performed a little dance step. "They manage to keep up with
me when I get the feeling!" she laughed.

"I'll see on Sunday," Travis teased.

"My, my. That will be something else! Travis Lee singing
at the Universal Church for All People!"

"How did you get this building?" Travis carefully closed
the piano top.

"Wilma Freelander. She sells real estate and is cochairperson of the March."

"I know. I saw her on TV with you." Travis looked at the
sun's rays sharpening the myriad colors of the stained-glass
windows. "How's the March shaping up?"

"Slowly, but surely. Wilma's in there working hard at it.
We have another meeting scheduled for tomorrow."

Outside, Myrtle turned to lock the doors. "Hungry?"

"Come to think of it, I am."

"How about a Wendy's hamburger?"

"Never had one. But any kind sounds good—with a big,
cold drink. This heat's terrific."

Myrtle started the car, turning the air conditioner higher.
"Nashville heat has a character all its own. Being inland, the

numidity makes it bad. Sticky like molasses. We'll get the food and go to Centennial Park and watch the ducks. I go there sometimes alone to sit and think." Glancing at Travis, she added: "Maybe you ought to put on sunglasses, if you have them, or else you might be spending your time signing autographs."

"Good idea." Travis took a pair from her purse. A tiny smile curved her mouth, as if cradling a fragile secret. "I've never been to a park before to watch ducks."

Myrtle drove easily through the thickening afternoon West End traffic. "I am sure you will find it relaxing."

"I'm finding it relaxing just being with you." The words slipped out in honesty.

"Hum-m-m. That *is* nice to know. Here is Wendy's."

They sat on a bench in the park eating near the pond where the ducks floated majestically by in the diamond-black, sun-sparkling water, heads arched on high-stemmed necks, beaks an orange knife blade.

"They're beautiful," Travis remarked, biting hungrily into the bun. "Look how graceful they are in the water. You can barely see their feet paddling."

"The beauty of nature," Myrtle said.

Finished eating, Travis crumpled up the napkin and empty cup into the bag. "Thank you, ma'am, for feeding a hungry stomach."

"The hungry stomach is welcome," Myrtle smiled, arm loosely curved behind Travis.

Travis leaned back against the bench, shoulders touching Myrtle's hand. "This must be a popular park by the looks of all these people."

On the other side of the pond, a long-haired bearded boy softly strummed a guitar, head low, immersing himself in his sound. A girl in shorts reclined on her back next to him, languidly smoking a half-camouflaged joint. From time to time, she would pass it to him.

"Student's haven and everybody else's, too." Myrtle felt Travis's shoulders through the sheer blouse. Her hand was warmed by the touch. To distract herself, she drank the rest of the Coke, sucking the ice in the cup. Initially seeing them approaching like twins, she thought they were a boy and girl with the same mid-length hair brushed to the side, walking hand-in-hand. But as they drew closer, she discovered the look-alikes—short, chubby, and dressed in jeans—were both females.

Travis saw the couple, too, and gave a nervous laugh. "So, they have *those* kind out here, too!"

Myrtle remained silent, fingers mashing the cup like an accordion.

"Does your church approve of *that?*"

"What?" She pretended ignorance, while covertly watching the kindred pair fade like a mocking chimera down the path.

"Lesbians."

"Yes, we have homosexuals, homophiles, gays in my church. Sexual preference isn't a barrier. We're all humans."

Travis detected the coldness in Myrtle's voice and chastised herself for causing the anger. Looking at her, she never ceased to be amazed that this attractive woman was a minister. Casual in her ice-blue slacks and blouse open at the throat, she didn't resemble one at all, or how Travis had always thought one should be. A disturbing frown was pinching Myrtle's deeply set eyes, making Travis want to brush it away.

A lone black duck circled past, perked his head high at them and piped a quacking sound. Travis playfully quacked back. A white girl and a black boy with "Vanderbilt" on his T-shirt paused beside the pond to look into the shimmering mirror of the water at their reflections.

Myrtle got up, depositing the paper bags in a waste container. "Ready to go?"

"Can't we stay a little longer?" A child's plea from a woman.

"As long as you like. I set aside today to entertain *you.*"

"It seems strange being here with you like this," Travis mused.

"How do you mean?"

"Eating hamburgers and watching ducks," she giggled, "with a minister."

"Ministers are human, too. We aren't God. We just interpret his word."

"I wonder if I would feel as nice and comfortable about it if I were here with a male minister?" Then answering herself: "I doubt it. I'd be expecting a pass to come somewhere down the line. Men seem to think they would think less of themselves if they didn't."

"Not all of them." Myrtle felt she should defend. "Here

comes Donald again." She pointed out the black duck paddling by, feet making narrow streams behind him in the water. "I believe he likes you."

"Hi, Donald," Travis called to the creature, a study in grace upon the waters. "He's gorgeous. Feathers so sleek and glossy. Why call him Donald?"

"Because that's the only duck's name I'm familiar with," Myrtle laughed. "We'll have to bring him something next time we come."

"Oh, yes, we must come again!"

"Bobby doesn't answer," Myrtle said, hanging up the telephone, "so I guess that lets him out for dinner."

"Knowing him, he's probably found his friend or a substitute. He can't be alone too long."

"Make yourself at home while I go put the pots on." Before going to the kitchen, Myrtle turned on the TV for the news, cuing herself to call George. She would do it in the kitchen. "Want something to drink?"

"Let's see. Do you have any of that wine we had at the motel that night?"

"Sherry. Yes, I have some in the refrigerator. Be right back."

In the kitchen, Myrtle telephoned George about Travis. He sounded surprised and promised to get it in the paper. One thing with George, she thought, turning away from the telephone, he was dependable. They had grown to like and respect each other, two ambitious people who knew what they wanted and were using each other to get it.

She set the wine and glasses on a tray, and went back into the living room. "Shall we toast our meeting again?"

Clinking glasses, Travis smiled: "To us!"

Myrtle was delighted to see the sparkle in Travis's eyes. "I am going back to the galley."

"Can I help?"

"No, thanks. You are my guest. I won't be long."

They ate in the dining room where Myrtle had set the table with candles glowing festively at both ends. Over the dessert, Travis smiled across the table at Myrtle. "The dinner was delicious. I think I'll hire you as my cook."

"Fine with me. I will be your cook, minister, or whatever," Myrtle ribbed back.

"Hum-m-m, my whatever. I like the sound of that. It gives me a lot to work with." Travis got up to help carry the dishes out to the kitchen.

Turning on the dishwasher, Myrtle said, "Shall we go back to the living room?"

"Yes, and drain the bottle!" Travis laughed, feeling light-headed. Pouring more wine into the glasses, Travis said humorously, "I think I'll get you tipsy."

"Rarely have I been intoxicated."

"I'd like to see a loaded minister," Travis sniggered aloud at the thought. "Like seeing a drunken Santa Claus."

"Most likely you have but didn't realize it." In the pulpit, on the streets, in bars, at funerals and weddings; more boldly at the church conferences away from home, parishioners, friends and families when collars are turned around and flies opened.

Travis looked at Myrtle in a strange way, tea-brown eyes half-narrowed. "Really, I'd like to see you high. Are you as self-possessed and verbally proper then?"

Myrtle laughed. "Are you trying to corrupt me?"

"No—loosen you up!" Travis emptied the wine bottle. "That's it."

"Would you like me to get another bottle?"

"Yes, bring on more wine, for I'm feeling fine-e-e!" Travis sang, making up a jingle. When Myrtle left, she got up to cut off the TV and turn on the radio. "Hey, there's nothing but country music on," she called out.

"Most of them play that. I will get something when I come in."

"Hurry; I feel like celebrating!"

In the dimness, they relaxed on the sofa with the soft music Myrtle had located playing in the background. Myrtle felt soothed by the warmth of the wine and Travis's nearness.

"I thought ministers were supposed to be talkative," Travis said, noticing Myrtle's silence. Curled up at the end of the sofa, she saw Myrtle's half-closed eyes, face withdrawn. "Don't you ever let go?"

"I am at ease now. I was thinking about you. Aren't you exhausted by now?"

"No." Certainly not. She could sit like this forever with Myrtle. "I hope my visit didn't interrupt anything—special plans..." A matter of conscience. Perhaps this was the cause for Myrtle's quietness.

"*Your* visits would never be an interruption."

Travis moved sluggishly into an upright position. "I am wonderfully tight! It's been a long time since I've drunk anything." She hiccuped. "Oops! Before I get worse, I'd better call Agnes. She's such a worrywart. Although I have a sneaking suspicion that Bobby's probably reported in already. Talking to Agnes will straighten me up."

"I plugged a phone in your room." Seeing Travis swaying slightly as she stood up, Myrtle moved to help her. "Here, lean on me." She braced an arm about her waist, feeling the soft pressure of Travis's hip.

"Lean on me, lean on me—" Travis sang. "That's really a song, you know."

"Yes. Here, lie down." Myrtle eased her onto the bed.

"I'm happily lit. I used to get bitchy tight, yelling and cursing everybody out."

"It's all right to overindulge sometimes, but not to make a habit out of it."

"Reverend Myrtle Black—my friend, my minister, my whatever—I have had a glo-ri-ous day!"

"Good. I have, too." Myrtle helped Travis off with her shoes. "Can you get undressed?"

"Sure. Simple. Just pull off my clothes. I didn't say that I was drunk! Besides, I've got to talk sensibly to Agnes, or she'll be here like a policewoman on the next plane. Dear old Agnes—"

The unpleasant thought of Agnes suddenly appearing caused a hint of a frown to trouble Myrtle's face. "If you need anything, I will be in the next room." Myrtle looked down at Travis on the bed, breasts pointed toward her, straining her blouse. Turning away, she said huskily, "Rest comfortably. See you in the morning."

Closing the door, Myrtle went to her room with the image of Travis haunting her. It was going to be a long sleepless night.

Chapter 14

B OBBY went with Clyde to the Everything Goes Cabaret, the local gay club most often frequented by straights who came for the show and sights. The cabaret was weekend crammed, hazy with smoke, and heavy with earsplitting disco music to which same-sex dancers gyrated amidst flashing kaleidoscopic lights.

"This place has some of the best female impersonators in the good ol' southland!" Clyde bragged to Bobby. "Flaming Dark Sugar is one of the finest!"

Studying the crowd, Bobby noticed the preponderance of males over females, and whites surpassing blacks. Sipping the watered down scotch, he drummed his fingers on the table to the beat of the music.

"You know, I never thought I'd ever see you again," Clyde grinned, covering Bobby's hand briefly with his own.

"Shows you never know."

"We didn't have much time together, did we?" Clyde moved his chair closer to talk over the din of the music.

"Not nearly enough."

The music stopped and in a few minutes, lights lit up the stage. The curtain drew back, and a blonde impersonator in high spirits came forward to announce the beginning of the show. Everybody was advised to sit back, get drunk, and enjoy the performances.

Then, with background music, a tall, slim shapely brown-skinned figure dressed in a skintight red dress with slits up the side, and hair cascading over a Diana Ross face, slinked sexily out on the stage to voicelessly mouth words to a song.

Hearing it, Bobby broke into choking laughter. "Oh, Lord, Travis's song, 'Love, Love, Love.' She should see *this!*"

"That's Flaming Dark Sugar doing it."

"The lip movement is right on time with my piano playing."

"I'm looking at the *hip* movements!" Clyde chuckled, picking up his beer.

Following the loud applause, howls, and whistles for Flaming Dark Sugar came similar acts of lavishly gowned performers with made-up faces, smooth skin, and firm breasts, who would have been taken for females anyplace else, wordlessly vocalizing songs with expertly improvised dance routines. All had a personal group of devotees who clapped wildly and encouraged them on.

When the acts were completed, the stars could be seen posturing and parading like colorful peacocks around the tables and bar, chalky powdered faces, garish clowns' masks, luminescent in the dimness. A strange sadness permeated Bobby as he viewed in hypnotic silence the Wilderian fantasy. The spectacle prodded open a painful gap in his memory, calling to mind himself as a college music professor's boy of ten whose familial lineage stemmed from white Virginia plantation masters to the old-line, blue-veined black Virginia closed society. The panorama of transvestites and drag queens opened the time when, whether through curiosity, or adoration for his mother's beauty, or a playful prank or subconscious psychic motivation, he wandered into his mother's bedroom to lipstick and powder his face, and wrap himself in the perfumed sanctity of her clothes.

In a rapid reel of unfolding memories, the amused laughter of his mother reverberated in his ears, to be abruptly drowned by the backwash of his later cries of terror at the painful whipping given him by his father. To be called a sissy by his boy peers because he was made to play the piano did not matter as much to his father as the dress masquerade. Since birth, Bobby had been destined to fulfill his father's lost dream of becoming a concert pianist.

After the fading sequence of the beating, women's clothing became a repelling attraction of evil and good to him. Sitting here surrounded with the bizarre chorus of chattering, restless queens, he repressed the strong desire to get up and join them.

Contemplating Bobby's prolonged silence, Clyde cast a wary eye over at him. "Hey, you still here with me?"

Clyde's laughter cut into his brooding introspection. "Sure—where else?"

"Look, Flaming Dark Sugar is coming this way."

The entertainer was trying to plow through a crowd of admirers. Seeing Clyde, she stopped to speak.

"You were great!" Clyde offered.

"You liked me?" Flaming Dark Sugar gushed, responding with pleasure. Smiling brightly, her eyes flitted from Clyde to Bobby.

"Sure did, and so did my friend, who is the piano player on the record. Bobby Blane in person!"

Flaming Dark Sugar's face lit up. "Well-l-l, *do-o-o!* I'm simply thrill-led!"

"Want a drink?" Clyde asked.

"No, thanks, honey. Someone's waiting for me at the bar. Can't keep my public waiting," she laughed, straightening a shoulder strap. "Mr. Blane, you tell Travis Lee that I just *love* doing her song." She waved back at them.

"Flaming Dark Sugar goes to that church sometimes your Travis is into." Clyde took out a stick of gum to offset the beer taste. "It's rumored the minister is a lesbian."

"What!"

"At least that's what Flaming Dark Sugar says is whispered on the gospel circuits. Seems like some young females have gotten awfully upset when Rev leaves town."

Bobby threw back his head to laugh uproariously.

"What's so funny about that?"

"Imagine! Travis unknowingly staying with a lesbian. After all those slurs I've heard she's made about *me.*"

"Maybe after this, you won't be hearing them anymore." Clyde laughed along with him.

"I need another drink on that," Bobby said, turning to signal the waiter for refills. As he did, his eyes were suddenly drawn to the opposite side of the room where a man sat with two women, one black and the other white. He had on a burgundy suit and rust tie with a diamond stickpin. His eyes were fixed hard on Bobby in a face cold and ominous. He was oblivious to the white girl stroking his hand, holding a half-forgotten burning cigarette.

When Bobby stared back transfixed, the man's bearded mouth formed a mocking saluting sneer. Bobby shook his head in disbelief, hoping that it was a trick of his imagination.

Anything but who the man looked to be. *Rudy!* Rudolph Valentino Jones back in town.

"You feeling sick?" Clyde questioned, upon seeing Bobby's face pale.

Bobby licked his dry lips. "You remember the guy we took to the bus station to get rid of?"

"Yeah. That was real comical."

"He's sitting right over there near the stage."

"Is that bad?" Clyde asked low, slowly chewing the gum.

"With Travis in town, too, it could be a catastrophe."

Clyde paid for the drinks brought by the waiter. "He wouldn't do nothing to her, would he?"

"I don't know," Bobby said warily, recalling that out of all Travis's succession of studs, Rudy was the meanest. "I'd better call and warn her."

On the way out, they took a twisted path to the door to avoid Rudy, whose eyes, Bobby was certain, were following them.

Chapter 15

*A*T the breakfast table, Myrtle could readily see that Travis's light mood of the previous day had changed. She hardly touched the toast and grapefruit set before her. Myrtle hazarded a guess that the letdown in spirit had its origin in Bobby's after-midnight phone call, for which she had to awaken her.

"You look worried," Myrtle said warily. "Is something bothering you?"

Travis blew on her coffee. "Bobby called to let me know that Rudy's back in town."

Myrtle looked at the troubled lines on Travis's face, and wondered who Rudy was.

Travis solved her puzzlement by going on to tell about him. "Agnes was supposed to have gotten rid of him. Apparently he found his way back," she said wryly.

Myrtle poured more coffee, since that was all Travis seemed interested in. Always there had to be someone or something to interfere, disturb, when things were going well. Why must shadows loom in the light?

"I'm a little leery of him," Travis confessed.

Myrtle's eyes darkened. "Don't be. God is with you." And so was she. The thought vexed her: How much had Travis cared for him? She had to ask. "Did he mean very much to you?"

"As much as all the others, I suppose," Travis said, thinking of it as an earthquake tremor at the time, consuming, shaking, but quickly over, leaving only devastation.

Myrtle emptied her cup, pushing the menace of Rudy aside. "I have a rather busy schedule lined up for today." She paused to carefully pose the question: "Do you mind if George comes over to interview you? It would be wonderful publicity for the church," she added quickly. "People would know that we have someone important like you worshiping with us Sunday." Myrtle slipped the idea in.

Travis stared down at the yellow place mat with "God Bless This Table" on it. "I—I don't know. With Rudy around, maybe I shouldn't be too exposed."

"If you don't want to, I understand."

"But, if *you* think it will benefit your church—" Travis smiled, making Myrtle's heart skip a beat. "I'll talk to him. It will give me an opportunity, too, to rejoice about finding Jesus again."

"Thank you." Myrtle relaxed. "While talking to Wilma to confirm our meeting this morning," she began, getting up, "I told her you were here. She wants to meet you. We are invited to dinner this evening."

"My, it *does* sound like a full day!"

Myrtle started clearing the table, but Travis stopped her. "You go on. I'll clean up. I don't have anything to do but wait for George."

"Some way to treat a guest." Seeing that some of the tension had eased from Travis, Myrtle smiled. "You look very pretty this morning." She did, in the loosely tied pink robe revealing the tops of her breasts.

"Why, thank you, ma'am." Travis pondered why she was flustered by the compliment. Agnes gave them to her all the time.

Myrtle glanced at her watch. "I have to go. You won't mind being alone?"

"Of course not."

"Here's the number where I'll be, in case you need me," she said, writing on a kitchen pad by the phone. "Ask George to please wait for me, if he can."

Before she left, Travis called: "Hey, you look pretty, too, in that dress!"

"Compliments all around. I'll try not to be too long."

Another woman was with Wilma when Myrtle walked into the office. She was introduced as Rita Stennette, national president of Women United for Action. "Rita flew in from San Francisco to meet with us this morning."

Rita Stennette was tall and rangy with flaming, loose red hair. Brittle emerald eyes shone intensely at Myrtle from a sharply pointed, homely face. She had on straight-leg jeans and a denim shirt with the women's symbol embroidered on the pocket. "It's good to meet a female of the cloth in the struggle," she smiled. "May I call you Myrtle?"

"If you like," Myrtle said, a trifle stiffly, disliking the premature informality common to whites.

"I'm really excited about this March, particularly since one of our chapters will be involved."

Wilma took a cigarette out of a pack and lit it. "We've been talking, and Rita thinks we should include additional objectives for the March."

"Most certainly," Rita took up, scissor-crossing her legs, toenails gleaming red digits trapped by string-thin leather sandals. "We need to put it in the political logistics of the overall Women's Movement. Focus attention on the *oppression* of women by male patriarchs. Bring to the forefront woman *power*—the power to control our lives, our bodies, our identities, as well as the destruction of sexism in our institutions!"

Myrtle listened to Rita's rhetoric which was not new to her, an avid reader who had participated in a few women's workshops. Here was a woman who plainly possessed a zealot's ardor. The fervor of Rita's words reminded her of the Black Movement's once fiery oratory, a movement whose eloquence was now reduced to ashes without even the heat of the flames.

"Don't you agree?" Rita challenged her silence.

"I am against sexism," Myrtle replied. "But my plan was simply to march against crime, corruption, and vice in the city. A moralistic concept."

Rita's green eyes flashed in exasperation. "Myrtle, how can you *separate* the two? Corruption, crime, and vice are embedded in the institutions that are controlled by *males*. If this is to be a Women's March, it should also highlight women's concerns!"

"Look," Wilma interrupted, waving her cigarette like a mediator's staff of office, "let's see if we can't compromise."

"*Compromise?*" Rita said incredulously, getting up to pace the floor like an unsettled pony. "What is there to compromise about? If women are going to come together and march on a patriarchal establishment, then it should have a *political* connotation. Getting the 'Bad Notes Out of Music City' to *me* means *males!* The WUFA is a *politically* oriented organization founded on the principles of obliterating women's oppression."

"As a *black* woman," Myrtle said icily, "I *know* about oppression, being victimized by racists *and* sexists alike. I catch it from those black women who are prime endorsers of black male chauvinism, white sexists and racist women. I know *all* about oppression!"

"Ah-ha!" Rita's voice rose jubilantly. "You *are* aware. So how can you ignore the importance of—"

"I am not ignoring it," Myrtle said firmly.

"Why don't we wait to see what the others who join in with us think?" Wilma recommended hurriedly.

"Sounds reasonable to me," Myrtle said. "We need to form a steering committee to assist in deciding central points. However, as the one who conceived this idea and as a minister, I am going to *insist* that there be moralistic and humanitarian objectives. We must not lose sight of intrinsic human values. All too frequently they are what get lost in movements."

Rita retraced her steps back to her chair. "How many groups have expressed interest?"

Wilma leafed through the papers on her desk. "Hum-m-m, to date, only the Women's Independent Voter's League."

"What about feminist organizations?" Rita inquired.

"Ours is the best organized in the city," Wilma relayed. "Southern women haven't rallied around the cause yet."

"What about *black* organizations, Myrtle?" Rita pressed on.

Myrtle took a deep breath, undertoning the Lord to forgive the prevarication. "I am waiting to hear from those contacted." Part truth. Basis in fact: Barbara had gone down the list George had provided of social, civic, and women's church groups, only to have the presidents respond by not being in, promising to return the call, or saying that an answer would be forthcoming. No concrete commitments from any.

"What about other Third World women? Indians, Chicanos—"

"Very small minority here, Rita," Wilma pointed out, coughing from her smoke. She put out the cigarette. Too much smoking here of late.

"This is to be a local undertaking," Myrtle said curtly. The woman must think she is still in California.

"I tell you what," Wilma said, trying to bring calm. "Why don't we wait until the steering committee is formed and then settle the basics?"

"Yes, then we will have more input," Myrtle concurred, thinking it was the democratic way to handle it. "We are going to have to find at least three or four women to work with us."

"I'll start this afternoon by making some more calls. Something tells me this is going to be more difficult than we anticipated," Wilma groaned.

George waited for her, chatting with Travis in the living room, his medicinal half-pint of bourbon on the coffee table with a glass of water. Travis was drinking ginger ale.

"Thanks for waiting, George," Myrtle said, tossing her briefcase on the table and sitting down beside him on the couch. "Interview over?" She smiled at Travis, who had changed into a dress.

"Long ago," George said.

"George is one of the few reporters I've enjoyed talking to."

"Keep on, I'll make page one yet," he said, mixing another drink. "How's the March shaping up?"

"Complications with folks wanting to get other things in. Do you have any more black organizations for me?"

"Nope, you have all I know."

"Is there a black feminist organization here?"

George stretched out his legs under the coffee table, red socks straggling around spindly ankles. The limp creases in his brown pants caused them to hang flat against his legs. "Not that I know of, but there is someone who might be able to help you. Contact Iffe Degman, an instructor in the history department at Vandy. She's been connected with some women's conferences."

Myrtle sighed in disgust. "I am thinking about the irony of it. Black women are the most exploited, but you can't get them together to demonstrate against it. Who gets raped, robbed, beaten up, and taken advantage of the most? I can't even get the black male ministers to encourage their churchwomen to join in with us."

"That's because they aren't heading it," George grinned. "Black men don't like being upstaged by black women. Take, for example, the Civil Rights Movement. Those women who could have been dynamic leaders were pushed back. They were trapped into doing paperwork, making the men comfortable, or subdued through love affairs and marriages. We should have had more Fanni Lou Hamers, Daisy Bates, and Gloria Richardsons."

"Is there anything I can do?" Travis felt inadequate, listening to them.

"Your being connected with us is enough for now," Myrtle assured her. "I am going to call Iffe Degman. I hope she is listed."

"If not, try the university." George finished his drink and got up, sticking the bottle in his coat pocket. "For the record, I tried to recruit my wife, but she said that she's tied up in an upcoming baby contest. Anyway, you can see not all of us black males are chauvinists!" He laughed good-naturedly. "Got to go write up this interview. Good luck with Iffe Degman."

Myrtle went to the study to call Iffe as Travis cleared the coffee table of the glasses.

"I got her. She is coming right over!" Myrtle returned to see Travis looking pensively out the window. Going to her, she said, "This hasn't been a very entertaining morning for you, has it?"

"It's been different. I feel connected with something that is meaningful for a change, but I don't like to see you so harassed."

The way Travis was looking at her made Myrtle want to take her in her arms. She shrugged it off by saying, "That is a part of life. Want some lunch?"

"I'll fix it."

"You are my guest—"

"I want to—for you."

By the time they sat down to the salmon salad and mint iced tea, Iffe Degman rang the doorbell. Ushering her in, Myrtle saw that she was a dark, attractive young woman with a close-cut Afro outlining a finely-shaped head. Bright, expressive eyes met Mrytle's from behind aviator glasses. She imbued a youthful effervescence that was contagious. She was a diminutive woman who wore a colorful African dress to her ankles. Gold dagger-pointed earrings dramatized her face. Myrtle introduced her to Travis.

"*The* Travis Lee! This is my lucky day, meeting both you and Reverend Black. My horoscope said that it would be. I'm an Aquarius," she appended.

"Sit down and have some lunch," Myrtle invited.

"Thanks. I'll take a glass of iced tea to cool me off. I have a Volkswagen without air conditioning, and it's hot as blazes outside."

Myrtle handed her a frosted glass with a mint spig and moon slice of lemon. "I asked you to come over because I heard that you have links with black feminists in the city."

"What black feminists?" Iffe scoffed, thirstily drinking the tea. "This is the South. When I came here last year from Chicago to teach and work on my doctorate in history, I did manage to get a small group organized. But guess what?"

"What?" Travis prompted interestedly.

"We met a few times, then they voted to change the name from Black Feminists to the Black Women's Improvement Club. You see, the word feminist was anathema. It antagonized their black men, and men *are* important to black southern women, you can believe it! To top that, they equate the word feminist with man-haters, white women, and lesbians. And, like wow! Lesbians are something that can't be dealt with in the black community—queers and funny people."

A hot flush went through Myrtle at Iffe's remarks about lesbians. It was such times as these, by her locked-in secrecy, she felt a traitor to herself. This silence she justified by weighing the burden of the consequences. She had her career as a minister who headed her church. Together with that, her sight was set on expanding her secular leadership role, an aspiration that was beginning to materialize. For her to come out now, declare her lesbianism, could be disastrous for both herself and her church. The core of her existence was rooted in black life. Black people had not yet come fully to grips with homosexuality. For these reasons, she had to conceal her sexuality. Religion and race mattered first to her.

The salad lost its tastiness.

Travis, caught up in what Iffe was saying, had stopped eating, as if not to miss a word.

"I resigned from the club, because it became like the others around here, engaging in safe, acceptable activities like sponsoring baby contests, card parties, fashion shows, bakes, and doling out scholarships. Nobody wants to rock the boat among their peers."

"Jesus made waves," Myrtle said, half to herself. He did, but she could not where she was most vulnerable.

"Now, I just work with the whites occasionally. I'm their

token nigger for the women's cause," Iffe laughed self-depre-
catingly. "Black women elsewhere are ahead of the southern
sisters in the women's thing. It's odd, too, for black southern
women are fighters. They were right in there getting their heads
knocked and butts kicked during the racial demonstrations,
freedom rides, and school integration, but they seem somewhat
slow about going out on the limb for their own women selves!"

"Fear of perpetuating the myth of castrating matriarch,"
Myrtle deplored. "Anyway, Iffe, another reason why I asked
you to come is that I would like for you to serve on the steering
committee for the March we're planning."

"I've been reading about it, Reverend. I'll be glad to do
whatever I can. It'll be great to be involved again."

"Iffe, I need *black* support. This is an academic city. How
about students?"

"I may be able to round up a few. Black female students
have been rather conservative, too, when it comes to the
women's issue. They're wrapped up in their families' middle-
class bags, and those who aren't, don't want to provoke boy-
friends or be too radically different."

"What about teachers?" Travis submitted hopefully.

"Good question. Their main interests seem to be playing
politics with male chauvinistic administrators, putting their kids
through college, and drawing a paycheck to promote black
bourgeois living to the hilt."

"There must be some who care," Myrtle insisted hopefully.

"I don't want to sound too pessimistic. I'm sure there are,"
Iffe nodded thoughtfully.

"The lower economic group," Travis tried again.

"They're enmeshed in the economics of everyday survival,"
Myrtle said slowly. "I don't care how bleak it looks, I am
going out there and *preach* up some supporters. Work through
my church. In the final analysis, if I have to lean more toward
white women to get female backing, I will do that, too. I am
going to devise a populist movement of white and black women
coming together in the South!"

"Hey, I go for that." Iffe's earrings jiggled as she moved
her head approvingly. "Reverend Black, I'm not much of a
churchgoer, but you can believe it, I'm in your pew!"

That evening, seated at the cherry wood dinner table in the
dining room of Wilma's spacious home in Belle Meade, Rita

monopolized the dinner conversation while continuously replenishing her glass from a personal pitcher of martinis at her side. "Do you know that the women who are most active in the movement are lesbians?" she stated, green eyes sparking a challenging flame at her statement.

"Come now, Rita," Wilma pooh-poohed, attempting to make light of the allegation. "That's a broad generalization. *I'm* not a lesbian." Looking smug, she took two rolls from the silver bread tray being passed by the elderly black maid in a white uniform. "Thank you, Flossie."

"There is some of the lesbian in *all* women," Rita theorized flatly, splashing part of the martini on the linen cloth.

There it was again, Myrtle thought, eyes downcast on the blue-bordered Dresden china plate. Travis, seated opposite her, was watching Rita intently, and seemed fascinated by either her declaration or capacity for alcohol.

"Going back to my original point," Rita pursued her discourse, "lesbians have more time to become active. They are independent women not hindered by husbands and home cares. And, as *you* know, Wilma, I'm a lesbian and proud of it!"

At this disclosure, Travis's knife clanked noisily against her bread plate. Myrtle's face was closed. When it came to who was what, she had long ago resigned herself not to be surprised. It wasn't an overly difficult thing for Rita to affirm her sexual preference. She was white, self-sufficient, and had an organization behind her.

"Are there many black lesbians around here?" Rita pumped Myrtle.

"I suppose there are lesbians everywhere. It is a matter of who is in and out of the closets." Again, a Judas to her own. She felt Rita's eyes burning on her, heating the frustration already within her, the conflicts, the deception of masking. But no one had asked; therefore, she hadn't denied. There was comfort in this.

"I don't know why people have to stay *in* these days," Rita complained disdainfully.

"For personal reasons, I imagine," Myrtle furnished. Had she sensed an innuendo, or was it her conscience?

"Myrtle's church has gay people in the congregation," Travis spoke up, remembering their conversation in the park.

"Oh?" Rita's eyes narrowed.

"My church is open to everyone, regardless of race, color,

creed, or sex preference." The maid gave her a sharp, hidden look on the way back to the kitchen.

"We're coming to your church in the morning," Wilma informed Myrtle. "How's it going?"

"Fine. You won't recognize the building. New paint and all. When you come, tell the usher to show you to my reserved pew."

"I hear you're quite a preacher," Rita said, finally starting to eat her food.

"She is!" Travis verified enthusiastically.

"I see she has you in her corner," Rita leered slyly.

"As I always say, Flossie, you make the best beef Wellington in town." Wilma smiled affectionately to the servant bringing in a steaming dish of fresh creamed peas and onions. "Flossie has been in the family for years. We have a kind of mutual admiration society."

Myrtle transmitted a friendly smile at the maid, thinking of others like her, heirlooms of the South. "The dinner is delicious."

"By the way," Wilma addressed Travis, "what brings you here to our city again? Cutting another record or giving a concert?"

"I'm visiting Myrtle."

"Nothing like visiting good women friends, I always say!" Rita burped.

"She's my minister, since I've gotten renewed faith."

"Faith in women is exactly what we all need," Rita advocated cheerfully. "Myrtle, do you have many women who come to you with problems about being lesbians?" It was as if she were determined, despite Wilma's consternation, to pursue her conversation on gays, a subject relevant to her.

Flossie hovered near, pouring coffee. Myrtle thought, since the big house days of slavery, black women were reservoirs of information for blacks and whites alike because of what they heard and saw. "A few. I find that most black women have a tendency to keep that to themselves, their lovers, or same kind of friends. I have had more males confide this to me as a problem."

"What kind of guidance do you give them?" Rita's eyes were hard upon her.

"It depends on the individual and the nature of their frustrations. If they are comfortable with themselves being homosexual, I tell them they have a right to their sexual preference, as long as they are not infringing upon or hurting someone else. God's heaven is open to all believers."

"A minister after my own heart." Rita drained the martini pitcher and raised her glass in a toast to Myrtle. "Female, too!"

"Travis, I bought your album made with our own Willie Frye," Wilma cut in, weary of the gay topic. "When we finish, we can go into the living room for dessert and brandy and listen to it."

"As the old amenity goes, we hate to eat and run, but I have a sermon to prepare for in the morning. We won't be able to stay too long," Myrtle cautioned.

"Since I'll be there, base it on women," Rita said.

"Women are always in my sermons."

"And in my heart!" Rita laughed loudly.

"That was an interesting evening," Travis mused in the car, as Myrtle drove home.

"It was," Myrtle mumbled absently, mind more on Travis sitting close to her in the darkness of the car. The front seat was an intimate cocoon sheltering the two of them. Hearing Travis chuckling, she said, "Can you share it?"

"I was thinking about Wilma. She may be a new breed of southern woman, but she still holds on to the convenience of the past. Namely her black maid."

"Why sho' nuff, chile," Myrtle spoofed in black minstrel style. "Dat dere is dey *roots!*"

Laughing, Travis rested her head back on the seat near Myrtle's shoulder. "I'd better catch up with Bobby to ask him to play for me in the morning. I should give Agnes a ring too."

"Agnes—" Myrtle repeated, always Agnes. She turned a corner too sharply. "Doesn't she believe you are in good hands?"

Travis closed her hand over Myrtle's hand, tight on the wheel, a brief transitory touch, like a butterfly's, there and gone without a trace. "I believe that I'm in very good hands."

Myrtle wished Travis had kept her hand there, warm on hers. Travis shifted, it seemed, closer to her. "Is there any special song you want me to sing tomorrow?"

"Sing what you want to."

Lights of passing cars glanced over Travis's face like fireflies. "White women are really into the lesbian bit, aren't they?"

Her voice was faint and distant, coming from some faraway mind place.

Once again, that invisible haunting specter, following her through the evening. An answer had to be given. She made it casual: "More openly, I suspect." Pulling into her parking space outside the apartment, she turned off the lights. "Here we are, home again, home again. Now you can make your calls and I will work on my sermon."

Upstairs, she quickly bid Travis good-night and went into her study to get ready for the morning.

Chapter 16

*E*ARLY Sunday morning, Bobby had Clyde drop him off at Myrtle's in order to go to church and play for Travis.

Travis greeted him warmly, kissing him lightly on the cheek. He noticed there was a new radiance about her, an aliveness different from the depression he had observed on the plane. Being with the Reverend was apparently good for her.

Myrtle was cordial, offering him coffee while they finished dressing. Waiting for them, he covertly regarded Myrtle, searching for any so-called stereotypical traits visible in her mannerisms of her rumored sexual orientation. All he could perceive that did have meaning to him was the admiring way Travis's eyes followed her. Looks at and between people were usually unconscious giveaways.

When they prepared to leave, he smiled at them approvingly. Travis had on a soft, sheer rose dress, and Myrtle was chic in a green linen suit, carrying a garment bag that contained her robe.

"You two ladies are looking good," he commented on the way out.

"Looking good for the Lord," Travis smiled sweetly.

Myrtle parked her car at the rear of the church so they could enter through the back door. Heavenly Delight was waiting excitedly in her white stewardess uniform. Her hair had a fresh, blonde tint, setting off a face that had lost some of its hardness since she had gotten out of the life. The exotic hair coloring was the sole souvenir of her past.

"Oh, Reverend Black, the TV people are here and the church is packed!"

"Good, Heavenly Delight, that's the way it should be—packed. Would you escort my guests to the reserved pew? I have to put on my robe."

Heavenly Delight glowed at the sight of Travis. "It'll be a pleasure. Travis Lee, you're my favorite singer!"

Myrtle locked her purse in the desk drawer of her study and went into the bathroom to change. She took off the suit and put on a gold robe, dazzling in its sunburst of color. Through the door, she could hear the pianist beginning a soft prelude. Too bad the church could not afford an organ. Organ music exuded solemnity. In the hallway, she could hear the busy drone of her assistant pastor, Ralph Casey, rising slightly above the music, as he also prepared for service.

Having a male assistant pastor contributed to her image, even though she had a sneaking suspicion he might be gay. Ralph was light-skinned with sculptured Roman features, sandy short-cut hair, and was thin as an arrow from constant dieting. Antiseptically clean and neat, he regularly smelled of Brut Shaving Lotion. He was genteel, which appealed to the elderly women, youthful enough in appearance to be adopted and trusted by the young congregants, and equipped with the necessary intelligence to lead. All in all, he fit in perfectly with Myrtle's organization.

Arranging her robe, Myrtle made a final swift inspection of her appearance in the mirror on the door. Hastily she got her notes, which she rarely used, for words came spontaneously, a family legacy. Before leaving to take her place on the pulpit, she closed her eyes and bowed her head to commune with the Lord and herself, activating her inner thoughts for revealing His word.

In the cavity of the pulpit, she stood erect before the hushed congregation. Voice strong and resonant, she began: "Let us stand and prepare for worship." Head bowed, she prayed: "The Lord is our helper, our redeemer. We come here this morning to praise him and give thanks and reverence to His glory. To learn the truth through His word, so the truth can make us whole. We worship in His name, a-men."

A-men, the congregation resounded.

"We will join our voices in song. Turn to page sixty-two in your hymnals." The large, tightly-corseted pianist struck a chord and the congregation, along with the purple-robed choir, sang out three verses of "O Worship the King, All Glorious Above."

"This morning, we are honored to have with us a visitor whom I am sure is known to most of you, Sister Travis Lee, from New York City. Sister Lee, out of the goodness of her heart, has offered to sing a solo. Her personal pianist, Brother Bobby Blane, will accompany her."

Instant murmurs of muted elation scattered throughout the church like birdwings flapping in unison. Bodies twisted and necks craned to glimpse Travis in person. TV cameramen scrambled for better positions as news photographers readied cameras.

With Bobby's introductory notes on the piano, the fluttering was transmitted into quiet expectancy. Travis commenced to sing "Just A Closer Walk With Thee" with a vibrant burst of melodious sound in a slow-moving blues tempo. Bobby improvised a background beat replete with intermittent treble trills. The music suffused out to the congregation, locking them in with the rhythm and words as only black soul-stirring religious songs can do to black people. Some swayed in languid motion to cadence, while others patted their feet like padded drums in measured time with the rhythm.

Sing it, sistuh!

Un-n-n-hun-n-n!

At the song's end, grateful bouquets of cries went up: *Bless-s-s you! Beautiful!*

Myrtle awarded Travis a look of appreciation. The song had set the tone, putting the congregation into a righteous state of mind for hearing the word. They were bolted in the emotional fold to be receptive to her propagation of the faith. "Thank you, Sister Lee, for that wonderful song. Later on in the service, she will honor us again." She would have Travis sing a second time after the collection was taken. That would keep them in their seats.

"The text of my sermon this morning will be on unity. Yes, brothers and sisters, *u-ni-ty!* The unity of people in love, respect and sovereignty. I am going to dwell especially on women, for *all* our brothers need to know about women. Some might *think* they already do, but *don't*. Because brother-r-rs, there is *more*—I tell you—to knowing about women than the art of making love!"

Muffled laughter punctuated Myrtle's remark with sisters looking satisfied and the brothers stonefaced.

Turning the pages of the large black Bible on the rostrum, Myrtle read: "Psalms 133, verse 1: 'Behold, how good and pleasant it is for brethren to dwell together in unity.' Brethren, my people, meaning *all* humankind—women and men. Ev-er-rybody in unity. But as I look around me at our everyday lives, I am sorry to say that I do not see-e-e the presence of un-i-ty. No-o-o! I do not *behold* it as in the eyes of Jesus. There are brothers against sisters, sisters against brothers, sisters against sisters, and brothers against brothers!"

Ain't it the truth?

Amen.

"Getting on *down-n-n* to the *root* of this evil of divisiveness—to the *cause*—is *in-equa-li-ty!* The unequalness of men and women and of races, festering sores on a nation that prides itself on being democratic. You cannot have unity where there is inequity, for unfairness breeds discontent and hostilities!"

Lord, yes-s-s!

Myrtle paused to let the words soak in, eyes winging over the congregation like talons. "The Book of Genesis, chapter 5, verse 2, says: 'Male and female created He them; and blessed them.' Yes! Male *and* female, He created alike in His image. But, there are among us some who believe the Bible teaches that women should be subjugated, *sup-press-ed* because they are inferior to men. This is the patriarchal interpretation of the Bible, used for selfish reasons. These believers will point you to the Apostle Paul, a man of *his* time, who reflected the patriarchal *background* and *thinking* of his time. Paul wrote in the First Epistle, Book of Timothy, chapter 2, verse 12: 'But I suffer not a woman to teach, nor to usurp authority over the man, but to be in silence.'

"*Silence?* What would have happened if the woman of Samaria, the first to get the message from Jesus about his being the Messiah, had kept silent? Had she not gone to tell-l-l both men and women? This was a *woman* who spread the *word*, and it was a *woman* to whom Jesus spake. If Jesus had wanted women to keep silent, he would not have chosen a *woman* to deliver that important message, but a *man!*"

Ah-h-h yes-s-s!

"There are men *today* who believe like the Apostle Paul in the subjugation of women. That women should be subordinate to men, walk *behind* them instead of *beside* and *in step* with each other for the fulfillment and enrichment of both their lives! There are sisters, too, who follow this line of thought, and believe in the servitude of women, in taking a backseat, for they have been led or rather *mis-led* to believe in their *own* inferiority! I say, *read* your Bible and see if you can find any passage which depicts Jesus as being disdainful or contemptuous of women. He looked upon them as *per-sons!*" Myrtle's voice roared like thunderclap above their heads as she moved from behind the rostrum, a gilded robed evangel of truth. "And *rightfully* so as persons, *glor-ri-ous* persons, for we are all-l-l *equal* in the sight of God, as we should be among *ourselves!*"

Prea-ch!

Out of half-lowered lids, Myrtle glimpsed Travis sitting mesmerized. Seated with her in the special pew were Wilma, displaying a go-to-it advocacy; Rita, pants leg crossed, lips forming a half-knowing smile; Flossie, perplexed dark face partially concealed by an alpine hat; and Bobby at the end, eyes downcast on his Gucci shoes.

Prancing back and forth in the pulpit, Myrtle's arms flailed the air, the sleeves of her robe unfolding into billowing sails. "Let us go on-n-n to Galatians, chapter 3, verse 28." The bookmark was already in the Bible, so without hesitation, she turned to the spot without losing time. "'There is neither Jew nor Greek, there is neither bond nor free, there is neither male nor female: for ye are all one in Christ Jesus.' Yes, dear brothers and sisters, we are all *one!*"

Amen!

Hallelujah!

Abruptly she stopped to glower piercingly at them. "We are all *supposed* to be one. Only look around you. *Look!* What do you see? I see people *di-vi-ded.* Division and disunity are rampant among races—white, black, red, and yellow. Why? Because of inequality. Where there is this disparity, there is oppression by those of the majority in control. Look around you again. *Who* is *in* control? Who controls our government? Business enterprises? Media? Lives? *White males,* that is who!"

Un-hun-n-n!

Yes-s-s!

"What does this control do? It breeds *power!* Too much power in the hands of a few leads to corruption, greed, selfishness, and subjugation of others. My brothers and sisters, we *all* know who suffers the most under this kind of system: those in the minority—black people and women!"

True!

"Women and blacks suffer in employment opportunities, housing, government, and day-to-day living. You elect *male* politicians who *say-y-y* they are going to *change* things. But *noth-ing* changes!"

Lord have mercy!

"Let *me* tell you, things don't *have* to stay the same. Oh, no-o-o! Women and blacks can *exert* themselves by coming to-ge-ther to *fight* the system. *Unite* to place ourselves in the sun of our society instead of the shade!"

Hallelujah!

"Above all, *women* must give vent to their talents, abilities, and skills to get an equal share in the civil, religious, and familial spheres in our society to establish a fair balance of male and female power. This is the coming of age of women in *all* her glory! Sisters, white and black, must help each other to overcome. To overcome and *break* the shackles of racist and sexist control. And brothers, you good-thinking Christian brothers, must *support* the sisters, for in freeing us, you are freeing yourselves!"

Freeing!

Praise God!

"You white sisters with Christian hearts, you must join your black sisters. Join us in God's unity to combat the forces of bigotry and corruption. Join us in our Women's March—a pilgrimage of liberation—under God's banner against the unjust evil forces of this city. We will form a Christian coalition of right-thinking sisters of *all* races. Form a different kind of populist movement of women in the South, right here, for we are all-l-l God's children!"

All God's children!

The response grew louder, propelling Myrtle to a frenzied climax, heightened by the show of togetherness before her. "I am calling you and you and *you-u-u*, brothers and sisters!"

Yes-s-s!

Striding back and forth on the pulpit like a swaying pendulum, Myrtle inhaled great swallows of air, which when expelled, gushed forth words that rasped fire: "We *need* you, good brothers and sisters, to follow the Christian example of Jesus towards humanity. We need you to come *together* in His

spirit. For in un-i-ty, you will find peace, strength, and salvation!"

Hallelujah!

Agilely springing from the pulpit, Myrtle confronted them.
"I am asking *you* who have been *touched* by the spirit of God
this morning, who feel the *need* to become a part of *Him,* to
come forth and let me receive you into this congregation of
the Universal Church for All People. A church which has no
barriers, a church that offers the interpretation of His word in
the context of *today!* A church of un-i-ty. Come and be saved
and help us to save each other while the choir sings."

The pianist sounded the key and the choir rose to blare out
a rock-shaking gospel song of faith. Myrtle raised her arms
high like a shelter over the fold. "Come, come, *come!*"

The choir's voices hurdled the rafters in tingling, spine-
moving harmony: "Oh, come to Jesus!"

Myrtle threw back her head and began to move her body
in the rhythm of the music. Her head shook and arms thrashed
in the way of the sounds, feet shuffling back and forth in
intricate dance steps. "Oh, yes-s-s, I *feel* the spirit! All those
wanting to be saved, Say Jes-us and *come* to me-e-e!"

"Jes-us!" Travis leaped up from the pew to fall weeping for
the second time of holy divination into Myrtle's arms. "I want
to become a *real* Christian again. To *live* the life God intended
for me to live. A *good* life without sin! I want to join *your*
church and come back to Jes-us!" she cried against Myrtle's
bosom. "Help me . . . oh, help me to be saved again!"

Myrtle was startled to find Travis once more miraculously
huddled in her arms for consecrated absolution. With rapture,
she felt the soft fullness of Travis's body smothered warm
against her own, face buried in her shoulder, the familiar perfume she had been breathing all weekend filtering into her
nostrils like an aphrodisiac.

"Yes, I will save you!" Myrtle said, delirious with the sensuous carnality of clasping Travis and the magnitude of the
moment. Involuntarily, her hips ground into Travis's crotch in
time with the music, pushing and rotating in slow agonizing
motions, while arms squeezed breasts to breasts and mashed
nipples to nipples. Myrtle caught the magnetic shudder fusing
Travis as her twisting hips answered back. Then with one final
thrust, Travis's loins stilled to lodge deep between the limbs
of Myrtle. Heat inundated Myrtle like a raging fire, sweeping

her in the throes of desire. Mercifully, by the sheer force of willpower, she managed to tear away from all the ecstasy in the world, secreted in the palm of a few moments of bliss.

"Confes-s-s your sins, my child, and come to Him through *me. He* will cleanse you; *He* will save you. *Love* Him. The Lord blesses those who dwell in His house and who sing His praises forevermore. *Praise* the Lord—Travis Lee is one of *us!*" With the heat from the physical closeness of Travis still lingering, Myrtle's voice sounded tremulous and overly strident in her ears. "Our new member—Travis Lee!"

Travis Lee! Travis Lee!

Through passion-glazed eyes, Myrtle stabilized herself to receive the others coming to her—men, women, children, young, old, sick, and well. She hugged them—but not the way she had Travis—kissed and blessed them all, the new recruits into her army of believers. A young, sloe-eyed woman with a too-wise face and big buttocks cramped into a sausage-skin dress, tried to crowd into her closely. Tactfully, Myrtle patted her on. Thirty redeemed passed her way.

Motioning to the congregation to stand, Myrtle blessed and extended the right hand of fellowship to the new members. "Welcome to the Universal Church for All People!" Myrtle spread her arms wide to embrace those on the benches at the front of the church. The choir sat back down, and Ralph, in the capacity of assistant pastor, went quickly over to the mourners' bench. Information had to be obtained from the professed followers of Christ.

Myrtle turned her attention to what she claimed (but to no one except herself) to be the most important part of the service—the offering. "For us to continue the work of *this* church, a *special* church, a *different* church which welcomes everyone, we need your financial blessing. We are asking you to give what you can, all you can. Blessed is the giver. With *your* giving, we can improve our church. Please, *please* give! Following the offering, we are going to ask Sister Lee to favor us again with a solo." She hoped it wouldn't be an imposition on Travis in her conversion state. If Travis didn't feel up to it, she would understand. Myrtle looked questioningly at her, and Travis, wiping her face with a handkerchief, nodded affirmatively. "Will the ushers please come forward to take the offering."

At that instant, Travis got up from the bench to face the

congregation. "I want my brothers and sisters to know that I'm presenting a check in the amount of three thousand dollars to Reverend Black for *our* church!"

Momentarily stunned, Myrtle stood paralyzed. The congregation reacted before she did with shouts of *God bless you!* and *Hallelujah!*

Rising to the announcement, Myrtle moved smiling happily toward Travis holding out the check. "Thank you, Sister Lee!" Flashing cameras emitted light flares at them. "God is certainly with the Universal Church for All People," Myrtle cried. "Jesus is pointing the way for a bigger church!"

A-men!

Smiling back, Travis said, "I'm going to sing my mother's favorite song, one she used to sing on Sundays at the church we went to in Detroit: 'His Eyes Are on Me.'"

When Bobby got up to go to the piano, the church quieted into a vacuum. Travis's music came out sweet and plaintive, an undiluted melancholy sound, analogous to a lonely, pliant voice floating from a cabin window beneath a waning, pink southern sky. As she sang, a cauldron of emotions engulfed the church. There were those who eased tears and others who listened in joy and sorrow.

> His eyes are on me-e-e
> Making me hap-py
> In my soul . . .

When she finished, pleasure and appreciation was indicated in the ancestral African custom of feet patting the floor and the praises: *The voice of Jesus! Truly beautiful!*

Overcome also by Travis's solo, Myrtle's voice quivered slightly. Her mother had liked that song, too. "Thank you again, Sister Lee."

Yes, indeed!

Myrtle's attention turned to her reserved pew. "We have some special guests I want to introduce. Wilma Freelander, president of the local chapter of the Women United for Action—" Wilma stood and smiled graciously. "Rita Stennette, of San Francisco, president of the National Organization of Women United for Action—" Rita half rose. "And Flossie Robinson, an employee of Ms. Freelander." Flossie, surprised at being singled out with the rest, darted up shyly and sat back down quickly. "Our Assistant Pastor, Reverend Casey, will make additional announcements and recognition of visitors whose names have been submitted."

Myrtle went back to the pulpit and sat down. Clutching the check Travis had presented to her, she looked at the date. It had been made out the previous night.

Ralph performed his functions in his usual refined way, black clerical robe a monk's cassock shrouding his reedy body. Upon completion, Myrtle gave the benediction: "May the grace of the Lord and His spirit be with you forevermore. Amen."

Going over to Wilma, Rita, and Flossie, she thanked them for coming.

"Good sermon, Reverend," Wilma lauded. "Hit the nail right on the head!"

Rita wanted them to meet again before she left on Tuesday, and Myrtle agreed. Flossie, hovering near, made no comment, looking away.

When the three edged into the crowd, Myrtle beckoned for Heavenly Delight and asked her to rescue Travis from a ring of admirers by escorting her and Bobby to the study. Myrtle then went outside to shake hands with the departing parishioners, a procedure she labeled her political performance.

Poised by the church door in the midday heat, robe a glittering metallic sheath in the sun, she smiled, talked, and shook hands. A man emerged, prominent in the departing flock, dressed in a white silk suit, zebra-striped pink tie, and white hat with tie-matching band. Two pretty women balanced each side of him, one white and the other black. Both were stylishly attired in knee-length, long-line dresses, high-heel shoes, and floppy hats. The man did not linger to shake hands, but tarried long enough for his eyes to hold Myrtle's in a padlock gaze before he moved on with the surge of departing people. She tried to search her memory as to where she had seen the familiar black bearded face. A minister should have a ready catalog for faces. People liked to be recognized.

In the study, Heavenly Delight charmed Travis and Bobby with her light chatter. Being entertaining had been a requirement of her past. "Everybody gone, Reverend?"

"Yes, Heavenly Delight. With the congregation getting larger every Sunday, I know we are going to have to get a bigger building."

"One thing for certain, Reverend, your name must sure be gittin' 'round town. Who would have thought the Sheik would darken the door of a church," Heavenly Delight giggled.

"Who is the Sheik?" Myrtle asked casually, unlocking the desk to deposit Travis's check in her purse.

"Rudolph Valentino Jones—"

Before Heavenly Delight could finish, Travis gasped, *"Rudy was here?"*

Bobby looked aghast. "I didn't know he was in church this morning."

"He was sitting on the back row," Heavenly Delight said, "with two women."

The man staring so hard at her must have been he, Myrtle concluded. Immediately she remembered Rudy from being in the hotel hallway that night carrying a poodle and leading Travis's procession as they changed suites.

"He's supposed to be one of the biggest players in town," Heavenly Delight resumed her conversation about the Sheik. "He ain't been here long, but he's sure in the bizness. They say he's even tryin' to move in on King. You 'member hearing Earthly Treasure talkin' 'bout her King, don't you, Reverend Black?"

"I remember," Myrtle was made uneasy by Travis's perturbed look.

"Maybe he's gittin' religion since he came here," Heavenly Delight smiled, undertaking to clear the air of gravity surrounding them.

"Knowing Rudy, if *he* came to church, it was probably for a purely unholy, selfish, and vindictive reason," Travis said forebodingly. "He probably read in the paper that I would be here and came just to let me see him."

"Don't worry, I don't think he'll make any trouble," Bobby said.

As Myrtle went into the bathroom to take off her robe, Ralph came into the study to hand Travis a membership form. Eyes slanting at Bobby, he smiled under a toothbrush moustache. "Mr. Blane, I'm a musician, too, of sorts. I teach music at Carter High School. If you're going to be in town for a while, come by." He handed Bobby his card. "You can reach me at home after four, or at school in the mornings. I'm teaching in our summer session."

"Ready to go?" Myrtle was dressed with her robe back in the bag. It would go to the cleaner's in the morning. She only wore a robe once.

"We collected fifteen hundred dollars, not counting Ms. Lee's check," Ralph said proudly. "Mrs. Higgs is putting it in the money bag."

Mrs. Higgs, prim and businesslike, brought the bag to Myrtle. "It's ready for the bank, Reverend Black."

Myrtle placed the bag in the oversized pocketbook she carried on Sunday for that purpose. "Thank you, Mrs. Higgs. I will drop it in the bank deposit. I don't like to have such an amount around until Monday." Looking at Ralph, she said, "Will you take charge of the young people's program this evening for me?" She knew he would be happy to do it. He liked to be in the limelight. All ministers did, or else they wouldn't be ministers.

"Be glad to, Reverend."

"I'll see that the church is in order," Heavenly Delight guaranteed. The worship of Myrtle and loyalty to her shone like a beacon light in Heavenly Delight's face and actions.

Settled in the car, Myrtle turned to Bobby in the back. "Going to my place with us?" She hoped he had another place to go.

"I'd like to Reverend, but a friend's going to meet me at the hotel." Clyde was coming for him again. Recalling that Travis and he were to leave the next day, he said, "Travis, what time do you want to start out for the airport tomorrow? Our flight leaves at four in the afternoon."

Travis was so quiet that they wondered if she had heard. "I'll let you know in the morning, Bobby," she answered finally.

Myrtle drove under a cloud having been reminded how little time remained for them. "Here you are." She pulled up in front of the hotel.

Bobby got out. "Thanks. I'll check with you in the morning about nine, Travis." That was best, for he was to spend the night with Clyde.

"Have a good day," Myrtle waved. Maneuvering the car into the after-church traffic, she said, "I am sorry you are leaving tomorrow."

"Agnes made up the schedule."

A battered Honda wheeled abruptly in front of them and

Myrtle blew her horn loudly. "Silly fool!" she snapped, surprised at the outburst of temper. She liked to drive and was usually patient with careless drivers. The anger had been provoked by the thought of Travis's leaving. Weekends go much too swiftly. She gripped the wheel in frustration as a hot flash flushed through her body. *Your age is showing with your anger,* she grimly chastised herself.

"What are you doing, praying to yourself?" Travis laughed a sparkle into the gloom.

Take advantage and be thankful for the time you have with her, Myrtle Black. "Not exactly. Want to go sight-seeing?"

"That should be fun. What's there to see?"

"There is the Hermitage, home of Andrew Jackson, the Upper Room Prayer Center, and Opryland. For the black sights, we could ride by the universities and American Baptist Theological Seminary. Before starting the tour, I have to stop at the bank. I do think we ought to go by the park to visit the Parthenon and let you say farewell to Donald."

"Let's take him something to eat this time."

Turning on West End, Myrtle headed into the drive-in section of Third National Bank where she dropped the money in the night deposit. Then she swung onto the busy thoroughfare, heading to Centennial Park. Both she and Travis were quiet on the way, isolated in separate cubicles of thought. The sunny day had become overcast by the tomorrow.

Chapter 17

*A*T Centennial Park they had fun mingling with the tourists visiting the Parthenon, then stopped to feed Donald and his proud-necked companions.

Leaving the park, they explored other sights, ending up at Opryland where they gleefully rode the train like fun-seeking children, eating pink cotton candy and viewing the sweep of the park. Afterward, Myrtle treated Travis to a champagne dinner at the Old Hickory restaurant.

It was almost dark when they returned home exhausted, filled with rich food and in a lighthearted mood. Right away, Travis got out of her clothes to put on a loose-fitting robe that she said would let it all hang out.

Myrtle donned a pair of slacks and tank top, and slipped into house shoes to relieve her tired feet. Closing the drapes, she blotted out the lights of the darkening skyline.

"Want something to drink?" Myrtle asked. "Iced tea, coffee, wine?"

"Wine!" Travis sighed wearily, half reclining on the couch with bare feet drawn up beneath her. "You don't think I'm becoming a wino, do you?" she joked.

"Not hardly," Myrtle laughed. "Frankly, I would like some myself." She went to get the bottle kept chilled in the refrigerator. "I want to thank you again for that generous church contribution," she said, making space on the coffee table for the tray.

"It was nothing. I wanted you to have what you deserve."

"One of these days, I hope to work up to a fantastic new

building," she murmured wishfully, gazing into her glass as if the vision were there.

"You will, I'm sure of that." Travis sniffed the tangy aroma of the chablis. She had only drunk wine with dinner before meeting Myrtle, or the red sweet kind when puffing on a weed with Rudy to send them on imaginary downy heights of euphoria.

"Would you like the TV or radio on?" Myrtle asked.

"Radio. Some nice, soothing music."

Myrtle turned the dial to an FM station that continuously aired easy sounds. An old Wes Montgomery filled the room, a combination of jazz guitar, strings, and harp enmeshed in melodic smoothness.

"Being here has been good for me," Travis said thoughtfully.

"I am glad to hear that." Myrtle settled beside her on the far end of the couch. "I love having you here."

Travis's eyes rested vacantly on the African wall prints, as though seeking security from what was bothering her. After a while, she said solemnly, "I really got carried away this morning, didn't I?"

"We all did," Myrtle replied gently, mollifying whatever was plaguing her. Was she remembering the time in her arms?

"You can really preach. People join your church in droves. You have the power of persuasion."

"So do you, through your music."

"Perhaps I do, but it's not as important as what you do."

"Indeed it is! Just think of what your music does to people. How it moved them this morning. Music and sermons go hand-in-hand. Music sets the tone and holds the mood." She smiled over her glass. "Spirituals and gospel music have aided many an itinerant black preacher along to set the good old spirit in motion. Including my parents."

Travis's eyes moved from the wall back to Myrtle, a smile tipping her lips. "Who do you take after, your mother or father?"

Myrtle laughed aloud at the question. "Why, I guess my father."

"What was he like?"

Myrtle refilled their glasses, thinking she should have placed the bottle in an iced wine bucket to keep it chilled. Slowly tasting from her glass, she tried to form an answer. "He was a dynamic preacher, proud and an impeccable dresser down to ironed boxer shorts. Strong in his way. My mother was, too."

"Like you." Travis took Myrtle's free hand, inspecting the long, slim fingers, nails perfectly clipped and shining with a subtle glow of natural polish. "Your hands show strength."

Travis's fingers interlocked with Myrtle's, a peach glaze over dark caramel. The touch was like a warm glove. Because she did not want Travis to feel her tremble, Myrtle withdrew her hand. Going into her minstrel routine, she quipped: "Why, chile, don't y'all know all us black women 'spose to be strong!"

"Strong for our men," Travis bantered back. "Only we're weak in that strength, or else we wouldn't be taking so much dirt from them. Like I took from Rudy." Travis ran a finger up and down the stem of her glass. "But that's all over. No more Rudy's—no one. I guess that I'm like Agnes now."

"You have the joy of *yourself*."

"And you!" Travis smiled. "But look who you have—all those people in your church who worship you. Why Heavenly Delight simply adores the ground you walk on."

"I furnished Heavenly Delight a way to a new life."

Travis looked mischievous, face impish. "Did your father have all the sisters in the church crazy over him? Most preachers do."

"They liked him." Her father handled the Jezebels delicately, succumbing to a mere few discreet liaisons. This she later came to understand. Men in the public view constantly had women after them, and being men, they could only withstand so much female pressure. She knew he loved her mother. That was the most important thing.

"Knowing men, what do you do when they make passes at you? As attractive as you are, I'm sure they do."

Myrtle shrugged. "I ignore them, or if the pass is too gross, I handle it with divine diplomacy," she laughed.

Travis finished the contents of her glass, as if for courage, before posing the next question. "You welcome gay people into your church. Have any women made passes at you?"

Myrtle's face grew guarded. "Occasionally."

"This morning, when I was in your arms"—Travis hesitated, seeming flustered—"I felt something that I hadn't before for a . . . woman."

Myrtle's composure was of stone, not wanting to break the flow of words, an enlightening discourse of self-revelation.

"I was . . . well . . . sexually aroused by you." At Myrtle's silence, she asked quickly, apologetically, "Am I being offensive?"

"No, you are not," Myrtle said softly. How could Travis offend when she was saying at last exactly what Myrtle wanted to hear? But don't pounce too soon, she warned herself, because it may not yet be the time to cross the waters. Assume the role of counselor. "Sermons can sexually stimulate people, for they appeal to the emotions as well as intellect. This in turn can project to the listener a physical attraction for the minister."

"What does it do for you?" Travis turned fully to face her, eyes wide. With the movement, the loosely tied robe fell apart, exposing a mound of breasts enclosed in a web of lacy pink brassiere. "I had a feeling you—you felt like I did. The way you held me."

Looking everywhere but at Travis, Myrtle was tense. "I, too, am human, my dear. Ministers aren't icons, as I have told you. We go to the bathroom, eat, sleep, and make love like everybody else. People believing that ministers are an earthly deity is one of our major problems. Look at the priests and nuns who defect. They know they are not. For me to say I wasn't excited by you would be untrue. I was."

"Hey—" A tiny smile tagged Travis's lips as she reached for Myrtle's hand again. "I have a feeling we're wasting a lot of time, aren't we?" Moving closer, she brushed her lips across Myrtle's cheek, a touch light as wind. "Why don't we hold each other?" A weak beckoning in a tight moment.

Myrtle drew Travis into her arms, as Travis's head made a nest on her shoulder. Gently Myrtle's fingers traced caressing flights from the nape of her neck to tangle in the underbrush of her hair. Travis was warm earth against her, a miracle of perfume, softness, and woman. Tentatively she lifted Travis's face to scan the amber slanted eyes brimming with brightness. Myrtle's fingers traced the pattern of Travis's nose which broadened gracefully at the nostrils, and the gentle curve of her full lips.

"You are gorgeous," Myrtle breathed, misting kisses of flower petals over Travis's face. She hovered at the corners of her mouth before matching their lips as one and the same together.

Travis emitted a low moan, closing her eyes and tightening her arms around Myrtle's neck. The kiss was long, deep and exploring, wonderfully new and fresh to them as first lovers' kisses can be.

Myrtle contoured her face between the groove of Travis's breasts, inhaling the woman-smell of sweetness and salty dampness. "I want to take you to bed. To get closer, to cradle, to feel, and to love." She could hear Travis's heart beating unsteadily in her ear, a wee outcry of its own.

"I want you to!" Travis inhaled a hiss, hugging her in delight.

Turning on the bedlamp, Myrtle shakily pulled back the covers. When Travis started to undress, Myrtle stopped her with, "No—let me, please."

Tenderly Myrtle began to disrobe her, pausing to kiss, nibble, and lick unexpected places on bare flesh. Travis had a mole on her right shoulder blade which Myrtle now sucked gently. Hands deftly unfastened the flimsy tissue of brassiere to make the pendulous breasts fall freely in view. Myrtle bent, kissed and tongued the eye of each brown nipple. Easing down the sheer lattice of panties, she uncovered the coarse black curly bush of hair securing the Venus of loving. Lying her down on the bed, Myrtle withdrew momentarily to undress, herself, keeping her eyes a rivet of flame on Travis.

Nude now too, Myrtle slid down beside Travis, rolling over to let their breasts touch. Travis's hands moved to Myrtle's hair, shaking loose the bun. "I've never seen it loose." The waves of Myrtle's hair fell like a shawl across her shoulders and around her face. "My Indian part," she teased.

Nuzzling Travis's nose in an Eskimo kiss, Myrtle laughed. "Black folks have everything in them."

Travis wrapped her arms around Myrtle. "I want your mouth again. It's so soft." Myrtle's lips made tickling brush movements painting Travis's mouth before she kissed her hard, rocking her head from side to side, hands roaming a venturesome route along Travis's copious body. She caressed the broad stomach and thick, luscious thighs. The whole of Travis was a plunging, plush cushion where she sank into a gorge of pliable curves.

"I want you to like it," Myrtle said low, voice an intimate stroke. "I have wanted to do this with you for a long time." Myrtle blew a loop of warmth into her ear. "We'll do it this way—first." Her fingers tangled below in the moist crevice of Travis, sliding into the pit of her.

"God-d-d—" Travis gasped, closing her eyes to the pulsating hotness flooding her.

Myrtle straddled the swell of her hips to couple the lower

lips of Travis with her own. Here their bodies met in slow, cyclone movements, pelvis joining pelvis in love. Travis's legs clamped Myrtle as she moaned in ecstasy, face a distorted peekaboo of pleasurable sexual pain between the strands of Myrtle's hair. The ache of loving swelled through them like a heated saber, swathing wounds of flame.

"Is it good?" Myrtle rasped between clenched teeth.

"Ah-h-h, yes-s-s!"

In a few moments, a song of gratification burst from them in a paroxysm of bliss. Travis cried out first, squeezing Myrtle with a clasp of steel. Then Myrtle answered in mutual intensity, her exaltation a volcanic quake which subsided into a whimper.

They lay in a heaven of their own, the sweat between them like paste, cementing them together for a nirvana in time. Suddenly Travis strained upward, hips seeking Myrtle's once more. "I can't get enough of you!"

Myrtle responded by moving in rhythm anew with her. "Nor I you—"

Travis made small kitteny sounds in Myrtle's ear as the body movements of woman loving woman in a special way submerged them in the climax of Sapphic paradise. Drained, but happy in their discovery, they went to sleep braided in arms of love.

Before the early threads of dawn, they awakened to the wonderment and enchantment of each other. Travis's lips pressed a diamond into the hollow of Myrtle's neck, stirring her. Myrtle smiled, moving an arm slightly stiff from cradling Travis's head on her shoulder.

Travis ran a hand over the thin, flat plane of Myrtle's long body, fingers traversing the black woman's smooth regions of firm, straight back, tight buttocks, and tapered thighs. Myrtle had the lithe body of a dancer. Palming the two round cheeks, Travis wove an experimental finger between the cleft of them. "This is the first time I've made love with a woman."

Trembling, Myrtle's voice sounded trapped. "You *are* learning fast!"

"It's coming naturally to me," Travis said, moving deeper into her. "I know what *I* like. This in turn helps me to know what you want, doesn't it?"

Myrtle hid her face in the curly bush of Travis's hair, the scent of the coconut oil she used a sachet of sweetness.

"Lying here like this close to you is like being next to satin.

Your body is so sleek, silky and soft. I didn't realize what making love to a woman could do to you!"

"Don't go crazy and try it with everybody," Myrtle warned facetiously.

Hugging her in elation, Travis laughed. "It's made me hungry!"

Myrtle sat up. "What would you like to eat?"

"Let's go to the kitchen and find out. Something washed down with the wine."

"Which is warm now. I didn't take time to put it back in the refrigerator." Getting up, Myrtle stepped over the clothes left in a lascivious hasty heap on the floor to get a bathrobe.

Watching her at the closet, Travis giggled. "Don't put anything on. Let's be nudists. It makes me feel sexy."

"Sex maniac." Myrtle indented a kiss on her forehead.

At three o'clock in the morning with the radio still playing, they sat at the chrome kitchen table under the fluorescent light and ate scrambled eggs with cheese, and toast dripping with honey butter, washed down with wine cooled by ice cubes.

When Myrtle stacked the dishes in the dishwasher, Travis came up behind her and encircled her waist, breasts velvet naked prongs titillating her back. Travis pushed her hips into the pliant globes of Myrtle's rear. "I'm obsessed with you!" she purred, coupling Myrtle's breasts and kneading them gently as she moved her hips back and forth into Myrtle's. Whispering softly, she murmured: "If I keep this up, I'll be coming again— right here!"

"Nothing wrong with that," Myrtle said, "unless you would rather do it in bed."

"Un-hun-n-n, bed! And let's take the wine." Travis licked Myrtle between her shoulder blades, making an exclusive brand of wetness.

Back in bed wrapped together in a fold of arms, Myrtle's words came out in the sponge of Travis's cheek: "I wish you didn't have to go tomorrow."

"I don't have to."

"Then stay longer with me."

"Why?" Travis taunted, laughing.

"We have just found each other—you and me."

Travis stretched to get her glass off the nightstand. The bedlamp gleamed a private glow on their warm corner. "I'll have to call Agnes."

"Yes, by all means, call Agnes," Myrtle murmured a groan.

Raising her head from the pillow cushioning them as one, she said, "Give me a sip, please, darling."

"Darling—" Travis repeated, savoring the endearment. "I like that word coming from you." She drank the wine, held it in her mouth and leaned to kiss Myrtle, who drank the liquid from the fountain of Travis's mouth.

"Delicious! Filled with you."

Travis's face mirrored the contentment of a cat. "Who would ever guess that the cool Reverend Myrtle Black could be such a terrific lover?"

Myrtle nuzzled her tenderly. "I am glad you think so." She should be, from the experience with the others whom she would never tell Travis about. Maybe one or two, if asked, but not all. There were things that should be kept even from lovers. Compared to the past line of mostly transitory young and a few old things, Travis was vintage wine. "Call Agnes first thing when you get up."

"*If* I get up!" Travis laughed. "I like being in bed with you."

"My sex pot." Myrtle took the glass from her and placed it back on the stand. "Lie back and relax. We are going to do it another way," she commanded softly, moving above her and down.

"Yes, ma'am," Travis said obediently, closing her eyes with a smile on her lips.

Chapter 18

R ITA stretched out on the webbed lounge chair beside Wilma's pool, a gin and tonic at hand. Dior sunglasses and a wide straw farmer's hat shaded her face from the blistering Monday morning sun. Her lean body, already a mulatto's toasted tan from the frequent weekend trips to California beaches with her lover, Toni, was barely clad in a polka dot bikini swimming suit.

Wilma sat opposite her at the wrought-iron table shielded by a green and white peppermint striped umbrella. Petulantly, she nursed a Bloody Mary while pouring over the two piles of paper neatly stacked before her. The largest mound on her right pertained to Women United for Action, and the smaller group on her left contained new leases to be signed. Because of her various activities, she had developed a habit of working on dual tasks at the same time. For her convenience, Flossie had plugged the phone at the table. This she picked up intermittently to call her secretary at the office.

Although Wilma wore a pair of Catherine's Stout Shop Bermuda shorts and a tissue paper sleeveless blouse, perspiration dampened her face and back, causing her to be uncomfortable on the patio. If she had to stay home this morning, she would have preferred being ensconced in the air-conditioned coolness of her den. What people had to do to indulge houseguests.

Pulling her glasses down midway to her ski-sloped nose in Bella Abzug style, she glared at Rita. "I don't know why in hell you wanted to come out here as hot as it is. You haven't been in the pool."

"To soak up nature's sun and air," Rita said, wiggling a knobby foot with paint-peeling red toenails. "It helps me to think, staring up into the sky like this."

"So? I haven't heard any pearls of wisdom come forth yet." Stomach making a growling sound, Wilma glanced over her shoulder at the kitchen window to see if Flossie was preparing lunch. She glimpsed the woman's white head by the refrigerator.

"As long as we've been friends, Wilma Freelander, from the setting up of the chapter here, you should know that I'm loaded with profound thoughts and words. All writers are. These are tools of the trade."

Wilma looked askance at her, trying to recount how many gin and tonics Rita had consumed after the light breakfast of coffee and English muffins. Rita usually referred to herself as a feminist political theoretician and activist, rather than as a writer, having only edited a paperback on feminism.

"Right now, Wilma, my thoughts are on the Reverend Myrtle Black and how she can utilize words."

"Ministers, like writers, deal with words."

"Yes! But *good* ones are endowed with the gift and skill to use them *effectively* for convincing. You can readily see she has all of this by the way people flock to her church."

"They do that for sure," Wilma conceded, lighting a Winston with the silver butane lighter Flossie had also retrieved from the den. She finished signing the new leases and put them on the left, then reached for the Women United for Action papers on her right. Apparently, by the drift of Rita's discussion, it was finally time to get down to business.

"With the Reverend's charisma and sharp intellect, she is just the black image we need for attracting black women to our national organization. We have to get more black women's support to counteract the notion that ours is essentially a white women's movement."

"I won't argue with that," Wilma said. "But with what I've been experiencing here, I'm wondering if it isn't basically a northern, eastern, and western women's movement. White southern women seem slow in upsetting the apple cart. It may be a throwback to the old antebellum days of white male chivalry, which they want to retain in their fancies. It's easier to stay home, be placed on a pedestal and let the husband bring home the bacon and fight the everyday battles."

"And easier to let the black women do the work at home," Rita injected sarcastically.

Wilma's lips tightened at the gibe as she hastily looked again toward the kitchen window. This time, to her relief, she didn't see Flossie. "If that was intended for *me*, I need someone to take care of the place, since I *do* work."

"Tch, tch, no offense to you," Rita apologized, leaning over lazily to pour Tanqueray gin into a tall glass. "It was merely an observation after looking out my window this morning at all the black women, going to work." Rita took a long drink from her glass. "It made me wonder about your southern white women."

"Some southern white women, unlike myself, are anachronisms. Those who aren't are country and western music singers!" Wilma laughed heartily at her joke, sipping from the Bloody Mary she had barely touched. She didn't like to drink before noon.

"A regional tragedy, no less," Rita lamented solemnly. "Returning to the Reverend Black, who is indeed a phenomenal *black* southern woman, she is exactly what we need. Can't you just *see* her on *The Tonight Show* or sparring with Phil Donahue? She would certainly hold her own with the best of them as articulate as she is. Why, I could even get her picture on the cover of *Ms* magazine. We could prove to them all that the movement is not racist, classist, or elitist!"

"She may not be interested in acting as our token black," Wilma said, fanning herself with a piece of paper. The liquor had made her warmer. "Remember how you tried to get the widow of that deceased Civil Rights leader to join?"

Rita waved her glass in the air and pshawed. "Now, Wilma, you know that widows of national figures, no matter how much they have on the ball, don't want to do too much. Somehow they feel more obligated to the sun of their husband's past than the light of their own."

Wilma looked furtively in the direction of the kitchen. She knew enough of southern slave history to keep in mind that black servants should not be regarded as deaf, dumb, and blind.

"Myrtle is neither married nor widowed," Rita resumed, "which makes her a natural for us."

Wilma lighted a second Winston from the burning butt of the other before putting it out. Rita, excited over her idea, got up and came closer. Wilma tried to read the expression on her face, for oftentimes, these told more about what a person actually meant. With the big frame sunglasses and sun hat, however, it was hard to see any of Rita's small profile, a bird-visage of beaked nose and sparse mouth. Leaning both elbows on the table, eyes hard on her, Wilma said, "I don't like your implications of using somebody."

"I didn't mean it in a self-seeking way. What I meant was we could do for her what we did for Cynthia Braxton in Washington. Cynthia is our outspoken and declared black female lesbian in the movement, and you are aware of how difficult it was for us to find one of *those*. She has been published in *Off Our Backs, Sinister Wisdom,* and *Conditions*. We promoted her and she has helped us. She is our triple jeopardy symbol!"

"God, Rita," Wilma groaned in agitation, "you don't get people to join organizations to fill specific promotional spots. We need to induce Third World women to join us by addressing ourselves more specifically to *their* concerns."

Rita shook the ice cubes in her glass. "Wilma," she began too patiently in an adult to child explanatory tone, "the movement issues relate to *all* women. Sexism, jobs, equal pay, child care, health needs—"

"You haven't mentioned job training, welfare, and drug problems; the black women in prison and the black men there who should be out helping their women take care of families; blacks in prison because they can't afford high-powered lawyers. And what about racism in society—in all of us to some extent? That may be the reason why they're not coming to us as sisters. They, in many cases, I suspect, are really not made to feel welcome."

"*We* welcome black women," Rita said adamantly, slightly riled because a bit of the truth had touched home. In inviting blacks, she had been selective. There were some blacks she felt more comfortable with than others. Wasn't that the case with people in general? "It's the South that's known for its racism."

"The whole country, Rita, is racist," Wilma hurled back defensively. "You forget that in my younger years, I was one of those rare southern white women who took part in the Black Movement. How I remember the young, white female students from elsewhere coming down here on their white steeds to help the blacks. What has happened to them? They went back, finished college, got married, had precious white babies, and are probably now fighting busing!"

"We're getting off the subject." Rita did an about-face to replenish her glass and get more ice cubes from the silver bucket. Like a fish, she flopped down at the table. "I think Myrtle should be invited to become a member of Women United for Action. We can place her on the advisory board. As I said, she's what we need. Moreover, she's a mature woman. We don't have many mature black women."

"Mature black women are most likely bound up in their own organizations. You'll have to make do with harvesting the young and making stars out of them."

Tight-lipped, Rita stirred her drink with a forefinger. "Sometimes, Wilma, you can make me damn mad!"

"Sorry about that." Wilma squashed out the cigarette she had partially smoked.

"Since you seem to be our black expert," Rita smirked, "tell me: Do you think Myrtle will go along with us about the March?"

"How do you mean?"

"Stressing women's issues."

Wilma brought the organization papers level with her chin on the table. "I'm not a mind reader, particularly for a woman as shrewd as Myrtle Black." She had fathomed this astuteness on their first meeting.

Rita suddenly jumped up and began a series of toe-touching exercises, hat falling off and rolling to the edge of the pool. "Stirs the blood to the brain cells," she said, facing down to her knees. "You ought to try it sometimes."

"I'd rather go horseback riding," Wilma answered curtly.

Rita progressed into arm stretches. "Did you see all those fags at her church? A regular camp!"

"I believe she said that it was a church for all people." Adjusting her glasses, Wilma perused the list of chairpersons for local women's groups.

"Fags are brazenly obvious with their mannerisms."

"Spoken like a true lesbian sexist."

Ignoring her, Rita continued: "There were so many people there, I couldn't really spot any lesbians."

An instant silence fell between them. Eventually, Wilma looked up questioningly, knowing something was on Rita's mind that she was hesitant to bring out. "What now?"

Mindful that Wilma didn't like to discuss lesbians in connection with the movement, claiming that the word "feminist" was sufficient to frighten off southern women, Rita debated if she should tell her about her vibrations concerning Myrtle. As the old grapevine cliché went: It takes one to know one.

Rita performed a couple of vicious knee genuflections and head twists, causing her glasses to topple to the concrete. Stooping to retrieve them, she decided to use a different tactic. "The Reverend certainly has that singer, Travis Lee, under her spell." When Wilma made no comment, she opted to drop her innuendo. "Wish we could get *her* in the movement."

"Born-again people don't make good recruits. They have one-track minds." Wilma's stomach rumbled. "Wonder how long it'll be until Flossie has lunch ready."

Rita put down her glass. "Have you ever asked Flossie to join the chapter?" she inquired vindictively.

The paper in Wilma's hands shook like a leaf impassioned by wind. "I have talked with Flossie," she said tersely, "and found that she prefers her asylum of work, family, and church."

Rita stared at her strangely before pointing her face to the sky. "Doesn't this sun feel good? I'm getting as black as a black person."

"Rita!" Wilma jerked around toward the kitchen window.

"What's wrong with that? Isn't black supposed to be beautiful nowadays?"

Wilma tried to figure out if Rita was getting high. There wasn't time for that; work had to be done. "I'm going to call Myrtle to find out when she can meet with us tomorrow. The rest of the day, you and I are going to look over this list and see who we can call to serve on the committee. Also, we need to round up some funds and marchers."

"I'm not one to shirk work, Wilma, drunk or sober," Rita said righteously. "Let's get on with it!"

Myrtle and Travis slept the morning away after loving from night to dawn. Myrtle was the first to get up and shower, leaving Travis resting in bed. Sudsing under the hot spray of water, she was glad that she had remembered to tell Barbara not to come this morning. A trespasser was not welcomed to share her precious days with Travis. For Myrtle, there was a time for work and a time to do other things. Today was an extension of her holiday for other things.

Going back into the bedroom freshly smelling of soap and powder, Myrtle saw that Travis had opened the blinds to the radiance of the day. Traffic noises ascended through the windows, alerting them to the business of the streets below.

Pulling on a pair of yellow shorts and blouse, Myrtle asked, "Have you called Agnes yet?"

"I telephoned the airport and Agnes, and told Bobby when he called, all while you were in the bathroom!" Travis ticked off, lying in bed congratulating herself. Usually, Agnes made all the arrangements. She was coming of age. "I told Agnes that I wanted more time to be with my lover."

Myrtle stiffened, then relaxed on seeing Travis wink. "Wonder who *that* could be?" she jested, standing over the bed to plant a kiss on Travis's forehead.

Travis glided a hand up and down the glossy sheen of Myrtle's thigh. "Hum-m-m, did you put on those shorts to tempt me?"

"No, merely to keep cool and be comfortable. Aren't you going to get up?"

"Aren't you going to take off that shower cap?"

"This instant!" Myrtle stood in front of the bureau mirror to brush her hair in the habitual one hundred strokes her mother had maintained kept the scalp alive. "You don't have to get up if you don't want to. I will serve your breakfast here."

"Breakfast? Woman, what planet are you on? That time there"—Travis aimed a finger at the bedside clock—"says twelve-fifteen—lunchtime."

"Lunch it is." Myrtle plaited her hair into two Indian braids which made her look deceptively youthful. She felt the same way. People weren't supposed to feel old anymore, particularly if they were healthy and imbued with *joie de vivre* like she was.

"While you're slaving in the kitchen, Pocahontas, I'm bath-tub bound. What do you say we both have lunch in bed?"

"Anything you say, my darling!" Myrtle laughed in accord.

It wasn't too long before they were propped upright against the walnut headboard of the bed, clad only in panties and brassieres, feasting merrily on a vegetable salad and cottage cheese, wheat toast, and coffee, decoratively laid out on a tray. Travis, full of fun, acted out an impromptu scenario of feeding Myrtle like a baby.

In the middle of it all, the phone rang. "Wonder who would dare interrupt this bacchanalian festival?" Travis feigned indignation.

"I hope it isn't a sick or deceased parishioner," Myrtle said. It was Wilma wanting to set up a meeting for the following day. Myrtle acquiesced, deliberately arranging it for two o'clock. Mornings were for Travis. Aside from that, she had to arrange for Iffe to go with her.

By the time Myrtle hung up, Travis's winsome mood had changed to seriousness. "This March means a lot to you, doesn't it?"

"I want it to be a success." Anything she did had to be. Success was a predominant goal of her nature.

"I'd never really thought about some of the things you brought out in your sermon yesterday. Like sexism in male and female relationships." Travis drank her coffee. "In dealing with Rudy, I can see where he was a sexist, as well as full of black male macho. I was supposed to sit back and let him do what he wanted. Take his abuse without a whimper, because men are expected to run other women while you sit at home and say nothing." She crumpled her napkin in her empty plate. "I imagine all women become feminists when they quit taking it, put their feet down and stand up to their men and for themselves."

"Yes, darling, you are right. But a funny thing, many would never dare think of themselves as feminists." Myrtle set the tray of empty dishes on the floor and leaned back on the pillow, needle lines pinching the space between her eyes.

"You're worried."

"Thinking." Myrtle drew Travis into the half-circle of her arms.

With bare legs touching beneath the cool sheets, Travis rested on her side, a leg and arm thrown across Myrtle. "Thinking about what?"

"The March. Reaching out to include other issues. That is why I brought sexism and racism into my sermon yesterday. I am going to take a gamble. I know that I will step on the toes of some fundamentalist groups who don't approve of the Women's Movement or the pro-abortion stance. But those objectives are important to me. I am not going to compromise myself for numbers."

"I don't blame you."

"For black and white women, this is an opportune time to act. Our major concerns are the same in some key respects, politically and economically. In looking back, I can't afford to go for a one-dimensional issue like the old Civil Rights Movement. This March to me has snowballed into something bigger, and it's especially significant that it's taking place in the bastion of the South where black and white women will publicly join together to assert themselves. That March is going to represent southern women of all races who are unafraid, independent, capable, and strong!"

"Masterminded by a black woman!" Travis said exultantly, caught up in the fervor of Myrtle's voice, overflowing with vitality, excitement, and promise. "What can I do?"

Myrtle's arm tightened around her. "Be here with me."

Travis's body moved closer to Myrtle in the familiar intimacy of woman to woman. "I always believed the Women's Movement was made up of a bunch of bored white women fighting with their men to get out of the house and go to work. My mama used to wish she could stay inside it. She got so tired of that hospital sometimes."

"Black women have always been out there, for better or worse, whether they wanted to or not. Black men should be real proud of their women."

Travis's head, ringlets of tickling fleece, moved slightly beneath Myrtle's chin. "Do you . . . dislike men?"

Myrtle laughed loudly at the question coming timidly from Travis. "Why? Because I fight against sexism? No, I don't dislike men. I can answer that the way some whites do when they are asked if they dislike black people. I have some good male friends. Take George, who has been behind me since I came here. I just don't like to be taken advantage of, or overpowered by males." Myrtle's face softened, looking down at Travis. "And why else? Because I like this?"

"When did you first realize you were gay?"

Myrtle chuckled. "The so-called experts are saying today that a child's sex orientation is usually established by the age of five. For me, a long, long time ago."

"Have you ever been with a man?" She couldn't imagine Myrtle with one. It seemed a desecration.

Myrtle brushed her fingers through Travis's hair, uncombed and tangled from the loving. Famous stock questions from the novice in the Sapphic love. "Yes—once." That was enough. The botched-up prom night with LeMelle. "I don't want men sexually. I have no desire to go to bed with them. And it isn't because I haven't found the right man. For me, there is only the right woman. Satisfied?"

"Not quite." Travis raised her head slightly. "Suppose your church members find out."

"Darling, some, I am sure, already know, or have guessed. In the black world, it's more horrendous when admitted." It wasn't the church members she was worried about, as much as her leadership appearance in the community. Leaders were supposed to be without blemish, for people to look up to and follow. Their private lives, if contrary to the norm, had to be lived in the shadows.

Travis mused over Myrtle's answer. There were those in the entertainment world whose homosexuality was whispered about. What would happen if this were made known to the public? The female performers about whom the gossip was most rancorous would surely suffer. How would it be with herself, who had turned to loving her own? She felt like shouting it from the housetops: It just went to prove, you never know where your heart is going to lead you. A low sigh escaped from her.

"Why that?" Myrtle asked tenderly.

"I was thinking about all that time I wasted before finding you—thanks to Jesus!"

"And still are. Kiss me."

Travis raised up to meet Myrtle's mouth. "Now you lie still. This one is on me!"

Chapter 19

*B*OBBY hung up the telephone in disgust after Travis called to say that she had changed her mind and wasn't leaving until Friday. That meant four more days in Nashville, which wouldn't have been bad if Clyde were going to be around, but his group had left to play out of town.

He lay down on top of the unmade bed, shoes and all. His suitcase was packed beside him. Leave it to Travis. Unpredictable as usual. Being born again hadn't changed that. He, too, should at least call Agnes.

For some reason, he dreaded going through the motions. Agnes could sometimes cop an attitude. But, after all, she was the brain trust. To brace himself, he poured a stiff drink of scotch before dialing.

Agnes's voice dripped with acid. He could tell she was pissed off. She firmly instructed him to make certain Travis got on the plane to get back to sign the Las Vegas Labor Day contract. The till needed replenishing and the Ding-a-Lings were getting restless.

Not wanting to add any more fuel to the flames, he didn't mention about Rudy's being in town. Hanging up, he felt relieved, for the chore was over. Outside the corridor, he could hear the maids pushing linen carts and opening the doors. He felt lonely, preferring to be on the move with people—with someone. A number of options occurred to him. He could go downstairs to the bar and pursue. Or take a walk along the tenderloin, the sleezy section of lower Broadway, clotted with peep shows, adult movies, and massage parlors, interspersed

between furniture outlets, guitar-glutted music shops and souvenir stores. (Driving through the section one night with Clyde,
he had been told it was a good place for cruising.) Or, as a last
resort, he could get a cab and go to the Everything Goes Cabaret. There, company would be guaranteed, for inevitably
someone lonely like himself would be present, too.

He needed to get some traveler's checks cashed. Taking out
his wallet to count his money, the white card of Reverend
Ralph Casey fell out. He had forgotten the invitation, being
occupied with Clyde. He checked his watch. Casey was in
school. Better give him a ring there to see about making later
plans. The choice was made, simpler and safer than cruising
in an unfamiliar city.

Ralph invited Bobby to go out to dinner, and afterward to
the Gospel Music Jubilee at the Municipal Auditorium. The
concert was crowded with a predominantly black audience.
Sandwiched in line between clerical collars and laypeople
smelling of liquor or with dope-screened eyes, they gradually
inched into the auditorium.

Women and men were decked out in the latest fashions. A
sociable, big night atmosphere prevailed, characterized by
friendly hellos, backslapping, kissing, and handslapping.
Necks craned to see who was there, who was with whom, and
who wasn't. Church was in session, a revival meeting with a
pulpit stage for the musical catechists.

Ralph pointed out to Bobby those whom he knew were gay.
"That's Jimmie Jones, a female impersonator whose stage name
is Flaming Dark Sugar. He belongs to our church."

Bobby hardly recognized Flaming Dark Sugar in a neat suit
and sport shirt, minus the wig and makeup. He and his companion, a short, chubby dark-skinned bald-headed man, took
expensive seats up front. "I've seen his act," Bobby said.

The lights dimmed and a handsome emcee, suave in a white
tuxedo clashing with his natural suntan, walked out on stage.
With a smile wide enough to capture all, he blared in the
microphone: "Goo-ood eve-nin', la-dies and gen-tle-men, my
good friends of the gospel sounds..."

"That's Lord Sherry, the sponsor," Ralph whispered hurriedly. "One of the few black music producers in the city. He
has an office on Music Row."

"We want to welcome you to another one of our *fan-tas-tic*

Gospel Music Jubilees. Tonight, you'll be hearing some of the *best* gospel music singing in the South. Y'all *know* that gospel music is part of our roots!"

The audience sanctioned him with *right-ons*.

"Music coming down from slavery. *Our* music that is straight from *here!*" Lord Sherry pounded his heart with a hand displaying a sparkling ring. "Music that tells it like it is and then some more!"

No lie!

"So, we want y'all to sit back, sit up, jump up or whatever, and enjoy what we have here for you to-night. Put on your shouting shoes for the Gospel Music Jubilee! First that famous group, the Susie P. Clark Gospel Royalettes from Atlanta!"

As the curtain drew back, the audience clapped enthusiastically for the six women strutting briskly out on the stage in green robes and elaborate black soaring wigs. An instrumental group consisting of an organ and drum was set up behind them. Two women in the group held tambourines.

Susie P. Clark stepped to the front of the group, gripped the microphone and began talking sweetly to the audience as the organist played softly in the background. "Children, I know how it is with some of us. Hummmmm, sometimes life can get real-l-ly bad!"

Sure can!

"It can get so-o-o bad, that if we didn't have Jesus-s-s, we'd all-l-l just have to lie right down and die!"

Tell it!

"Especially when people start talking about you, putting you *down*. *Bad*-mouthing you—"

"Lordy, Lordy, Susie P., how *we* know!" The response was from two women in the first row who wore green shirts and pants the color of the singers' robes, and short Afros.

Ralph nudged Bobby. "She's got her groupies there."

"And for all-l-l those bad-mouthing, putting-down people, we dedicate *this* song: 'Say No More.'"

The organist and drummer suddenly whipped up the tempo as Susie P. Clark laid her head back, opened the heart of her mouth and blasted:

> You can talk mean all you want
> And be real unkind
> But I got Jes-us in *my* mind

Her groupies leaped up and shouted: "Hallelujah!" and "Sing it, Susie P.!" Others in the audience swayed with the beat, clapping their hands and patting feet in time with the music.

Finishing the song, Susie P. swung right on into another and another, sermonizing and counseling before and in between musical bellows of pain, despair, hard living, and hope. "Now-w-w!" she pealed out. "Have you ever seen the Saints do the Holy Dance!" And with that, the drummer and organist and women with the tambourines began a foot-stomping beat as Susie P. and her Royalettes sang: "Come On in the House." Shaking, moving and dipping to their own frenzied sounds, the group, led by Susie P., danced off the stage and into the aisle.

It was a housewrecking, shouting shoes number. The crowd went to pieces, crying out, jumping up in their seats, arms flailing, heads back, getting with the feeling. As Susie P. snake-hipped with her Royalettes down the aisle, her groupies got up and fell right in line behind them, extemporizing body movements and footwork. A slick-haired boy in form-fitting red pants and shirt opened Harry-Belafonte mode to the waist, screamed and sprang up on the stage to do a twisting wiggle in front of the male drummer. The groupies followed Susie P. up and down the aisles, until the singers returned to the stage to end their performance with the finale of the holy dance. The audience shouted them to heaven.

Next were the Space Gospellaires, the featured attraction who were to appear near the end of the program, but had their slot switched because of new travel arrangements. Lord Sherry presented the four men and three women resplendent in purple robes with gold hoods.

The lead singer, a robust shiny-faced man, quieted the applause. "My friends, it is certainly a pleasure to be here tonight with you, to perform for this wonderful event. As soon as we finish, we will be on our way to the airport heading for the Apollo in New York City!" Smiling proudly, he waited for the magnitude of his announcement to be digested. "We are going to start off with a song composed by our black father of gospel music, Thomas A. Dorsey, singing his 'Precious Lord, Take My Hand.'"

A different musical accompaniment had set up, and the organist started off slow and easy in a blues tempo, mellowed by the soft plucking of a guitar, as the group crooned mournfully.

Suddenly the voices accentuated the upbeat, while the drum, organist and guitar grew louder and the rhythm completely changed to a pulsating rock sound. The lead singer's bass escalated to alto and almost soprano heights as he opened his mouth to scale the music. Clapping his hands, he instigated a soft-shoe foot tap that equaled Bill "Bojangles" Robinson.

People shouted and rose in their seats. *Do-o-o it!* came from a second groupie section in the third row of the left aisle.

The singers, caught up in their own sounds and the harmonious spirit of the crowd, erupted into sliding spine-tingling notes approximating musical instruments. Waving his arms, the sweating lead singer pushed his hips in and out, singing to the Lord. A woman stood up, hallelujahed, and rotated her hips back and forth in unison with his.

Bobby was swept up by the music, a myriad complexity of polyrhythms. His hands and feet went into motion. Ralph was on the edge of his seat, clapping hard with the rhythm of the sounds.

Some of the obvious gays seized the place, getting up in the aisles, bodies bumping and grinding in erotic abandon. Here they could come out and be themselves under the guise of getting happy for their Jesus. They could be seen and act out their stage dramatics right along with the straights. Nobody cared as all were behaving alike, expressing themselves in homogeneous accord to the Lord. The gospel scene offered the freedom to unleash volatile emotions where an atmosphere of community existed. Bobby could readily see why they came— out of pain and joy, belonging, and soul-caring for Jesus and themselves.

To Bobby, the music brought back the little storefront Holy Roller and Sanctified churches in Virginia that he used to pass on Sundays with his staid middle-class parents, who hurried him on. Those places held such sounds of singing and shouting and musical instruments pouring out through the walls and into the streets.

Intrigued by the sounds, he would sneak back in the evening to stand outside in the darkness and listen, the music flowing through him as deep as the earth, an umbilical cord to a musical past. It helped to lay the foundation for his blues and jazz.

"Nigger music," his father would snort in disgust. "Nothing but a bunch of hollering and noise."

Niggers to his father were black people who didn't conduct

themselves or try to live like whites. He supposed, in that case, it was as his father had said—nigger music—for it was made by those further down on the economic totem pole, who couldn't live or didn't want to act like whites. Hymns were sung in the Congregational Church he attended as a boy.

Looking critically at the audience surrounding him, he could see that the majority were not well-to-do blacks. Those here were the day-to-day livers who knew of helplessness and despair to and of which gospel music spoke. The gays were not of the black elite. Lower-class gays were more out in public. The middle-class black gays stayed in closets.

The slick-haired boy in the red pants, who had danced on the stage, got up from his seat, shouted and abruptly keeled over into a faint. Two ushers carried him out. Bobby heard a woman behind him laughing: "That sissy does that all the time. Just wants to be seen!"

During intermission, Ralph kept Bobby occupied with meeting people and pointing out local celebrities. As he talked, his eyes constantly roamed over the crowd.

"You've pointed out a lot of us here tonight," Bobby spoke his thoughts aloud.

"There're *plenty* of us on the gospel circuit and in the churches. Choir practices take the place of gay bars for some!" he laughed.

"In that case, church must be simply heavenly," Bobby smiled.

They went back for the rest of the program which lasted well over its allotted time.

After the concert, Ralph took Bobby to a party at the home of Lord Sherry in the suburban black Gold Coast of exclusive homes. Wall-to-wall people circulated through the well-appointed rooms, drinking, eating soul food prepared by a caterer, and sharing joints in obscure niches.

Some of the guests were friends of Lord, business acquaintances, gospel singers, and a few party sniffouts who had overheard the word. Many were gay and males. The scattering of females comprised members of gospel groups, Lord's personal friends and closeted sisters of the gay brothers. It was a formal atmosphere of unspoken gay nuances and heavy innuendoes, for there were a number of straights present.

The males appeared to be having the most fun, while the

females milled around and tried to assist Lord by seeing that
drinks and ice did not run out and cigarette trays were emptied.
In corners, the gay sisters listened as mother confessors to the
joys and woes of their gay brothers lamenting about their on-
and-off love affairs. There was the unspoken communication
of identification among them, but the sisters did not talk about
themselves, for they believed gay men were too gossipy.

Throughout the party, Lord patrolled his house, watching
out that no one spilled anything or got sick and threw up on
his rugs and expensive furniture. His second host care was
monitoring any outbreaks of arguments.

On the stereo, pop-gospel music played, variegated with Al
Green, Johnny Mathis, and Nancy Wilson. Bobby, a celebrity,
too, among them, found himself the center of attention. Male
singers, still with stage makeup and eye shadow, quietly
flocked around him. A Reverend Summerfield, towering and
black as night, kept rubbing against him. He was reported to
be, by a green-eyed Ralph, married with three children. Lord
approached him about the possibility of cutting a record with
one of his local groups. A straight woman, magazine beautiful,
tried to flirt with him. All this transpired with Ralph hovering
possessively near.

Bobby began to feel dizzy from the scotch he had consumed.
Perhaps it was because Lord didn't buy the best. Marijuana
smells escaped from under doors. He wished that he had a
joint. Two men came in from the patio outside. One had forgotten to zip his fly. Male eyes darted about the room, seeking,
questioning, inviting like predatory spiders. The gay action was
subdued among the unwitting straights, who seemed to be enjoying themselves at the party of a host whose sex life they
cattily overlooked. In show business, even of this kind, a little
of everything was found.

"Here comes Flaming Dark Sugar!" someone called out.

Flaming Dark Sugar entered, smiling greetings around the
room, followed by his companion at the concert. Spotting
Bobby and Ralph, he immediately went over to them. "Hello
there, Reverend Casey and Bobby Blane." Looking at Bobby,
he asked, "Mr. Blane, why didn't you bring Travis Lee? I'd
lo-o-ve to meet her. I thought her singing was *fan-tas-tic* in
church Sunday."

"Travis is with Reverend Black," Bobby said.

"Oh?" Flaming Dark Sugar's eyebrows shot up as a crooked

smile curved his lips. "Well, I'm sure she's being *well* taken care of. I hear our Reverend Black can really show the women a *gay* time. Hah, hah!"

When Flaming Dark Sugar moved off, Ralph asked, "What did he mean by that?"

Bobby glanced sharply at him. Could it be that he didn't know? "The grapevine has it that Reverend Myrtle Black might be gay."

Ralph frowned down at his glass of wine. Being new to the church and her assistant, he really hadn't taken time to speculate or care for that matter. It would be nice if she were, then he wouldn't have anything to fear.

"You hadn't heard?" Bobby asked incredulously. But some parents and spouses didn't know either. It was highly probable.

Suddenly Ralph laughed. "It *would* be funny if she were, wouldn't it?"

Bobby joined in with his laughter, thinking it would be funnier if the Reverend Myrtle Black got her amorous hooks into Travis. But then again, it might not be so comical to all concerned. With that dark thought hounding him, he grew more sober as the evening wore on.

The party broke up at 4:00 A.M., and Ralph drove Bobby back to the motel. From experience, Bobby knew what was on both their minds. Ralph didn't move him with earth shakes, but it beat an empty bed. Taking the initiative, he rested his hand on Ralph's leg. "Want to come in with me?"

Without a word, Ralph got out and locked the car.

Chapter 20

*L*EAVING Travis at home, Myrtle and Iffe went to the meeting at Wilma's office on Tuesday afternoon. Rita was there, along with three other women whom Wilma had persuaded to serve on the steering committee. They were introduced as Lois Goldstein, a beehived blond with a bluenosed air, president of the Independent Women Voters, and calculated to influence the Jewish community; Kate McCain, thirty-six-year-old chairperson of the Women's Studies Center, who appeared coolly perceptive and attractive in a summer dress; and Nikki Townes, president of the Student Feminist Alliance, adding a touch of youth with her jeans and frizzled dark hair.

All were seated at the table in Wilma's conference room with Myrtle placed at the head. "Here we are, ladies," Wilma began, laughing in her cigarette-tinged voice, "preparing to tackle a city!" After distributing legal pads and pencils, she leaned back in her chair to face Myrtle. "I haven't had any luck as yet in convincing the goodly church folks in serving on the committee. I guess their fundamentalist minds must think we're radicals or loose women. I even tried the Unitarians. Of course, the Catholics are almost hopeless."

"*I* am here, and *my* church is behind me," Myrtle reminded her, dispensing optimism at the head of the table.

Later, breaking for a brief respite, Wilma had her secretary bring up refreshments from the cafeteria below. Myrtle took the time to telephone George to come over with a photographer.

Back at the conference table, they wrapped up the meeting by forming subcommittees with chairpersons to be named.

These were to hurdle the details of selecting and training parade marshals, preparing posters and leaflets, and to make mail and telephone contacts. Funding was left in the hands of Wilma and Myrtle.

The March slogan was to remain as Myrtle had originated, and the target date was set for the third Saturday in September. The objectives were resolved to be: (1) to fight crime and vice in the city; (2) to fight corruption in government; (3) to appoint more women of all races, creeds, and colors to responsible positions; (4) to elect more women of all races, creeds, and colors to local, state, and federal governments; (5) to fight racism and sexism; (6) to band against rape; (7) to defend the right of women to control their minds and bodies; (8) to strive for more job opportunities; (9) to encourage women of all races, colors, and creeds to become more involved; and (10) to bring about Christianity, morality, and love for all people.

When George came, the photographer took group pictures of what the committee purported was a history-making event in the South—black and white women joining forces for women's rights and issues. Before adjourning, they scheduled a second meeting for Wednesday of the following week at the same time.

Outside, Myrtle invited Iffe to her place for dinner and a private black caucus session. To Myrtle's surprise, Travis had dinner ready when they arrived home. Pungent odors circulated throughout the apartment.

"I never dreamed that I'd be cooked a meal by *the* Travis Lee!" Iffe breathed in delight, as they sat down to eat.

Travis had the table spread with a roast lamb dinner. "It's been quite a while since I've done this," she announced, looking pleased with her accomplishment. Her strict diet had negated such fares.

Myrtle, sitting down at the head of a table for the second time that day, gave a short blessing.

"How was the meeting?" Travis asked, thankful no diet warners were around as she filled her plate with food. Damn the calories, full speed ahead. Agnes would have been horrified. Basking in the sun of rebelliousness, she took an extra roll.

"I think we accomplished quite a bit for an initial meeting," Myrtle said.

"Un-hun, after all the bickering ended about male participation and including gay rights in the objectives," Iffe added, refusing the meat, for she was a vegetarian.

Travis kept her eyes down on her plate. "What did they decide about the males?"

"It's to be strictly a Women's March," Iffe said. "Nikki and I wanted males along to show support, but we were outnumbered."

"And gay rights?" Travis asked slowly, stealing a quick glance at Myrtle.

"Now *that* was the biggest and longest hassle," Iffe answered, shaking her head in dismay. "I have to give it to Rita Stennette, she doesn't bite her tongue expressing how *she* feels about it." Iffe burst into laughter. "You should have seen Lois turn red as a beet when Rita said that southerners were sexual charlatans. Then, she went on to back up her statement by saying how placed-on-the-pedestal southern belles had lesbian affairs with their slave women, while the masters were copulating in the slave quarters!"

"Sounds like Rita," Travis said, recalling the dinner conversation at Wilma's. "But what was the decision?"

"No gay rights," Myrtle cut in sharply. "Gay women will be invited to take part, however. That is, as long as they don't identify themselves." The closet again; a swinging door of out and in—out with your lover, in with the public. Was Travis so burdened now, too?

"I had to go along with that," Iffe said candidly. "As Nikki pointed out, we might have a tough time getting students if the gay issue were brought aboard. And Lord knows, I'd have an awful lot of explaining to do to get black support."

"We need all of us we can get," Myrtle said. "That's where I am depending on you, Iffe."

"I'll do my best, Reverend. There's a friend of mine, Betty Perry, in the mayor's office who might be able to help us with the grass roots."

Crumpling up her napkin, Myrtle smiled at Travis. "You're a good cook."

"I'm glad to know my efforts were not in vain," Travis said, eyeing the empty plates.

"Let us go to the den and map out some strategies," Myrtle said.

Following them, Iffe remarked, "Reverend Black, I must say that you handled the meeting quite well."

"I tried to be effective. Sometimes white people like to take

your ball game and run away with it. That is why I stood my
ground on the headquarters site being at my church." There she
could control and keep a vigilant eye on the operations.

Travis pushed her chair closer to Myrtle at the desk. "Where
did she want it?"

"In one of her vacant offices near Green Hills," Myrtle
replied, liking Travis's closeness. "In the back of Wilma's
mind, God bless her, was the thought that some whites might
not want to go into a black neighborhood—the high crime risk
factor. You have to think ahead, as well as along with them."

"I learned something from the meeting today," Iffe laughed.
"Southern white women think the Women's Movement is a
Yankee invasion!"

"And gays are like the bubonic plague," Myrtle said, bit-
terness tarting her words.

Iffe frowned. "I don't have anything against gays."

"That's nice to know," Travis intervened, clearing the air,
hand fleetingly grazing Myrtle's on the desk.

"We are all alike in the sight of God," Myrtle said, wondering if Iffe had seen Travis's touch, as brief as lightning.

When Iffe left, Myrtle and Travis, both tired, went to bed.
Snuggled cozily in Myrtle's arms, Travis murmured drowsily,
"I'm experiencing something that I never have before."

"What is that, darling?" Myrtle's hand was a feather brush
in her hair.

"What it means to wear a mask."

"And to have one foot in and one foot out of the closet."

Travis closed her eyes, enjoying Myrtle's hands gliding
through her hair and down over her face. Now she knew why
cats liked to be stroked. She wanted to purr in contentment.

"Will you be able to come and sing for the March in September?"

Travis opened her eyes to meet the question in Myrtle's.
"You know I will." A will-o'-the-wisp smile flitted across her
face at the notion titillating her thoughts. "I think that I'll bring
Agnes. It would be good for her." Myrtle's caresses ceased,
and Travis laughed, reading her mind. Straightening up, she
bloomed a kiss on Myrtle's cheeks. "Have no fear. She'll stay
in a motel!"

They laughed together, Myrtle hugging her, a bundle of
fleece, nose muffled in the cap of curls smelling of coconut

oil. She breathed in the scent with copious whiffs, for it was Travis.

Moving her head, Travis's gaze swallowed her, as one lone fingertip copied the shape of her eyes, nose, and mouth. "I think that I'm falling in love with you."

Myrtle looked away from the woman with love in her eyes above her to peel apart the word love. There was love for Jesus, love for people, love for yourself, and love for a person. The last she frowned over. Had *she* really *loved* anyone? She liked being with Travis, holding her like this with her body melting against her own like heat. Was that love?

"I want to tell everybody how I feel about you!" Travis exhaled happily, smiling down at her. "Would that be so awful?"

Myrtle's arms tightened around her, hearing the warnings in her head. It would be, if everybody knew. All might be ruined for her. "Perhaps. Let it just be our secret. There are some not ready for us yet."

"We'll make them be," Travis insisted stubbornly, toying with Myrtle's earlobe.

Like making the Ku Klux Klan accept blacks, Myrtle thought wryly. "Be patient. Right now, I am involved in something very important to me—to us."

"Which means I'm secondary."

"You aren't listening—" Or understanding. Travis was one who put her emotional feelings first. She could afford to do that, for entertainers were not expected to be as circumspect as ministers—especially female ministers.

At the silence falling like a curtain between them, Travis drew away. "Don't—" Myrtle said, bringing her back, pelting kisses over her face like dew-glossed rose petals.

"Feel." Travis guided her hand below where the dampness was beginning.

In this curly brush of forest, Myrtle made a love song of her own. To it, Travis's heart beat in tune as she coiled like a snake around Myrtle.

"I like it better each time," she said, breath warm against Myrtle's mouth.

"Close your eyes, darling," Myrtle whispered, "and let me enter the pearly gates."

Chapter 21

*I*N a sparsely furnished two-bedroom South Nashville apartment, Rudy, in black silk monogrammed pajamas, stretched back on his king-sized water bed to read Wednesday morning's paper at four o'clock in the afternoon.

He was late waking up because he didn't get to bed until 9:00 A.M. Last night had been a good working one for Popora, and when she brought home a bundle of bread, it had put him in a good mood. They went to a bang-up coke party, and afterward he let her sleep with him for a change, having denied his affections to her for the past week. Withholding his loving was one of the tactics for keeping her in line, making her peddle tail harder to please him.

All the night and early morning fun had left him hung over, and the steady beating of the rain battering the windows didn't help in the least. Popora came in with a tray of food for him— steak, eggs, biscuits, and coffee. She put the tray on a corner table beside the TV. With arms crossed in the loose housecoat, she stayed to see if he wanted anything else.

Deliberately ignoring her, he let her stand there, not looking above the paper or acknowledging that she was in the room. Leisurely he turned the pages, aiming for the sports page and stock market reports for numbers tips. He had in mind to let the bitch wait until he was ready to say something to her.

Suddenly reading the page before him, he lost his affected coolness. "I be Goddamn! That woman preacher really meant what she said Sunday." The shaking of the paper indicated to Popora an oncoming rage. "She's goin' to have a March

Against Crime and Vice in the city..." he read aloud a part of the article.

Popora remained a mute statue as Rudy slammed his feet to the floor and began pacing up and down, scowling. "Look at them bitches!" He waved the paper at her so fast that all she could glimpse was a photograph of women posing together. "Bunch of crazy hags. Somebody needs to rape them and dump their asses in the Cumberland River." He stopped to glare at her. "You know what this means?"

Popora was more wrought up about whether she should keep her silence than what the picture meant. Rudy had the habit of talking to her, but not expecting a reply, like she was a backboard to sound his questions on.

"Do you?" A demand to respond.

She shook her head negatively, believing it to be the better of her two options. This way, she answered but said nothing.

"It means they're goin' to crack down on us pimps for a while to shut those bitches up and make themselves look clean. At this time, damnit, when we gittin' the tourist trade." He glowered at the picture again, then threw the paper on the bed.

Popora dug into her robe for a cigarette, found none, and left her hands buried in her pockets.

"That preacher got my used-to-be-woman all wrapped up in religion. *Born* again, shi-i-t! Up there in church singin' for *free*. On top of that, giving three thousand dollars to the *church*. Hell, I got to give it to that woman preacher"—he refused to call Myrtle by any other name—"she sure knows how to run a game. Pimpin' for Jesus!"

Popora wished he would stop ranting and raving about religion and the church, and eat his food which was getting cold. She had taken such pains to prepare the steak the way he liked it. Furthermore, she didn't want him feeling mean after the good time they had together last night. She watched him stop pacing to look out the water-smeared window. Because of the rain, the afternoon was dwindling fast into a dull, putrid gray. Thunder rumbled in the sky. A bad night for working. Maybe since she did so good yesterday, he would let her off.

In front of the window, he made slapping sounds with his fist in the palm of his hand, as his thoughts raced in anger. He wouldn't ever get over Travis kicking him out. She was the first woman to do that—and he vowed the last. He had let his game get out of hand. He was the one who was supposed to do the leaving, splitting, cutting out. And that Gloria, tricking him out of town. If he ran across *her* ass again, she was going to be one fucked up bitch. Turning away from the window, his eyes fell on the tray. "That shit's cold. Take it back and fix me some more."

Popora got out another steak and turned on the broiler. The kitchen was small and compact, equipped only with six glasses, a six-piece Woolworth set of plastic pink dishes, a couple of aluminum pots, and an iron skillet.

Rudy took more interest in buying clothes and paying for the Cadillac outside. Nevertheless, the place was a whole lot better than what she had before. Living on welfare with her mama, six brothers and sisters, and her son M.L.K., in the projects. They ate in shifts since there weren't enough dishes or food either.

Preparing the second tray, she moved slowly, tired from the previous night of working and partying. But it had been a fine night. Rudy had been nice to her for a change, taking her out and coming home and loving her. Brightening times like that were few in her life. She was beginning to feel weary, dispirited, and old. Not seventeen at all, more like one hundred and seventeen.

Beholding herself in the bathroom mirror this morning, she realized that her face was hardening, darkness fringed her eyes, and that she had lost some of her youthfulness since meeting Rudy in the station that day on the way to Knoxville. On the bus she had wondered what was wrong with him, cursing and running up and down the aisle, looking out the windows as if trying to see somebody. The driver had gotten mad and ordered him to sit down and shut up, or he was going to put him off and call the cops.

Grumbling, he sat down in the vacant seat beside her with M.L.K. curled in her lap. She could tell he was half-drunk, looking and smelling like he had been on a two-day binge. He slouched in the seat, muttering to himself about women being bitches until he fell asleep. He slept with his mouth open, tongue cherry red in a bearded face, head lolling from side-to-side with the jerking movements of the bus. Light snores emerged like distant fog horns.

When he awoke, he sat up, blinked and looked around, red eyes dazed. Noticing her, he smiled in recognition. "My, my!

It's sure nice wakin' up to a pretty little mama like you beside me. Makes me think I woke up in heaven with the angels!"

She blushed, pulling M.L.K. closer to her, keeping him out of the way. She thought Rudy was funny.

"Popora Bell King, didn't you say your name was back there at the bus station? And this is your son, M.L.K." He tickled M.L.K. under the chin. "Cute kid. Just like his mama. Where y'all headin'?"

"Knoxville," she said shyly.

"Well! What's a pretty thing like you goin' to do in Knoxville? Got some lucky dude waitin' there for you, I'll bet."

Embarrassed because she didn't, she said no in a half whisper. She wished there was someone waiting, a prince to carry her off and care for her and M.L.K. No prince was there, but a grandmother with whom she was going to live. Spurred further by his cagey questioning, she related this and more, while the Greyhound bus streaked through the countryside, hugging the road and passing everything on the highway with unyielding ease. It was making time, as Rudy was making time with her.

The family history spewed out of her, released by his warm attention and interest. She was born in Nashville and had dropped out of school after becoming pregnant with M.L.K. Tired of the same everyday monotony of poverty, waiting for welfare checks and stretching them, watching TV, baby-sitting for her mother in the imprisonment of the ghetto project surrounded with those like herself, she decided to leave. In Knoxville she was going to stay with her grandmother and find a job to make life better for herself and M.L.K.

Rudy listened sympathetically, nodding his head understandingly, making mental notes as he blew smoke rings vengefully toward the driver's thick black neck. At a rest stop, he invested his meager unspent change in hamburgers and soft drinks for them. With his willing ear and good-natured rapping, he made the trip less lonely and the end less fearful for her.

When the bus pulled into the Knoxville terminal, he decided to end his journey there, too. Getting off, he helped her with the bulging cardboard suitcase, holding all of her and M.L.K.'s belongings. He took her address and pledged that as soon as she got settled, he would be around to check on them.

The next day, he came by the single-story unpainted frame house in Lawnsdale where her grandmother lived. Her grandmother disliked him on first sight. In her "been living longer than you" sage advice to Popora, she psyched Rudy as a no-good nigger with a mean streak showing like a skunk; she could see it in his beady eyes. He wasn't nothing but a cockhound, which you could see by that lump sticking out in front of his pants. If he was any good, he'd wear a jockstrap.

Rudy didn't like her grandmother either, who was younger than most grandmothers, for she too had started out having babies at a tender age. She worked as a cook in a soul food restaurant where she saw all kinds of men and could smell a no-good apple ten feet away.

Since Rudy and her grandmother didn't like each other, Popora started going over to his place to see him. In the cheap, roach-infested, black-owned motel room he rented, she confided her problems and worries. He was patient, giving out an impression of wisdom and compassion as he heard her frustrations and woes over trying to find a job so she could get a place of her own. Rudy was her sole friend.

Inside two weeks, she knew that she was in love with him. One night in the cramped, peeling walls of the room, she kissed him and exhaled petals of love.

He laughed, pushing her away. "Girl, you know who you wantin' to make love to? *Me*—Rudolph Valentino Jones who's had some fine chicks. I come *high*. Now, if you want *me*, I can show you how you can make some money, and maybe then, we can get together."

She left M.L.K. with her grandmother, who wanted him to stay, and moved in with Rudy. By the end of the week, she was amazed to find out how much money she could make from what she had been giving away.

Back in bed again waiting for his food, Rudy puffed on a cigarette while thinking hard. Popora's banging of pans in the kitchen was phased out as he concentrated on a plan of action. Something definitely had to be done about those bitches running around loose harping on cleaning up the city. A simmering hatred for the woman preacher who started it burned through him like a forest fire on a dry, summer day. A *woman* preacher at that.

He had deliberately gone to her church that Sunday with his two classy whores, Lanette and Deidra, draped on both his arms, after reading in the paper that Travis was going to be there. He wanted her to see that he was where *he* wanted to be and not in Atlantic City or the gutter. Church had been a real trip, a regular circus with Travis crying and carrying on about Jesus. Then that woman preacher putting down her spiel, hugging and kissing people, getting all those converts in her stable.

But that woman preacher wasn't going to spoil his game in this town, not when he had built up a reputation as a boss mack. He had two foxy hookers, Deidra and Lanette, stashed in a pad in North Nashville, which he visited to dispense his favors and keep the situation cool. They worked out of the pads and motels. Popora stayed with him, for she was weak-minded. He caught on to this from the git-go when taking application on her during that bus ride. He had to keep her around to watch over her.

Everything had worked out fine since he came here. He wasn't about to pick up his women and leave for someplace else, like he had to in Knoxville when the city officials got holier-than-thou and clamped down, netting out jail sentences. Popora hadn't wanted to come back here where her family was, but who in the hell was she to tell him what she wanted to do. He had heard that the city was jumping, and money could be made in Music City, a place where the action was, and one which didn't hand out jail terms, but delighted in the revenue from whores' fines.

Luck and his own know-how made him a top nigger in no time. He pulled Lanette, a pretty yellow chick copped from King, into his stable with his fast-talking jive and good-fucking self, and his top star, white Deidra, once a go-go girl in Printer's Alley. In time, he was going to move in on King's other dealings, too. People were starting to know who he was—a top dude and smooth operator—because he knew that pussy ruled the world. Those Johns—black, white, poor, old, young, rich, lame, blind, and can't-get-'em-ups—proved it by how much they were willing to pay for it. Selling pussy was a business, and he was a businessman who got the commodity to the consumers. The success of the business showed there was a need for it. If there wasn't, he wouldn't be in business. Simple as that.

From the money his women brought in, he splurged on his wardrobe of silk shirts, tailor-made suits, jewelry, pastel socks, homburg hats, and alligator shoes. He had ordered a full-length, fur-trimmed leather coat for winter. His natty dressing had caused the boys to give him the name "The Sheik."

No sir, no stupid, square broads were going to ruin *his* business.

The cigarette was burned down, heating his fingers. He leaned to stab it out in the flaky ashtray on the floor. The movement redirected his thoughts to the matter at hand. He wanted a drink. "Bitch, bring me a drink!" he yelled to the kitchen. "Scotch, and hurry up with it."

Popora came on the double with a bottle of Johnnie Walker Black and a glass of ice. "Where the hell is my food? You sleeping in there?"

"It's ready, Rudy." She scurried back to the kitchen.

Disregarding the glass, he tilted up the bottle and drank from it. The rain continued to whiplash the windows. Popora bought in another tray of steak, eggs, and biscuits. The liquor set his thoughts aflame more. Getting up to eat, he carried the bottle to the table. Popora lingered around in case there was anything else he might want. He ate as if he were shoveling coal, loading his fork to dump food into his mouth, washing it down with liquor. The whole time he ate, his thoughts were fired by Myrtle. He had to stop her somehow. He would bet she was a bulldagger, with her church full of faggots, dykes, squares, and Jesus freaks, hugging on Travis like that while pretending to be praising the Lord.

Suddenly his eating movements stopped as a wide grin spread over his face. Snapping his fingers, he said, "I think I'll have a little talk with that faggot, Flaming Dark Sugar, who I saw hootin' and hollerin' in her church. I got to find out if she's what I think she is. And if so, I'm goin' to ruin her shit and *her*."

"What do you mean?" Popora asked, perplexed.

"Stupid!" he yelled at her. "I'll let everybody know she's a *bulldagger*. Then we'll see how much those high and mighty sanc-ti-mo-nious broads'll follow what she's puttin' down. I'll make her name stink like shit!"

Popora was stunned. The bulldaggers she knew on the streets were whores, or looked and dressed like men. The Reverend Myrtle Black didn't impress her like that.

"The Sheik ain't got no time for people gittin' in his way. I'm moving up. Soon as I move in on that simple pimp King's game, there won't be no stoppin' me. I'm goin' to be the biggest and baddest player in town!" Smiling with satisfaction, he poured another drink. "Now to get with that Flaming Dark Sugar."

Chapter 22

"*HUM-M-M*, this is the way I like to wake up in the morning," Travis murmured, luxuriating in the short nipping kisses Myrtle was bestowing upon her, sprinkles of dewdrops on her face.

"You taste like love." Myrtle mouthed on the jewel place where Travis's heart beat. An arm was thrown across Travis's naked body, entangled in the crumpled damp sheet.

Travis's hand smoothed the burnished brown of Myrtle's back. "We ought to join a nudist camp."

"You and your wild ideas." Myrtle's mouth opened wide to enclose a warm cave around one of Travis's breasts. Travis trembled, clutching Myrtle tightly, absently gliding a fingernail down the narrow path denting her spine.

Suddenly Myrtle broke away in a spasm of laughter. "Stop, that tickles!"

"Ah-ha! Now I know where you're ticklish!" Travis said gleefully, delighting in her discovery, repeating the playful torture while Myrtle squirmed, laughing, begging her to stop.

"You have found my weak spot!" Myrtle leaned back, breathless from laughter.

"Why—!" Travis feigned indignation, "I thought that *I* was your weak spot."

"You are, my darling." Myrtle kissed her reassuringly, a deliciously tormenting, slow and erotic kiss that left them weak, but wanting more. "See?"

Travis's mood unexpectedly became somber. "I'm going to miss you."

"Me, too."

"Me too *what?*"

"I am going to miss you, too," Myrtle translated against her temple.

Travis closed her eyes. "How much time do we have?" The eyes opened, misted with the thought of the void to come.

Myrtle turned her head slightly to see the clock. "Eight o'clock. Enough time. Your flight doesn't leave until four thirty-five."

Travis pushed her nose between the ravine of Myrtle's breast. "You smell like me."

"A good smell."

The tip of Travis's tongue flicked out to lick up the salty dampness she had caused on Myrtle during the night's loving. "You said that we have plenty of time." Her hand tangled and made a hard knot in the flow of Myrtle's hair, loose down her body.

Myrtle gently pushed Travis back and raised up on an elbow to take in the whole of her with the camera of her eyes.

Travis smiled, lowering her lids sexily. "Shameless hussies. We did this practically all night, and here we are, waking up horny again."

"Two horny people at morning's early light—" Myrtle sang, substituting words to an old song. Partings incited passion among lovers.

"One can sing, too!" Travis quipped. "I want to make love again and again, all the way up to the time the plane leaves, on up to the runway!"

Myrtle smiled, enjoying the sensuous fire kindled by Travis's feather light lips roving her face. "Shall we start now?" Saying this, she did, locking in all parts of Travis's body with her own, the visible and invisible, arms folded wings engulfing her.

"You mean... like this?" Travis began moving her body up and down in slow, measured patterns. Underlying lips met, merged, and stroked with slender spears converging together in a manner distinctive to them, the friction of movements extending electrical currents of ecstasy between them.

Travis embraced Myrtle, her shaft of fire. "Talk to me, please—"

Myrtle brought her mouth to the core of Travis's ear, sucked tenderly on the lobe, and blew a whiff of warm breath into the hollow of it. Keeping her mouth close to the crevice, her voice siphoned low, funneling an intonation of a Sapphic muse into the depths of Travis.

"You, my darling, are beautiful. Lovely! You feel so good to me in my arms, my angel—soft, wonderfully sweet. I rejoice in making love to you, sinking into the core of you to become you, too. I can feel the length, breadth, magnitude of you, the roundness of your breasts entwined with mine, the fullness of your stomach bedding me, the pillars of your thighs, the hairy, crispness of the most intimate flower of you, the wet flush of your face against mine, the love-heat of your body. I love being with you, holding you, wanting you, inflaming you, *having* you! I want to taste the nectar of you with my lips and tongue. Like this . . . like this!"

Travis moaned and writhed to the soporific chant of Myrtle's love ode, inducing a narcotic opiate of somnolent magic. "My lover . . . yes, like that . . . like that! It feels so good. Jesus . . . *Jesus!*" She cried out on the thrashing waves of her breath, clutching Myrtle in a mercurial steel vise of shattering emotions, strangling on her voice and words as she was carried to the highest plateau of loving.

Myrtle loved her until the tremors ceased in a feeble, delicate, final quake. Then she kissed her gently and held her like a goddess of love.

On the way to the airport, Myrtle drove with one hand, for Travis was holding tightly to the other. Both were tired, exhausted, satiated with lovemaking.

"I'll call you as soon as I get home," Travis said, splintering the stagnant, forlorn silence.

"Will you be back for the March?" A plea leaked out in Myrtle's question.

"I'll be there. I wouldn't miss it. I have to fill that Vegas slot, or Agnes will have a fit."

"No more guilty feelings about the music?"

"I'm leaving all my guilty feelings in the hands of my minister. And such nice hands they are!" Travis toyed with Myrtle's fingers, kissing each one individually. "They're beautiful lovers—all five of them."

"They have something beautiful to love." A car honked warningly in passing. "See, you vamp, you made me leave my lane!"

Travis patted the cleavage between Myrtle's thighs, leaving

an invisible hand-print creasing the flowered dress. "Take care
of Patsy for me."

"Cut it out! Why Patsy?"

"Because I like patting it!"

"You had better stop, or I will be forced to find a deserted
road."

Travis looked pensive. "If you need anything—money for
the church or March—let me know."

For reply, Myrtle kissed her hand.

"I hate good-byes."

"This one is not forever." Myrtle turned off Briley Parkway
to the Metro Airport, passing the Cambridge Square apartments
and cluster of service stations, motels, and restaurants.

Bobby was waiting for them. "Good timing. The motel
limousine just dropped me off."

Myrtle hoped he wasn't angry because she hadn't picked
him up. She and Travis had wanted to be alone, even for that
short amount of time, with no intrusions.

Travis and Bobby checked their luggage, and while Bobby
waited for his claim check, Travis gave Myrtle a covert look
of love. Myrtle walked up to the gate with them to be with
Travis as long as she could, until the sky separated them in
their farewell.

Restless, Agnes wandered haphazardly around her living
room, forging patterns by her repetitive movements of lighting
a cigarette, putting it out half-smoked, refilling her glass with
scotch, and firing another cigarette.

Her tenseness, although she would have denied it, was gen-
erated by the anticipation of Travis's arrival that evening. She
had not yet admitted to herself that she missed her, but those
few days Travis had been away seemed an excessive amount
of time.

Rhoda, curled up in a snowy white fuzzy ball on the sofa,
watched her surrogate mistress curiously. She had been to the
vet and properly poodle-groomed for the homecoming—
bathed, dipped, hair and toenails clipped. Almost as if there
were a mental connection of thoughts between them, Agnes
went over to sit by her and pat her head.

"Your mama will be home soon, Rhoda," she said, thinking
she had talked more to Rhoda than people the past few days.
Rhoda had helped to break the monotony by taking her for

walks and rides. Rhoda liked to ride, leaning her fluffy head out the window, eyes alerted to the scenes passing in motion, air flooding her nostrils.

Agnes raised her glass, drinking without the effects of a high. With her thoughts working like this, sometimes she never even got a buzz on, no matter how much she drank. Weighing the time spent while Travis was away, it wasn't all wasted or fruitless, in spite of the dullness. She had performed long overdue business functions—putting accounts in order, collecting rent, paying bills, answering correspondence, looking into bookings, and conferring with Travis's publicity agency. For her social life, she had been out to dinner a couple of times.

Travis must have been engaging in more excitement than she, and obviously didn't miss her or Rhoda since she had postponed her return. Over the telephone, Agnes could detect an animation that hadn't been there when Travis had gone. Being with the Reverend must have done some good. Whatever it was, she was keeping her fingers crossed that it wouldn't interfere with Travis's singing career.

Mechanically she stroked Rhoda, who made low sounds of contentment. Rhoda enjoyed being petted and shown love the same as people. She started to light a cigarette, stopped and retrieved the glass from the coffee table. Rhoda sniffed at the glass and retreated to the foot of the sofa. Agnes guessed liquor fumes reminded her of unpleasant parties in the past.

Her mind went back to recapture the broken thread of her thoughts of love, a sentiment she found difficult to come to grips with. Dogs liked to be loved and so did Travis, as she had amply demonstrated by her recurring love affairs. At that reflection, a thunderbolt of apprehension jarred Agnes. Had Travis fallen in love with somebody while she was out of town? There was no mistaking the happy lilt in her voice.

She set the glass down and Rhoda eased back to curl warmly against her. Agnes smoothed her back. Loving animals was different from loving people. There was less to give and less to take and, foremost, loyalty. Animals did not hurt loved ones. Love for people, too, was fine, for those who had time for the luxury.

Taking note of her empty glass, she moved Rhoda aside, got up and went to the kitchen to splash liquor over ice. She didn't drink as much when Travis was around, primarily because she was too engrossed in looking after her. Her existence was centered around Travis, personal and otherwise. She had become bound up in Travis, more than Travis with her.

She went into the living room again and put the glass on the table. "Life's a bitch," she assessed, peering out the window at the graying New York skyline.

Sensing her morbid musing, Rhoda whined, jumped off the couch and came over to her. "We miss her, Rhoda," she finally acknowledged. "It won't be long before we go to meet her."

As if understanding, Rhoda wagged her tail and licked Agnes's hand.

Chapter 23

F RIDAY night, Rudy caught Flaming Dark Sugar between shows. He took Popora along to keep away the cruising fags. Displaying what he considered his most winning smile, he invited Flaming Dark Sugar to their table for a drink. He didn't spend money on fruits, but this was business.

"You're somethin' else on that stage," Rudy said, thinking Flaming Dark Sugar in that black wig and sequined gown looked better than Popora. "I'll bet you'd knock them out on the West Coast. Why you want to stay 'round here?"

"I like it here," Flaming Dark Sugar said, bracelet hand languidly holding a smoking cigarette. He had heard of "The Sheik," and was wary of him. In the back of his mind, he was trying to determine the reason behind Rudy's sociability. There had to be an angle somewhere. One thing for sure, he wasn't going to let Rudy con him into doing any freak tricks for him. He hated pimps. One beat him up a long time ago, accusing him of ruining his whore's play. He couldn't help it if the dude had preferred him.

"I guess this is a pretty nice place for you to be, since you got religion and all." Halfway turned in his chair, Rudy feigned an interest in the disco dancing. "I got to give it to that woman preacher—she's got a good thing goin' for her with that church."

"She's a wonderful minister," Flaming Dark Sugar said, eyes steady on Rudy. He had barely touched his drink. "She appeals to my sensitivity. You see"—he smiled at Popora, drawing her silence into the conversation—"I'm a female allusionist. I can *relate* better to women, for I am one in fantasy. I admire the Reverend Myrtle Black as a minister and woman."

Popora seemed fascinated by Flaming Dark Sugar. If it weren't for his tenor voice, and her knowing, she would have sworn he was a female. The beer left an acrid taste in her mouth.

"Have you been to my church?" Flaming Dark Sugar questioned Popora.

"Naw, she ain't," Rudy answered for her, cuing Popora to stay voiceless. She was here as a prop, not a partaker. Shaking the ice in his glass, Rudy undertoned confidentially: "Is it true what I've heard about her?"

Flaming Dark Sugar's eyes half closed as he blew out a streak of smoke. "I don't know what you've heard."

Grinning lopsidedly, Rudy said, "That she's a bulldagger."

Slowly, Flaming Dark Sugar put out his cigarette, twisting it into a coiled tobacco twig. "Oh, honey, now wouldn't that be just *beautiful* if she was?" Laughing he stood up. "Thanks for the drink. I have to get ready for the next show. Have fun!"

Watching him slip smoothly through the dancers, Rudy spat out: "Damn cocksucker!"

Shuddering, Popora finished her beer. She hated to see him angry. It meant a rough night for her.

"Birds of a feather stick together. Com'on, let's get out of here."

It had begun to rain, an unexpected warm weather deluge. Hurrying to the car, the water soaked Popora's one and only dress.

Drying out at home, Rudy changed into silk lounging pajamas, and Popora put on her old housecoat. Opening a fresh bottle of scotch, Rudy began pacing the floor, immersed in his thoughts of Myrtle. "That fag don't have to admit to me she's a dyke." He stopped to light a cigarette from a gold monogrammed lighter. The flame shot up like a spear. The flickering fire held his attention for a long moment before he put it out. "What I ought to do is burn down her church with *her* in it!"

Popora opened her mouth to cry out: "Oh, no!" But managed to choke the words back. *Burn a church and the preacher!* She could hear her heart palpitating fiercely within her chest in disapproval. That would be the devil's evil work. Despite the fact that she had quit going to church long ago, she considered herself a Christian. The idea of what Rudy intended to do made her flesh crawl.

"What the hell you standin' there lookin' at me like that for?" he glowered. "G'wan and put some clothes on. It's git-down time."

"Rudy, it's raining cats and dogs out there," she whined, startled at herself.

As if all of the frustrations he had encountered that evening were directed at her, his fist shot out knocking her to the floor. "Bitch, didn't I take you out and spend money on you? Now git up and git out!"

In a few minutes, Popora was back in her working outfit of tight hot pants revealing sprigs of curly black pubic hair, halter, bare midriff, and boots. Her Afro was covered with a brown wig, and fresh blue eye shadow and lipstick had been applied. She pulled on a cheap, clear plastic raincoat and umbrella. The rain on the roof sounded a dirge in her ears.

Sprawled on the bed with a drink in his hand, Rudy didn't even look up when she left.

Popora walked slowly in the rain which had thankfully slackened. In a strange way, the wetness felt good to her, like baptismal water purifying her from Rudy. Her boots made squishing noises on the pavement. The streets were deserted and dark, illuminated only by the streetlights and neon signs. The liquor store and bar signs were the brightest.

She had been out on the block thirty minutes and hadn't turned a trick. A black Chevy cruised up beside her with two white men in it. She slowed down, surveying them out of the corner of her eyes. The one on the passenger's side rolled his window down and called to her. They looked suspicious. She had been busted once and Rudy had gotten her out. Head straight ahead, she quickened her steps. The car drove on into the rain pit of night.

Being inside might be better. The desolate rain and lonely streets were making her sadder. Lately, she had been getting depressed. Thinking of M.L.K. was part of it. Rudy gave her money to send back to her grandmother for him, but she would rather have him with her. This was the first time they had been separated. He was everything that was entirely hers. She never told the social worker who the daddy was—Michael Lang, the math teacher, who made her stay after school one day for misbehaving in class. He offered to give her a lift home, and on the way, took her to his apartment. The visits progressed into regular ones. Due to M.L.K.'s daddy being "somebody"— a school teacher—she wanted her son to be "somebody," too. She named him Martin Luther King, initials after his daddy, M.L., combined with her last name, which also gave him the name of the greatest black person she had heard of. She wanted to get out of the life someday and raise her son right. Rudy had promised her this, as soon as they got enough money.

She went into the Rooster Lounge, where there were only two regular male customers drinking and talking to Charlie, the bartender. The air conditioner was on, but the place was stuffy and steam fogged the windows. The lounge was the hangout for pimps, their women, as well as a front for pushing dope, collecting numbers, and a market for boosters. On weekends, it was an oasis of fun and gaiety and activity. She didn't spot any macks tonight at their corner of the bar rapping and bulljiving among themselves. One of the men, nearest the juke-box, put some money in and Travis Lee came up singing "Love, Love, Love." She paid for a beer and took it back to a table by the door. Lighting a cigarette, she smoked and waited.

The door swung open and Earthly Treasure breezed in pro-tected by a red vinyl raincoat and floppy hat pulled down around her face. She closed a black umbrella, which spattered rain puddles on the floor, and headed for the bar.

From the time Rudy had copped Lanette, Popora was ill at ease around Earthly Treasure, King's bottom woman, and went out of her way to bypass her. She liked Earthly Treasure; most everybody did. Earthly Treasure had been nice to her when she first started out here on the streets, giving her advice to keep herself safe. Earthly Treasure didn't have to do that, but she did, laughing about how young and green Popora was.

Remembering what Rudy had bragged about before she left, Popora was more uncomfortable than ever. She dropped her eyes to the foam in her beer, hoping Earthly Treasure hadn't seen her, but she had. The flash of red was back with a gin sling to sit with her.

"Bad-assed night," Earthly Treasure groaned, taking a long taste of her drink. Picking up Popora's cigarette from the ash-tray, she lit one from it. "What you lookin' so down in the mouth for? Tricks that bad tonight?"

Popora shrugged, drinking out of the side of her mouth that wasn't sore from Rudy's fist. By rights, Earthly Treasure shouldn't be speaking to her because of what Rudy had done to King.

"You look like you done lost your coochie-patch," Earthly Treasure guffawed, heavy lips wide in laughter. "Long's you got that down there, you in biz'ness." To Popora's lack of response, Earthly Treasure's popeyes softened. "Somethin' the matter, honey?" Her black hand covered Popora's clamped around the beer mug.

The contact was tender and comforting, the kind of touch that spoke of woman's concern for woman. Warmth flowed through her like those rare intervals when her mother held her protectively against her bosom if things went wrong. She had the impression of being a little girl again, placing herself in the hands of someone who cared, someone she could confide in. The long-stored tears finally broke over the dam.

Earthly Treasure squeezed her hand. "Cry, honey. Help yourself to a good cry. We got to cry sometimes, or we might forgit we human, too." She reached into her purse and handed Popora a Kleenex. "You knocked up? Got the clap? Or cut loose?"

Popora's head wagged negatively, meaning that it was none of those things. Earthly Treasure was being kind to her when she shouldn't be. Kindness was a benevolence Popora realized she'd lost along the way.

Without aforethought, Popora told on Rudy. As she explained, he was mad at the woman preacher, called her a bulldagger, and said that he was going to hurt her. He even talked of setting her church on fire. Popora was frightened, for preachers and churches were holy, and the wrath of God might strike them both dead.

Earthly Treasure's eyes bulged. She was on the way to lifting her glass, but she had seemed paralyzed. That man must be crazy to want to do something like that. Above all, to the church where her old friend, Heavenly Delight, worked for Reverend Myrtle Black, who had gotten her off the streets. Bulldagger or not, she would never forget how Reverend Myrtle Black came to the hospital and prayed for them, brought her smokes before King did.

Caught in the waterfall of her words, Popora's exposé continued. "He's going to move in on King's numbers and dealin's too!" Quickly her hand pressed over her mouth. She had talked too much.

Shrewdly sensing her alarm, Earthly Treasure's face went blank at the last, pretending she hadn't heard. The girl was trembling like a leaf, alarmed at her betrayal. "Popora, drink your drink. Make you feel better. Ever'thin's goin' to be all right."

Popora tried to drink the beer gone flat, which went down like swill. She wiped her face with the Kleenex a second time, careful not to mess up her false eyelashes. With the mirror in her compact, she applied a thick, new layer of powder and lipstick. Their cigarettes had burned to nubs in the tray, forgotten during the talking. She pushed them around in the gray ashes, smothering them. Ashes to ashes, a requiem to life.

The same customer stuffed more money in the jukebox. Travis Lee did an encore. Earthly Treasure cocked an ear toward the music, tapping a finger on the table with the beat. "Travis Lee belongs to that church. I like her singin'," she said vacantly, lifting her glass.

A white man came in, baseball jacket halfway zipped, cap low, faded bell bottom jeans flapping sails over muddy brown shoes. Chewing on the bottom end of a match, he looked over Earthly Treasure and Popora. At the bar, he ordered a beer.

"Straight from the boondocks and out to change his luck with some dark meat," Earthly Treasure sized up. "You go on. My night off. Got comp'ny down there," she grinned.

Popora threw off her raincoat, lit another cigarette, and went to the jukebox to scan the selections. Standing by it, she began to dance and sway sexily to the music, eyes half-closed, cigarette a torch between her fingers.

The white man, who had come in, eyed her shapely brown legs, tarried at her groin where the lips of her sex creased and pinched the shorts. Licking his lips, he got up and crossed the room to her. Seeing him through lowered lids, Popora knew that she had broke-luck for the night.

Chapter 24

RUDY slowly drove down the block, taking in the physical structure of the Reverend Myrtle Black's church. A flurry of Monday morning activity surrounded it with telephone and delivery trucks pulling in and out. One car, which he took to belong to the woman preacher, remained parked. It had a minister's sticker on it.

Cruising along, he made a mental map of the neighborhood. The church was on the corner with a parking lot on the side. There were a few second-rate stores in the vicinity, a shoe shop, mom-and-pop grocery, and dry cleaners interspersed between older homes. He had decided that he would do the job himself. It would give him personal satisfaction, and too, it wasn't always safe to have too many involved.

This kind of operation called for a well-designed plan, utilizing the skills he employed when getting a new whore into his stable. He would take his time. First off would be the harassment of the woman preacher. Treat her like he did his whores, scare the bejesus out of her. Badger her to no end like a cat playing with a mouse.

The thoughts stimulated him to the point of an erection. He reached down and tugged at the bulge in his pants, which represented his alter ego, his livelihood. He could never figure out why women wanted to go to bed with each other, pretending they had something which they didn't. He knew some of the whores did it together, but his male chauvinistic logic based it on the fact that there were no men around.

He wouldn't hate that woman preacher so much if she

weren't a woman-lover, getting Travis into her fold. She was messing up his program. He intended to make enough money from his whores to go back one day to Travis, looking big, bad, and rich. Then gloat when she begged him to come back. He had no doubt in his mind that she would beg. This vision of return-and-conquer was his layout for the future. Afer a certain age, pimps wore out, too, like whores.

The sun made a purple cast against the tinted windows of the Cadillac. He would make a second circling of the block and leave, not wanting to become conspicuous. Nearing the church again, he saw Heavenly Delight going out the back door to empty trash. She had on a cleaning outfit with a dust rag covering her head. He snorted in disgust. Just think, a whore giving up the easy life of spreading her legs to clean up. That bulldagger must sure put down a mean rap.

Stopping at a light, he noticed a gas station a block away with a phone booth outside. It was time now to let that woman preacher know he could put something down, too.

In the basement of the church, Heavenly Delight helped Myrtle to arrange the new office furniture and put away supplies. "Reverend, you say this is goin' to be the March headquarters," Heavenly Delight said, pausing to look around proudly at their morning's progress.

"Yes. People will be coming in and out of here everyday until the March."

"That's sure goin' to be a big day, Reverend."

"It will be a high point for our church, Heavenly Delight."

The phone rang and Heavenly Delight laughed. "Phone's just been put in and people callin' already."

"Answer it, please," Myrtle said, arms full.

"It's for you, Reverend."

The voice was a man's, gruff, obviously disguised. It uttered threats and obscenities at her. Myrtle hung up quickly, cutting him off.

"Anythin' wrong, Reverend?" Heavenly Delight shot Myrtle a searching glance.

"No—a crank call." She tried to smile reassuringly. She could bounce off the threats against the church and March, but not the vile name-calling directed at her. No one had ever head-on called her a bulldagger, the coarse street epithet. It had left her shaken. "We will be getting some of those. But don't worry, we will put our trust in the Lord."

* * *

Arriving home with the phone call plaguing her, Myrtle didn't have much of an appetite for supper. She prepared a light salad and glass of iced tea. Eating in the living room, she mulled over the dilemma of being who and what she was. Living in the shadow of her sex life was beginning to become more and more of a burden. She could relieve it by coming out, by admitting. If she did this, she was confident that there would be loyal church followers who would stay with her. But to do this *before* the March could be disastrous. She could predict the cries of I-told-you-so's and I-thought-it with the troops deserting—this foremost coming from the blacks, whom she needed. Following one like her, to them, meant you had to be one, too. Times were critical when a person's sex life overshadowed all else.

She finished the salad and drank her tea with the quietness of the apartment inducing further ruminations. Already she was beginning to miss Travis. Missing someone was a new experience for her. She ought to get a dog or cat, now that she was stationary. She moved to turn on the TV, but stopped. What she really wanted to do was to call Travis.

Succumbing to the urge, she reached for the phone. When Travis answered, the response hit her heart like a dart. Myrtle smiled into the phone: "Hello, my darling."

"Myrtle, I was just thinking about you!" Travis sounded pleased.

"I am glad. That means we were thinking about each other. Are you all right?"

"Of course, except for being lonely without you."

Travis was lonely too. She felt relief. "I miss you."

"How—how do you miss me?" A mischievous laugh through space.

"I miss the feel and touch of you. I miss your perfume, those smoldering eyes looking into mine, the way you curl into me when asleep—"

"Hum-m-m," Travis murmured over the wire, "tell me more. I'm lying on the couch and visualizing you here beside me."

"I wish that I could be there, then I could do what I want."

"Like what?"

Myrtle closed her eyes tightly, the love-ache surging through her, pressing down, down, down, spreading a fine web of fire as the words came out almost in a whisper. "Kiss you, run my hands over that fine luscious body while I breathe my passion on your face and kiss the tips of your breasts. Holding you close to me to make you want me as I want you. I miss the clinging hotness of us together—of me into you—to show how I feel, and make you happy in my happiness."

"Oh-h-h-h!"

Myrtle heard Travis's gasp over the telephone, one she had heard when they were in bed together and the world came to an end. The cry made her shudder into a moment of blinding weakness. Finally she spoke: "Travis—?" A wee search over miles. She listened to the strangled laughter.

"Myrtle, darling...I didn't know making love over the telephone could be so enjoyable!"

Neither did she know that she could care so much. "Good night, my dear. Sleep and dream of me." Hanging up, Myrtle sat immobile, overcome by the strength of her emotions. The evening was waning, shading the room.

She got up to close the blinds. As she did, she caught sight of a man across the street staring up at her window. He had a broadbrim white hat pulled low over his eyes. Seeing her, he turned quickly down the street.

Far into the night, the phone rang, awakening her. The same guttural voice repeated its verbal abuse. Lying awake in the early dawn hours, it suddenly came to her that the man in the street resembled Rudy.

Chapter 25

*E*ARTHLY Treasure sat pensively at the kitchen table drinking gin, oblivious for a change to the pulsating bass of her neighbor's record player invading the walls. She had started drinking early in the evening to placate the moody feeling of depression that had become increasingly pervasive ever since talking with Popora last week. Their conversation had lingered like a singing mosquito in her ear.

Tonight she didn't feel like going out into the funky streets to turn a trick, and she *wasn't*. Being King's bottom woman gave her that leeway, long as she didn't fall short on bringing in the money. King kept this apartment and let her stay in it alone, mainly because he used it for other transactions and needed her there to help take care of business.

King had been her sole pimp, and at this stage in the game she couldn't conceive of life without him. The years together, which were short but seemed long, hadn't been easy. She had her knocks and bruises to prove it. Yet he was her man, and she loved him. He was all she had.

She was happy for Heavenly Delight getting out of the life. She doubted if Heavenly Delight would have made it without the Rev supporting her. Lifting her glass high, Earthly Treasure toasted Heavenly Delight for achieving what some whores dreamed of doing, but never did.

She lit a cigarette, blowing out a gale of smoke through her nostrils. That Rudy sure must hate the Rev's holy guts, especially if she was a bulldagger. Black men despised women lovers, for they were a threat to them. Bulldagger or not, *she* liked the Rev. Anyway, what difference did it make? There were plenty of male preachers in town who were out-and-out fags.

Earthly Treasure refilled her glass, stirring the remaining half-melted ice cubes. Being in the streets, she knew that some men were just naturally crazy, but Rudy was one for the books. It was bad enough having white folks burn down black churches and hurting black preachers. But niggers, too?

She realized that King didn't like Rudy, who was younger, better looking, and a go-getter. Rudy was becoming a menace to him. She had witnessed others in the past who had been also, but King, in his methodical way, managed to get rid of them.

For a brooding period of time, Earthly Treasure fitfully smoked and drank, while assessing the situation. Eventually, what she had to do loomed before her. God didn't like doing ugly to good people, and neither did she. She could make decisions, too, although King would never admit it.

Rising from the table, she pounded angrily on the wall, her signal to turn the damn music down. Emptying the ashtray and setting her glass in the sink, she prepared to pay Heavenly Delight a visit.

Heavenly Delight had just turned off the small black-and-white portable TV set she was buying on time, and was about to let out the sofa bed, when the knock came on her door.

Rarely did she have company in the little place she rented, attached to one of the church member's rambling, old-fashioned houses. She had her own entrance at the side, and was careful about whom she invited to visit, making sure that no past friends from the life were informed, only present ones she had made at the church, now her life. She wondered who it was at this time of night.

"Who is it?" she asked through the door.

"It's me, Earthly Treasure."

Surprise seized Heavenly Delight in a tight vise, preventing her from answering immediately.

"Heavenly Delight—" Earthly Treasure called again.

"Un-hun." A bare squeak managed to come from her. What was Earthly Treasure wanting with her? A slew of thoughts cycled through her head, totally devastating, bad, ominous. She hadn't seen Earthly Treasure since they got out of the

hospital together and went to court for something they were
completely innocent of that time. They had to pay a fine, but
the law couldn't catch the ones who shot them.

"I got to talk to you 'bout somethin' important."

"You by yo'self?" Heavenly Delight had the presence of
mind to ask cautiously. She didn't want nobody setting her
up—namely Sticks, getting back at her for leaving him.

"Yeah—let me in."

Heavenly Delight removed two chains from their bolts and
took out a key to unlock the dead latch.

Earthly Treasure was there in person, smelling of gin and
cigarettes. "How you doin'?" Her face expanded into a broad
smile, for she was indeed happy to see Heavenly Delight.

"I'm fine. How you doin'?" Heavenly Delight responded
in kind, peeking warily into the darkness behind Earthly Treasure before she let her in. Swiftly she replaced the chains and
locked the door. "Sit down."

Earthly Treasure sat on an overstuffed chair with a print
throw cover and looked around. A faded picture of Heavenly
Delight's mother, now dead, in a five-and-dime frame was on
the dresser. At the end of the couch, which became the head
of the bed when let out, was a large calendar with a picture
of Jesus holding a lamb. A Bible was on the table beside the
clock–radio. The high-ceilinged room was small, but clean
and neat, decorated with fresh wallpaper of pink roses. A portable electric fan hummed in the one window.

"You want somethin'? Tea or coffee?" Heavenly Delight
asked politely. It was a long way to her place from where
Earthly Treasure lived. She thought that there must really be
a reason for her coming.

"Got any gin?" Earthly Treasure asked, smiling unevenly.

Heavenly Delight frowned, puzzled as to whether Earthly
Treasure was being serious or funny. "Don't drink no more
since I'm back in the church." She wanted her to know that
she had had church upbringing in the past, regardless of what
happened afterward.

"Soft drink?"

"Sure, got that." Heavenly Delight went into her pantry-
sized kitchen.

Earthly Treasure could see her looking in the refrigerator.
"Cute place you got here," she said, taking the can of Seven-
Up and glass Heavenly Delight held out to her.

"Thanks." Heavenly Delight seemed to loosen at the compliment, face showing pleasure. "Reverend Myrtle Black got it for me. The people who own the house have a grocery store down the street. Real respectable folks."

Earthly Treasure blinked. Nobody was respectable. Heavenly Delight should know that from all those so-called respectable weirdoes she had gotten money from. Earthly Treasure did not speak her mind.

"What you want to see me 'bout?" Heavenly Delight perched on the sofa near the lamp.

The light's glare brought her into full view. Scrutinizing her, Earthly Treasure envied her looking young again, less haggard, clear face devoid of makeup. Her hair was rolled for bed. One thing about Heavenly Delight, she would keep that hair pretty with the blonde stuff in it. Before lighting a cigarette, she started to ask if she could smoke, but changed her mind and went on and lit it. She *wasn't* smoking a joint.

Leaning forward, Earthly Treasure began pointedly: "This is hush-hush. If I ever hear 'bout where you got it from, I'm goin' to lie."

Heavenly Delight turned the fan's button from medium to low so she could hear better, for Earthly Treasure was talking real soft. She could spot by the way Earthly Treasure's bulbous eyes were fixed on her and the serious look on her face that this was something important.

"What is it?" Heavenly Delight questioned, dreading the answer.

"Rudy—The Sheik. You heard of him."

Heavenly Delight's lips mouthed a yes. Who hadn't? She had been surprised to hear that he had been a friend of Travis Lee.

Earthly Treasure drank some of the soda, wishing it were gin. Taking a long drag on her cigarette, she squinted over the smoke at Heavenly Delight. "He's plannin' on doin' somethin' bad to your Rev and her church. Talkin' 'bout burnin' the church down. He's mad at her 'cause of the March and for stirrin' up trouble."

Heavenly Delight sat stunned.

"You hear me?" Earthly Treasure asked loudly, for Heavenly Delight was sitting like a mummy, eyes wide, mouth agape.

"I heard you," Heavenly Delight finally managed to whisper.

"I thought you ought to know," Earthly Treasure continued softly. "Rev's been good to you—good to me when I was in that hospital flat on my back, layin' there hurtin'. What other preacher in town came to pray for us two whores?"

Heavenly Delight shuddered, hating the past, the remembrance of which she had blacked out, only now to have Earthly Treasure open it up again. She loathed the word Earthly Treasure had used of what she had been.

"Shouldn't noboby hurt a woman of God and her church," Earthly Treasure asserted emphatically, reflecting on what she said and liking it. She was proud of herself for what she was doing, almost like being saved. Doing this should get her a star in heaven. Lord knows, she needed one.

"Thanks for tellin' me, Earthly Treasure."

Happy, Earthly Treasure momentarily envisioned herself a saint. She thought about the name her mama had given her—Earthly Treasure—a longtime joke among her young schoolmates and friends. At this moment, it was a name she deserved. Way back there, she and Heavenly Delight used to get high and sad, too, with it, cursing their names, a mockery to follow them the rest of their lives. Sitting here, she could see nothing bad was meant by it. That was what they were to their mamas at the time of their birth—a heavenly delight and an earthly treasure.

They sat in silence with their thoughts. They had been together before, but not like this, where respect and liking poured between them in the strength of knowing each other. Earthly Treasure was glad that she had come. She had faith in Heavenly Delight, who would handle what she told her in the right way. Heavenly Delight had a smart head on her.

Earthly Treasure stayed a while longer in the company of her old friend. As they talked of school and growing up days, nostalgia blinded Earthly Treasure's eyes. In that brief encounter, they were two young and innocent school girls anew.

The bubble burst and the fantasy disappeared. She had to go. "Call me a cab?" Earthly Treasure asked, finishing her soda and stubbing out the cigarette in the one ashtray in the room.

The cab came, its horn sounding loudly on the quiet street.

"Take care of yo'self," Heavenly Delight said, hoping she would.

"Got to do *that* for my King!" Earthly Treasure laughed, back in the dregs of her life. "Bye." She kissed Heavenly Delight. "Girl, you lookin' good!"

Going down the steps to the waiting taxi, Earthly Treasure heard Heavenly Delight bolt the door. Before getting into the cab, she took a deep breath. Telling King the other part wasn't going to be as easy.

Chapter 26

MYRTLE was pleased by the progress in setting up the March headquarters. They had a volunteer staff, except for Barbara, who was paid by Myrtle to be her personal secretary.

Everything was going smoothly, save for the continuous hounding calls of the past two weeks. They came in the middle of the night, and sometimes during the day at church. Apparently, someone was keeping close tabs on Myrtle's movements.

The calls were making her edgy, and the uneasiness was becoming evident by the darkness beneath her eyes and her increasingly frequent brusqueness with people. Around females, she became restrained, careful of any looks that might be misinterpreted, and of being alone with them. She did not want to have any erroneous instances which could point to impropriety.

Her tormentor was causing her to become nearly paranoid. When she looked into faces, she was beginning to imagine hidden sneers of knowingness. And when her back was turned, she fancied furtive labeling whispers about her. It was like an unseen forest fire creeping up behind to engulf.

Saturday morning, unable to sleep, she arose early to go to her church and bury herself in work. Keeping busy helped to relieve some of the pressure on her, along with the telephone calls from Travis. She hadn't told Travis about the threats. There was no need to have her distressed miles away.

Heavenly Delight also came earlier than usual to work, surprised and glad to see Myrtle sitting at her desk. "Reverend

Black, you must've got up with the birds. You had somethin'
to eat? There's coffee and doughnuts in the kitchen I can get
for you."

"Thanks, Heavenly Delight, but not now."

Heavenly Delight turned on more lights to brighten up the
basement. "You look like you workin' too hard, Reverend
Black," she observed, eyeing Myrtle with concern.

"That is the only way you get things done, Heavenly Delight—by working hard."

Behind her, Myrtle heard Heavenly Delight grunting fitfully
to herself as she opened the utility closet. It was a while before
she realized that Heavenly Delight had stopped her cleaning
and was hovering over her. Looking up, she asked, "Did you
want something?"

Heavenly Delight's hand tightened around the broom handle. "Reverend Black, I got somethin' to tell you." With con-
straint, for she did not want to upset her any more than she
had to, Heavenly Delight relayed what Earthly Treasure had
told her the night before.

Myrtle listened quietly, not surprised, putting the pieces of
the puzzle together, berating herself for not fingering Rudy as
a prime suspect all along.

"He's sayin' some awful things 'bout you, too." Heavenly
Delight did not go on to reveal what they were. She looked up
to and loved her minister, whom she had chosen to follow.
Wasn't anything going to turn her away.

"I know," Myrtle said, eyes distant.

"What we goin' to do?"

Myrtle pondered the question. She could call the police, but
there was no proof, only hearsay. Then, too, with her past
sermons and the upcoming March on city officials, she would
hardly get much sympathy or cooperation there. Another line
of action would be to confront Rudy himself, but he surely
would deny.

"Well, Heavenly Delight, it may not be as bad as it seems."
She tried to sound light. "We will hire a part-time security
guard for nights until things simmer down." She would worry
about paying for one later, relying on her age-hardened belief
that the Lord will provide according to Saint Matthew, chapter
7, verse 7: *Ask, and it shall be given you; seek, and ye shall
find; knock, and it shall be opened unto you.* Rising from her

seat, Myrtle said, "I think we both should have some coffee now, Heavenly Delight."

When Ralph accidentally dropped by later in the afternoon, Myrtle led him away from the office clamor to the privacy of her study for a talk. Finishing, she added: "Cranks are always around when plans like ours are being implemented."

"Yes, but it's so ridiculous!" Ralph shook his head in bewilderment.

"To adversaries, it isn't." For all his intelligence, Ralph was somewhat naive about human nature, a trait ministers could not afford. "Ralph, people will go to great extremes to preserve their kingdoms—themselves—when it is a point of sheer survival and expediency to them."

Ralph looked gravely at her. "If that's true, I'm worried about *you*. Maybe we should have somebody to watch over you."

"No, I have Jesus as my protector." Leaders could not afford to show fear. "It is the church that needs to be kept safe," she smiled shakily, trying to reduce the tension.

"All right, if that's the way you feel about it, but—"

"And Ralph, keep this between us. No reason to get everybody else upset." Noticing his grim look, she smiled. "Just trust in the Lord, Ralph. He will see us through."

The afternoon sun blazed through the telephone booth in front of the gas station where Rudy had been trying to place a call for the past fifteen minutes. He did his undercover calling on public phones to deter any tracing. Hot and irritated from having to wait for the line, perspiration wetted his face and dampened his white suit. He would have to take a shower and change clothes again.

Dropping a coin into the slot, he got another busy signal. Damn! The Reverend Cross must be praying for somebody or begging for money. That was all preachers did—pray and beg. He would wait five minutes longer.

Looking out of the booth, he saw the station attendant gassing up his car. The man was short, black, and shapeless in greasy coveralls. His hair was plaited in corn rolls, making Rudy instantly take a disliking to him. *Men ought to wear their hair like he thought men should.* Subconsciously, he patted his Afro.

Turning back to the phone, he tried again. This time the line was clear. When a woman answered, he placed a handkerchief over the receiver and asked for Reverend Cross. The woman must have had a hard time understanding him, for she kept repeating: "What? What?" When he did get through to her, she said that her husband wasn't home, but she would be happy to take the message.

Peeved because the Reverend wasn't there after wasting time in the cramped booth, a streak of anger shot through him at her. Pushing his mouth closer to the receiver to make sure she would know what he was saying this time, he gave her the message with sadistic delight, wishing he were a fly on the wall at the other end to see the bitch's expression: "That preacher woman who stole all those members out of your old man's church is a BULLDAGGER!"

"A *what?*"

Shi-i-it! Either the woman was hard of hearing, or she was too goddam stupid to know what a bulldagger was. "A WO-MAN LO-VER!" he shouted into the phone.

There was a pause before the woman replied stiffly: "Sir, *all* of us Christian women *love* each other—"

Hell! Rudy slammed the receiver down in disgust. He hadn't asked for no sermon. Wiping his face with the handkerchief, he went over to pay the service man imitating Stevie Wonder.

"Sharp hog you got there, my man," the attendant said, handing him change from a fifty-dollar bill.

I ain't your man, Rudy wanted to say. "It ought to be. Paid 'nough for it." As the man stood there admiring the car, Rudy thought: *Look on, you motherfucker, for you'll never get one.* Stepping on the accelerator, he found the car wouldn't start. Annoyed, he pumped his foot up and down.

"Won't turn over?" the attendant asked.

"I wouldn't be sittin' here if it did," Rudy snapped.

"Open the hood." The man went around to the front.

Rudy released the latch, watching the braids disappear under. In a few minutes, the man poked his head up and called out: "Try it now."

When the motor started, Rudy pressed his foot down hard to the floor, causing rushing motor noises.

Grinning, the man wiped his hands on a greasy black cloth hanging like a tail from his back pocket. "Battery cable was loose. Happens sometime to the best." Coming up to the window, he said, "If you ever need a good mechanic, just come back and ask for me—T.J. I guarantee a good job every time!"

Glaring at T.J. with a *fuck you* in his eyes, Rudy took off in a burst of speed. Glancing back in his rearview mirror, to his amazement, he saw the fool laughing his head off.

With the air conditioner cooling both him and his temper, Rudy sank back in the seat, reviewing the happenings as he drove. He was getting bored with the telephone calls. It was time to get down to the nitty-gritty of action. He would head for home, kick Popora's ass out into the streets to be alone, and map out his major tactic.

Chapter 27

S TANDING before the mirror, Rudy was pleased with himself. For a week he had meticulously planned, and now everything was set for tomorrow night. Sunday there wouldn't be any church or preacher. Elated by his thoughts, he smiled broadly, adjusting his tie and fastening the first two buttons of his new two-hundred-dollar plaid jacket. It was 2:00 A.M., and he had to pick up Popora in North Nashville.

The smile was still on his face when he turned the key in the ignition and stepped on the accelerator. At that moment, the bomb planted in his car detonated a smattering explosion, killing him instantly.

During the time of the incident, King was seated at a table by the door in the Rooster Lounge with Earthly Treasure. In unusually good spirits, he laughed and talked, trading rounds of drinks with acquaintances.

Earthly Treasure barely touched her gin sling, tight with the knowing gnawing inside her. Understanding her tenseness, King reached over in an unfamiliar gesture of kindness and patted her hand. Although the touch was brief, it made Earthly Treasure feel like a queen. She lit a cigarette and relaxed, watching the men and women playing out their Friday night games with each other, the relentless music throbbing around them. She could spot the bullshitting cool pimps dressed to kill, their predatory hookers, and the unsuspecting squares out for a good time. The brainless squares giving it away for a night of fun, or the daydream of love. The maelstrom of gaiety mingled with cigarette smoke, liquor and beer fumes, and people odors of cheap perfume, powder, shaving lotion, and underarm sweat. Black talk rapped like a volleyball in a jive swirl around her:

Hey, man, what's hap'nin'?
You got it all.
Hey, baby, you lookin' good!

Holding up two fingers, King signaled the waitress for a refill. When the young, cute waitress brought their drinks, King, acting on instinctive reflexes with an eye for business, immediately turned on his charm. "Say, baby, you must be new. I ain't seen nothin' as pretty as your fine self in here in a lon-n-ng time."

The girl smiled with toothpaste teeth, as she set the drinks down and wiped the table of glass sweat rings.

"I'll bet you drivin' all-l-l the dudes crazy tonight." King paid for the drinks, tipping her with a crisp, five-dollar bill.

Earthly Treasure pretended not to hear his talking trash, the sound-out of the trade. The stable could always hold one more.

King sat back also to view the crowd, but not for entertainment. His street eye was catching sight of the shady deals going down, and new women prospects. Now and again, he would glance toward the door. When a man eventually came in, wearing army fatigues and sporting corn rows, he said low, "There he is."

Getting up, he followed the man into a back room stacked with empty cartons of liquor, wine, and beer amidst broken pieces of tables and chairs. A light bulb with a noose string gave off a weak yellow gleam in the center of the room.

Locking the door behind them, King asked, "Well?"

"Old T.J. guarantees to get the job done. The U.S. Army'll vouch for that. I didn't spend all that time in Vietnam doin' nothin'.."

"That's why I hired you niggah!" King laughed, patting his back. "Here—" He counted out a roll of bills. "Take a trip for a while."

"Yeah-h-h. Goin' to go out and buy me a hog, just like the one that *was!*" he winked.

Opening the door, King peered out cautiously before ducking across the hallway into the foul-smelling men's toilet. On the way back to the table, he paused by the bar to whisper shit in the young waitress's ear. To his bottom woman, Earthly Treasure, he said, "Ever'thin's all-l-l right!"

* * *

In front of Monday's Restaurant and Lounge, Popora waited for Rudy to come get her. She was tired, but excited, for she had had a good night and Rudy would be happy. She wished he would take her to a party like the other night, or better, let her sleep with him.

Friday nights were always busy, but this weekend a national black business group was having a convention at the Hyatt, and tricking had been especially good. Monday's was filled with men eating and drinking after the sessions were over. One had laughingly remarked that he had to get away from that white hotel for a while and get down-n-n and be around his own for some funky fun. Some of the men had their wives traveling with them, but tonight they were having a fashion show at the hotel, and the men were "on their own, hah, hah."

With the faint sounds of music and laughter from Monday's around her, Popora looked up and down the night street to see if Rudy was coming. He didn't like to be kept waiting. When he drove up, she was supposed to be ready to hop right in. The parking lot was jammed with cars. He could be parked somewhere in-between them. She started walking around the lot.

"Hey, baby—" a man called to her out of a parked car.

From the rays of the lounge's lights, she could see he was middle-aged and had a heavy moustache. He resembled the businessmen in his summer suit and tie.

"How much?" he asked.

She hesitated, wondering if she had time. Rudy should be here any minute. He wouldn't wait for her to finish with tricks, preferring to stay out of sight.

"Twenty."

"Get in." He got out, handed her two tens, and opened the back door of the car.

He wanted a blow job. But first he wanted to play with himself. He had her hold a flashlight while he unzipped his pants, pulled from his purple boxer shorts his short, thick penis with a circumcised head, stroked it lovingly, and started pumping.

Breathing fast, he said, *"Watch*—keep your eyes on it!"

She fixed her eyes on his jerking movements and out the window, too, for Rudy. When his cock grew long and inflated, he grabbed her hand. *"Feel* it! Big, isn't it? Isn't this the biggest dick you ever seen in your whole whore's life?"

She flinched at the word, nodding dumbly, lying, for it wasn't the biggest one she had seen. *"Squeeze* the lemons—" He made her feel his balls while his cock twitched and shot upward on his hairy belly. Grabbing her by the nape of the neck, he pushed her head down so quickly she thought her neck was going to snap. The cock, like a live, pulsating fat sausage, filled her mouth.

"Suck it—suck it, whore. *Suck it good!"*

Mouth stuffed with his meat, she could feel his hairs against her face and smell him as he farted in excitement. He came, spurting a gushing emission of fluid in her mouth. She tried to break loose to vomit out the window the gummy taste she detested, but he held her head tightly. "Swallow it. *Swallow* it, I said!"

She ingested the thick, white mass and gagged, tears brimming her eyes. Her mouth felt as if it were coated with dried cement.

Wiping his cock with a handkerchief, he arranged it back inside his shorts and zipped his pants. When she started to get out of the car, he stopped her. "No, honey—Metro vice squad."

Shocked, she gasped, seeing his sneering grin, the badge, a glistening sliver of indictment. She wanted to scream at him, tear him apart, spit all of his nasty, slimy come back on his handpainted tie and into his grinning face.

"You son of a bitch! You motherfucker! You bastard—!"

"Tch, tch, honey. Nasty, nasty." He handcuffed her. "No point in crying now. You should have thought of this before selling ass." His hands searched her, finding the money she had made. "Un-hun, looka here! Haven't gotten to your pimp yet, hun? I'll just keep it instead." He put the money in his pocket and started the car. "We got orders to crack down for a while; do our part to help that Reverend Black clean up the city," he laughed. "Might as well get my fun out of it." The car exited from the parking lot. "I don't ever screw you whores. Don't want to stick *my* dick in your filthy holes. Could catch anything. So I let you suck it off." He took her clasped hands, pushing them down between his legs. "Here, give it a little action on the way to the station."

Tears rolled like miniature glass marbles down her cheeks. Rudy would get her out.

* * *

Heavenly Delight couldn't sleep that night. At 4:00 A.M., she was still awake in bed reading the Bible. She had turned off the TV, for she had seen the repeat late night movies. Her inability to sleep was caused by worrying about the church. Once she had been tempted to get up, put on her clothes and call a cab to go there. It would be a sin and a shame if something happened.

Eyelids getting heavy, she closed the Bible, and set the clock–radio for six o'clock. In the darkness, it was a while before she finally drifted off into a restless sleep.

The radio awakened her with the news. She sat up and stretched in the early morning daylight glossing the room. Getting out of bed to the whiplashing voice of the news announcer, she half listened, nothing really penetrating: "A man was killed in an early morning explosion in front of his South Nashville apartment building. The name of the victim is being withheld until the next of kin can be located."

Heavenly Delight cut off the news, which to her was never good news, and got down on her knees to say her morning prayer. She prayed for Reverend Myrtle Black and the church. It wasn't until seven o'clock when Earthly Treasure called that she learned that the man in the car was Rudy.

Heavenly Delight immediately called the person whom she thought should know first of all. Myrtle was quiet for a long time before she said, "That's terrible."

"Terrible?" By Heavenly Delight's thinking, in a way it was, and in another, it wasn't.

"Yes, even though he was our enemy, his death is regrettable. As the prophet Habakkuk beseeched upon Shigionoth: 'In wrath, remember mercy.' I will say a prayer for his soul."

Hanging up, Heavenly Delight got down on her knees for the second time that morning to pray, like her minister, for Rudy's soul.

Chapter 28

*A*FTER talking with Heavenly Delight, Myrtle called Barbara at the office to let her know that she would not be in. All the rest of the day, she tried to reach Travis without success.

Ralph, having learned the news of Rudy's death from Flaming Dark Sugar, came by to see her. Feeling drained, Myrtle asked him to take charge of the church services for Sunday. She saw that he was pleased, smiling as he left to work on his sermon. Now that the worst of her problems were over, she hoped to get a full night's rest for a change.

Rudy's death was on the front page of the evening's paper. The police believed the killing may have been gang related, connected to prostitution and drugs. They were investigating, but had no leads.

She had just finished reading the account when the phone rang. Harold Thurman, Jr., a local undertaker, had the body of Rudolph Valentino Jones. The remains had been brought from the city morgue by Misses Lanette Miller and Deidre Folini, since no relatives had claimed it. It seemed the deceased had taken the ladies to Reverend Myrtle Black's church once, the only one they knew of his having attended. Because of this, they would like to have her officiate at a small service for the deceased in the undertaker's chapel on Tuesday evening.

Listening to the bizarre request, Myrtle was thrown for a loss. She didn't know whether to laugh or cry at the ensnaring tentacles of fate.

"Reverend Black?" The undertaker was waiting.

227

"Mr. Thurman, may I call you back?" She needed time to think it over. "I have to check my schedule."

"Of course; I understand," he replied politely.

It was ironic: Rudy following her even in death. She tried to reach Travis again, and found her home. With relief, she unburdened all that had transpired, ending with Rudy's death. "Should I conduct a funeral service for a—a hustler?" she asked despairingly.

"Doesn't your church and you stand for a savior of the rejected?" Travis reminded her.

"The rejected, not the enemy," Murtle replied bitterly.

"Darling, you are forgetting your own and God's teachings to love thine enemy."

She had slipped, letting malice enter her heart. But Travis didn't know what she had been through. A seed of hate had been planted within her for the man who had hurt Travis and was on the verge of ruining her. Ministers, too, could be flooded with a fountainhead of enmity. Weakness is alive in everything human.

To diffuse her own animosity, Myrtle inserted an airiness of light teasing. "Look who's giving advice to her minister!"

"In this case, I feel that I should. Rudy was once a part of my life, although not a nice one. And then he became a part of yours because of me. What are lovers for, if not to share other things in the loving, too?" Travis asked.

Myrtle frowned, puzzled. "But what can I say about him?"

Travis breathed a deep sigh into the phone. "Myrtle, Rudy had a tough life when he was a kid. Making it on those sidewalks hardened him. Since you have helped me, I can understand him a little better now. I feel sorry for him." Travis became quiet. "Do it for me—please."

The appeal in Travis's voice touched her. "All right, my sweet—for you." Kissing her good-night over the telephone, Myrtle sat silently in thought for a prolonged stretch of time. Was it Shakespeare who wrote that there was some soul of goodness in things evil?

She would call Mr. Thurman to let him know that she would perform the service.

The Harold Thurman & Son Funeral Home was the oldest and most prestigious black one in the city, having a fleet of

Cadillacs to bolster its image. The home was a stately white colonial structure with columns. It had wall-to-wall carpeting, a private family room, and chapel. A mansion facing a crumbling housing project in the ghetto, it stuck out like a sore thumb.

Harold, Jr., was a slightly built man with a dispassionate face the color of a pineapple, and thinning, naturally straight brown hair. He had the undertaker's polished formality, and a quick way of smiling and cutting it off equally fast.

On Sunday afternoon when Myrtle entered his comfortable but cluttered office decorated with certificates and plaques of civic awards, she detected an odor of liquor as he held out a chair for her.

In going over the arrangements, he seemed unduly concerned with wanting the rites to go smoothly. He kept to himself that he really hadn't wanted the body. He favored burying only the traditional black—Nashville aristocrats—but the ladies had ordered a deluxe burial, and money was rather tight these days, even for burying the dead.

"Could I talk with Miss Miller and Miss Folini?" Myrtle asked, "for they should be counselled in their sorrow."

"Uh, I believe the . . . ladies desire privacy—not wishing to see anyone."

"Not even the minister?"

Harold Thurman looked pained. "That is correct. I asked them, but—" His glance dropped to his desk. "Now they just want a short service to begin at seven o'clock in the evening. We will bury him Wednesday morning."

"Do you have any information for the obituary?"

Fumbling through papers, he handed her a sheet. "This is all I have on him." His hand shook as the smile flicked on and off again.

As Myrtle reached for the paper, the liquor smell was noticeably stronger. "May I have the ladies' telephone number?" There wasn't much on paper.

Clearing his throat, he looked embarrassed. "I am sorry, but I don't have it. They call me, you see." Pushing his chair back, he crossed his leg, eyes on the wall. "I do think it's nice they are . . . ah . . . burying the deceased. They are just friends of his, you know, not relatives." A marked distinction to him indeed.

"Sometimes friends are better than relatives," Myrtle said, folding the paper and slipping it in her purse. "May I see the body?"

The undertaker jerked as if a string had been pulled inside him. "Oh, no-o-o, not now. I haven't quite finished. He isn't in very good shape. The bombing—horrible, yes, horrible. A lot of work..." He threw up his hands in dismay.

"Please convey my condolences to the ladies. If they do need to talk with me, tell them to feel free to call anytime. I will do my best to see that the deceased has a decent burial."

"Thank you very much, Reverend Black. I thought you would do this for them. I have heard some fine things about you and your church."

"Good evening, Mr. Thurman. I will get back with you." Leaving, Myrtle's mind lingered on the women, who were continuing to look after Rudy, even in death.

Tuesday was a dreary day, holding the threat of rain. By the time of the funeral, the air had cooled and the swollen clouds mobilized together, seeping moisture. A prying neighborhood crowd, composed mostly of young people, gathered outside the funeral home. The curiosity seekers bunched like crows to gape at the glittering line of expensive cars with flashily dressed, jewel-bedecked men and women alighting. The youngsters, versed in street lore, guessed accurately that they were pimps with their whores, and others linked to the street world.

The men came in deference to one of their brotherhood, conscious of their own demise someday. Some knew Rudy and some did not. It was time to flaunt their wealth and whores to each other in a communion of male solidarity. Others drifted in from the Rooster Lounge. They were the ones for whom Rudy, in his exhibitionist moments, bought drinks, and the ones he had business dealings with.

They filed into the chapel, some with dark glasses, glazed eyes and liquored breaths. As the seats were filled, Ralph softly played the organ. Harold Thurman, Jr., was like an obsequious fly, lighting everywhere, giving orders in low tones, a store manager in his dark suit. Liquor polluted his breath, his undertaker's self-embalming fluid. Solemnity reigned in the place of tears for the mourners.

Because of Myrtle, George came for a story. A reporter and

photographer from *Jet* magazine covered the event because of Rudy's past ties with Travis, who was always news. Two black undercover vice officers attended to take heed of who was there, and to check license plates. It was a rare treat for them when the underground phalanx crept above ground to emerge visible.

Dressed demurely in white with large, stylish veiled hats screening their perfect model faces, Lanette and Deidra led the small procession with King in between, conservative in a black-and-white three-piece pin-striped suit. Popora and Earthly Treasure were behind. It was whispered street knowledge that King was paying for the funeral. He had already taken over Rudy's stable, and through Earthly Treasure's subtle pleadings, had paid the Metro fine for Popora's release. The pimps thought King was one boss nigger for what he was doing, burying a dead brother in spite of their suspicions concerning the motive.

Myrtle stood on the dais behind the rostrum, looking distinctive in her black silk robe with an embroidered white cross that she had designed for funerals. She began the service on time. In a subdued, but clear modulation, she commenced: "Jesus said: 'I am the resurrection, and the life: he that believeth in me though he were dead, yet shall he live; and whosoever liveth and believeth in me shall never die.' Let us repeat the Lord's prayer." For the convenience of those who did not know it, she had the prayer printed on the program. At least they would have said a prayer for the deceased, as well as themselves before it was over. "Let us stand."

Shuffling movements rended the air as they sat back down. Outside, the rumble of thunder and lightning foretold rain. The chapel lighting was dim, made more so by the fading twilight suppressed by the stained-glass windows. Children could be heard playing wildly on the streets, a parody to the presence of death within.

The expensive bronze casket, capturing attention, bedded through the dexterity of the undertaker what was left of Rudy. Rudy's skin appeared ashen and taut against the gold velvet lining, lips dry and bloodless, encircled with a neatly trimmed beard. The ladies had buried him in his favorite suit—fuchsia with tiny gold glints, and a pink shirt and plum tie. Out of his three diamond rings, one was on his little finger, left hand. A modicum of floral arrangements enhanced the area around the coffin. A large heart-shaped wreath of roses from the ladies and Popora was prominent among them, as were King's gardenia wreath, and a spray in the shape of a rooster from the Rooster Lounge.

"Sister Mary Haynes will sing, 'Father, I Stretch My Hand to Thee.'"

A lumberous, dark woman with a melodious soprano, Sister Haynes was narcissistic about her voice. She never refused to sing for weddings, concerts, special programs, with other choirs, birthdays, and funerals. A defector from the Reverend Amos Cross's church, she believed that people were basically good; only some had just gotten off the right track. For this reason, she agreed to sing for Rudy's funeral, and because she felt her minister was a wonderful woman to do this for the Lord.

When she sang, tears glassed the eyes of a few of the women in recognition of beauty touching their lives. The men sat in Spartan silence, legs crossed or spread, arms folded, imagining such a voice singing for them—whenever. Black people liked the best of grandeur in their funerals.

After the musical selection, Ralph, in his black robe and clerical collar, read the brief obituary. Thunder smashed the sky as the rain came down heavily against the windows. Cries of children abandoning play to run home arose from the streets.

Myrtle paused momentarily, commanding silence, before she began the eulogy. "Someday, we all must die, leave our loved ones, our family, our friends, this earth, to go to the great beyond. When that time will come, none of us know, but of certainty, it *will* come. The well-known English writer, William Shakespeare, wrote in his play *Julius Caesar:* 'Death, a necessary end, will come when it will come.' It has come to Rudolph Valentino Jones, who died young. His life, although short in the span of time, has—as all-l-l of our lives at some point—touched others. Some more, some less. For this encounter, for better or worse, we are responsible to ourselves and to our God.

"When facing our maker, it should be asked: 'Remember not the sins of my youth, nor our transgressions: according to thy mercy remember thou me for thy goodness' sake, O Lord.' The God above is a just and merciful one. Rudolph Valentino Jones—sleep in peace within the arms of His mercy."

Sister Haynes rose again to sing "Nearer My God to Thee." The body was viewed and mental notes taken of the cost of the casket, burial clothes, and the work of the undertaker. The onlookers were clearly impressed. Rudy had been put away in style.

Myrtle said a short prayer, and the group of mourners left the chapel with the rain falling upon them like a benediction.

Wednesday morning was bright with sun shining on the polished black hearse and Cadillac family limousine carrying the group to the gravesite. Myrtle followed in George's car with the *Jet* reporter and photographer in the back seat.

The grave was on a hillside, and Harold Thurman, Jr., quickly jumped from the hearse to assist the ladies up the muddy mound. King did not come; only the women—Lanette, Deidra, and Popora—were present.

Standing above the open grave surrounded with flowers, Myrtle said, "'Earth to earth, ashes to ashes, dust to dust; in sure and certain hope of the Resurrection unto eternal life.'"

For the first time, the ladies spoke to Myrtle from behind the cover of their veils, showing admiration as they thanked her. Deidra pressed a sealed envelope into her hand.

In the car, George said, "You are to be congratulated. No preacher in the city wanted to do that funeral."

"You'll see yourself in *Jet* soon," the reporter said.

"I can assure you, it was no easy task." All to please Travis. She thanked God it went well. And she drew some comfort from the luster it added to her fame and reputation.

Opening the envelope at home, she counted out five thousand dollars in cash. The amount took her by surprise. Replacing the money, she smiled. Rudy had just bought an organ for the church.

Chapter 29

*T*HE following weeks found Myrtle in demand for local and out-of-town speaking engagements. In line with these, she and Iffe made personal appearances before black civic and church organizations to drum up support for the March. The groups' responses ranged from cool to lukewarm.

To meet the needs of her growing church, Myrtle, Ralph, and members of the trustee board met with a leading architectural firm to go over a design for a larger and more modern facility, suitable for new innovative programs. The kind of structure they envisioned was going to be costly, which called for future fund-raising activities.

A few subversive innuendoes sewn in the wind by Rudy among a vicious group were raised in an attempt to cast aspersions on Myrtle and her work. These were mostly ignored or looked upon as titillating gossip. At this stage, she had become too powerful to be really touched by rumormongers. Also, not being out, she was tolerated by those who frowned on such sexual identities.

Everything was moving along fairly smoothly for Myrtle, except for her private life with Travis. Distance began to raise havoc between the lovers. Each night after twelve midnight, Travis called to lament about how much she missed her, how lonely she was without her, and how she wanted to see her.

In response, Myrtle tried to make Travis understand how busy she was, detailing what she had to do. But Travis refused to listen, believing *she* should come first in Myrtle's considerations. In one tempestuous conversation, Myrtle gave in and made a tentative agreement to see her in New York. Subsequently, she had to cancel out because Barbara reminded her of a speaking engagement in Louisville. Infuriated, Travis slammed down the phone. They did not talk again for a week, until Myrtle broke the silence.

Jealousy reared its head, too, in the quarrels. Travis began to intimate that perhaps Myrtle's busyness stemmed from an interest in someone else. To this Myrtle retaliated by saying that she had seen photographs of Willie Frye escorting her places. Travis, in turn, assured her that it was strictly to promote their country music album.

As a follow-up to Myrtle's postponed trip, Travis suggested that Myrtle come to New York the third week in August, prior to the Vegas engagement. Myrtle maintained that since it was getting closer to the March, it would be better for Travis to come to Nashville, in case of any unforeseen emergencies.

Unmoved, Travis stormed about how it was a nuisance for her to travel. Agnes would insist on Bobby or herself accompanying her. And besides, she wasn't in the mood to be harassed by celebrity hounds. Myrtle could come on a Tuesday or Wednesday and leave late Saturday night in time to be at church on Sunday morning if she had to. Anyway, Travis would be in Nashville for the March, wouldn't she?

Weary, Myrtle conceded. She would go to New York.

The evening before departing, she packed with her mind filled with Travis. This was one relationship that had gotten out of hand. She had never been involved with anyone this long, always breaking off previously before it got too binding. This was a part of her nature—a female *bon viveur*. Always, she put herself first—her feelings and desires.

Closing the bag, she poured a glass of wine and settled down beside a photograph of Travis. Like the wine, Travis was of a special vintage. It was difficult for her to interpret exactly what it was she felt about her. True, she had a deep fondness, and the lovemaking was as strong as heat between them. For the first time, she found herself in a rare state of confusion about a person.

She ran a caressing finger across the glass enclosing Travis's face. To be seen with her too much would certainly inflame the smoldering intimations. Was it worth it? She had her goals, her ambition. How could she explain to Travis? Did she really want to?

Picking up the picture and holding it close, she groaned, "My dear, what am I to do about you?"

Travis's announcement that Myrtle would be flying in Thursday evening caught Agnes completely by surprise, causing her to spill some coffee. The abrupt news was disturbing, suggesting too many unaskable questions. Taking her time to wipe up the liquid on the kitchen table, she decided that the visit shouldn't have been too unexpected in light of the numerous Nashville calls on the phone bills. Seeing them, she had supposed that Travis was seeking spiritual advice not to be found in the Bible, since she didn't seem to be reading much of it lately. Because there wasn't anything she could do about it, she concluded that if the minister's visit would help to keep Travis happy—fine. She just didn't want Travis getting uptight before they got to Vegas. Travis had lost some of the exuberance she had had upon first coming home from Nashville. Oddly enough, sparks reminiscent of it returned in the wake of the long distance calls.

Spooning waves in her coffee, pieces were trying to fit together in knotty places for Agnes as she concentrated on the Reverend Myrtle Black. The woman seemed to have cast a spell over Travis, as the old folks back in New Orleans would say. "Is the Reverend coming for any special reason?" she asked, trying to appear nonchalant.

"She's coming to see me." A hint of defiance was in the set of Travis's mouth as she bent over a grocery list, a task rarely undertaken by her. "Incidentally, Agnes, while she's here, I don't want to be disturbed by anyone."

"Just as you wish." God, she hoped the Reverend wasn't a spiritualist.

Pushing the list across the table, Travis said, "Would you see that I get these? The wine is on the back."

Agnes scanned the items. "Quite a high-price order."

"It's *my* money."

"So it is."

"Now, let's see, I have time to get my hair done, a facial, manicure," Travis enumerated.

Agnes's eyes looked quizzical at this sudden interest in her personal appearance. Since when did women start wanting to look good for women? A murky thought began to haze her mind, as dark as the coffee in her cup.

* * *

With Agnes driving, Travis met Myrtle at LaGuardia. Immediately upon seeing Myrtle, Travis ran to greet her, hugging her excitedly. Before going home, they stopped at Justine's Sea Food Castle for dinner.

In keeping with her festive mood, Travis went overboard in ordering the meal. Eating, she talked with Myrtle about the church and March, while her eyes, radiant, spoke of other things over their glasses of white wine.

Myrtle, distinguished in her clerical collar bordering a tan suit, answered Travis's questions as she tried to make a show of eating the food for which she had no appetite.

Agnes was quiet during the meal, a remote spectator to the exchange between them. Travis's face held a perpetual smile as she threw what was to Agnes undisguised adoring glances across the table at Myrtle. Venturing into the conversation at one point, Agnes asked Myrtle if they had found out who killed Rudy.

"Unfortunately, no," Myrtle said, cutting into the baked trout. "The police are at a dead end." She omitted that the investigation seemed desultory. One less black pimp for the police to deal with.

Looking closely at Myrtle, Agnes saw that she was an imposing woman, highly attractive with a face tastefully made-up. However, her reserved demeanor gave off a touch of coolness. An intelligent conversationalist, she made the dinner interesting, chatting with Travis.

Insisting on their having dessert, Travis also ordered another bottle of wine. For a tiny fraction of a second, Agnes could have sworn she saw Travis purse her lips in a kiss to Myrtle. What she did not see was Travis grasping Myrtle's hand in her lap.

Disquieted by the scene charged with subtle byplays, an ever-brighter dawning of recognition of what was taking place numbed Agnes for a split second into a small state of shock. Drawing heavily upon her social decorum to help her through the rest of the evening, she somehow managed to maintain her balance to cope with the gay deceivers until the dinner was over.

They stood in the living room hungrily drinking in the sight of each other before embracing happily. Lifting Travis's face,

Myrtle kissed her crushingly, opening her mouth with her own to let their tongues meet, coiling, looping and sucking into wet caverns. When Myrtle withdrew, their lips stuck together for a tying moment, as if peeling away from adhesive.

"I missed you, I missed you—" Travis sang in Myrtle's ears, arms tight around her neck.

"It's wonderful to hold you again," Myrtle breathed in her ear, surprised at herself, for the words rang true. She reveled in the softness pressing into her of a luscious body known so well by touch. Blindfolded, she could identify every nook and corner and pocket. She ran her hands lovingly up and down Travis's back, rediscovering, feeling the hips and thighs which had added weight since the last time. The increased heaviness felt good to her, like holding a warm bale of cotton.

"Darling . . . darling . . ."

Travis licked Myrtle's face. "My chocolate ice cream cone; my goody!" she laughed.

They were locked into each other, breasts, stomachs and thighs cemented together. Myrtle trembled from the wave of passion coursing through her, rocking and bending Travis in her arms. Lovingly, she made small bites on Travis's neck.

"Yes—*bite* me!" Travis threw back her head for the nibbles which became harder as Myrtle's breath quickened.

Once more, Myrtle brought her lips back to Travis's mouth as her hands squeezed and pushed the round globes of Travis's buttocks into the cave of her. Suddenly Myrtle uttered a low moan: "Oh, baby, baby!"

Clinging to her, Travis felt like a Lilliputian in her arms. The only time she got the impression of being short was when standing beside Myrtle. "I'm ready to go to bed, Reverend, and let you take me to heaven."

Gently, Myrtle's hand slid down, making circling patterns on her stomach. Inserting a leg between Travis's thighs, she murmured huskily, "Why not here first, standing up with our clothes on?" Low, evocative, fire against the lobe of Travis's ear.

Caught in the throes of a rushing tide of desire, Travis sucked in her breath. "Yes-s-s, right here!" Closing her eyes, she felt Myrtle move away from her as she kneeled to bring love.

Downstairs, Agnes tossed and turned in bed, reviewing the mammoth significance of the evening. If the implications were valid, as she saw them, Travis was having an affair with the Reverend, a female, which could be more devastating in some ways than with a male. Any kind of public leak could have repercussions. Female singers were sex symbols to males and models for women.

The Reverend was absolutely not one to be taken lightly. The woman had a tremendous influence on Travis, and for herself to get adversely entangled with her could turn out to be a marathon tug-of-war, which Agnes feared she might not win.

Travis's having an affair with a lesbian—a minister at that—created a predicament that she did not know how to handle. Women, enamored of men, still sought the benefits of female companionship unique to women. With Myrtle, Travis had the dual physical and emotional satisfaction in a woman-to-woman relationship which could leave Agnes out.

She recalled how she had looked with disdain on the few lesbian liaisons in school. She had viewed them as ridiculous— silly girls playacting, imitating the legitimate drama of love. But now, she was beginning to have second thoughts. They were just as real.

She debated whether to get up and take a Valium or smoke a joint. The full moon cast a bright path to her bed. Round moons were for lovers and loving. She stretched out in a slow, sensuous movement, nightgown sliding above her thighs, columns flanking a patch of darkness. Smiling down at herself in the moonlight, her hand glided over her stomach like a wiggling snake. A joint was just a drawer away. God bless the woman who knew what to do with her own.

"I have the damn cramps!" Travis moaned, coming from the bathroom. "Of all the times. Four days early! I'm usually late."

"Too much action last night," Myrtle smiled sleepily, turning over in the bed. They had made love practically all night with Travis taking the initiative in the infancy of the morning hours.

Travis crawled back into bed, drawing up in a knot. "I have them awful this time."

"Did you take anything?" Myrtle asked solicitously.

"The medicine my doctor prescribed. I didn't have them too much when I was taking birth control pills, but I got afraid of the things. Repercussions, you know." Travis gave a small laugh. "I think I'll get a hysterectomy and put it all to rest." She twitched as a pain knifed through her. "God, why do women have to go through this mess every month?"

"Because of the curse on Eve—Genesis, chapter 3," Myrtle said sarcastically. "So saith the male ministers."

"Humph! If men had to do this every month, somebody long ago would have come up with a solution. Can you see a man going around with his jigger wrapped up in a sanitary napkin or with a tampon stuck up him?"

"Or having babies. If men had to carry them for nine months, go through the pains of the birth process, and have the major responsibility of taking care of them, there wouldn't be any problems with male legislators in passing abortion laws," Myrtle said sarcastically. Travis nestled against her, and as if to take the pain, Myrtle placed her hand flat on her stomach. "Anything I can do?"

"No, I'll sleep awhile. It'll wear off." Closing her eyes, Travis asked, "Do you ever have the cramps?"

"Seldom. Anyway, mine will be over soon, and I will be relieved of it all."

Travis's eyes opened. "You mean by the change?"

"We all have to go through it sooner or later," Myrtle replied philosophically. "If women would stop looking at it like men, for their own sadistic, contemptuous male reasons, as an end to women's function in life, there would be many fewer despondent middle-aged women."

Travis sucked in her breath. "Keep your hand there on my stomach where it hurts."

"Anything you want, darling. Try to go to sleep," Myrtle said, pulling her closer into the blanket of her.

"Hum-m-m," Travis murmured, kissing Myrtle's cheek, "such a nice way to sleep."

After Travis went into a deep sleep, Myrtle got up, showered, and dressed. Finding her way around the kitchen, she made a cup of instant coffee and read the *New York Times*.

Agnes knocked on the door around noon. "Travis up yet?"

"No, she isn't feeling well," Myrtle said, letting her in.

"Must be that time." Rhoda ran to Agnes, barking happily. "Has Rhoda been for her walk?"

"She's been asleep, too. Should I have taken her?"

"No, no. I'll do it. Come on, girl, let's get the leash and the pooper-scooper."

On the way to the kitchen to get Rhoda's things, Agnes passed the guest room. Myrtle pretended not to have noticed that she had seen Agnes observe the unutilized bed and room in perfect order with none of her things visible. In their hurry last night, no one had bothered to close the door.

"We'll be back soon," Agnes said, leading Rhoda, face inscrutable.

While Travis slept, Myrtle worked on her sermon for Sunday in the room swollen with records, an elaborate tape recording system, stereo, record awards, and photographs scaling the walls and occupying tables. A sectional black leather couch curved in front of a huge TV.

While working, she considered getting in touch with the press. She telephoned the *Amsterdam News* and the *New York Times* to sound them out concerning an interview. The *Amsterdam News* editor was enthusiastic and was going to send a reporter in the morning. The *New York Times* connected her with someone vaguely interested, who would get back in touch with her. The publicity would be good for the March and church. For once, she left herself out of that company.

Travis had not awakened by the time Agnes returned. "Would you like to come downstairs to my place and have lunch?" she invited, unleashing Rhoda.

"Thank you, but I had better finish this sermon while my thoughts are flowing. I ought to stay here, too, with Travis, in case she wants something."

"Give me a ring, if you have any problems," Agnes said, going out the door.

Travis stirred from her drugged sleep around three o'clock. "How do you feel?" Myrtle sat down on the bed.

"Better. Groggy." She held Myrtle's hand. "I'm sorry. You're here and I have to be like this. Have you eaten?"

"I had coffee."

"I'm hungry, but soup is probably the only thing that'll stay on my stomach."

Myrtle got up. "Soup is on the way."

"Eat whatever you want. I filled the refrigerator with lots of goodies for you." Travis pulled on her robe. "I'm beginning to bleed like a cow." Red spots dotted her gown.

Rhoda, lying on the couch in the living room, heard her

mistress's voice and ran into the room. Travis kissed her. "Hi, honey-bumpkins. You been to wee-wee and poo-poo?"

"Agnes took her around noon," Myrtle said on the way to the kitchen.

When Travis came out of the bathroom, Myrtle had almost finished warming a can of turtle soup for her and broiling a lamb chop for herself. They were eating when Agnes came up again to inquire about Travis and take Rhoda for her after dinner walk. Delivering the dog back, she stayed for a while watching TV and talking with them. Travis was curled up on the sofa, a light blanket thrown over her by Myrtle, who felt she should have it.

Before they retired, Myrtle changed the bed sheets. Aching in Myrtle's arms, Travis said, "I'm mad as the devil. I haven't seen you for weeks and this mess!"

"We are together. Holding you like this, kissing you, having you near is enough. I am loving you like that."

Travis laughed a small puddle splash in Myrtle's neck at the thought flitting through her mind. "If I were lying close to a man like this, he'd have a hard-on sticking in my stomach, wanting to get it off somehow, ruining it all."

"That is the difference in loving women," Myrtle smiled, tucking the cover closer around Travis's back. "And there is a difference!"

To Travis's annoyance, early the next morning a young female reporter from the *Amsterdam News,* face smothered by large, round glasses, came to interview Myrtle. When she left, Travis flared out angrily, "You know we don't have much time together. You leave tonight."

"Good publicity, darling, for the church and March. You want to belong to a church you are proud of, don't you?"

"Church—March! Can't you *forget* all that for one day?" Sulking, Travis paced the floor. "Sometimes I wonder if *I* mean as much to you as those things?"

"You mean a great deal to me." Myrtle put her arms around her. "My dearest."

The top of Travis's head brushed Myrtle's chin. "Do you love me?"

The ringing of the phone was a saving grace for Myrtle, who was afraid to answer Travis's question. It was the *New York Times.* Vexed once more, Travis handed Myrtle the receiver. Because time was getting short, Myrtle talked to the reporter over the telephone. Yielding to the unpreventable, Travis went to the den and turned on the stereo, inundating her disgust with her own music, volume high.

"Am I to expect the *Village Voice* next?" Travis said derisively, cuddling Rhoda.

"Be nice and clip the articles for me when they come out, please. I will put them on the church's bulletin board." Myrtle joined Travis on the couch, kissing her lightly.

"If you'll be nice to me the rest of the afternoon—"

"That won't be a hard promise to make," Myrtle laughed, "as Jesus is my witness."

Chapter 30

O N Tuesday, free of classes, Iffe met with Myrtle in her church office to go over the day's schedule of visits to solicit more black support for the March. "I've set up a joint meeting at twelve noon with the student Pan-Hellenic Council and female officers of the Student Government Associations," she said, showing her appointment book to Myrtle. "Then at two o'clock, I talk to Les Femmes Club, and last, I have an appointment with Betty Perry, black community relations officer with the mayor's office."

"Sounds great," Myrtle said, pleased. "We really need to get more black participation. Nikki's doing wonders with her Students Feminist Alliance." Myrtle thoughtfully tapped her pencil against her chin. "You may have some difficulty with Les Femmes. It is an old highbrow society club and very selective about members."

"I hear they're mostly teachers and wives of professionals."

"Yes. Those kind sometimes have an insulated kind of conservatism." Myrtle shook her head sadly. "I just pray that we get good vibrations today."

Iffe nodded in agreement. "So do I." Rising, she said, "Well, here I go to seek and find."

"I will pray for you."

"Thanks. Something tells me that I'll need all the prayers I can get," she laughed. "I'll check back with you later."

Entering the Ida B. Welles Barnett Building on Tennessee University's campus, Iffe compared the faces of the students in the hall with those on the campus where she taught across town. There, she saw mostly all whites. Here was a semblance of Africa, awakening nostalgic memories of her undergraduate days at a predominantly black school. She had attended Howard University in Washington, D.C., on a scholarship, much to the delight of her widowed postal clerk mother.

The students were milling about waiting for her in the classroom. A slender poised medium brown girl in a mid-length flared tan skirt and blouse came over quickly to her. "Ms. Degman?"

"Yes—" Iffe smiled, thinking bull's-eye—identified by age and materials in hand.

"I'm Shirley Sawyer, president of the Pan-Hellenic Council of sororities." Her friendly, intelligent face smiled back.

"Hello, Shirley. It's nice meeting you after all of my worrisome telephone calls."

"You can sit here." Shirley escorted her to a scarred teacher's desk in front of the room. The wall behind contained a blackboard with an English composition assignment. Iffe pulled out a chair and deposited her materials on the desk.

"I guess they're all here." Shirley moved farther to the center of the room to begin her introduction of Iffe and the purpose of the meeting.

Iffe was impressed by her articulateness. As Shirley talked, Iffe perused the faces of the girls before her. In the same curious manner, they too looked back at her in her African dress and matching headscarf. The group did not look the same as her peers of the sixties, who wore dashikis, tikis, and Afros. These young women were fashionably and neatly dressed in pantsuits, dresses, and skirts. Only a few had Afros now.

By the light handclapping, she realized Shirley was finished. Standing up to speak, she suddenly felt ancient in front of a pool of youth. To establish rapport, she told a student joke on herself, which drew laughter. Afterward she launched into her talk. "We are all conscious of the crime and vice in the city, especially around our black communities. Robberies and rapes are frequent with black women being the victims. The Women's March, initiated by the Reverend Myrtle Black, will allow us to confront, as a group, our city officials about this problem that must be *stopped*."

Continuing in an easy conversational way, she went on into the black women's issues of racism and sexism. Concluding, she appealed to them to urge their sorority sisters and sister students to join in the March of white and black women demonstrating together for common issues.

Sitting down, the only sound heard was the scraping of her chair against the tile floor. Breaking the silence, Shirley got up to open the floor for questions.

A fair-skinned girl in the rear stood up. "I'm Thelma Pruitt, president of the SGA at DuBois College. I'm all for marching against crime and for concerns of *black* women. I think this is a new day for us black women, and we're finding out more and more that we're going to have to look after *ourselves*, for nobody else's going to do it. And that includes the black *man!*"

"Tell it like it is, Thelma!" some of the girls laughingly chorused.

Spurred by her friends' rousing record, Thelma's voice rose: "We're going to have to learn to be our *own* selves and do what we want to do and not worry about what somebody *else* thinks. To do this, we have to stop worrying about the so-called castrating of the black man, which to me is passé. We need to *be* who *we* want ourselves to be, do what we want to do and not feel guilty about it."

"Go-o-o, Thelma!" A voice called out cheerfully.

"But, Ms. Degman, getting back to the March—I'm for it. Only, why do we have to march with *white* women?"

Resounding applause broke out.

"In substance, *all* women are oppressed by sexism in hiring practices, wages, promotions, overbearing male advances, chauvinistic attitudes, and discrimination. We know black women are doubly victimized by racism as well as sexism—"

"We're oppressed also by racist white women!" a girl shot back.

"Indeed, that too. But thankfully, some white women are attempting to face up to their racism and are trying to do something about it here in the South." Looking imploringly at them, voice low-keyed but taut with meaning, she said, "We cannot afford to take on the onus of our racist oppressors and become racists, too."

"Are the brothers to march?" Shirley asked.

"No. This is to be strictly a Women's March. However, we welcome our brothers' backing it." She held up one of the leaflets. "Here are some endorsements by prominent male leaders—black and white."

Shirley glanced at the wall clock in the back of the room. "Time's running out. I need a motion."

The quiet was tangible, until Thelma got up. "I move that we take part in the March."

A second girl seconded the motion.

"It has been moved and seconded that we take part in the March," Shirley said. "All those in favor, please raise your hands."

Iffe steeled herself, not looking up at the voters, wanting to close her eyes. Youth could be as unpredictable as hell. Shirley's voice cut through to her.

"Opposed?" She paused. "A unanimous decision to participate."

"Thank you!" Iffe said, the knot in her stomach disappearing. "You students here today are beginning a new era in the history of black women in the South. I'm proud of you, my sisters!" God, were her eyes clouding up. "I'm going to leave some of these leaflets and posters for you to pass out on your campus. We'll be in contact with you about parade marshals, routes, and other things."

Iffe was late leaving because some of the students with free time stayed to further explore some of the points she had made. Driving along with the afternoon traffic, she kept a watchful eye out for the exit off the interstate.

Les Femmes Club was meeting at the home of its president, Jacqueline Hightower, who taught, along with her husband, at Tennessee University. Judging by the directions the woman had given, she lived in a new condominium in a predominantly white area.

Leaving the interstate, Iffe had little difficulty in locating the house. Parked in front was a line-up of Buicks, Cadillacs, Porsches, and Mercedes-Benz. At the sound of the chimes, a woman answered the door.

Smiling, Iffe said, "I'm Iffe Degman. I'd like to see Jacqueline Hightower."

"Oh, yes! I'm Dr. Hightower. Do come in."

Walking into the strikingly well furnished house, Iffe had the eerie sensation of stepping into the home pages of a slick woman's magazine. Suddenly she remembered that she had left the leaflets and posters in her car.

Dr. Hightower blended with the decor—gracious with hostess smiles, exquisite in her billowing print fashion pantaloons.

The aroma of Bal de Versailles and scotch scented her. "We're out on the patio." Guiding Iffe through unlived-in-looking rooms, she kept up her rivulet of chatter: "We have our business meeting first, eat and end up with a little card game. The meeting is just over."

On the patio, women were lounging on lawn furniture and mixing drinks from a portable bar. "Would you like a cocktail?" Dr. Hightower had a Mediterranean face that shone a sharp yellow in the sun.

"No, thank you," Iffe said. "I have another stop to make, and I'll need a clear mind."

"I understand." Bending her head down, the woman whispered: "Are you Doctor, Mrs., or Miss—?"

"Ms.," Iffe said flatly.

A crooked smile twisted Dr. Hightower's lips. "Ladies, this is *Ms*. Iffe Degman, history instructor and graduate student at Vandy, who, as I told you, wants to talk to us about the upcoming Women's March."

Iffe found herself among a completely different assemblage from the one she had left. The women were mature prototypes of the black bourgeois. Their colorful dresses and pants combinations set an elaborate tapestry backdrop beneath the clear blue sky. Despite the variations of dress and Soul-Sister's-Beauty-Salon auburn, black, brown, and silver hairdos, homogeneity merged them like a landscape of the sea. Their gazes plucked at her in unflinching stares. Iffe felt as if her slip were hanging, provided she had one on. The women smiled tightly at her as some made their way back to sit down, holding glasses like teacups.

"Sure you won't have a drink before we start?" Dr. Hightower asked again.

A drink was probably what she did need, Iffe thought, but she refused. Taking a deep gulp of air, she drew herself up stiffly and faced the women. As she talked, they languidly smoked and sipped cocktails, listening patiently. When she finished, their faces were frozen.

Finally, a voice seared with irony said, "Honey, do you *really* think this Women's March is going to do any good?" The last part was almost drowned in the drink at her mouth.

"If we didn't, we wouldn't be having one," Iffe replied stiffly.

"Personally, I don't think we should embarrass our city like this. We've come a *long* way since I was a girl. Why stir up things?" A silver-haired aristocratic woman scowled at Iffe.

"You have to stir things up, or they'll remain the same." Iffe was starting to heat with anger. The women were being abrasive in their patronizing way.

Dr. Hightower quickly intervened. "Ms. Degman, we're in sympathy with your efforts, but our organization's primary function is to promote the education of our youth. Why, last year we sent three girls to Spelman, Bennett, and Fisk through our scholarship program. Today, we planned a fashion show for next month to initiate a music scholarship to Julliard."

Iffe knew when it was hopeless. These women were comfortable in their tranquil world. Racism barely touched them, for they were cloistered in their own circumscribed physical and mental ghettos. The whites they came in contact with were the ones like themselves, whom they met formally and informally in the same working environs and similar integrated social milieus where their professional paths crossed. They would hardly have an encounter with the Ku Klux Klan, and sexism was not even in their vocabulary, although rife in their day-to-day existence.

"Thank you, anyway, for letting me come," Iffe said, but she had already been dismissed. The women had gotten up to move to the table where the black caterer was in motion bringing out trays of food.

"Oh-o-o," someone squealed in delight, "those won-der-ful cream crab sandwiches again! Don't you just *love* them?"

"Yes, but they don't love me. Not good for the figure. But I'm going to cheat and take just *one!*"

Smiling at Iffe, Dr. Hightower put a motherly arm about her waist. "Stay and eat with us."

"Sorry, but I have to go." Even if she didn't, the food would have choked her.

The air, August-hot, smelled like a breath of life at the opposite end of the house.

Back at Myrtle's apartment, Iffe, feet propped wearily on a hassock, drank iced tea and reported on the day's outcome. "Betty Perry was a gem. She's going to be our house nigger in the mayor's office," she laughed. "Keep us informed of what the ol' massas are up to, namely the mayor and chief of police, who she says are real uptight about the March. The only happy city official seems to be the head of the city council who wants to run for mayor!"

"Good!"

"The students are with us." Iffe looked down into her glass. "Those two are my triumphs. My defeat was Les Femmes. To them, I was something straight out of Miss Anne's Fairyland. This reminds me that sutdents were the backbone of the Civil Rights Movement. It looks like the young black women are going to have to carry the ball for the Women's Movement, too."

"Not entirely," Myrtle said optimistically, pouring more tea into their glasses from the pitcher on the coffee table. "I had an unexpected visitor come by the headquarters—Alfreda Brown. She is a divorced mother of three children, and works as a school crossing guard. She is fed up with unsafe neighborhoods, especially for children, and wants to organize the mothers in black communities. I think she will make a fine grass-roots leader."

"You've just given me a new dimension," Iffe laughed. "I'm going home and rest. This has been a day!"

"But obviously a beneficial one," Myrtle added. "Get a *good* rest. We are about to get our show on the road!"

Chapter 31

RETURNING from a successful Las Vegas appearance, Travis's high spirits diminished after calling Myrtle to inform her that she was back in New York. Myrtle's responses were detached, as if she were only half listening, her mind on something else. Her remoteness was chilling to Travis, causing many questions to arise bearing upon their relationship. Stroking Rhoda curled on the sofa beside her, she supposed the same problems arose in loving women as loving men: the frustrations of jealousy, fear of losing, and eventual monotony setting in, which caused affairs to sour.

Myrtle had become an essential part of her, and had done much to help her to find herself. She had discarded the superficialities of the superstar role, growing into a settled maturity. She was more relaxed with people and herself. At times she would marvel over the love she had found, a different love, undreamed of, but yet one which meant more to her than any before. She was happy, loving emotionally, mentally, and physically.

But did Myrtle love her? She had never heard her use the word, not even when the loving became strong and beautiful, riding the crest of passion. Myrtle had said that she cared. But loving was deeper, more meaningful and lasting than caring. Loving, too, meant being open with each other. Every so often in their quiet moments together, she sometimes saw a shadow cross Myrtle's face. She wanted to ask what was troubling her. Burdens shouldn't be carried alone, if there was someone else close and willing to bear some of them, too.

She tucked the gray thoughts away. Agnes had to be told

about the trip. Whistling to Rhoda, they went downstairs to find her.

Agnes was going over a pile of mail in the two-room office across the hall from her place. When Travis walked in, she smiled in surprise, for Travis seldom came here. Business matters were an annoyance to her.

Sitting down on one of the chairs nearest the cluttered desk, Travis feigned a cough as she fanned away Agnes's cigarette smoke. Taking the hint, Agnes put out her cigarette. The last letter she had opened contained exciting news. If quenching a cigarette would help to keep the peace until she could bring it up, that was the least she could do.

"I thought you were asleep," Agnes said, for Travis had mentioned going to bed when they returned.

"No. I just talked with Myrtle."

"How is she?" Agnes asked politely.

"Busy preparing for the March." Rhoda whined and Travis picked her up. "I want you to go with me for it."

Recognizing an order when she heard one, Agnes asked, "Any special reason?"

"It's going to be history one of these days, and I'd like for you to be there."

"History is made every day, but people don't realize it," Agnes said.

"Also, I promised to sing."

"You did?" She should have known. More shenanigans of the preacher, no doubt.

"We need to be supportive of women's causes. Black women must learn to stick together."

"And not be like crabs," Agnes quipped, recalling an old black leader's expression "pulling each other down in a barrel." Now Travis was into social movements, a black Joan Baez. She debated whether to delay telling her about the letter. First, solve the business at hand. Consenting to go would soften things and avoid temper flare-ups, which, thankfully, there hadn't been too many of late. "When do you want to leave?"

"The March is on a Saturday. We could get a flight out on Thursday and come back Monday. I want to go to church Sunday." And at Agnes's cryptic expression: "I *do* belong to Myrtle's church."

"I know." An idea occurred to Agnes. "We'll take Bobby."

"Bobby—why?"

"He's good for taking care of little things." A veiled reply. Underneath, she was mindful that Travis was supposed to cut one more record for Abe Apstein. Maybe they could do it while there. If so, she would need Bobby to back her. He was the best accompanist Travis had ever had.

"All right, we'll take Bobby." He usually went along anyway. Bobby was becoming like a brother instead of the contemptible fag he used to be to her. Why not? Weren't they now of the same ilk?

"I'll get our plane reservations squared away."

"Get motel reservations, too, for you and Bobby. Myrtle has a small apartment."

That was smoothly done, Agnes applauded. Now for her immediate concern: "We just received a letter from World Wide Music. They want you, the Ding-a-Lings, and your backup band to go on a two-month tour of Germany the first of the year. It seems you have a lot of fans over there. I think it would be a great circuit."

Travis set Rhoda down on the floor. "That's a long time to be out of the country," she said slowly, lips in a tight line. "I'll have to think about it."

Putting the letter in her priority file, Agnes decided it was best not to press right now.

The first week in September, Myrtle conferred with Iffe, Lois, Kate, Nikki, and Wilma at the headquarters to finalize the March plans before meeting with group leaders on Friday. Everything was practically in order. They had the police permit, route maps, signs, loud speakers, bullhorns, and marshals. If needed, student nurses from Vanderbilt and Meharry had volunteered to offer First Aid.

The March was to convene at Myrtle's church and be joined by participating groups along the way. For those physically unable to walk the distances, cars were to take them to the termination place at Legislative Plaza.

"Everything's looking rosy!" Wilma said happily, lighting her third cigarette.

"Let's hope it doesn't rain on our parade," Iffe said.

Glancing over the projected program, Nikki frowned questioningly. "This Reverend Snead of the Metropolitan Church, who is giving the opening prayer—isn't she gay?"

"If she is or isn't, what difference does it make?" Iffe opined offhandedly.

"I asked her because she is a female minister," Myrtle said edgily. "She balances out the program—one black and one white female minister."

Kate broke the tension by saying: "Isn't this exciting? The first all-women's March in the South!"

"The South's goin' rise a-gin!" Wilma let out a rebel yell with yards of smoke.

"But in a different way," Iffe smiled sweetly.

For the remaining days, Myrtle worked late at the church with Barbara and Iffe staying with her, dining on hamburgers and coffee. Those times, too, Heavenly Delight refused to go home, hovering around to keep vigil with the security guard.

They were disappointed with the press coverage to date. News pertaining to the March was doled out in small items from nattily dressed tongue-in-cheek newscasters. Felicia Howard did invite the steering committee to appear on her TV *Sunday Ebony Roundup Show*.

Local newspapers cut their press releases and assigned them to the obituary page. Adverse news about the city was not conducive to Music City's booming tourist trade, nor respectful of the white male establishment. Furthermore, it was merely a women's gripe, wasn't it?

The national black presses were more considerate, seizing upon the March led by a black female minister with a coalition of whites and blacks as history making.

George was doing the best he could with his paper, managing to channel bits of news in his religious column. He called each day and frequently visited the headquarters. Myrtle could see his new confidence in himself. He walked straighter, smelled less of cigarette smoke and bourbon, and was matching his socks with his suits and ties. He was of the opinion that this was the best thing that had happened to the city since the Civil Rights Movement, and was pushing for a front page by-line.

Travis clipped and sent the small article in the *New York Times,* and the longer one in the *Amsterdam News* to Myrtle. The write-ups had kindled outside interest, and women called from various places wanting to come and march with them. Many sent financial contributions. This show of outside solidarity did much for their morale.

Despite the apparent smoothness of the operation, Myrtle had trepidations, hoping that nothing would happen. A bottle, rock or shot aimed by a dissenter could cause serious repercussions. Rudy's plans at the time of his death still hovered over her. He might not be the only man who hated them enough to try to cause trouble.

The whirlwind of activity kept Myrtle's thoughts from being too clouded by the turn of events with Travis. Their phone calls were becoming less frequent and shorter, admittedly because of her. Due to her increasing March functions, she was harder to reach, and when Travis did manage to get her, the call, in some instances, had to be brief, for she had an appointment. By the time she got home, exhausted late at night, she would fall asleep before making her proposed call.

God knows she hated what was happening to them, but she would make it up when Travis came.

Chapter 32

THE week of the March and Travis's visit arrived, catching Myrtle with a topsy-turvy house. In a bind for time, she hired Heavenly Delight to clean in preparation for Travis. To add to the confusion, a press conference was to take place at the time Travis's plane landed. Hemmed in, she asked Ralph to meet the flight for her.

Hearing that Bobby was coming, too, Ralph was overjoyed to do the favor. The scene at the airport dampened his pleasure. When informed that Myrtle was tied up and couldn't make it, Travis became closemouthed. Agnes struck him as being preoccupied, and worst of all, maneuvering Bobby aside, he learned that the musician couldn't see him that night. The happiest of the party was Rhoda, released from her flying kennel.

Spirits low, Ralph left Bobby and Agnes at the Andrew Jackson and took Travis to Myrtle's, where Heavenly Delight waited with dinner cooked. Morose, he drove back to the church to report to Myrtle that all were in their places.

At the hotel, Agnes and Bobby had a light snack and drink together. Agnes, mind on business, retired to her room. Bobby, alone, immediately called Clyde on the lobby phone. When he didn't answer, he dialed Ralph, who wasn't there either. Disgusted, he went to the bar to try his luck.

Myrtle got home to a smoldering Travis as soon as she could. For Heavenly Delight's sake, they ate dinner and made light conversation until Heavenly Delight went home. Following her departure, the fireworks exploded.

"*You* couldn't meet *me* at the airport!" Travis spat out, enraged.

"I asked Ralph to explain to you that I had an important press conference." Myrtle struggled for restraint at Travis's inability to understand. The phone rang, interrupting the ensuing quarrel. Turning to Travis, Myrtle said apologetically, "I am sorry, but I have to go back to the church. Rita Stennette just came and Wilma wants us to go over something together."

"It's a good thing I brought Rhoda," Travis said, lips curling, "or I'd be here all by myself."

"I will try not to be long."

Frustrated and growing angrier by the minute, Travis went into the guest room, where Heavenly Delight had deposited her bags, and began to unpack. Rhoda trailed behind her, sniffing the strange surroundings.

When Myrtle did not return within two hours, Travis went to the refrigerator for a bottle of wine, but stopped upon seeing the unopened scotch in the kitchen cabinet. She took the bottle and ice into the living room. With the radio playing, she drank, read the paper Myrtle had left on the coffee table, ate a cold chicken leg from dinner, and drank some more.

She was prompted to call Agnes to come over, but changed her mind and talked to Rhoda. The incessant interruption of people leaving telephone messages for Myrtle made the waiting worse. They were mostly women toward whom Travis was beginning to feel more and more jealousy. She resolved to put a halt to the calls and took the receiver off the hook.

It had been quite a while since she had drunk anything stronger than wine, and the liquor quickly stole through her like a possessing demon. Thoughts of destruction, like breaking dishes, overturning furniture, and throwing books on the floor of the den, plagued her. Getting up to put them into action, she discovered herself swaying. The better part of her intoxicated judgment advised her to go to bed. This she did, fully clothed, on top of the covers in the guest room, with Rhoda faithfully beside her. Lights burning, she fell into a liquor-induced sleep.

Before long, standing in the doorway looking at her in amusement, Myrtle said, "Maybe I should have prayed for you before I left. What are you doing in here?"

Rhoda's watch dog barking pulled Travis awake. Squinting at Myrtle through bleary eyes, she said icily, "Sleeping."

"There are no sheets on the bed."

"So? I'm on top. Me and Rhoda. Right, Rhoda? Right," she ventriloquized for the dog.

Myrtle sat down on the side of the bed, fatigued and in no frame of mind for hassles. "All right, we'll sleep here." She kicked off her shoes and stretched out, thinking she would later try to convince Travis to go into her room to bed. But the demands of the day plummeted down upon her like cascading rocks. In a few moments, she was sound asleep.

Friday morning, Myrtle was the first to be aroused by the early chirping of birds in the trees surrounding the apartments. Emerging from a deep sleep, she was initially disoriented, staring in bewilderment at the lights still burning, confused about not being in her own bed. In moving, her foot brushed against a form, which she realized was Rhoda. Memories of the previous night dawned upon her. Travis was asleep, tiny snores emitting liquor fumes. Myrtle got out of bed and Rhoda jumped down to the floor, yawning and stretching. She would shower, take Rhoda to find some grass and cook breakfast. Careful not to make any noise, she went to get fresh clothes out of the closet.

Walking Rhoda in the cool, morning air was invigorating to her thoughts. Appetite stimulated, she cooked Canadian bacon, pancakes and eggs for breakfast. For Rhoda, she scrambled an egg.

Travis ate sparingly, making her breakfast mostly coffee. "That's one way to get through the night," she said sarcastically. "Get loaded."

"How do you feel?" Myrtle's eyes held concern.

"I've felt worse."

She didn't look too bad, eyes slightly puffed and dark-ringed. "Why did you take the phone off the hook? I tried to call you."

"Because I got sick of its constant ringing." Slopping coffee in her cup, she asked, "Why don't you get an unlisted phone number?"

Myrtle stopped eating to say resignedly: "I am a minister, and ministers should be found when needed."

"Like doctors," Travis intoned grimly.

Dodging further confrontation, Myrtle opened the morning paper. Opposite the front page, Travis sneered, "Just like married folks."

"Hun?" Myrtle lowered the paper. "I wanted to see if they quoted us correctly from the conference yesterday."

A blistering silence covered the table. Suddenly Travis blurted out, "What's going to be next after the March is over?"

Frowning, Myrtle put down the paper. "How do you mean?"

"To keep us apart."

"Apart? We aren't apart."

"Aren't we?" Travis held her cup with both hands, as if it were as weighty as her words. "We're apart physically and mentally. You here, me there. Seeing each other between *your* church services, speeches, and March plans."

"As long as we know how we *feel* about one another, what does it matter? I can't give up what I am doing, and I am not going to ask you to. It wouldn't be fair." But in the long run, if it were to last, concessions had to be made by someone.

Travis's cup rattled the saucer as she set it down. "You could come to New York."

"My church is here." Why didn't Travis say that *she* could come *here?* Northern regional superiority was instilled even in black people. Besides, this was where she wanted to be. Her springboard was here.

The phone rang loudly in the kitchen. "Better answer it, Reverend. It might be a Christian soul in need."

"Agnes—for you." Myrtle handed Travis the phone. Tuning the conversation out, she went back to the paper.

"What's on my schedule today?" Travis shook the newspaper covering Myrtle's face.

"I have to go to the church. Would you like to come with me?"

Not replying, Travis said coldly in the telephone: "Nothing, Agnes."

To get away, Myrtle started clearing the table, taking dishes to the sink. Behind her, Travis's voice invaded her ears: "I'm going over to Music Row with Agnes and Bobby to see Abe Apstein."

Myrtle unashamedly felt relieved that Travis would have something to do. "Tell Agnes and Bobby I would like to take them to dinner tonight. I can make reservations for eight o'clock."

On the way out, Myrtle handed Travis a key. "In case you get back before I do."

Mellowing, Travis said softly, "You haven't kissed me."

Myrtle's lips grazed her cheek. "There will be more—later."

Bobby, who had a date with Ralph, couldn't have dinner with them, but Agnes did. Following the meal, Myrtle brought Agnes home for a while before taking her back to the hotel.

Lying that night in Myrtle's bed, Travis said, "I think Agnes knows."

"I am not surprised."

"We had an argument today. She thought that I should make one more country music album for Abe. I put my foot down, so we finally settled on gospel. Abe felt it would be a good idea. Another new sound from me."

"Wonderful." Myrtle kissed a perfectly arched eyebrow.

"I'll be thinking of you when I do it." She returned the kiss. And afterward: "Agnes wants me to go on a two-month concert tour of Germany the first of the year." Which took them back to where they had left off that morning.

"I am glad for you."

Travis snuggled closer, moving her foot gently up and down the calf of Myrtle's leg. "Do you want me to go?"

"I want whatever is best for you."

"Come with me! It'd be like a vacation for us!" Travis said enthusiastically, excited by the spur of the moment idea.

Go with her? Wouldn't that provoke hidden questions? But by now, they must surely have already risen about them. As Rita had intimated to her last night, eyes glittering: "It's marvelous that Travis has come all the way here to be with you." *To be with her.* How many thought like Rita?

At Myrtle's silence, Travis moved away, staring into the darkness. To the extended stillness, she asked gently, "Is something wrong?"

"How do you mean?"

"You're away from me—detached."

Myrtle kissed the tip of Travis's nose. "I was merely thinking about the March tomorrow . . . and myself, too."

"What about yourself?" Travis moved back into the curve of Myrtle's arms.

"Something that I will have to come to grips with sooner or later—to free myself."

"Free yourself? From what?"

"The self-imprisonment of being..." Who and what she was. To become a total person.

"My, you have heavy thoughts tonight!"

Myrtle's fingers curled in her hair. "Heavy with you and me in them," she said low.

Travis painted her face with a fingertip lighter than a brush's stroke. "You have a hard day ahead tomorrow."

"I got out my walking shoes," Myrtle half smiled.

"Don't forget the clerical collar. It makes you look sexy."

"I feel sexy around you like this."

"Then *prove* it!" Travis challenged, rolling over laughing playfully.

And Myrtle did.

Chapter 33

T HE day was framed beneath the lenses of a picturesque artist's sky, a brilliant blue with mushroom islands of clouds. Banded together in columns of twos, the women marched, twelve hundred strong by their estimate—nine hundred calculated by the press, and eight hundred gauged by the police.

They walked in solidarity, the New South of the young and old in eighty-eight-degree heat. They marched clad in jeans, pants, skirts, dashikis, shorts, and dresses with feet comfortably encased in sneakers, sandals, loafers, Dr. Scholl's, tennis, and clinic shoes. The rainbow faces of black, brown, yellow, red, and white stepped proudly into the rhythm of the day.

Helmeted, blue-coated motorcycle police rode discreetly with them, and closed-faced traffic officers, caps shielding hard eyes, stood wide-legged and arrogant at busy intersections, shrilly blowing whistles. Automobile horns honked impatiently, and a few cars, bearing red-neck Saturday beer drinkers, yelled out to ask if anybody wanted a good screwing before loudly gunning their rumbling cars without mufflers, laughter extending in back of them like smoke. The police, with sly grins, turned their eyes to the ocean of the sky.

Passing through the old neighborhoods, dogs barked at their heels, while towheaded, bare-chested sun-tanned white children rode bicycles too fast and too close. Mothers in faded housedresses, holding squirming babies, screeched like harpies to their own color: "Commies!"

"Nigger lovers!"

"Troublemakers!" and "We don't want no women libbers!"
To those of another hue, they spat out one of the first words
some learned at birth in the south: "Niggers!"

In the belly of the inner city, black people watched, some
reticently, remembering similar marches of not too long ago.
Males in broad hats, caps, colorful shirts and shades hiding
their eyes, laughed and called out: "Hey, baby, what you doin'
later on?"

"Com'ere, pretty mama, I got somethin' for you!"

"Bulldykes!"

The words of the more placid with despairing faces mouthed
a strident bleat: "Tell City Hall we black men need jobs!"

The men and the women and the children stared at the army
of women, reading their banners and signs of the contingents:
GET THE BAD NOTES OUT OF MUSIC CITY; WOMAN
POWER; DOWN WITH SEXISM AND RACISM; SISTERS
UNITED FOR A BETTER SOUTH; WOMEN SICK OF
RAPE; MAKE OUR STREETS SAFE FOR CHILDREN;
NEW SOUTHERN WOMEN; MY BODY BELONGS TO
MYSELF; WOMEN FOR POLITICAL POWER; WOMEN'S
RIGHTS; CHRIST BELIEVES IN WOMEN; PUT CHRIS-
TIANITY AND LOVE IN MUSIC CITY.

Student groups chanted:

> Women unite together
> To make our lives better.
> The earth on this land
> Wasn't just made for man!

And:

> Black, white!
> Can make things right!

And:

> The New South is here
> Help us to make it a place
> Without fear!

Undercover female police had been planted within the
groups, and intelligence and vice control division officers, disguised as reporters and television camermen, merged with the
marchers. George walked with a photographer, interviewing

bystanders, but staying close to Myrtle. Marshals, arms tied with identifying white bands, kept the lines orderly and moving on schedule, preventing major traffic jams.

Converging on Capitol Boulevard to Legislative Plaza, Myrtle walked with head high, eyes straight ahead, but seeing everywhere, too. She cut a memorable and striking figure in her black pantsuit, clerical collar and tiny gold cross necklace around her neck. Flanked by Wilma in a denim dress and Iffe in her usual bright African apparel, they led the marchers. The remaining members of the steering committee were behind them with Rita striding along in her jeans, hair a flaming torch in the sun. Travis walked with the first group, members of Myrtle's congregation.

They strode in pride, charged with the magnitude of the occasion. Emotion engulfed them, smearing their eyes with tears. They were making history. They *were* history, this moving blanket of women. The March showed strength and unity. Sisterhood in more than words, a political statement of determination in planting the seeds for a new southern woman.

Myrtle was inflated with self-esteem, for this was *her* creation. She, Myrtle Black, daughter of small-time evangelist ministers, was leading the first coalition of black and white women in a precedent-setting March in the annals of the South. She, a *black* woman, southern by birth, and an invisible lesbian. The thought haunted her: What would they think if they knew? No doubt, there was a silent legion of lesbians striding along with her, dreaming of a different southern march someday for another purpose.

From the spectators, Myrtle heard: "There's that Reverend Myrtle Black!"

"Hey, Rev, what you goin' to tell the mayor?"

"Take care of biz'ness, Rev!"

To them, she flashed a big Elijah Black smile.

As they neared their destination, Wilma and Iffe locked hands with Myrtle—white and black, and black and black. Myrtle's step quickened, back ramrod straight, chin jutted out. The day had come. God on his throne was looking down upon them.

The Reverend Snead, a tall, large-boned woman of fifty-five with a rugged, weather-creased face and unruly gray hair, stood on the platform and prayed. She prayed for women, their goals, and for putting the spirit of Jesus in hearts. She wanted them to "'Cast thy bread upon the waters for thou shalt find it after many days.' The Lord is with us. With his help, humankind can reach the greatest of heights 'to the measure of the stature of the fullness of Christ.' Amen."

After the Reverend Snead, Travis sang "Prayer Changes Things," a gospel that rocked and spilled into their souls and set their hearts aflame. Her voice rose to a tremble, the music intense, powerful, magnificent. Women wiped their eyes and said, "Oh, yes!" When the last musical vibrato died, a split silence prevailed before a bellow of appreciative applause and shouts burst into the air.

Travis knew she had sung her best. The music had come from deep within her, spilling out her thoughts, feelings, and prayers. She had exposed herself to them, naked in the throes of her own sound.

Wilma took over the microphone to talk about the March and the role of women in shaping a better South. She outlined the work of the Women United for Action, urging women of all races, colors, and creeds to join. Unity was the key, and the March was symbolic of what women united could do.

Iffe was next, sketching the history of black women in the South as slave, breeder, concubine, and workhorse. She extolled black southern women, such as Harriet Tubman, Sojourner Truth, Ida B. Wells Barnett, Daisy Bates, Rosa Parks, and Fannie Lou Hamer, as well as the unknown, who too had stood strong. Now was the time for a coalition of women of different colors to forget their prejudices and join up in sisterhood for strength to make and share in a new destiny by fighting racism and sexism. She concluded by quoting the black southern educator, Mary McLeod Bethune: "'The true worth of a race must be measured by the character of its womanhood'— and this means *all!*"

Lois read a statement on the importance of voting and of becoming elected officials to have a voice in legislation and government. She wanted women to know the voting records of officials in relation to blacks and women, to deluge elected officials with letters and phone calls, and learn to lobby for the issues of women. Voting organizations could shed light on candidates for office, make them aware of women's and black's demands, and provide voting blocs. Women should exercise the right of the nineteenth amendment and vote. Become involved to gain political power. Politics rules the nation, and it was time women got a piece of the action. The Independent Women Voters needed *them*.

Nikki spoke, representing the Students Feminist Alliance, calling upon students to become interested in their city, their government, and themselves as women. They were tomorrow's women leaders. As feminists, they should work to alleviate the burden of racism and sexism. The youth of today could not afford to repeat the mistakes of the past. Women who are feminists are feminists together and inextricably bound.

Cassandra Lane, sole female member of the House of Representatives in the legislature, a fading blonde forty-eight-year-old Baptist, appeared ill at ease as she approached the platform. Dressed smartly in a pea green linen dress, she hurriedly read a typed statement in a skittish voice. She spoke briefly and safely on the historic significance of the March, the gains of women and blacks in the city and state, lingering on the Christian mission of women in connection to home, children, and family life. Her most radical departure from the staid speech was on women and voting. She disregarded the March's objectives, for underneath she was a pro-lifer, closet racist, and believed in upholding the decorum of the southern past.

Myrtle was the last to speak. As usual, her height and presence commanded attention. Applause greeted her as voices shouted:

Reverend Black! Reverend Black!
We are standing in back
Of you, you, *you!*

Beaming, Myrtle let them demonstrate for a while, relishing the acclaim which bestowed the vestment of power, before motioning for silence. Positioning herself behind the microphone, her eyes sparkled like burning coals, sharp, embracing the hundreds of women as one. Fragmentary notes were spread on the dais.

"My sisters in Christ, spirit and soul, you have been told that this is an eventful day. It is! This day will be chronicled in history books, records, diaries, memoirs, films, and tapes. A day that participating mothers will relate to daughters, daugh-

ters to daughters, and sisters to sisters in blood and bond. There
will certainly be those who ask: *Why?* What precipitated this
day? To these, I can say: What precipitates *anything?*

"*I* can tell you: Being *troubled* did it! Troubled about the
city in which we live. Troubled over the vice, crime, and
corruption running amok and *overlooked* by those who *should*
be seeing and *do-ing* something about it!"

Right on-n-n!

"*I* am troubled, as *you*, over our young people getting
hooked on drugs and alcohol, resorting to crime to satisfy their
addictions. I am trou-bled, as you, by racism and sexism bla-
tantly and subtly displayed in our government, laws, jobs,
hiring practices, and everyday lives. I am trou-bled, as you,
about the unequal balance of political power controlled by *white
males*. I am trou-bled as you, over the abuse of women's bodies
of which women should have control. I am trou-bled for the
need of *Christian* principles, morality, and love that is lacking
in this city and others. Yes-s-s, I am trou-bled, for these are
troubling times. And this is why we are here to-day—to *speak*
out about our troubles!"

Go on-n-n with your fine talk!

Speak out!

"A great blues singer, Dinah Washington, used to sing a
song called 'Trouble in Mind'; Novella Nelson sings a song
called 'I'm Troubled'; that renowned gospel singer, Mahalia
Jackson, used to rock churches with the sound of her voice
singing 'Soon I Will Be Done With the Troubles of the World';
and our Travis Lee sings the spiritual, 'Nobody Knows the
Trouble I've Seen.'

"*Troubled* is what we are in our minds, hearts, and spirits.
And it is *now* we must raise our voices against these troubles,
these troubling times, these *worst* of times. To *speak* and no
longer be silent. If God wanted women to be silent, He would
not have given us voices!"

Yes!

"It is time for us to *lift* up our voices and *scream-m-m* our
outrage at these troubles, and to go out there among *them* and
do-o-o something!"

We're ready!

"In the book of the Prophet Jeremiah, it is written: 'Be not
afraid of their faces: for I am with thee to deliver thee saith the
Lord.' We are now ready, with the help of the Lord, to deliver

ourselves—to *liberate* ourselves-s-s in a new emancipation of blacks and women for equality and justice for all. The Bible says: 'Let the oppressed go free.' We are ready for change, for things *must* change and things *will* change!"

Change!

"We are starting our changing times with this March to take care of the business of change. Aileen Hernandez, one of our eminent black feminists said: 'We need to get about the business of becoming persons. We need to get about the business of addressing the major issues of society as full-fledged human beings in a society that puts humanity at the head of the list, rather than masculinity at the head of the list.'

"I, the Reverend Myrtle Black, am saying to *you*, my beautiful sisters, the business *is* at hand, the time has come, the mo-ment is now with us, and the clock is tick, tick, tick-ing a-way! We *must* stand up and reject the oppression of misogyny. The Greek philosopher, Euripedes, wrote: 'Woman is woman's natural ally.' We must all-l-l be allies in a natural alliance of women to achieve our goals, objectives and purposes.

"*I* don't want to be troubled for the rest of my life, and I know *you* don't either. Let us band together and work towards a future history of betterment. One of our black spirituals is entitled 'I'm So Glad Trouble Don't Last Always.' No, troubles *don't* if we can help it. And we *can*. By fighting for the *power* of sisterhood. God, the truth, and ourselves will set us free-e-e!"

Hoo-ray!

Hallelujah!

The women gave her a thunderous ovation, clapping and cheering and shouting. "Reverend Black, Reverend Black...!" Exalted and roused to soaring heights by their laudatory fanfare, Myrtle rose to the pinnacle of self-adulation, acknowledging their cries by smiles and waves, a reigning deity with both arms raised to the sky. Iffe leaped up to hug her, as the Reverend Snead and Wilma surrounded her, patting her shoulders and kissing her cheeks. Photographers snapped pictures. Scaling the wings of martyrdom, she loved it, gloried in it. This was *her* day, her heaven of triumph.

When the ringing response slowly died down, Myrtle said, "Dr. Kate McCain of our steering committee will present the Petition of Women's Concerns to the mayor's office."

Since the mayor had a previous commitment, Betty accepted

the petition for his office. Later, she informed Myrtle that the mayor was at the City Club getting soused, while watching the "Women's Circus" on TV with the boys. Representative Lane received the petition for the legislature.

To climax the event, the female choir composed of voices from various churches throughout the city sang "The Battle Hymn of the Republic." It was a crowning day of beauty and joy.

The crowd seemed reluctant to disperse, overcome by the magnificent occasion. Myrtle stood in the midst of it all, smiling and talking, surrounded by Rita, Wilma, and Iffe.

Patting Myrtle on the back, Rita said admiringly, "Great speech, Myrtle. I'm going to take it back to California with me. We can use it there, too!"

"Incredible!" Iffe summed up. "I can't believe we actually did it."

"Work and determination," Wilma supplied, affectionately embracing Iffe and Myrtle. "That's what it all boils down to."

"And God's blessing," Myrtle superimposed. Looking around, she searched the crowd for Travis, whom she had lost among the autograph seekers. Spotting her about to cross the street in her direction, Myrtle lifted her hand and Travis waved back, smiling happily.

Suddenly the loud gunning of a motor sounded as a car careened down the street, racing wildly through the crowd. Myrtle heard the shouts and cries of people scattering in fright to get out of the way. Someone screamed a warning, and like a nightmare unfolding before her eyes, she saw Travis lying in the street.

Frozen for a split second, she stood stunned in an icy glaze of shock. "Oh—my God!" she cried. The shrill siren of a police car giving chase blasted unheard in her ears.

She ran, pushing through the crowd, face contorted with horror and anguish. Student nurses rushed to the scene, keeping the people back. "Call an ambulance!" one of the nurses said, bending over Travis.

Myrtle leaned down, too, above the still form. "Travis... darling... darling..." Tears filled her eyes like a flood.

Chapter 34

MYRTLE, Agnes, and Bobby were assembled anxiously in the hospital's private waiting room for the doctor's report on Travis. Bobby sat bent over with his head in his hands, a stunned look on his face. Agnes smoked countless cigarettes while restlessly pacing the floor.

Myrtle, tense on the brown leather couch beside Bobby, found herself for the first time in her life at a loss for words. She had stared so long at the bland-colored walls and gray linoleum that she knew they would be forever etched in her mind. The sight through the half-opened door of white uniformed nurses whisking by with charts and medicine carts made the waiting more grim.

She had alerted herself for the possibility of trouble today, but not this. A sinking helplessness fused within her, causing her to feel impotent and worthless. Why did this have to happen to Travis and not to her?

The trauma had made her come to grips with how much Travis meant to her, something she had selfishly submerged and refused to face. In their closeness, she had given less and taken more. The waiting seemed ominous. Silently she prayed to her mentor above for her beloved.

Coffee was handed to her by Agnes. "I thought we could use this."

"Thank you," Myrtle said gratefully, taking the plastic cup.

Bobby listlessly held his cup, eyes vacant. A pregnant woman in a bulging smock and a harried-looking man passed by with an overnight bag, following a smiling nurse hurrying them along.

"I'm going to take a walk," Bobby said, getting up.

Sitting down in his place, Agnes lamented, "God, this waiting—"

"I know." Myrtle felt the coffee bringing strength to her, spreading currents of warmth in a weary body. She looked down at the patches of dust on the knees of her black pantsuit where she had knelt on the sidewalk to hold Travis. The ambulance ride had been a nightmare, siren screaming a cat's wail while Travis lay still.

Agnes set her cup on the wooden end table flanking the couch. Someone had left an opened *Time* magazine on it and an empty chewing gum wrapper. Seeing Myrtle's dark worried eyes, empathy flowed out to her. Extracting a cigarette from a fresh pack, she exhaled a sash of new smoke before saying in almost an undertone, "I know how you two feel about each other."

The words came unexpectedly to Myrtle, like a bolt of quiet thunder. She turned sharply to Agnes, whose yellow face was shadowed, angled away from her. The usually neat black cap of hair was in disarray, where her fingers had fretfully made nervous paths. Myrtle's hands tightened around her cup. Of course, there would always be those who knew.

"It doesn't matter to *me*," Agnes continued, gazing at the scuffed toes of the old brown loafers she had worn for the March. "I love her, too—like a sister. I like to see her happy. You've done that for her and lots more. Sort of made her into a new person in a way."

"She has done the same for me," Myrtle said.

Agnes flicked ashes in a glass ashtray filled with her red-ringed butts. "I just don't want her career hurt. You understand?" Her eyes locked with Myrtle's.

"You mean by the way we care for each other?" She, too, had thought of this and more.

Agnes finished her coffee, taking a long drag on her cigarette and putting it out. "The public isn't quite ready ... for *that* yet."

"The public wasn't ready for integration either," Myrtle snapped, thinking the only way to update society's mores was to go against the grain.

Bobby came back. "The doctor's on the way."

The resident physician was a slim young white man with a thin moustache. The name of Dr. Leonard A. Miles was written on his white coat. He gave them a professional smile. "Nothing to worry about folks. The X rays show a couple of fractured ribs. We've given her something for the pain and put her in a rib support." His smile broadened. "Lucky woman. We'll keep her until Monday for observation. She'll be all right."

Bobby breathed a sigh of relief. "That's certainly good to hear!"

"May we see her?" Myrtle asked eagerly.

"One at a time," the doctor replied, "for about five minutes."

"You go first," Agnes said to Myrtle.

On entering the room, Travis appeared to be asleep, but when Myrtle approached the bed, her eyes opened.

"Hello, darling." Myrtle lightly kissed her forehead, the flesh damp and warm to her lips.

Travis's amber eyes caressed her. "Groggy—" The response was weak.

"I was so worried—afraid." Myrtle pulled a chair close to the bed. Leaning over, she touched her cheek to Travis's face. "You mean so much to me—so very much." Myrtle's lips lightly brushed her ear. "Oh, my darling, I love you." The endearment was strewn like petals of roses from a soft breath of love.

Travis turned her head a wee bit to land a kiss on the side of Myrtle's nose. "What you just told me is the best medicine I could ever have."

Myrtle patted her hand. "I have to go. Agnes and Bobby are waiting to come in." Kissing her again, she said, "See you tomorrow, my dear."

"Say it again, please, before you go," Travis whispered.

Not needing to know what it was Travis wanted her to say, Myrtle said gently, "I love you."

A fragile smile brightened Travis's face.

Released from the hospital, Travis came home to stay with Myrtle until she was able to travel. Satisfied that she would be all right, Bobby and Agnes flew back to New York on Wednesday.

To Myrtle, taking care of Travis was a delight. She spoiled her, attending her beyond her needs.

"You make a lovely nurse," Travis laughed over the lunch tray Myrtle served her in bed.

"That's because I have a special patient," Myrtle said, glad that Travis was getting better.

Rita came by with Wilma on Friday afternoon to say good-bye. She brought her own shaker of martinis since she didn't think Myrtle had any. "Males—" she grunted, her longs legs in jeans propped on a stool. "Always try to spoil things organized by women. It could have been a perfect day."

"Rita's a female chauvinist," Wilma laughed, looking over at Travis stretched out on the couch with Rhoda at her feet. "It's good, Travis, to see you're on the way to recovery."

"With the help of my new girdle that I'm trying to get used to," Travis winced, moving a little.

"That is what she calls her rib support," Myrtle explained.

"The doctor tells me I can start singing again in six weeks."

"From all of those telegrams and flowers, your public proves it cares for you," Wilma said, glancing around the room.

"You should have seen the flowers we left at the hospital!" Myrtle threw up her hands. "Unbelievable!"

"I have to go and pack," Rita interrupted, finishing her drink. "Myrtle, you and Wilma let me know when you want to do something exciting again like having another March or something. I loved every minute of it!"

"Always the activist," Wilma wisecracked affectionately.

"Keep in touch—" Rita kissed Myrtle and Travis good-bye. "As the saying goes, I'm as close as your telephone."

Iffe dropped in later that day after classes and accepted Myrtle's invitation to dinner. Remembering Iffe was a vegetarian, Myrtle fixed a casserole and fruit salad.

At the table, Iffe aired the results of the March from her end. "The students are still talking about it," she relayed with delight. "I think we have them fired up about something for a change since the Civil Rights Movement," she laughed.

"Which goes to prove your efforts weren't in vain," Travis said.

"Efforts for principles are never in vain," Myrtle appended solemnly.

After Iffe left, George rang the doorbell as they were preparing for bed. He had on a new brown suit and his eyes were bright and clear, minus the telltale redness. "I apologize for my late visit," he said, "but I couldn't make it any sooner."

"It doesn't matter," Myrtle said, turning on more lights in the living room. "We are glad to see you."

Rhoda barked, sniffed George's pants legs, then ran to Travis entering the room.

"How's the patient?" George gave her a friendly kiss on the cheek.

"Doing well with a wonderful nurse." Travis smiled at Myrtle.

"Did you see my front page story on the March in Sunday's paper?" he asked proudly.

"We did, and it was an excellent job," Myrtle replied. Eyeing him reflectively, she said kindly, "We have come a long way together in a short time, haven't we, George?"

"Sure have," he acknowledged, warmly returning her look. To Travis, he said, "They caught the guys in the car that ran you down. It'll be in the morning paper. They had been smoking pot and drinking. It seems at the time they thought it would be exciting to run through a crowd of women libbers."

"They could have killed her," Myrtle said angrily.

"And others," Travis said. "Thank God that didn't happen."

"I just stopped by to see how you were and be the first to let you in on the news." At the door, he said, "Take care of Travis, Myrtle. She's got a lot more singing to do."

Watching Myrtle turning down her bedspread, Travis asked softly, "Why have you gotten so quiet all of a sudden?"

Myrtle helped Travis slip on the yellow gown whose color was so perfect against her skin. "I was thinking over what George said concerning your lifetime of singing."

"What about it?" Travis eased against the pillows Myrtle had propped up for her.

"How I fit into it." Myrtle's back was away from Travis as she reached into the closet for her own nightclothes.

Frowning, Travis said nothing.

"Remember when I talked to you about freeing myself?"

"Un-hun. During one of your thoughtful nights," Travis said, trying to lighten a somber moment.

"I have finally decided to do it." Pulling on her nightclothes, Myrtle slid into bed beside Travis. Lying on her back, eyes on the ceiling, she said, "When you leave, I am going to deliver the most important sermon of my life."

Travis faced her. "Why *after* I leave?"

"Because it affects you, too, and I don't want you to suffer on account of me."

Now Travis knew. The realization was stark before her, clear and meaningful. Her face tightened in thought. "I can take care of my end," she said slowly. Moving closer to Myrtle, she laid her head where the small sound of Myrtle's heart beat. "If your sermon is going to be that important to us both, don't you think I should hear it?" Then, teasingly: "I don't want you saying things behind my back."

Eyes glistening with tears, Myrtle's fingers stroked her hair. "Darling, I am glad you understand."

Careful to avoid creating pain, Travis shifted slowly upward and back against the pillow. Leaning over, Myrtle kissed each eyelid with a flower brush of lips. "All right, I will do it when you feel like going to church."

"Hum-m-m," Travis murmured, pleased that the weight had lifted from Myrtle. "I must be getting better. I'm feeling horny."

"Togetherness can do that," Myrtle smiled, burying her face in Travis's hair. "Lie still, do nothing. I will be gentle," she promised, moving down.

Chapter 35

SUNDAY, three weeks later, Myrtle, face clouded and eyes darkly lined, stood in the pulpit looking down upon her filled congregation. Travis in a front row pew watched her with concern, aware of the tension within. Seated next to Travis was the Reverend Snead, clerical collar a striking white coronet around her neck. At Myrtle's request, Reverend Snead had talked with her late Friday night on into early Saturday morning. Now she had come to be with her at this time.

Hands gripping the sides of the rostrum, Myrtle began speaking in a low, distinct tone: "My sermon this morning is on Freedom and Acceptance. Yes. *Free-e-edom and Ac-cept-ance,*" she enunciated slowly for the words to take effect. Fixing her gaze on the opened Bible before her, she continued: "I am going to read to you from the Gospel According to Saint John, chapter 1, verse 3: 'All things were made by him; and without him was not any thing made that was made.'"

Pausing, she looked up from the scripture for a long interval, before raising her voice to a loud crescendo: "In-dee-e-ed *all-l-l* things were made by God. *You* were made by God, and *I* was made by God in God's image. There are some who might say that all people are *not* made in God's image because they are *different.* True, there are different races, colors, and *kinds* of people. But are they not of God, too? We are all-l-l a part of God—each and ev-v-ery one of us. *Made by God!*

"Others might say that people of a different sexuality are not of God. These point to the Apostle Paul, chapter 1, verses

26 through 28, in which Paul spoke out against homosexuality—what *he* called vile affections against nature.

"As most of you know, in *this-s-s* pulpit, I have previously attacked Paul's view on women. This morning, I am refuting his teachings on homosexuality. You see, in making humankind, God gave us a physical nature—*sexual* feelings. If not licentiously abused, this can be one of the most beautiful, enjoyable, and loving of experiences, whether heterosexual *or* homosexual.

"To this, some will disagree, saying for heterosexuals: yes; but homosexuals: *no*—citing Paul. But let us look at it in this manner. In the dark days of blatant segregation, white racists pointed out that God didn't intend for black and white races to mix, to have sex, to marry. But I contend if God didn't, then God would not have made it *physically* possible for whites and blacks to join together in a physical union, or even to have attractions for each other. This, also, goes for homosexual unions. God created our *physical desires!*

"In accordance with this, I say to you that the church of today must update the teachings of Paul on homosexuality. Look at it *not* in the context of Paul's time. Paul's purpose was to warn the Hebrews against the Roman and Hellenistic sexual cultures, which he linked to idolatry."

Myrtle's hand struck the rostrum as she uttered, *"This is a new-w-w day!* Our society has gone through an upheaval of social revolutions brought on by people who want mental and physical freedom from oppression. We have had the Black Movement, the Women's Movement, and now the Gay Movement for liberation. Movements which challenge freedom and acceptance in all aspects of life. *Including the church!*

"But! Has the church responded? Not hardly, for the church has not lib-er-ated itself! To survive in this changing society, the church must meet the needs of people who are different racially, politically, and sexually. The church must become re-le-vant to *this* day and time!

"Of all the oppressed, gays are the most rejected by the church, although its pews are filled on Sundays by those hidden in the shadows. The church must alter its attitudes toward homosexuality and view it as a chosen way of life. We are all made of God and accepted by God. God accepted the lame, the blind, the sick, the weak, the adulterer, the ungodly, and the profane.

"First Timothy, chapter 4, verse 4, reads: 'For every creature of God *is* good, and nothing to be refused.' If God were standing here at this-s-s moment, I *know-w-w* God would *not* say I want this-s-s person to come unto me, but *not* that one. God is not a discriminating God, nor an incriminating one. God is a *just* God, and *just* you, too, must become to know and share in the beauty and goodness of one another.

"To those who are different, you must *open* your minds and hearts. By doing this, you are helping them to come out of the darkness of imprisonment. You are helping them to walk *free-e-e* into the light without fear of condemnation—those men who love men, and women who love women."

Myrtle stopped for a long silent moment before moving from behind the rostrum. Chin uplifted, she announced in clear-spoken words: "I am one of those people who imprisoned herself. I *locked* my tongue in silence and carried the weight within my heart. But this morning, I decided to *free-e* myself before you. *To walk in the light!* For in freeing myself, I hope to give courage to others like me to free-e-e *themselves,* too!"

Descending slowly down from the pulpit, Myrtle held herself erect before her congregation. *"Look at me,"* she beseeched. "I am of the same flesh and blood as *you*. I am still the same minister who gave you spiritual guidance and solace in the past. I have been your leader in the church, as well as in the streets. Standing here before you declaring unashamedly who and what I am—a lesbian—I feel cleansed, washed in the blood of the lamb, baptized anew in the sight of our wonderful savior, Jesus Christ—and *you!*

"Naked in spirit I stand, revealing my true identity—my *soul!* I feel *touched* by God's hand, made stronger and freer to serve my Jesus. Therefore, I ask of you: 'Let the words of my mouth, and the meditations of my heart, be acceptable in thy sight.'"

The church was hushed. Not even the birds sang outside in the Indian summer day. It was as if life had stopped in the throes of time.

Eyes half-closed in the privacy of prayer, Myrtle said quietly, "I want you to love and respect me as I do you—all of you." And opening her sight to them: "Those who do *not* wish to remain a member of *this* church are free to go—*now!*"

When there was no movement to leave, tears of joy wet Myrtle's cheeks. Raising her arms high to the sky, she shouted,

"Praise God! The Lord's goodness and mercy shineth down upon you! God bless each of you! Hallelujah!" Spinning around in a half-arc, she blazoned out, "Say Jes-s-sus and *come* to me-e-e!"

Jesus! The church responded with love.

Travis sprang forth first to hug and kiss Myrtle, and remain by her side as the congregation came to embrace her and shake her hand in union.

Looking pleased, the Reverend Snead rose to congratulate her on a sermon she thought well done. Ralph quickly motioned to the organist to start the choir to singing "We Are All God's Children."

In the evening after dinner, casually dressed in slacks, Myrtle and Travis went to the park to relax and watch the ducks. On the bench, Myrtle's arm was loosely curved behind Travis. From time to time, as if to reassure herself that Travis was actually beside her, Myrtle would lightly stroke her shoulder in a fleeting movement. Tiredness flowed within her, but she was happy. The gauntlet of her existence had been overcome.

The park surged with people taking advantage of the late autumn warmth before the chill crept in. Behind the trees, someone was practicing a flute. The soft clear notes gravitated to them in a melancholy sound.

"I was proud of you this morning," Travis said softly. "That was a brave thing that you did."

"I had you there with me for support. Loved ones give strength." With the toe of her sandal, Myrtle designed a "T" in the grass. "Two more weeks and the doctor says that you will be as good as new."

Travis shifted closer, wanting to feel some part of Myrtle touching her. Myrtle's thigh created a patch of warmth against her own. "Yes."

"Then you will be gone." But she had, through an unpleasant stroke of fate which had miraculously ended well, been with her longer. Myrtle looked at a crisp orange and red leaf falling from a tree. Even leaves, too, must separate from the singular part of them when the time comes.

Divided into separate chambers of thought, silence became an interloper. A ragged column of ducks swam by, making erratic patterns in the water darkening under a waning sky.

Risking her thoughts, Travis asked in a small voice, "Are

you going on the trip with me?" Myrtle's drawn out silence disturbed her. Waiting for answers, which were important, was always disquieting. "You deserve and need a rest." She hoped that would help to bring on the reply she so much wanted to hear.

Half turning to her, Myrtle smiled, and the smile, to Travis, was like a song. "If you want me to." Myrtle's fingers caressed Travis's shoulder and made heat.

Travis laughingly mouthed a kiss in the open space between them. Myrtle stood up, a slim silhouette against the lavender sky. "Darling, are you ready to go home?"

Travis nodded, eyes tight upon her. "Yes," she replied in almost a whisper.

Home to where they could be together as one.

A few of the publications of
THE NAIAD PRESS, INC.
P.O. Box 10543 • Tallahassee, Florida 32302
Phone (904) 539-9322
Mail orders welcome. Please include 15% postage.

LOVING HER by Ann Allen Shockley. 192 pp. Romantic love
story.   ISBN 0-930044-97-5 $7.95

THE BLACK AND WHITE OF IT by Ann Allen Shockley.
144 pp. Short stories.   ISBN 0-930044-96-7   7.95

MURDER AT THE NIGHTWOOD BAR by Katherine V.
Forrest. 240 pp. A Kate Delafield mystery. Second in a series.
                                         ISBN 0-930044-92-4   8.95

ZOE'S BOOK by Gail Pass. 224 pp. Passionate, obsessive love
story.   ISBN 0-930044-95-9   7.95

WINGED DANCER by Camarin Grae. 228 pp. Erotic Lesbian
adventure story.   ISBN 0-930044-88-6   8.95

PAZ by Camarin Grae. 336 pp. Romantic Lesbian adventurer
with the power to change the world.   ISBN 0-930044-89-4   8.95

SOUL SNATCHER by Camarin Grae. 224 pp. A puzzle, an
adventure, a mystery—Lesbian romance. ISBN 0-930044-90-8   8.95

THE LOVE OF GOOD WOMEN by Isabel Miller. 224 pp.
Long-awaited new novel by the author of the beloved *Patience
and Sarah*.   ISBN 0-930044-81-9   8.95

THE HOUSE AT PELHAM FALLS by Brenda Weathers. 240
pp. Suspenseful Lesbian ghost story.   ISBN 0-930044-79-7   7.95

HOME IN YOUR HANDS by Lee Lynch. 240 pp. More stories
from the author of *Old Dyke Tales*.   ISBN 0-930044-80-0   7.95

SURPLUS by Sylvia Stevenson. 342 pp. A classic early
Lesbian novel.   ISBN 0-930044-78-9   7.95

PEMBROKE PARK by Michelle Martin. 256 pp. Derring-do
and daring romance in Regency England. ISBN 0-930044-77-0   7.95

THE LONG TRAIL by Penny Hayes. 248 pp. Vivid adventures
of two women in love in the old west.   ISBN 0-930044-76-2   8.95

HORIZON OF THE HEART by Shelley Smith. 192 pp. Hot
romance in summertime New England.   ISBN 0-930044-75-4   7.95

AN EMERGENCE OF GREEN by Katherine V. Forrest. 288
pp. Powerful novel of sexual discovery. ISBN 0-930044-69-X   8.95

DESERT OF THE HEART by Jane Rule. 224 pp. A classic;
basis for the movie *Desert Hearts*.   ISBN 0-930044-73-8   7.95

SPRING FORWARD/FALL BACK by Sheila Ortiz Taylor.
288 pp. Literary novel of timeless love. ISBN 0-930044-70-3   7.95

FOR KEEPS by Elisabeth Nonas. 144 pp. Contemporary novel
about losing and finding love.   ISBN 0-930044-71-1   7.95

TORCHLIGHT TO VALHALLA by Gale Wilhelm. 128 pp.
Classic novel by a great Lesbian writer. ISBN 0-930044-68-1   7.95

These are just a few of the many Naiad Press titles—we are the oldest
and largest lesbian/feminist publishing company in the world. Please
request a complete catalog. We offer personal service; we encourage and
welcome direct mail orders from individuals who have limited access to
bookstores carrying our publications.